Prohibitions

Caron Freeborn

An *Abacus* Book

First published in Great Britain as a
paperback original in 2004 by Abacus

Copyright © Caron Freeborn, 2004

The moral right of the author has been asserted.

The author gratefully acknowledges permission to quote from 'Sweeney
Agonistes, Fragment of an Agon' from *Collected Poems 1909–1962* by
T.S. Eliot. Reproduced by permission of Faber and Faber.

A CIP catalogue record for this book
is available from the British Library.

ISBN 0 349 11383 1

Typeset by Palimpsest Book Production Limited
Polmont, Stirlingshire

Printed and bound in Great Britain by
Clays Ltd, St Ives plc

Abacus
An imprint of
Time Warner Books UK
Brettenham House
Lancaster Place
London WC2E 7EN

www.TimeWarnerBooks.co.uk

*To the memory of my father, and for those to
whom that memory matters.*
Cheers

Acknowledgements

I'd like to thank: Chris, who yet remains. Spell, who understands. Michael, who was such a generous technical advisor. Em, who listened to every detail of each back story without punching me. Anne, Catherine, Kev, Liz & Liz, Louise and Dr Steve, who heard me in other ways. Each of the above was also among those who supported me through my beloved dad's dying and my return to writing. I am fortunate as well in my students, especially those from 2002–3, who constantly re-invigorated my relationship with my language. And in the wider world, I greatly appreciated the good-humoured responses of Debs, Geoff, Nick Bolter, Richard Hopkins and Simon Mumford to my research questions; anything I might have misinterpreted is not the fault of their answers.

I owe more formally professional debts, too: Chris Bristow, for Cambridge. Patrick Walsh, for taking the first chance. Richard Beswick, for his guidance and patience. Sarah Shrubb, for her amazingly sensitive editing. Finally, mentors seldom get the recognition they deserve; I can't give Jonathan Martin that, but I do offer my gratitude for the way he rigorously employed his critical eye during the writing of *Prohibitions*, and more particularly, for all that he has taught me.

Prohibitions

Part 1

Diamond Lily

What is more base, empty of worth and full of vileness than harlots and other such pests? Take away harlots from human society and you will have tainted everything with lust. Let them be with the matrons and you will produce contamination and disgrace. So this class of persons, on account of their morals, of a most shameless life, fills a most vile function under the laws of order.

St Augustine

Chapter One

Angel had once bought him a bottle of absinthe. That was in the days before you could get it in Tesco, before the Internet even; smuggled in from what was then Czechoslovakia, a holiday souvenir suggesting weeks of hallucinatory excess. *Green and bitter, sucking the hell through sugar*: even Angel's postcard had been full of his excesses. Jacob had poured half the absinthe down the sink. Maybe a touch more than half. But then something had stopped him; he remembered abruptly righting the bottle, the feel of its weight as he held it up to the light. He could even see the bulb, greasy and too low a wattage. Couldn't get hold of what he'd felt, though, until the point he'd drunk some of the dreadful stuff. Where had Angel been at the time? Jacob thought he could hear that laugh, that, *Bloody hell, Jake, you a man or a bar mitzvah boy?* but Angel couldn't really have been in the room: he'd never have let Jacob tip alcohol anywhere except down one or both of their throats.

How long ago? Over twenty years, must be. The summer before Tripos, when finals had seemed too far off to worry about, and The Damned had been a bigger part of their lives than Dante. Or maybe that's just how Jacob saw it now. Yet the Cambridge you were given in films and novels, the sherry parties, the intellectual conversation over bad food and good wine, where had that been? And punting on the Cam, May Balls, secret societies with Latin names, weird initiations? Jacob didn't remember anything like that. Maybe they *had* gone punting once; he couldn't be sure. But he could easily feel that absinthe on his tongue, the taste of his secret timidity. What if he went mad? Saw reality distorted, had visions or something? He didn't, though, and he'd got a little kudos from Angel, who'd cracked up laughing when he'd seen how much of the bottle had gone. *Nice one, Mitzvah.*

Screw Angel. Just screw him. Jacob took the bottle and the box of sugar cubes out of the Tesco bag, got a glass from the draining board. He filled the small jug with water, adding some ice. That thick plastic was a sod to get off the bottle, but he had to because the special holed spoon was attached underneath. With everything on a tray, it looked as though he'd misunderstood something vital about tea-party etiquette; could just imagine what his grandmother would have said. Jacob carried it all through to the lounge, then looked along the shelves for an appropriate CD. Not too sure he *had* anything appropriate. Forget the classical, obviously. Bunny Wailer, Tom Waits, The Who, Deanna Witkowski . . . there must be something here. If he'd still had his vinyl, wouldn't be a problem. No *hippie bollocks*, and anything Jacob's own playing was featured on wasn't a goer either. He'd have to stick with the blues. Jacob clicked Billie Holiday out of her case, put the CD into the machine. *Call that blues, you dickhead? Thought you were meant to be a muso. It's fucking jazz.* Tough shit, that's what you're getting. Angel used to say all meaning contained slippage, anyway.

Jacob sat on the settee, pulled the stopper out of the bottle. Aniseed. A bit like pastis, but with an undertow. Undertone. Or maybe he was imagining that, adding what he knew to what he could smell. God, Jacob got on his own nerves. He tilted the bottle until a few drops of absinthe began to cover the bottom of the glass. How much was a measure? Perhaps you were supposed to make it about sugar cube height. Then balance the spoon along the glass, place the cube on top of that, pour the iced water through it, and watch the painfully slow dissolve, the drink gradually turning a greenish-yellow; ritual could make any bloody thing seem profound. *Mazel Tov. Go on, you know you want to.* Carefully, Jacob rested the spoon

4

on the coffee table, stared at the dirty-looking liquid, his heart beating faster than the music. What was happening to him? It was as though he'd lost twenty years, recovered all his uncertainty, his weaknesses. As though he'd never had jobs, relationships, any standing as an adult. Waiting to graduate to real life. After all this time, Angel could reach out and *with love* and three kisses write Jacob off.

He'd really kissed Jacob that once. In their kitchen. They'd both been stoned, but Jacob didn't think that had anything to do with it: Angel had simply wanted to see what Jacob would do. He'd done nothing. Just stood and taken the kiss, not kissing back but not pulling away either. Angel had laughed in his face then; Jacob had turned to put the kettle on. What had he felt? Not desire; Angel was great looking but Jacob was straight, and anyway, he knew Angel too well to be taken in. Yet he could remember feeling flattered, even as he knew that Angel was only playing with his head. And love, of course, he'd felt love; there was always that. Strange, to realize that nothing had actually changed after all. Although he'd seen Angel only a handful of times in the last few years, and not so very often in the ten before that, Jacob had apparently preserved everything, including the need for Angel's mocking approval and for his love.

Without putting his glass down, Jacob opened the drawer under the table, fished for the half-packet of cigarettes and his lighter. So much for giving up. Dear God, what did his friend want from him now? Seemed his demands never ended. *They're a family. That's the point, Mitzvah. The Dawsons. The linchpin is a hard-faced old bird called Maggie, but it's her niece you're after.* Jacob could practically recite the whole letter, even though he'd only read it twice. Shit, and there were still those videos to watch; whatever was on them might be easier to face drunk. Meantime, this one was for Angel. The Immortal. Who'd gone and bloody died.

L'chei-im.

* * *

5

'Look, Nana, that one in the picture there?' Fred'd switched off the telly, was flicking though Maggie's *Woman's Own*. 'My mates say she's really fit, they all well love her.'

'So they all love her, do they,' said Maggie. 'What about you?'

'Get off.' He shook his head. 'Don't love no one, yeah.'

'You will.' Course he would. Love was a word that belonged to men. They said it to get sex. Said it sometimes when they'd of got their leg over without, giving themselves a verbal insurance. Said it to excuse bad behaviour, *But I love you, darling.* And they counted on their women saying it, because men had them taped then. Although Maggie never believed in love, she still had the self-same troubles as if she was the biggest sucker for it there was.

'Nan?' Fred tapped her arm with the magazine. 'Are we having any tea?'

'Sorry, love, miles away.' Mind, Maggie's problems was worse than most, seeing as she had seven, no, eight relationships to get out of, if she went through with it. 'What d'you fancy? Got a nice bit of haddock.' She grinned, knowing he'd turn his nose up.

'Yeah, sure. What we really having?' Weren't so easy to catch Fred out, these days. Twelve was more grown up than it'd been even when his mum was young.

'Nothing, if you don't wash yourself.' No use pretending they wasn't relationships, that she never relied on the blokes. For a start, how was she going to get her meat, if she packed it in with the butcher? Or have things fixed around the place if she knocked the ex-electrician on the head? 'Dirty Dick from Hackney Wick, you are,' she added.

'Yeah, only cos nothing rhymes with Stepney. Go on, what we having?'

'Got a microwave pizza in the freezer.' Weren't just about the money, was the whole background to the rest of her life, the foundation even. *Love.* Couldn't hardly of told whether she liked them. Weren't a relevant question after all this time. 'Pepperoni. That do you?' Little marriages. Maggie'd never wanted even

6

one husband, and here she was contemplating eight flaming divorces.

'Wicked. But you don't like pizza.'

'I'll do meself some cheese on toast. You know I'm not a big eater.' Thoughtful kid, not like his mother at that age. Lulu'd took everything for granted, never thought to ask, *What about you, Auntie?* How Lu'd managed to of brung up Fred so different, Maggie couldn't say. Maybe he took after his nan – great aunt, whatever Maggie was meant to be to him. He got it from her side of the family only, for definite. Was looking like he had a chance of growing into a man you might almost respect.

'Could do our tea for you?' Fred got to his feet. Already a good bit taller'n Maggie – mind, she was a short-arse. But this one here was going to be a six-footer plus, if she weren't very much mistaken. Could do with a bit of filling out, though.

'You want to?' she said. 'Be careful of yourself on that grill, then.'

'*Nan.*' He done that rolling eye thing better'n Lulu even. 'Not like I don't know cookers're hot, in it. I'm not a baby? Do my own tea all the time indoors.' Stopping at the door to the kitchen, he turned round to her again. 'You want it with Worcester?'

'Smashing. And have that wash while you're out there.' Maggie patted her wig, checking it was still on straight. It was, it always was. Lulu said her keep doing that got on everyone's nerves, but Maggie was too old to break the habit of a lifetime just because it annoyed her niece. She lit a ciggie. The menthol felt cold in her lungs today, making her catch her breath. Really ought to cut down, weren't doing herself no good. Seemed so drastic, the idea of letting the men go. Weren't like she thought of herself as fifty-nine, didn't feel no different to how she had at thirty, except for the tiredness and her knee. Crikey, would she be entitled to a bus pass? She should bloody cocoa. Been a size eight all her life, never dressed old, never had to. Weren't about to get the other trappings of being a pensioner, not if she could be off of it.

She glanced over at the picture behind the ornaments on the sideboard. Got up to have a closer look. Been a smasher in her day, pocket Diana Dors someone'd once called her, and not just because of being so blonde. Maggie would of liked the long lallies, but other'n that, hadn't never minded being small. Helped you stand out, and in her game anything what made you that bit different was a bonus. Now what was she going to be, a little old lady? That's how Mummy'd got, in the finish. Or Nanny Wedge, with her skirt tucked in her drawers. Well, no thank you very much. Maggie leaned over, put out her cig. Checked her lippy in the glass over the mantel-piece. Might have to get her eyelids done again soon, maybe find out about that Botox. No real rush, she still had what it took. Question was, did she still *want* it took?

'Here are, Nan.' Fred come back through, handed her a plate. Cheese was just right, browned but not burned. His pizza looked soggy though – well, that was his look out.

'Ta, love.' Reached round for her glasses. 'Want the news on while we have it?'

'You mean you want it on.' Cheeky blighter. But he pressed B1 on the remote. Then he picked up her ashtray, put it over on the side. 'Don't know how you can eat with that near you,' he said. Making one of his disapproving faces.

'Give it a rest. When you're as old as me, you can tell me what to do.'

'But that's impossible, right. See–'

'I do know that, Fred. Now sit down and eat your tea. Want to hear this.' Kids was so bleeding literal, made you die. But that thoughtful expression suited him, in a comical way – with them dark, serious eyes and his hair sticking up from his double crown like a mad thing, he could be some brainy expert on an Open University programme. He really was sharp, and all. Course, wouldn't do to tell him that.

'Am I going back home tonight?' he asked, after a couple of peaceful seconds.

'Up to you. Mummy's got a date, remember. She's staying

up Soho after work, could be home late.' Or not at all, dirty cow. Was a disgrace, way Lulu left Fred to his own devices. 'I've no company due, you're welcome to stop here.' Far as flaming Lu knew, the boy could be all on his Jack. Neighbours would love that, they found out, not to mention Social bleeding Services. Nosy pokes.

'Okay.' His cheeks looked a bit flushed, even through the tomato shine he had from catching so much sun. Most probably didn't want to think about his mum with a chap. But he couldn't be sheltered from how the world worked, that just weren't fair. It'd come as too big of a shock if he found out all at once, later on. 'Can I go get a video, then?' he asked.

'Only if you shut your noise. And only if you get one with no guns in it.'

'Don't want a chick-flick, yeah,' he said, whiny. But then he smiled, quick as that. 'I know, I'll get a comedy, right. Don't tell me, I'll shut up now.'

He did and all, for a wonder. Maggie never minded the idea of watching a film with him, she'd even give him a few bob for some sweets and pop to go with. But he should be playing out with his mates. Not like he never had friends, just he'd rather spend his time with an old woman. Older, anyway. Funny bugger.

'Want me other slice?' she asked. 'Two's too much for me.'

'All right.' Like he was doing her a favour. 'But I bet you'll want half the mega Galaxy you're going to buy me.' Really did have a lovely saucy smile.

At first, Jacob thought it was the absinthe making him see things; wasn't that he didn't know what Angel was, but to send videos like this as a parting gift seemed weird even by Angel's standards. After the initial surprise of seeing an enormous dick being shoved into various women, Jacob began to think there was something else strange: he didn't know much about porn except from a couple of stag gigs, but wasn't this film quite old-fashioned? He switched it off, put another video

9

into the machine. Same Indian bloke, and two of the women were the same as well. Same eighties' haircuts, same lack of polish. These girls were pretty, but . . . well, ordinary. Big breasts, neat pubic hair, false-sounding ecstasy, yet they looked real, where the films Jacob remembered had been full of bionic women. Shaved bionic women. *The vids are rare, Jake. Valuable, even.* Maybe because they were old ones. Jacob watched for a few more minutes, wondering whether he ought to be turned on. If he strongly felt anything other than mystification, it was embarrassment; what had this performance to do with him, watching other people fake pleasure? Although suppose the man must be genuinely into it, else how could he keep it up: this film was surely pre-Viagra. Or maybe the industry got hold of that before it became legal. God, what if your cock did let you down? What if you just weren't good enough in bed, and they sacked you? Unbearable. Not that anyone would pay to watch any part of Jacob: his mother was right, he was always *grubby looking* no matter how often he washed, and more than one girlfriend had told him he resembled an elongated monkey. The only thing he found attractive in himself was that he had plenty of curly hair still, and somehow, he didn't think paying customers would give a toss about that. *Sweet essay that would make, Foxy.* 'On Narcissism.' Oh, bollocks. Jacob turned off the television, the film still running underneath the blank screen.

. The ice had melted in the jug; Jacob picked it up to refill it, then changed his mind, went into the kitchen to pour a large brandy. He stood by the sink in the dark, looking out at the lights, at the date-smart people making their way to the numerous restaurants on the high street. Hampstead these days was more comfortably in Angel's price bracket than in his, but Jacob had been renting here so long he couldn't give it up, the only place, other than Cambridge, he'd ever felt was home. Even though Mum was still in Guildford, that felt pre-life, most of its memories borrowed. He finished his brandy, leaned awkwardly against the edge of the sink. Everything was the wrong height for him. *Thought four-bys were meant to be short and fat? Weren't for that beak, I'd think you were one of us.* Angel wasn't anti-Semitic, though: he took the piss out of everyone. Maybe it was a defence mechanism, a way of looking down on anyone who might otherwise look down on him. Cambridge in the early eighties had still been full of public school types; whatever Angel was, it wasn't that.

He must have known. To leave that letter, the videos, with his solicitor to be *Sent on in case of my death*, Angel more than suspected he was going to die. *Bad gear doesn't rock, Jake.* But then junkies were hardly likely to be the oldest corpses in the graveyard, Angel wasn't the sort to kid himself about that. Even in the early days, Jacob had never heard him come out with all that bollocks about heroin being part of a creative community, that it was misunderstood by straight people. A lot of other kinds of bollocks, but not about drugs. Admitted once it was the risk that turned him on. Yet . . . the letter was dated only six weeks before he'd died, with further instructions that it not be forwarded until six weeks from his death; that seemed far too neat, too mathematically precise. This, he couldn't understand. *Don't lose your bottle, Jake, don't take it to the Old Bill. What I want from you is nothing illegal, cross my heart and hope to die. Oh, too late. But I just want you to meet her, for all our sakes. After that, it's up to you. I'm offering you both a legacy; take care of it. Remember, I know you, better than anyone has ever known you.* Arrogant prick. Jacob's throat was swollen with tears. Why was Angel still playing his stupid, childish games, even when he was dead? He could simply have told Jacob, in plain language, what this woman had to do with either of them, but that would have meant Angel relinquishing the power. Since their first meeting, it was obvious Angel had wanted Jacob's apostasy; later, he'd even put it in those terms. *Loyalty is what matters most to me, Jakey. For the Lord, whose name is Jealous, is a jealous God.* He'd been only half joking, if that.

Watch the videos and then take them to that address to sell

them, without giving Angel's name. Then go to the other shop, where he'd find the Dawson niece. God, he wouldn't put it past Angel to be posthumously setting him up. Well, Jacob could do the rest, but watch the films . . . what would be the point? He turned away from the window, rubbing the base of his back, which had begun to ache with him leaning so long. Seen one old porno film, you'd seen them all. Though he needn't decide tonight. Meantime, he'd switch the piano to headphones, work out 'Rhapsody in Blue' for tomorrow evening. He had to be at the bookshop all morning for the stocktake, visit his bloody degenerate father in the afternoon, there'd be no chance to practise if he didn't do it now. Okay, recently Jacob had chosen to become in some sense more solitary, yet his life was still crowded with obligation, he didn't have time to go chasing strange women for his dead friend. Angel had already cost him this evening's gig, a bloody Saturday night, his best payer. If he did do what Angel was asking, at least the door finally would be shut on that relationship, and Jacob's head would be his own again.

As he walked through to the lounge, Jacob found he was freezing cold; surely he didn't need to put the heating on in July, for God's sake. The weather in this country was getting silly, there ought to be someone you could complain to about it. For no reason at all, he started to cry.

'Nice summer holidays you're giving the boy.'

'I do have to work, you know.'

'Doing nights now?' Maggie stuck her hand on her hip, glared at Lulu. The girl said one sarky word to that, she'd had it. Look at her, Hammer Horror weren't in it – Sunday morning, still dressed up from the night before, eyeliner down her cheeks, the lot. If the new man'd see that, another one'd of bitten the dust before you could say how's your father.

'Don't start, Maggie. Any tea going?'

'What d'your last servant die of? And don't change the subject.'

'I'll do him a full Sunday dinner, make up for it. Got nice

chicken bits in the fridge. Presume I still have.' Lulu run her hand over her dirty face, sat down. 'Where is he?'

'Gone home. You should know that.' Maggie lit a cig, leaned her backside against the sideboard. 'Just assuming he stopped here the night . . . Well, he did do, but he rushed off first thing – to check you was there, if I'm not very much mistaken. Murder, you are.'

'Don't go on, I'll sort it. Fred's all right, I *want* him to grow up independent.'

'Mm.' Give her flaming independent. 'What was he like – worth it? This *man*.'

'Wash out. Won't be seeing that one again.' Lulu smiled then, what you had to admit made a lot of difference to her haggard morning face. Maggie eyed her niece. Yeah, could be an attractive enough woman, she was to make a decent effort. You had to say, had the height to be striking. If she'd just keep ahead with her roots and do her hair a less orangey red, maybe cut it shorter – that wouldn't be a bad idea, her age. Nor would wearing something a bit more dignified than a skirt showing half a mile of well-fed thigh. Mind, you wouldn't know Lu was thirty-six, but then good skin run in the family. Amazon type, when she didn't look like she'd been dragged through the bleeding jungle backwards.

'Keep telling you, don't put out unless there's something in it for you.' Maggie smoothed down her own skirt, as though that'd make Lulu more tidy. 'You always–' But a mobile interrupted her. Maggie and Lulu both went for their bags. 'Mine,' Maggie said, pressing the green button. To this day, Maggie never liked jawing to the men in front of the kids, so she popped out the kitchen to make her arrangements. Didn't take a sec – after more'n twenty-five year, they'd worked out a shorthand. While she was talking, she put the kettle on, got the chocolate digestives out the cupboard. Most probably getting on for pub time, by Lulu's normal Sunday reckoning, but that was her look out. She'd asked for tea, now Maggie'd bleeding well make her stop till she'd drunk it.

'Nothing to stick in it?' Lulu asked, with her chancing her arm face on. Maggie ignored her. Any booze in this flat was work only, Lulu should know that by now. 'Well, cheers anyway, Mags, I was gasping. Just have this, then I'll get going.'

'Take this with you when you do. Treat Fred.' Maggie fumbled round in her bag for her purse, give Lu a twenty.

'Thanks,' Lulu said. Looking at her feet.

'Don't do me no favours.' Maggie couldn't get over this girl. 'Oh yeah, my Garry and that Bathsheba said to ask if you want to come round theirn for your tea Tuesday. I'm going and all, don't hurt to remind her he's got a mother. Fred can show us what you got him with me money.' Lu was more'n capable of spending that twenty if she had to, even though the silly moo was too proud ever to ask for a borrow. Never make her out.

'I'll have to see.' Lulu got to her feet. 'Tell B not to make nothing with lentils, Fred won't touch anything like that, for some strange reason,' she added, grinning, going over to the nest of tables to grab a couple of biccies. 'For the walk home,' she said.

Fred was beginning to worry. Not loads, wasn't worth it, though anything could of happened. Thought about ringing her mobile, but, *You got to be able to take care of yourself in this life, Freddie.* She wouldn't see he was only looking out for her. Like Uncle Garry said, no telling women, once they'd made up their minds. Someone from school reckoned Fred's mum looked like a witch when she shouted, with all her bright red hair and spiky fingernails, that she was *one bad mother*. Crap, really, not like she'd ever even properly smacked Fred. She could just get a bit . . . loudish. Quarter past eleven. *Must* be home soon.

Telly was pants, Sunday mornings. Surfed for a while, got a couple of games cheats for Diablo II Expansion, but couldn't be bothered to think of anything more interesting. Couldn't even come up with a word to find in the dictionary, that's how bored he was. Wished he had something to read. Had finished his libraries and Mum's books were all stupid love stories. Not really any sex in them even, not with proper descriptions. Fred knew about sex, knew loads, but he didn't see why it had to be written about like it was a puzzle you had to solve. Couldn't even get cheat-sheets for books.

The flat was well quiet. Fred stuck the radio on. Chart stuff. Shit stuff. He liked some of the things Nan played better, Tony Bennett and that, but best to keep up with the charts so you didn't stand out too much. Trouble with having Lulu as your mum, you always stood out, in it. Still felt horrible for not telling her about the last parents' evening, though wasn't like she'd of remembered probably anyway, dozy cow. Then she'd of cried after when she did. One of his teachers asked why she didn't turn up, but Fred reckoned that was only cos the old pervy liked looking at her knockers. He must be at least forty-eight and all.

Going on half past. Fred started picking at a hangnail, *Don't do that, it's bleeding disgusting*, sucked the finger, stop it being sore. Was always . . . At *last*. About time.

'Freddie? Sorry, gorgeous, missed the last Tube, daft mare I am. Okay, are you? Just give us half-hour to get a bath, then I'll do a nice roast. Maggie sent you a tenner, by the way. Been all right on your own?'

'Course I have.' How come she looked such a minger? 'Not a little kid.'

'Well, precisely, that's my good boy. Where's my snoggeroo?' His cheek got wet with her sloppy kiss. 'Well, you'll be pleased to hear I'm not bringing you home a new uncle. Jesus, Fred, don't ever grow up into a slime ball.' She laughed, making him laugh and all, couldn't help it. Not that it was funny, her making jokes about *men*.

'Why'd you stay so late, then? If he was horrible.'

'Out of the mouths of babes.' Kissing him again. 'Tell you what, promise I'll be more careful in future. Think I was a bit out of practice – haven't had a date in months. You can be my next date, okay? Want to go the pictures on my day off?

Go on, say yeah. Else I'll feel rejected.' Putting her arm up to her forehead, swooning backwards, all dramatic.

'Can I choose the film?'

'Yep, and we'll have a little Indian after. There's my bonus due at work Wednesday, we can go Thursday, yeah?' Grabbing him tight as tight. 'Got a date, have I?' When she was like this instead of fed up with herself, could make Fred choked, didn't know why. *Big girl's blouse.* 'Missed you, chicken,' she said. 'Make your old mum a cup of tea and bring it through, will you?' She ruffled his hair before she left the room. Fred hated that.

The Sunday night crowd wanted a sing-a-long. Jacob didn't play many straightforward pub gigs these days; when he'd been asked for classy, hadn't realized that would mean songs from the McMusicals as opposed to 'Any Old Iron'. Forget the Gershwin, obviously. Screw Angel. Jacob had been forced to swap gigs only because of him. Somehow, he muddled through, eliding notes, making too much use of the sustain pedal; another hour, he'd be free. Meantime, he played Angel's letter over in his head, without coming to any decisions.

'Give us "Don't Cry For Me, Argentina".'

They're a family. That's the point, Mitzvah.

'D'you know "I'm Going To Wash That Man Right Out Of My Hair"?'

I just want you to meet her, for all our sakes.

'How about "I Don't Know How To Love Him"?'

Do it because you love me; I'm asking because as much as I can love anyone, it's you.

Eventually, it was over. Jacob was grateful he didn't play an instrument you had to pack up, that he could walk away from the piano, even though it was to the disappointed slow hand-clap of the party. Thank God he was so near Golders Green, just one stop from home; all Jacob wanted to do was to crash out soon as possible. He made himself jog quickly past a pub that looked similar to the one he'd just left. Tempting to stop, in the hope of catching last orders, but he needed sleep even more than spending time around a conviviality for which he had no responsibility. But then, of course, the Northern Line was full of idiots; didn't people have jobs to go to on Monday mornings, that they could be out getting slaughtered on a Sunday night? Jacob kept his head down, but by the time he got off at his station, he was totally wound up. Racist crap, sexist crap, aggressive crap, had the lot in that few minutes on the Tube. Now he'd need a brandy to help him sleep.

The flat felt empty. Too quiet. Jacob had meant to get another cat after Duke died, but that was over a year ago. Once there wasn't a woman around to remind you about stuff like that, it got left until it seemed too late to bother. He'd probably live in a cat-free universe for ever, unless he got into another serious relationship. Jacob poured his drink, considered sticking some sounds on to make the place feel more lived in, but after this evening, he was musicked-out. Was always a video. Angel's letter had been pretty insistent Jacob see them all, and sure, might be an elaborate joke, but by the same token it could be important. Jacob didn't feel he could take the risk, ignore the instructions; guess he'd always intended, on some level, to obey. Susie would have called it *closure*.

Glancing over, seemed as though the video machine was poking its tongue out at him, like it was on Angel's side. Jacob ejected the tape, which had obviously played right through, although he hadn't watched it. He took another video from the little pile by the television; this one had a label in Angel's handwriting: *Last*. Meant nothing to Jacob. He turned out the overhead light, keeping only the fibre optic on, lit a cigarette and, taking a huge gulp of his brandy, pressed the remote.

More of the bloody same; if these were Angel's personal stash, didn't he get fed up with them? Jacob remembered him as having the lowest boredom threshold in the country. Where Jacob could sit for hours, fishing, or listening to one track over and over, or just thinking, Angel always wanted to be on to the next thing. *Drink up, let's go get some whiz.* Like a toddler, distracted by anything brighter, shinier, quicker. A mystery, how Angel had gone on to get his PhD in only the three years.

Lighting a cigarette from the stub of the one before, Jacob felt his lids get heavy, scratchy. Never make it to the end of the film, they were only just past the knicker-flashing stage. But the next thing he knew, he was leaning forward, eyes wide open. Bloody . . . bloody *hell.* Angel, a young naked Angel . . . that Lucinda Luscious . . . Oh, shit. Some other bloke sucking her breasts, then somehow being by her face, but Jacob couldn't spare him any attention. Close-up. Longer shot, where you could see her apparently loving it. Was it Jacob's imagination, or did it look less fake than before? God. Jacob felt his own cock grow hard; how could *this* be turning him on? Shit, no. Did that mean he was gay after all? Fancied his oldest friend, who was *dead*, for God's sake? As he continued to watch, his erection became unbearable. He unzipped his jeans, pulled them and his pants down to his ankles, started to stroke himself. Stop it, you freak. But he couldn't. The scene seemed to go on for ever, prolonging the torture, but eventually, they came. All four of them: Angel, Lucinda, the stranger into the girl's face, and Jacob. Then without warning, Jacob retched, violently, a spurt of yellow bile over the coffee table.

Maggie was well aware it was always going to be hard to retire. You heard of people popping their clogs a week after getting the carriage clock, or turning right old and not bothering to put on their make-up, just because they weren't working no more. But how the bleeding hell d'you sit back and wait for your pension when some of your clients'd been in your life over twenty year? More than tricks and less than lovers. Suppose that's why they reminded her of husbands.

Retirement. It was such a . . . final sort of word. Maggie'd always been honest with herself – even a good many years back, when she'd been more of a semi-pro, she'd known she was on the game. Funny expression that. Weren't clear who was playing with who. Or who won. But if she was a prosti-tute, then that made her a working girl, and no one done their jobs for ever. There was her tiny trust fund, but how was she going to manage on that and the state? This job mostly give you up rather than you giving up it, though trouble was, if you hadn't never been a one-pant-leg-down street brass or even a brothel whore, you could pretty well go on till your men couldn't, till they was six foot under.

Maggie sprayed herself with the perfume Lulu'd give her at Christmas. Miles too heavy, but it did her for work. Was a suspicion in Maggie's mind Lu'd brought it for that reason, like she was helping out her auntie's job. And Maggie didn't appreciate other people being part of that, specially the kids. Proud to be able to say, hand on heart, she'd always been her own boss. Well, almost always.

Better get her sheets off, Clifford'd be here in half-hour. On the dot, knowing him. *No one trusts a tardy solicitor. Procrastination is the thief of time.* Maggie stripped the bed, put her own sheets in the laundry bin, got the work ones from the chest. Funny, no matter how many times she washed them, could of told the difference between hern and the work sheets just by smell. Only the ones she put on the bed for sleeping smelled like her.

Chapter Two

Fred wasn't meant to go Up West on his own without saying. No way was he going to look for someone to ask this time though, not when Bathsheba had offered him lunch. *More fun if no one knows where we are, sweetie.* Their meetings were well crunk, they only didn't happen often enough. Everyone else had private stuff, why not him? Staying round Stepney was boring anyway, and when the whole family was together, like for tea last week, the grown ups took Bathsheba off him. She had a brilliant job, and all. No one else had an auntie, or sort of auntie, who was a *contortionist*. He'd never seen her, you know, actually contort, but she'd shown him the odd thing, putting her arm over her shoulder and bending so's she touched the back of her knee. Wicked. Fred had tried it, loads – could nearly do it now, a special thing between her and him, in it. Maybe more than she had with Uncle Garry, even though *they* were meant to be getting married next year. And she was buff, with her black shiny hair, and all little and neat and thin. Not like most people over twenty, where their insides seemed too big for their outsides and tried to burst through. Like in that old film – *Alien*? Yeah. But Bathsheba was . . . in the right container. Even had an ace name.

This was the first time they'd met in Oxford Street, they normally went nearer home. Fred had taken a lot of trouble with gelling down his hair, trying to beat that skank double crown, and put on his best jeans that Mum called his clown trousers. She didn't know about fashion. Her stuff was so tight you could see everything, all her lumps and everything.

Bathsheba always wore way smart trousers or skirts, never anything tarty. Her clothes cost a lot and all, Mum said you could tell. Fred knew to meet Bathsheba outside the station, but he was a bit nervous, case he got there first and looked a saddo. Not that he wanted to be late. It was a bit of a problem.

'Hello, darling.' She was there, lucky for him. Gave him one of her butterfly kisses on *both* cheeks, made him go well red. Then almost straight off she started walking. 'And how's Freddie?' Always sounded just like a famous actress.

'Um . . . fine, thank you.' What was the right thing to say? *Freddie's fine* or *I'm fine*? How did you get to know that stuff? Bathsheba stopped walking, sudden as she'd started, and pointed down Poland Street to a *café*. Full of done-up mums with their poncy kids. Sort of place none of Fred's mates would be seen dead in.

'Is there okay?' Bathsheba asked. 'Does masses of veggie sarnies, really scrummy.' She smiled. Her lipstick was dead pale, had to look twice to see she was wearing it. 'Pity McDonald's doesn't do much veggie, might have been more of a treat for you.'

'No, this is all right.' *McDonald's?* If Bathsheba started treating him like a kid, then . . . then all grown ups were the same after all. And her making out like Fred was a veggie too – she knew he wasn't. Unless she couldn't be bothered to remember.

Bathsheba ordered a Greek salad roll, but Fred wasn't too sure he'd like whatever that was, so he asked for egg and salad cream. They only had egg with mayo. Couldn't even get that right, saying the proper thing to want in a pants dump like this.

'How's your summer holidays going then, sweetie-pie?' Bathsheba was picking the black olives out of her roll, eating them first. Totally sophisticated. What's the word he'd found the other day? *Gastronomic*. Maybe Fred could get to like olives.

'All right, bit boring,' he said. Perhaps it wasn't so bad in here. 'Mum's always at work, right, and it gets a bit . . . boring, hanging round with your mates all the time.'

'My mum died when I was exactly your age.' Her voice gone all serious. 'Might sound bizarre, but one of the worst things was so how boring it was without her. Suppose because I was much, much younger than my brothers.' She'd never told him anything like that before. No one had.

'Bummer,' he said.

'What about Maggie, though?' she asked. 'You spend a lot of time with her.'

'Yeah. But not always.' Fred had a big mouthful of his Coke, tried not to burp. 'Sometimes I'm not allowed. Got things to do, in it. She can't be . . . at my becking call.'

'Beck *and* call. Your Uncle Garry told me she seems to be thinking of retiring? *Again*. So he gathered, anyway.' Bathsheba put her serviette on top of her roll. If that was all she was going to eat, she'd starve to death. 'But she doesn't give much away, does she?' Even her laugh was neat, like she could control it. 'Come on, just between us, is Maggie going to give up work this time? Can she truly afford to?'

'Maggie? Thought you meant Mum, then. That'd be brilliant, if Mum stopped work.' Fred pulled a bit of cucumber out his roll. Rank. 'Nan doesn't work, B.'

'No, silly me.' She reached over for Fred's serviette, dabbed the corners of her mouth with it. 'I meant do less, that's all.'

'Like looking after me?' Wasn't good news.

'Oh, I shouldn't think so, sugar plum. Just . . . less.' Bathsheba put her hand out, squeezed his arm. Fred had a glance round, see if anyone'd noticed. 'Maybe your Mummy *will* be able to give up work. Might come into some money, you never know your luck.'

'Yeah, right. Mum never even does the lottery.'

'It could be yooooou,' Bathsheba said, making the poncy kids stare. 'Freddie, do Mummy or Maggie ever mention my daddy?'

'Don't know.' Fred shrugged. 'Mickey McGowan? Well, yeah, no, she doesn't?'

'What about my brothers?'

'Don't know. Why?' Fred felt a bit funny, like he was grassing

22

Nan up, even though he didn't have anything to say, and so was letting B down at the same time.

'Just wondering about Christmas,' Bathsheba said, picking up her coffee. She had it black. 'Thought it'd be nice for us all to get together, one big family. Like that, wouldn't you, darling? I know you love me, and it's what *I* want.' Looking at him over her cup. Fred's mouth went dry.

'Yeah, wicked.' But Nan never liked Bathsheba's family, even though Uncle Garry worked with them. That Mickey McGowan was a *nasty bugger* – one time, Nan shouted at Garry that McGowan was a murderer. Couldn't of meant it, but it had to stand for something bad. Nan wasn't too keen on B, neither. Was blatant. 'Christmas is ages, though.'

'Let's face it, we so ought to start building some more bridges before then.' Bathsheba nodded at a waitress and the bill came, like the credits at the pictures. Fred's guts went empty. Even compared to normal, this was a quick meeting. Wasn't fair. Not worth coming hardly. He shovelled the rest of his roll down fast, save wasting it. Bathsheba took some money out her purse, got to her feet. 'Come on, Freds, time to go, sweetie.'

Definitely no afters, then. Those cakes didn't look bad.

Outside, it was well hot. Fred wished he was wearing shorts, he could easily of got away with them in that rubbish café. Bathsheba didn't look like she ever sweated, ever, though course she must do. She gave Fred a massive hug. Was he meant to hug her back? He settled for sort of patting her shoulder. Wished she'd been arsed to stay a bit longer.

'Bye-bye, sweetie,' she said. 'Must dash, I've got a rehearsal near here.' She turned away and walked off through the market, without looking back. People *always* had a reason for rushing off, like there wasn't a choice. Fred couldn't be bothered going home yet, no law to say he couldn't walk the same way B had. Better be careful, case she noticed him and thought he was following her. Which he wasn't. Could go fuck herself, if she reckoned he was. He started off well slow, though he could still see Bathsheba's back. Not that good round here, didn't know

23

why people got excited. If you went down the other way and along, wouldn't that take you to Mum's shop, where she worked? He wasn't going there. Way embarrassing, clothes made out of rubber and stuff – for perves, it was. Mum reckoned it wasn't a sex shop, but Fred knew the clothes had to do with doing it, right. They *did*. No one would wear things like that going down the street or even to a party, would they? So they must have to do with it. Stupid. Made more sense if you wore nothing. Anyway, the shitty shop didn't interest him, and Uncle Garry's shop didn't neither, though Fred wouldn't of minded a look in the club sometime. Uncle Garry said he could, if he didn't mention it at home, but it hadn't happened yet.

Bathsheba nipped through a little street, one with dirty book-shops and that, and when she got to the top, where the bigger road with proper shops was, she hung back to look in a window. Fred went to the end of the side street again, hoping she wouldn't turn round – make him look a right tit, lounging about here. He stared, all casual, down the way they'd just walked. A man roughly Uncle Garry's age, only in a well flash suit and with all the bling bling, was striding along swinging his briefcase like his shit didn't stink, like he didn't know it was pervy alley. He stopped in front of a shop, then went in. Obviously didn't care one bit if anyone saw him going to buy toss-off magazines. Fred glanced over his shoulder, but Bathsheba was looking away from him, along the road, like she was waiting now for a cab or something. He'd just stay till B was gone, then carry on. Few minutes, and the pervy bloke came out again, this time with no briefcase, and went back the way he'd come. Funny, leaving your stuff behind in a place like that. Where'd he put his dirty mags? Sounded like a taxi pulled in nearby then, so Fred turned to see if it was for Bathsheba.

Sky blew up.

End of the world.

Pavement under his face.

* * *

At the last minute, Jacob took the Angel video out of his music case, put it in the drawer. The one place where Angel still breathed, moved, smiled; Jacob felt weird, keeping it, but he couldn't stand the thought of letting it go. The address in the letter could have the rest, all five; he'd watched them, and there was nothing of Angel there. Not that Jacob was planning ever again to look at the one he'd held back, but he didn't want it to belong to anyone else. It'd be like throwing the last of Angel's life away. The past two days had given Jacob some perspective: of course he'd been ostensibly turned on by what he'd seen, it was the shock, the reaction to Angel's death. It was grief. Having Angel return for those few minutes . . . the feeling had come out physically, that was all. Most people would have responded the same way. *You reckon, do you, Mitzvah?* He did, yeah, and nothing Angel or anyone else could say would convince him otherwise.

He dreamed them, though. Jacob desperately hoped that would stop, the images of Angel, Lucinda Luscious, the strange bloke, fucking in the night. Meantime, he'd try to achieve what Angel had wanted; not only the least he could do, fulfil his friend's last wish, but Jacob felt it would somehow clean out the other night from his mind. Make him recognizable to himself as a man who did the decent thing. Had Angel known those people in the video? Were they his friends, or simply work colleagues? Maybe the whole episode had been a cold, academic experiment. Jacob couldn't imagine sleeping with someone who wasn't his friend, not in reality. But then, porn wasn't real. It was made-up feelings, invented sensation; perhaps you could fake even friendship, liking, in that context. Couldn't begin to think what made people go into porn. Especially women. All the women Jacob knew thought pornography was stupid at best, even degrading and dangerous. He tried to imagine Susie in a movie, but the vision wouldn't appear. She'd have hated him for even attempting to conjure it, more than she did already. *Jesus, stop fucking thinking, Jake, just get going. Dolly bloody Daydream.* Surely that couldn't be one of Angel's expressions?

Jacob hadn't often been up that way. He'd laid down a few tracks there once, for Mark Five, and he'd played several times round and about, God, must be a good couple of years ago now. But he couldn't say he was familiar with the place. He'd looked up the street in the *A–Z*, saw it was best to get out at Tottenham Court Road. At least, he thought that was right. Maybe he'd make a day of it, have a bite of lunch, couple of pints. Though he *was* working tonight, wasn't he, perhaps better keep a clear head meantime. Since Angel's letter, Jacob had been drinking twice as much as usual, as though they were both still twenty with livers of steel. Yet at forty-one, he ought to be able to play out his natural caution rather than some bad variation on Angel's bloody signature theme. *You fucking wimp. Scared of what Rebbe Kosher might say? Go on, live a bit.* Not the sort of advice Jacob would be likely to take from a dead man.

All the same, it was a difficult gig to face sober: Jacob didn't even know if the videos were legal, and here he was, taking them to some dodgy shop. In the three days since Jacob had received Angel's letter, it had come to seem less bloody melo-dramatic, less a potentially humiliating game than a reason-able request. The final request. But as he walked past neon lights that were surely unnecessary in the daytime, heavy bass beating the air, he began to feel that old, familiar anxiety in his stomach; what the hell was Angel up to? After a couple of false hopes, Jacob turned right at Walker's Court, down one of the seemingly identical back roads, and found Peter Street. God, as though personification would lend it an identity. The shops all looked the same, too: blacked out windows, brightly painted signs, a mixture of hiding and boasting, of cover-up and display, a weird kind of tease. Embarrassing, having to read those signs rather than being able to pretend he was just cutting through the alley. Gay Knights. Everything But The Girls. Domino. The Book 'n' Film Emporium. Well, here he was. Couldn't hang round outside deciding whether to go in, that'd make him look even more a voyeur. Jacob pushed open the door.

It only bloody jingled. Like a chemist's or an off-licence. Jacob was so taken aback, it took him a couple of seconds to register the inside of the place. Brighter than he'd expected, almost like the Hampstead Bookstore, with rows of videos and DVDs and paperbacks: yeah, he could be at work, except these all had lurid covers. Not as full-on as he'd envisaged, though; perhaps the heavy stuff was out the back. Next to the till, a portable television was facing the wrong way, so customers couldn't see the screen. There were red velvet curtains along one wall, a tiny sign above declaring Booths. Were there punters in there now? That, he didn't like to think about. Before he had time to worry too much, a man came through from the door behind the counter, holding a bunch of keys. Late thirties, carrying a little too much weight, receding fair hair worn a touch too long. He had nothing like Jacob's height . . . then, comparatively, not many people did. The man nodded, but barely. Maybe he expected Jacob to browse. There was something familiar about him, though it was probably just the generic type that Jacob recognized: a drinker, in a suit that would be cool if it were made of the right schmutter, conventional good looks disappearing inch by inch under flab and two-tone.

'Uh . . . Hi.' Jacob went over to the counter. 'Are you the manager?'

'We're licensed.' The bloke nodded again, more perceptibly.

'Right.' Shit, was he being offered a drink? 'This might sound a bit strange—'

'Nothing sounds strange to me, mate.' He took a cigar from his jacket pocket, lit it, waited. Bloody disquieting; if Jacob had been a genuine punter, he'd be terrified.

'A friend of mine . . . ' *You're a nebbish, Jake.* Oh, screw it. He'd just come out with it, and if the bloke had a problem, Jacob would simply leave. 'I was given some videos. They . . . I was told they were worth something.'

'Selling?' Sounding bored, but his small eyes all of a sudden piggy, greedy.

'Not sure I care.' Jacob put his music case on the counter.

'There's five of them, see?' He opened the case to show the contents.

'Yeah.' The man puffed on his cigar. Nice little chat they were having. Jacob shook the videos out on to the counter. The manager took one of the films from its blank case, stuck it into the machine underneath the television. 'Let's have a butcher's, then.' He pressed a button. Jacob heard the opening bars of the cheap music, the first sighs. The man watched, his face not changing. A few minutes in, he switched it off. 'Early Rami Tardah, introducing Lucinda Luscious,' he said. 'A wind-up, is it?'

'If it is, I'm the one being wound up,' said Jacob. Surprisingly firm. *Ask for the manager and don't say I sent you. Sell the videos if you want, that's up to you. But keep schtum.* 'If they're worthless, just say.' Either way, he wanted them gone.

'Speaking true, they're not a total loss. Course, Luscious has been retired years now. That helps.' Eyeing Jacob. 'Could give you . . . two hundred notes for the five? Assuming they're all the same quality. Have to check.' He smiled then, showing slightly stained teeth. 'No, tell you what, they're your gold-fish, make it two-twenty. Best touch you'll get, mate.' He changed videos, running the next one for just a minute or so.

'Two-twenty.' How did Jacob know what was meant by valu-able? He'd admitted he didn't know what they were worth, the bloke was bound to be ripping him off. 'I thought more like three,' Jacob said.

'Aw, *mat*e, can't be done.' Putting his cigar in the ashtray on the counter, the third video into the machine. 'Look, you want rid? Struth, if you do, you could trawl round every shop in bastard London, and still finish up back here, begging for me two-twenty.'

'Two-fifty.' Where was this coming from? Never bartered in his life.

'Hang about.' In silence, the manager ran a few seconds of each of the other tapes. 'All right,' he said, when he'd finished. 'Two-fifty. But that's your lot.'

28

'Done,' said Jacob. *You have been.* But he didn't care. He'd gone through with the first part of what Angel wanted, and meantime got himself a few quid. What would he do with the tapes anyway, if he were to keep them? It wasn't as though he was selling Angel. He watched his money being counted out. 'Thanks,' he said. The manager's handshake was firm, businesslike; weirdly, Jacob was reassured, as though he hadn't been too badly ripped off after all. 'Uh . . . Bye.' He turned to go, walking quickly from the shop, the door-jamb jingling behind him. It was like being Mr Ben. Angel had loved that programme.

Outside, the street was swamped by the sun; Jacob squinted, wishing he hadn't lost his shades. That was the third lot this summer, and it was only July. Still, he could afford a decent pair now. What his mother called *mad money*: it came unexpectedly, so you didn't feel you had to spend it on essentials. Jacob always got by, he had to concede that occasionally he even did quite well, if he tucked in some serious studio hours between the gigs and his three days in the bookshop, but it wasn't often two hundred and fifty quid came his way, just like that. For the first time since Angel's letter, he felt quite cheerful.

The noise was incredible.

As if the whole city had blown up.

Glass and videos.

Took Jacob a couple of seconds to realize what he'd seen: in the street opposite, across the road from where he was standing, a shop-front had exploded. Outwards. People knocked off their feet by the blast. No flames, but a dense clump of smoke drifting down the street on top of the debris. God, oh my God. If Angel had given him a different address, Jacob might have been in that very shop. And in *yeneh velt.* How long since he'd last prayed? Years. Twenty years, probably. Now, Jacob prayed.

'Well, you're a bleeding pickle.' Maggie tipped some TCP on to a bit of cottonwool, dabbed at the scrape on Fred's cheek. He hardly even flinched. Was her that was the bag of nerves – say he'd been killed? Didn't bear thinking about. What she couldn't make out was why Fred'd been up there in the first place, him being on his way to see his mum at work just didn't wash. Least Lu'd had the sense to send him home in a cab, though you'd think she could of got the rest of the day off, come with him. Half Soho was bound to be shut because of it, anyway. 'There are, you're done. Nothing much wrong with you, a nice cakey won't cure.' Please God. She binned the cottonwool.

'Nice *cakey*? I'm not five.' But he grinned and sat down. 'Fancied one all day, as it goes. What sort of cakey?'

'I got some Battenberg . . . no, you're not struck on that, are you? There's a couple of them mini-roll things, if you've not had them already, or a proper swiss roll. Chocolate.'

'Can't I have both?'

'Coming it, ain't you?' Maggie kissed the top of his head and went to get his cakes, patting her wig to see it was straight. 'Don't think you're getting this treatment every time you nearly get yourself blown up,' she called through. Making her voice purposely light.

Didn't know what the world was flaming coming to, shops being bombed, no one caring who got hurt. Wicked. Suppose it was a rival lot – there was loads of funny takeover stuff at the minute, so Garry said. Outsider businessmen, respectable types, behaving like tinpot gangsters to get their hands on the shops and clubs. Well, and course, council licences coming in took sex places right away from the workers. Red tape. Enough to turn you commie. Thank God it weren't Garry or Lulu in there. Made Maggie's heart go over. Soho was getting so flaming dangerous – mind, whole of London was, if she weren't very much mistaken. Them nail bombs a couple of year back, one was in Old Compton Street and she seemed to remember there was one in Brixton, but the other was bleeding Brick Lane. Couldn't go anywhere and be sure you'd come home safe. Fred was only a baby, and he could of been dead by now. Dead. Out of nowhere, Maggie burst into tears, but she blew

30

her nose quick on a piece of kitchen roll before the crying got hold. Mustn't let the boy see her fear. She took the bits through on a tray.

'Just children's programmes on now, in it,' he said. 'Better than nothing.'

All drugs and violence everywhere, nowadays. Not like when Maggie was young. Then it'd been classy clubs even in Soho, people looking out for their own. Where the brasses had a bit of something, offered a proper service. She'd had that room off Wardour Street herself for a year or so, maid and all, way back when. Yeah, there'd always been a few bad apples, blimey, Maggie knew that better'n anyone, but it hadn't been like today.

Maggie worried for the kids, she really did. Specially Garry. Weren't at all convinced she'd done the right thing letting his engagement to that Bathsheba go on. If she hadn't, doubt he'd be working for her family now, but it was hard to put your foot down when your boy seemed happy for the first time in his life. Something funny about that girl, something not quite right about all of them. The bleeding McGowans weren't no angels anyway, whatever Garry made out. Dreaded to think what they might be into, if the boys was anything like their father. Though surely even that family wouldn't blow up a place where a kid might be near. As for Lulu, she didn't ought to work up there at all, she should get herself a nice little job round here somewhere, the Tescos in Bethnal Green maybe. Have more of a chance to keep an eye on Fred, then. Nine o'clock she finished, some nights, and that's without the getting back. Weren't on.

Maggie lit a cig, ignoring Fred's massive sigh. He'd have to lump it, after nearly giving her heart failure.

'Nice programme?' Maggie asked. Reaching for her glasses off the nest of tables.

'No, bit boring.' He gulped the last of his Coke. 'Nan . . . does it matter if you see something and not say? If it might not of got anything to do with anything?' He touched his cheek. 'You shouldn't grass, should you? Ever.'

'What you bleeding on about?' Having a conversation with Fred could be worse than trying to do one of Mr Piozzi's cryptic crosswords with her drawers round her ankles.

'Just wondering, you know. Can I get some more Coke?'

'Wondering what, love?'

'Nothing.' He stood up. 'Can I get a can, then?' He went out the kitchen, come in drinking his pop. 'See,' he said, sitting down again, 'I *think* . . . I saw a man go in that shop, just before. When he came out, he never had his briefcase. He went in with one, definitely.'

'Well, that don't mean nothing.' Maggie felt she might cry again, what was ridiculous, he was safe. Doubted the man he'd see was important, but she didn't want Fred bothered by the Old Bill. Or by whoever done the damage, more to the point.

'You sure?' His sharp eyes looked into hern. 'I mean, right, he might of had to do with it? You know, he might of had something in his briefcase, yeah.'

'Even if he did do, he's long gone by now, love. Don't worry your head about it, nothing to do with us.' She put out her cig. 'You always did have a vivid imagination.'

'And you always say that.' Looking at the screen again. 'Can I have *Friends* on later, at six, or do we have to have the news?'

'Chancing your arm now, you know I love me news.' But anything to stop him thinking about some bloke he most likely wouldn't recognize in a strong light with an arrow pointing. Besides, the explosion was bound to be on the news, she didn't want Fred seeing that. 'Have to get you home after, though,' she said. 'I'll give you some money for fish and chips, to have indoors. And I'll walk far as the chippy with you, case you come over queer.'

He only nodded, and even though he was still facing the telly, Maggie could see he was choked. But Welsh Adrian was due over with his nappy – until she retired, she had a living to make. Not like she was the boy's mother, after all.

* * *

32

After three large brandies, Jacob felt a little better. He'd watched the police arrive to cordon off the street, the market stalls turned into festival attractions, then made his way out with the other evacuees until he'd come across a paper shop, where he'd bought a king size Mars bar. Weird how slowly he'd eaten it, really tasting each mouthful, standing in the holiday-feel sun; difficult to comprehend that the same sun was shining on the wreckage, that the weather hadn't darkened, that tourists were still smiling, picking up tans. Carefully, Jacob had put the chocolate wrapper in a bin, found his way to this pub. Would have expected the whole area to be closed, but that was probably impossible; maybe this was so regular an occurrence that they knew exactly how to contain it with the least inconvenience. He'd stopped shaking now, might even get to his gig later, be able to play after all. One more brandy, and meantime he'd decide what to do about the Dawson niece.

'I heard it was a takeover bid. Or someone hadn't been paid.'

'Wouldn't be surprised if it was Arabs. Fundamentalists.'

'Wasn't even all that bad, the copper told me, more mess than anything. Hardly September eleventh. Someone's going to get good copy, though.'

Although this was obviously a professionals' pub, heaving with suits, all the conversations at the bar seemed to be crass speculation about the explosion. Jacob slipped between a red-cheeked bloke and a blonde woman whose skirt was even redder, waved his fiver at the barmaid. Strange how there wasn't more shock, more outrage; people were interested, but detached, as though it were something that had happened in another city rather than a mile or so away. Totally different from Jacob's experience of '74, when the IRA had blown up the Seven Stars and the Horse and Groom: the whole of Guildford had been rocked for months. Mum hadn't liked him going into town for ages. Clearly London was more blasé than Surrey, had probably learned to be. Maybe it was because the blast *had* occurred in this city that there wasn't any hysteria or even particular surprise.

33

Impressive. The barmaid must be good at her job, seeing that she could remember a stranger's drink in a crowded bar. He knew he was too fussy about bar staff, probably because he met so many of them. But as his mother always said, there wasn't any excuse for giving a job other than your best. *Fucking mummy's boy*. Great, Angel could have got him killed, and was still taking the piss in Jacob's head. This, he could live without.

He took his brandy back to the tiny round table. Lit a cigarette, the last in the packet. Before all this, he'd been down to a few cigarettes a week, if that, now he was back on nearly twenty a day. Jacob took his *A–Z* from his pocket; as far as he could work it out, the shop he wanted was much nearer to Dean Street than to the explosion, so was probably still open. *Don't ever learn to drive, Jake, you'll have a head-on down a one-way street in the first five minutes.* Oddly, his mother had said something very similar when he was young. Trouble with most people was they believed what they were told about themselves; he was no different. Perhaps Angel was telling Jacob he wouldn't have the bottle to find the Dawson woman, to speak to her, without knowing why he was being asked. Could be a test after all, and yeah, one Angel knew Jacob would be bound to fail. Well, screw that, not this time. *Don't tell me, more fucking closure. Can we say the words 'cod' and 'psychology'?*

Swallowing his drink, Jacob stood up, ground his cigarette into the ashtray. As he pushed his way out of the pub, his heart sped up; stupid, it wasn't as though he was likely to walk into another explosion, this wasn't Israel. Or even 1974. Calm down, calm down. Couldn't be that he was nervous about this meeting: he didn't even know for sure he'd actually get to speak to her. *Don't mention my name.* No idea what he'd say, even if she were there and willing to talk. Angel was beginning to piss him off again; here Jacob was, years on, and still he was running incomprehensible errands for his so-called friend. Though for the last time. That, he promised himself.

Must have been because he was thinking of other things

that Jacob found himself in the right street without any problems. Once he realized he was there, he started to breathe a little too fast; wasn't much more than an hour since he'd seen the window blown out, only natural that his body would remember. It did help that this road was much nicer: a café with pavement tables on the corner, the thick smell of coffee, a bar, lots of clear, clean glass fronts. The people walking along looked normal, rational, and as though they belonged rather than were visiting. Jacob held his breath for a couple of seconds, slowly exhaled, then began to look for the name Angel had given him. Heaven Scent.

A women's clothes shop. Jacob hadn't known what to expect, but he'd thought it would be worse than this, especially after having been in the video place, that it would at least sell gadgets, if not girls. Yet when he went in, he found all it held was a small collection of expensive-looking PVC, rubber, leather. Jacob checked out a couple of random price tags: God, yeah, *really* expensive. There were a few people in the shop, browsing.

Then he saw her.

Oh. My. God. *Gotcha*. Of course. Was Jacob a congenital idiot? *Remember, I know you, better than anyone has ever known you.* Angel totally believed he had Jacob's number: he'd be taken to this woman only by stealth, when he might otherwise have walked away. Jacob was being played with. Again. Arrogant fucking bastard. Bastard. Bastard.

Hadn't registered before that she was tall, must be five nine or more, even without the little heels she was wearing; he'd only have to drop his gaze to look directly into hers. She'd put on weight since those videos, was obviously ten, maybe fifteen years older, but still she was much more sexy in the flesh: long red hair caught at the side with a bow, perfect fingernails, a classy black dress, tight and low-cut, showing an impressive cleavage. Her smile was the thing that got to him though, lighting up her pale blue eyes, making her seem kind, infinitely hospitable. Stopped him from walking straight out. She came towards him. He smiled back at her.

'Hi,' she said. 'Can I help you, or are you just looking?' Her voice shop-bought, carefully laid over East End sounds. Gentle. He glanced at the name tag on her dress.

'Lulu? Maybe you *could* help me. What time do you get off?' That was the most upfront thing Jacob had said in his life. It was as though Angel had spoken for him.

Bathsheba smiled at her reflection in the big mirror. Thank goodness the silly lapdog hadn't been hurt. She was certain Fred could be trusted not to mention her name in the story he was undoubtedly telling (with masses of embellishments), he deserved the little pressie she'd send him. *And* he'd practically walked into a bomb for love of her. Had to admit, the boy might be as irritating as thrush, but he was loyal. Occasionally useful, too. Made her fond enough of him, in a way. Hardly surprising that Fred had latched on to her, adored her – his fat mother and that ancient control freak were (if you were going to be honest) so just a pair of selfish slappers. Probably hadn't even registered that Fred was a bit shaken up.

It *had* to be something to do with Stephen Hopkins. He'd already got ISU's paws completely round lots of the smaller outlets, and nobody thought their legit status made them squeaky clean (well, big business was borrowing oodles of techniques from the more *traditional* Soho vendors, these days). Pathetic old Nozzer's shop was his only income, yet he'd have to sell to Hopkins for buttons now. If her brothers were right, Nozzer had been losing money hand over fist (and let's face it, they were always right about things like that), no one had been hurt by the bomb . . . how was that going to look? Like an insurance job, that's how. Especially as he didn't have a council licence to sell hardishcore – no way could he compete with the shops that did. Or raise the twenty-five grand to get one. Bathsheba laughed, pulled her thumb back to touch her wrist. You had to admit, assuming it *was* ISU, they were a neat operation. If Hopkins weren't black, his hands would be practically lily-white. Yet it was a bloody extreme thing to have done, even without the risk of being pulled up – there was something intriguing about a businessman who'd resort to a villain's mindset, in some flashy display of how far he was prepared to go just to buy a property.

Humming that catchy Spandau Ballet thing she used to love, she leaned into a hamstring stretch, pointed her toe to the ceiling to get a better pull. Lifted her head to look at herself reflected in that position. Not bad, but her bum could do with a bit of work. Bloody tiring, staying down at six stone thirteen, making sure that every muscle kept its tone (mm, and almost thirty was getting a tad old for that to remain practical). There had to be more fulfilling ways to spend her time. If she could turn her own nominal slice of the McGowan business into a proper advantage, she'd be independent. Have the life she deserved. Garry wasn't doing badly (all things considered) but he needed a pushlette to really make it. Needed to stop being a *good bloke*, to become the man she so knew he could be, away from their families. If Bathsheba had to do many more corporate gigs for the bloody Japs, she'd scream, although obviously she could never bear to do nothing, to end up like Mama. Still, she was almost sure now she'd landed the dinner show at ISU. Everything these days was about networking, about *displaying* the right mindset. Daddy's ruthlessness might not save him, but she'd show him how much he'd (unwittingly) taught her, and it was so going to save her. She'd make her 5 per cent of *his* firm work for her and against that bastard, or perish.

Curving her spine into a backbend, Bathsheba looked between her legs at her smiling face. Didn't the stupid punters realize that every smile cost them? She knew people on the circuit who lived for what they did, performing ever more ridiculous contortions. Not her. She had other unique gifts. If Daddy would give her some credit for once, offer her a position, there might be no need to look elsewhere. But the vicious old git never would (no one changed in their sixties, did they?), and Bathsheba had no time for fantasists. Besides, she didn't give the McGowan united front much chance of long-term survival. Oh, they so didn't know how much those lost shares were going to cost them . . . not that anyone else in the family even knew yet they were gone. Idiots. In one easy movement, she stood up, started on her triceps. When she was out of this, she'd never put any of her limbs through anything outside the ordinary again.

A knock on the dressing-room door. She knew whose that was. Didn't like Garry visiting her before a gig, but she was in too optimistic a place to remind him.

'You look terrific, B.' He eyed up the new costume (or what there was of it), kissed her lightly on the mouth. Nice, how he still looked at her as though she was the most beautiful woman in London. That no matter what she said to him, he'd never lay a finger on her in anger, or just for the hell of it, that he'd keep worshipping her. Accepting her. No matter what she did. 'You hear about Nozz?' he asked. 'Poor bastard. Aw, *mate*, guess what? Caught some punter today, make a nice bit of bunce on that.'

'That's fab, darling.' Didn't it occur to him to wonder about the explosion?

'Paid two-fifty for some vids worth a couple or three hundred more'n that, easy.' He laughed, obviously delighted with himself. High time she set his sights . . . well, higher. 'Yeah, but guess what they was?' Garry took out a cigar, though he knew better than to light it in here, the sweetheart. But had that suit always been naff? *So* nineties. She'd give it to Oxfam. Would get him to have a Bruce Willis, as well – he'd look great with a close crop, he had the cheekbones for it. A teeth-bleaching wouldn't go amiss, either. Reaching her fingertips towards the ceiling in a final stretch, she raised her eyebrows at him. 'They're Lu's,' he said. 'Her first films, more or less. That a coincidence or what?'

Bathsheba stared. Her skin went goosey. Didn't he think it at all odd (though face it, for all his masses of good points, imagination wasn't his strongest) that it was Garry those videos had found their way to? And today.

'A real coincidence,' she said.

Chapter Three

Lulu had forgotten, in those few days since she'd met him, how good-looking Jacob was. He wasn't the sort of bloke she'd notice straight off, not precisely, even though his being so tall did make him stand out. But now she was sat across a table from him, them enormous dark eyes, and all that curly hair, and the way his smile got reflected in loads of creases down his cheeks . . . she realized again how they added up to a seriously attractive man. Was like he had to get – what's the word? – animated, for you really to be able to see him. He looked his age, maybe even a bit older than forty-one, but he seemed in terrific nick at the same time. Wiry body, not much grey among the dark, no stiffness in his movements. And there was something about his eyes that could belong to a much younger person. Lulu wasn't clever enough to say what that was, but she knew it was there. Jacob Fox. Yeah, and he was one. Suddenly, she wished she'd bought this bra in an F, it was too tight, that was going to mark her. Thirty-odd quid just to get four bosoms, like a cow. Was possible she might need to worry about that later, despite Maggie's warning to hold off.

'Do you mind if I smoke?' Jacob took out an unopened packet of fags. Oh great, weren't they them stinky French things? Though Lulu couldn't remember any bloke asking if she minded before. About anything, really. Maybe some posh blokes were different.

'No, course not,' she said. He hadn't smoked at that first meeting, but then they *had* gone for just the one swift drink then, of course, where she'd had to get back, see Fred was all

39

right after his fright, and Jacob'd had to get off to work. A pianist. Hard to believe she'd be seeing him play in a bit. 'Funny, I've never smoked myself,' she added. 'Not even when I was young. Never fancied it, I think because my auntie smokes so much. She more or less brought me up, see.' Shit, was she gushing on? She smiled, pushed the ashtray across the table to him. Jacob lit his fag, picked up his pint.

'Well, I'm pleased you don't mind anyway, I really need this cigarette,' he said. 'Comparatively nervous about playing with you here. Better watch how much booze I have beforehand, or I'll be doing the "Volga Boat Song". A crap version.'

'Nervous? With me? Why?' This was good news. Lulu let her look stay on him for – *one elephant, two elephants, three elephants, four elephants* – four exact seconds before asking again. 'Why?'

'Don't know,' he said at last. 'It's been a while since a woman saw me perform.' Then he laughed. 'Didn't mean that how it sounded.'

'Yeah, I realize that.' If he'd blushed, or made some crude joke, Lulu would of been put off. But what he'd said was just right.

'Though come to think of it . . . ' Jacob drew on his fag, his eyes still smiling. 'I'm not exactly Mr Casanova,' he added.

'Mr Casanova most likely wasn't Mr Casanova, if you'd of asked his wife,' Lulu said. That made him laugh again. Lulu had a warm feeling in her tummy – Jacob liked her, she knew he did. There were loads of women in the bar, but he obviously wasn't bothered by their opinion of his piano playing, only by hers. She believed him that he hadn't brought anyone to a gig lately. Funny, the way he'd asked her out in the shop, she'd never of had him down as a bit shy, though he was. Hardly said anything at their first attempt at going for a drink. Till he'd asked to see her again, she'd thought he was regretting saying for her to meet him. But this time felt better, more like a proper date. And his shyness wasn't over the top, just a nice change from most of the cocky gits she met. This club was nice, too – plush seats, decent glasses, and her favourite thing, dim lighting. A girl needed all the help she could get after thirty-five. Lulu finished off her Chablis. 'Can I buy *you* a drink?' she said.

'No, stay where you are, I'll get them.' Jacob signalled to a waiter, holding up two fingers. Lulu couldn't help smiling. This was great, she didn't even have to get her round in. And everyone knew him. All right, he worked here, so they would do, but it was still a nice feeling, that he was known and it wasn't because people were scared of him or he had something on them. Been a long old time since Lulu had been out with someone normal. Just have to hope he never found out who she used to be. What she used to be. Somehow, she didn't think he'd be one of them blokes who were turned on by the thought of fucking an ex-porn actress. A lot were, but not someone like Jacob. Didn't even seem to fit with him that he'd come into Heaven Scent.

The waiter brought their drinks over. Out of habit, Lulu rested her look on him, but only for two elephants. She didn't think Jacob would like the woman he was out with to flirt with the bar staff. He had manners.

'Tell me something about yourself, Lulu.' Jacob stubbed out his fag. 'Go on, anything you like.' Staring at her embarrassed silence with friendly eyes. What was she meant to do, come out with her life story? That's one thing she wasn't going to talk about. 'Okay,' he said. 'What's your favourite food?'

'Food? Jesus, can't you see I like bloody everything?' She patted her podgy waist. Then she heard Maggie's voice in her earhole, *Say bad things about yourself, men'll believe them.* 'But what I really like is steak and chips. Pudding and custard. Eels, mash and liquor. That sort of thing.'

'Old-fashioned grub,' said Jacob. Grinning.

'Well, precisely.'

'Me too.' He rubbed his tummy, like a little kid. 'My favourite's dreadful illicit stuff, like bacon sandwiches. Want to get something to eat afterwards? I can't stand people who don't like to

41

eat, can you? Give me Nigella Lawson over Geri Halliwell any day.'

'No. I mean, no, I can't either. Thanks, I'd love to go out after.' She'd never had a conversation like this, not with a man. Oh shit, she was really starting to enjoy herself, but she hadn't mentioned Fred yet. And that might well turn him right off, never mind what she said about her appearance. Get it over with, girl, if it was going to make a difference, it would. Better sooner rather than later. Fred might be a nuisance sometimes, but he was a fact of life. And he was *her* nuisance. Anyway, after him being nearly caught by that bomb, it'd be tempting fate, denying she had a son. 'My boy eats like there's no tomorrow,' she said. Her voice a bit too high. 'He's twelve, going on thirteen. Good thing he's an only, or I'd be skint before I started.'

'Growing spurt,' said Jacob. Looking completely unfazed. 'I was the same myself at that age. Meantime, my mother said she couldn't keep enough bread in the house, the amount of toast I got through. A whole loaf for a snack. Is his dad around?'

'Nope. Never has been.' She wasn't going there.

'You must be close, then.' Jacob lit another fag, smiling, easy. He was just too bloody good to be true. Maybe he'd turn out to be a psycho, one of them people the neighbours claim always kept themselves to themselves. 'I'm an only child, too,' he said. 'My father left us when I was about four. I see him, but it's my mother who's my . . . primary parent, even now.'

'You got kids?'

'I haven't, no.' Told like it was a pity? 'What about the rest of your family?'

'Nothing to say there. It's, you know, ordinary.' Lulu sipped her wine. Not a lie, it was ordinary enough to her, wasn't it? 'There's my Auntie Maggie, who's like my mum – my boy even calls her *Nan* – and my cousin Garry, who's like my brother, and then he lives with a girl.' The acid test. Most men got overexcited when she mentioned Bathsheba. 'She's a contortionist,' Lulu said.

Jacob creased up. As if it was the funniest thing he'd ever heard.

'Don't know what the hell to say to that,' he managed to get out. 'For a living?'

'Oh yeah. Think she started in a trendy circus thing. She's quite well known in—'

'Contorting circles? Wouldn't call that ordinary.' Jacob was still laughing. Unless she'd lost her radar, that wasn't sexual interest he was feeling. Or if it was, it was directed to herself. Was such a shame Lulu had never really liked actual sex much at all.

'She's called Bathsheba. It's her real name, believe it or not.'

'This just gets better.' Jacob tried to draw on his fag, and coughed, where he still had some laugh left in his mouth. 'God, I'm sorry, it must sound like I'm taking the piss. It's just so . . . surprising. Bathsheba what?' He took a gulp of his pint.

'McGowan. Bathsheba McGowan.'

'Nice.' Jacob put down his glass. Then another waiter appeared, gave Jacob a nod. 'I'm sorry, I've got to play. Will you be all right on your own? The piano's just over there, look.' He sounded . . . distracted or something. Most probably gearing up for what he was about to go and do. She felt a small clutch of excitement in her tummy. And nerves – what if he was rubbish? 'Lulu? I said will you be okay?'

'Oh, course. Looking forward to it.'

'Good.' He smiled, and kissed her on the forehead, for some strange reason. Just soft. Hardly a kiss at all. 'Wish me luck,' he said.

Finishing her rice cake, Bathsheba carried her plate through to the kitchen. Garry was late tonight, better not be with his bloody mother. Well, retiring or not, that washed-up tart would soon learn where Garry's real loyalties lay. No, actually he was more likely to be playing snooker with Stan and Del. Or with them at the Holly Blue, ogling the women. Her brothers did their absolute best to corrupt Garry, they really did. Not that she'd ever have anything serious to worry about on that score (he had a lot in common with Fred when it came to devotion), which was part of why she'd decided on him in the first place. Of course, Garry had so been gorgeous three years ago – he was a bit too content these days and it showed in his figure, she needed to put some hunger back. Perhaps a diet, as long as it didn't sap his sexual energies – his cock was the one thing that made her feel full. Made the humiliation go away. She rinsed the sink round, put the kettle on for some chamomile tea, chewing on a piece of kitchen roll to stop her raiding the fridge herself. Yeah, they were so having a nice boys' night out – she'd get a phone call around midnight, full of drunken apologies and the confidence of the always-forgiven. Stan and Del were no better, they should be having serious discussions about what Hopkins had put on the table, not dismissing the whole thing and going off to shoot a few frames with her fiancé.

How her family could be so *stupid* . . . She was especially surprised at Daddy. Even now he was semi-retired, leaving such big, public decisions to the infant school was scandalously out of character. So much for the Commandant. If he got himself and all their properties blown to smithereens, wouldn't be him she'd be in mourning for. Since the funeral he'd seemed to care less and less, and suppose he thought that at forty-three, Stan ought to be given his chance, and even Del was thirty-four now, too old to be just a lacky – though she doubted Daddy truly believed in either of them any more than he'd ever done. Bizarre. She could so wipe the floor with both of them. Daddy had actually seen her, more than once, switch in a split second from one way of being to another because a dodgy situation demanded it, and he'd never said anything in praising her other than, *Two-faced little cow*. Bet he actually still believed her living with a Dawson was some tragic revenge – he didn't have a heart capable of recognizing why people might need each other. He'd only ever loved one person apart from his bloody self – Bathsheba hoped she'd be there to see the look in his eyes when he realized what his precious favourite had done to the firm. She took her tea through to the sitting room, flicked on the telly. Well, *she* could see the writing on the wall, if they couldn't. Angel had made it clear to her that when hardcore had gone legalish (and, admit it, with relaxation of drugs laws on the cards), that the days of the medium players . . . Right, Garry had decided to come home after all. He'd better not be in the mood for sex, because Bathsheba so wasn't. Yet.

'Hello, beautiful. You still up then, is it?'

'Observant as ever.'

'Aw, *ma*te, could do without the agg. Been with your brothers – ain't bothered, are you?' He kissed the top of her head. Too hard. 'What sort of day you had?'

'Murder, actually. Was coming back from a *nightmare* at Stevenage, waiting for a cab at King's Cross, and some stupid old bag wanted to be taken right over to Epping, can you believe it? Then when the cabbie said no, she didn't even get to the back of the queue.' Ugly bitch she'd been, too. How a woman could let herself get so fat, Bathsheba would never know. 'Bruised my leg with her poxy case, as well.' She took a sip of her tea. 'What about you?' she asked. 'Good night?' But if it had been, he'd hardly have come home before closing. 'Much talk about ISU's offer, was there?'

'Bit, I suppose.' Garry sat heavily on the sofa, tried to push one shoe off with the toe of the other. 'What you watching?' Peering at the telly.

'You're *all* quite sure about it, are you, darling? Turning them down?' Bathsheba felt her body tense, despite the chamomile. 'Seems to me a good price for the freeholds and so on would mean you could all start thinking about doing something else. After all, sweetie, the sex industry was so Daddy's choice, not ours.' Rubbing her sore calf. 'And if you tell Hopkins no, he might just find other ways to persuade you. Don't you think, my love?' That should be clear enough, even after a boys' night. Garry shrugged.

'We ain't Nozzer, B. They wouldn't pull a stroke like that with us, not with your old man's name.' He scratched his head, ran his hand over the crop. 'That tea you got there?' Looking hopeful. Jesus, he reeked of whiskey.

'The boys at least should sell their shares.' She watched him struggle with that. 'Everyone admits there's not much mileage left in being a smallish business round there.'

'Your Stan reckons giving in's kamikaze. We can get fully legit ourselves.'

'Mm, easy as winking, sweetie.' She rolled her shoulders. Garry was like a used-car salesman who hadn't realized his showroom was filled with something a lot more powerful than bloody bangers. If he knew how many McGowan shares had been signed away, he'd so change his tune. But it wasn't *quite* the right time to tell him, not until she'd sussed out this Stephen Hopkins. Garry hadn't even considered that those horrible Lulu videos were a tad likely to have been delivered as a warning that ISU wanted Soho for itself – fully licensed, clean and corporate. Yet her love wasn't anyone's fool, he just took his time getting there with new ideas. She *had* eventually persuaded him to keep those films, anyway, just in case they were important. Once he'd grasped something, he was a proud mother with it.

She tried to explain now, though without the classic mistake of talking down to him – he had enough of that in his life. An established holdings company could always afford to license *all* its outlets, and the council would never turn it down, would it? Without secure licences, it'd be even dodgier than in the old illegal days, selling hardcore. Prosecutions galore, sweetie, the big legit boys would so make sure of that. Don't think a few friendly Old Bill – Jesus, even the years-long permission they'd had to trade so damn graciously granted by the real Faces in the area – would cut it any more. Didn't matter how dirty ISU played, it had the disguise of top-drawer briefs and respectable property divisions and (for all they knew) the bloody Freemasons. Yes, clearly some people *would* survive legalization but . . . Didn't Garry remember those old

American movies, where the end of prohibition meant the end of masses of firms? James Cagney. Garry liked him. But no amount of coaxing was going to get through tonight – too much of her brothers' companionship in his gut. And too much interest in her body, without a doubt.

'Don't fucking worry so much,' he said. 'Come on, babe, let's go up. Please.'

She stared into her tea, let her eyes unfocus, allowing herself see Garry's weak, handsome face reflected in her cup. Stabbed at it with her spoon. But he was a sweetheart. Her brothers kept forgetting he was a Dawson, which counted for masses. She'd never had faith in anyone's commitment like she had in his, ought to be able to manipulate that rather than her limbs (nicely, of course), for their future. All she'd to do was to figure exactly how.

Her gig at the ISU dinner would be a start. Bathsheba would make certain she met Hopkins there, and she'd make it crystal to him that she didn't take the same line as the rest of the McGowans. After all, Hopkins was a man, wasn't he? He wouldn't be immune (especially after seeing her bloody act), she was sure of getting him talking. She only needed a teeny in. Yet it would be nice to have some other real brains around for support, she had to admit. At times like this, Bathsheba almost regretted Angel. Though. If she could just find whether Lulu had actually got any of Angel's money, she could persuade her that sharing was the only safe option, which would be a nice bonus. After all, by this time next year Bathsheba would be a Dawson, she and Lu would be practically sisters-in-law. But Fred didn't seem to think there was any money around in his home (yet). Jesus, if she didn't find a way to stop it all bombarding her, she'd never sleep tonight.

'All right then, bed,' she said. Couldn't bear to disappoint those needy eyes for long.

'Sad retro bastard! Hey, I love this one – ch-ch-ch-ch-ch-ch-ch-ch . . . '

The mad bloke was in Jacob's earshot, somewhere close behind his left shoulder. Too close. At first, Jacob thought he was commenting to his mates, but glancing round a couple of numbers in, saw that the guy was alone, chatting away happily to himself. And loudly. Being members only, they didn't often get the deeply strange or the seriously slaughtered in Padley's, yet this guy was both. At least it was something for Jacob to focus on, an external something that helped keep at bay what Lulu had told him. Though it wasn't a full cure. During the middle eight of 'I Only Want To Be With You', Jacob suddenly became conscious of the fact that he was playing, seeing his hands on the keys, not knowing where the hell he was in the song. Lightheaded. Panicky. And the bloody thing was repeated; God, which part *was* he in? Somehow, he got through it, then abruptly changed his set to the jazz standards he usually played on quieter nights than this, where people wanted to talk rather than shout at each other. Surely he could do those even in his sleep.

'Al-riiiight!' screamed his new best friend, as though Jacob had launched into a rock number and this was Wembley Arena. 'Way to go, man . . . Here, get off, what have I done?' A bouncer must have come over to have a quiet word. Jacob was sorry, in a sense.

'Take five, Jake,' said the bouncer in his ear. 'We'll get this nutter calmed down or slung out. I'll get someone to bring you and your lady a drink over.' Jacob sped up the final dozen or fourteen bars of 'Jeepers Creepers' and shut the lid. He barely noticed whether there was much applause, slipping out quickly to splash some cold water on his face.

Okay, calm down. So Angel had a sister. That must be what the connection was, they were both such pretentious *first* names. Of course, Angel never talked much about his family, Jacob had certainly never met any of them except his parents briefly at graduation, but hadn't there been a picture? That, he did remember. Sure, Jacob had definitely seen a photo, of Angel with . . . two brothers, and God yeah, a much younger girl.

Never think I'd be related to such a fucking ugly bunch of retards, would you? Look at that schnoz on little Bea. Looks more like one of your lot. Bea. Shit, no, not *Bea*, he must have said *B*, a diminutive. Jacob had been led by the balls to two women.

'That was brilliant, Jacob.' Lulu was smiling at him as he made his way through the half-hearted backslaps over to their table, her face flushed either with pleasure or wine. For a fraction of a second, Jacob thought again that he might faint; everything was too weird. Here he was, with a woman who'd been in *porn*, the ties between her and Angel appearing stronger all the time, yet when she'd spoken, Jacob had at first simply felt pleased that someone so pretty had enjoyed his set. Sitting down, he took a long drink from his pint.

'Thanks,' he managed to say. More than a touch late. Watching the swell of her flesh as she breathed: a Titian painted over by Degas. 'I'm back on shortly,' he added. 'Meantime, better get a cigarette in. Some people can smoke and play, but I can't.'

'You seem jittery,' Lulu said. Putting her hand on his arm. She had incredible skin, white and smooth, like a girl's. Obvious she dyed her hair that shade of red, that she wore a lot of make-up, but her face was barely lined, her hands naturally young, beautiful. Given the life she must have had, couldn't be lack of experience that kept her so unblemished.

'God, your hands are lovely.' He hadn't meant to say that, had meant to ask more about Bathsheba. But he couldn't take his gaze from those long fingers resting on his sleeve. Wished he'd worn a tee-shirt, then he'd be able properly to feel her touch on a bare arm.

'They are?' She lifted up her free one, examined it, wrinkling her nose.

'Yeah.' He held out one of his hands for her to take. Still looking surprised, she did. Jacob felt the start of excitement, blood moving from his head to his cock. How could he be turned on by something so simple? Especially after what he'd seen her do in those films. Or maybe that was why. 'Need that cigarette,' he said, pulling away. Lulu picked up her glass, leaned back in her chair.

'You feel all right?' she asked. Sounding pissed off. Perhaps she felt he'd rejected her. Jacob lit his cigarette, drawing hard. Had a strong feeling he shouldn't tell her what he more than suspected now, didn't want someone that sweet to be a move in Angel's endgame.

'Sure,' Jacob said. 'But, well, the first person I ever really loved had the same surname . . . They died, really recently.' Shit, since he'd begun this bloody charade, it was as if he'd suddenly developed Tourette's. 'Shook me a bit, when you told me . . . Probably just one of those things.' *Don't mention my name.*

'Same surname as what? What you on about?' Lulu leaned forward again. 'I haven't said anything.'

'Before I played. You know, all that contortion stuff.'

'Oh, right. Bathsheba.' Her expression thoughtful. 'And she's got the same surname as someone who just died, you mean. McGowan, yeah?' A smile that to Jacob looked totally sarcastic. Crap. Lulu had really seemed to like him up till now. 'Yeah, coincidence,' she added. 'Got another one for you, mate.' She looked right into his eyes. 'First person I ever really loved had the surname McGowan and all. Get what I'm saying?'

'Uh . . . Not really,' he went with. If Angel had hurt this woman . . . Oh bollocks.

'Leave off, course you do,' Lulu said. 'Not a bloody coincidence, is it? Christ, I'm a prat.' Almost whispered. Then, louder, 'Jacob, I'm not being funny, but are you queer?'

'No. God.' He shook his head, too vehemently. Shit, this couldn't be going more wrong. 'I'm straight. That, I promise you, Lulu. Always have been, before you ask.'

'Just wondered. He was bi, see. You're talking about Angel, though.'

'I am, yeah.' A relief, in a sense, and she *had* got there on her own. More or less. Lulu obviously wasn't stupid; that was another relief, although Jacob couldn't have explained why. 'It wasn't sexual, but I loved him,' he told her. 'Looked up to him, maybe?' *Angelniu.* 'And now he's fucking dead. Sorry.'

'Don't be.' Nodding, her hair falling across her face. 'What is it, seven, eight weeks now? Still freaked myself, and I hadn't seen him in years. Told you, I loved him, too – a long, long time back.' She sipped her wine.

'*My salad days, when I was green in judgement.*' But sod it, he must be coming over superior, dreadful: wasn't a possibility Lulu could understand that reference. So she'd really cared about Angel, more than professionally. Jacob put out his cigarette, moved round the table, to the chair that was next to Lulu's. He took her hand. 'You okay?' he asked.

'That's why you came into the shop.' It wasn't a question.

The only thing Jacob could think of to do was to kiss her.

What the bleeding hell was she meant to do with a chandelier? Swing from it? Flaming thing'd make this room look like a knocking shop, she weren't having that. End of the day, they didn't call it a living room for nothing. Maggie touched the crystals, smiled at him.

'Don't you like it?' he asked. If she didn't know his eyes watered the whole time, would say they was bright with worry. 'Too big, isn't it?' He looked at the chandelier, like he'd just noticed its size. How'd a porky midge like him drag it up here?

'Be truthful is, a bit,' Maggie said. Smiling again. Wonder how Lu was doing on her date? Sounded a bit more promising that most of them. Maggie liked a nice piano.

'And not your cup of tea.' He sipped his dry sherry.

'Not really, dear.' She leaned over, patted his knee. 'Not unless I change me name to Queenie and call this place Buck Palace.' That made him laugh. He was easy enough to manage mostly, provided you never made him feel a fool. Some men liked that, but it weren't . . . well, as he'd say, his cup of tea.

'Not to worry, I'll hold on to it myself. It'll remind me of you.'

Sent shivers down her, him keep saying stuff like that. Be saving used johnnies next. Sooner she got out of this, the better.

In a funny way, that bomb the other day'd made it much more clearer in her mind's eye. Choker, leaving the poor blighter in the chippy after what he'd been through. Maggie had to take a firm decision, stop all this shilly-shallying about. Not for Fred's sake, she weren't about to turn into Supergran, but . . . Weren't like she meant she was packing it in tomorrow, dear, just thought it fair to give warning, after all this time. Notice.

'You've said that before.' He sipped his sherry. She picked up her orange juice, held the glass against her neck. That was warm in here.

'This time I mean it.' She'd made the concession, having their chat in her living room, but she weren't going to let him not see she was serious. He'd not long retired hisself – he should understand. Should appreciate and all that seeing he'd been visiting her so long, she'd give him more courtesy than the others. 'In a few month, I want to be clear, spend more time with me family.' Sounded like a sacked MP. Putting her drink down, she touched her wig. 'Come on, chin up. Not the end of the world, is it?'

'You *are* my world.' Clifford's face seemed to sink in, fat sucking at the skin, his eyes damp. Reminded her of a tortoise.

'Oh, I'm sure that's not true.' Giving him her biggest smile, blowing him a kiss. He brightened for a sec, like she'd kissed him for real. Maggie fiddled with the earrings he'd brought her the other day. Course, they wasn't diamonds, but she never let on she knew.

'I'd feel I'd been served a divorce petition.' Clifford finished his sherry, held his empty out for a refill. Comical, the little glass waving about on the end of his short arm, as if it was made to measure. Most unusual for him, though, one drink was his limit as a rule. 'But you won't go through with it.' Catching hold of her hand, squeezing her fingers, hard, with his horrible little plump ones. 'I love you.' Here we go, the L-word. 'Besides, I'm not a well man, you wouldn't have to put up with me for long.'

'Don't talk daft.' Bleeding faker. He was looking at her silly now, as if she had a magic potion what'd cure his imaginary ills. Been at death's door for twenty-six year.

Maggie fetched him another sherry, stuck some more ice in her juice. Course, she'd known Clifford'd be the one not to make it easy, but he didn't seem to *believe* her. She fixed her stare on the picture opposite. A Constable, that was. Not the real thing, obviously, but it was pretty. In the hall was one Clifford had got her – 'Birth of Venus', though she could never remember who painted it. Maggie'd grown used to it over the years, even to like it, but she still felt embarrassed having a naked lady up on her wall.

'Clifford, dearie,' she said. Silence'd gone on too long. '*You* wouldn't of wanted to of worked for ever.'

'Is that all I am to you? Work?' His eyes had gone angry.

'Course not. But . . . ' She rattled the ice in her glass. 'I'm too old for all this.' Should be able to see that for hisself.

'Nonsense.' Clifford drained his glass. Going some, weren't he? 'Of course you must stop seeing your other . . . men friends. But with me . . .' He shook his head. 'It'd be like when Princess Diana died. An atrocity, if you were taken from me.' Sounding outraged.

'Could get you the name of someone else.' Felt a bit sorry for the soft sod.

'She wouldn't be you, Maggie.'

'She'd be younger,' Maggie pointed out. 'Look, I've had it, dear. You don't know how tired I am. Not of you,' she added, quick. 'Of this being me life.' She watched his tongue come out, flick across his lips.

'Let me look after you, then,' he said. 'Informally, I've been your legal advisor for a quarter of a century, if you take my point.' Pulling at the loose skin round his throat. 'We've always helped each other out, Maggie. I still want to help you.' More

53

pulling. 'A man like myself . . . I'm different from all the others, I just need time to make you see that.'

'Said I'm going to retire, and I will do.' Hearing indecision she hoped he never.

'Sorry, but I can't let you,' Clifford said. He smiled then. Fishy-eyed now. 'I don't care about my own reputation, since I haven't been working. I just care about you.'

'Sounds like it.' Flaming cheek, him making out he was doing her a favour.

'Oh, Maggie,' he said. Sadly. 'I've never wanted to resort to this, but what choice are you . . . Importuning, of course, tax evasion, possession of an unlicensed firearm, endangering a minor . . . have I ever taken you through the Children and Young Persons Act of 1933? Protection of Children 1978? Do I really need to go on?' Course he never. This was a go at flaming blackmail, unless she was very much mistaken. Never would of thought it of him. He was behaving as though she genuinely had no right to change her life, that it weren't even hern to change.

'It's not illegal to sell sex,' she told him. Contemptuous.

'Not *as such*, no.'

'Well, I ain't retired yet,' she said. Trying to sound cheery again. He'd never go through with blackmail, weren't the type. Course not. Bluster, that's all. But no point upsetting him more before she had to. 'You want to come on through, then?'

'Okey dokey.' He helped hisself to his feet by pushing down on the arms of the chair. Furniture'd be ruined, everyone done that. 'Just let me get my wind,' he said, pulling out his hanky, holding it to his mouth. 'Carrying that chandelier quite took it out of me. Have I ever told you my mother used to be a dancer?' Only about a million times. 'Stayed as slim as you do, all her life. Wish I'd inherited some of her stamina.'

Maggie smiled.

But they did get to the bedroom in the finish. Maggie switched on the lamp, turned the overhead light off. Forty watts was quite enough, thank you very much. Clifford got rid of his jacket, tie, unbuttoned his shirt, before easing hisself on to the bed.

'Do you know, Maggie, I think Little Clifford might want a kiss tonight.' He patted his crotch. 'Wasn't sure he was up to it, but it occurs to me it'd do him good.'

'Smashing.' Yeah, smashing. At least half hour on her poor knees trying to get *Little Clifford* excited. Why Clifford took it regular to that strip joint was beyond Maggie. Like a diabetic going to Cadbury World. Tickled her, way he boasted about the Pussy Parlour as if he was trying to make her jealous, silly old fool. 'Pass us that cushion.' Kneeling on the velvet pad always took her back to when she was a little girl, and Nanny Wedge'd made her go to church. Praying to a God Maggie used to get confused with the Good King in fairy stories. Now, she just prayed for a quick delivering from the evil what was the stink of old man's penis.

She unzipped Clifford's flies. He raised his backside, so's she could slide his trousers and pants down round his ankles. Clifford's legs'd got skinnier over the years, as his belly'd got fatter. Elderly piglet. Maggie took a johnnie from the work drawer in the bedside cabinet. Have to go some before she could even get that on him. But least there *was* a sign of life, tonight. When there weren't none at all, he got right upset, stroppy even.

Johnnie was on at last, though the tip flapped about like a little flag. Handcream on her palms. Cupping her hands to her mouth. Thank you God, for making Avon – only the tip of any dick'd ever passed her lips, and the men never bleeding realized, even after years of it. Felt like years to her and all, stuck down here. But *eventually*, Clifford come, for a wonder, a thin drizzle of spunk what Maggie was sure'd be like eating olives, if you let it in your mouth. And who could truthfully say they liked them?

Bli, her knee was giving her gyp tonight. Heaved herself on to the bed, lit a cigarette, letting the menthol take away the taste of rubber. Clifford coughed as he sorted hisself, but she made out she never noticed. He'd had a good night, for him, she could afford to take a liberty. Come to something, when the men thought they was buying even your air.

'I'd like to give you a little extra.' Clifford fetched his jacket from the back of the dressing-table chair. 'Treat yourself to something pretty for our *next* assignation.' A fifty-pound note. Oh, blow this. But she could do with the bunce. 'You're an amazing little lady, Maggie Dawson.' Right. Now bugger off, and take that crystal hideousity with you. 'As your legal advisor, I'm going to insist on something,' he said. 'One kiss before I go,' he said. 'Our first.' He said.

All through the meal, Lulu had been waiting for Jacob to kiss her again. Was he going to ask her back to his? But now he'd gone to the toilet, said he'd call for the bill on his way back, and it felt precisely like being out with someone from work, not romantic in the slightest. Maybe her scoffing so much tandoori had put him off. Still, just as well the evening seemed over, she wanted to look in on Fred, check he was asleep. Even days on, made her heart feel funny, how near she might of been to Fred being killed. Though she would of preferred to of been able to say to Jacob, *Thanks but no thanks, some other time maybe*, rather than him losing interest almost as quick as he'd found it. Thanks but no thanks – Jesus, hark at it, Lady Muck. Who was she kidding? You had to laugh. Wouldn't of told him no. About as cool as his vindaloo, her.

Lulu put a few of them little coloured seed things in her mouth – not that there was much point in freshening her breath. But they were a nice flavour. Aniseedy. Course Jacob didn't want to sleep with her, he'd been told to meet her by bloody Angel, for some strange reason. Though it did make her feel a bit soft towards both blokes, as if her life hadn't been as shit as she'd reckoned, and there were men in the world who'd bother telling you that. Lulu didn't want to end up like her auntie, without a man of her own just because she wouldn't dare give any a chance. Maggie's work must make it difficult to see men as people, but then how come she'd got into it in the first place? Tight-lipped on that subject.

Only one other couple left in the restaurant, the poor waiters must want to get home. Christ, Jacob had the firmest lips ever, the gentlest tongue. She'd kill Angel if he'd told Jacob about the films. Well, no, obviously she couldn't do that now, but it would kill the bit of tenderness she'd let into her memories tonight. Angel had been the love of her life, presumed there must of been something worth that in him. At least, Jacob was letting her remember there must, and that made her feel less of a prat. But she didn't want to get stuck again in her own past, taken years for her to move on. Real pity Jacob was only a messenger boy. Way he'd kissed her in the club had her fooled, for a minute.

Someone turned off most of the lights, Lulu had to finish her lager without being able to see it hardly. Jacob was taking his time, most probably the curry had gone through him. Garry was like that, always spent ages in the toilet at Indians – Bathsheba had a right go about it. Maybe Lulu had been wrong, perhaps Jacob was more excited by exotic women like Bathsheba. Horrible witch, kept Garry on so short a lead, surprised he didn't choke. But nothing was special about Lulu, she'd always been Miss Average. Even when she'd been doing films, hadn't had the life that went with. *Big heart, that's what you got*. Yet Maggie must know they were two a penny. Besides, Lulu just as often heard from her auntie, *Only think about yourself, you do*. And, *Red hat, no drawers*, though Lulu had never worn a hat in her life.

'I've paid.' Jacob had crept up on her in the half dark. Funny, how such a tall bloke could move so quiet. 'Think they want us to go.'

'How much do I owe you?'

'Don't be daft, my treat. Come on, let's find you a cab.'

'Yeah, course.' Trying to sound breezy.

'I'll see you again soon, anyway.'

'When?' she asked. Shit, could of cut out her tongue.

* * *

57

You couldn't respect none of them. All men would sell you down the river to get what they wanted. And then smile, ask for a kiss. Maggie'd known that a long old time. Though at twenty-three, suppose she'd been a late starter. She'd thought that a great age then, making her a real grown up, with a baby, a man, a little flat, never even minded about no ring on her finger. *Be your own fault, you get left with a babe by your ownio.* Mummy'd nagged and nagged, but what she know? *Leave off, it's 1966, not the bleeding dark ages.*

Only then her Ron'd lost his job, and course things got harder, bound to. Maggie'd offered to go back to Cohen's, though like Ron said, who'd of looked after the baby? Well, Mummy would of kept an eye, but it weren't fair to ask, not with Nanny Wedge how she was, and their Dolly expecting now. Maggie was glad she'd had a boy – Mummy had a point, girls bought you home nothing but trouble. They'd manage, Ron was sure to find something soon, weren't like it was diffi-cult to get work.

But somehow, they never managed. No jobs about, he said. Not what he was suited to, he said. Not what wouldn't drive him up the wall, so's he'd pick up his cards before he'd been there an hour. He flaming said. Had to take money off Mummy for the tally man, and it got to the stage where Maggie was hiding from the rent, holding Garry close against her chest to drown out his crying. Slowly, she'd started to look at Ron different. He'd always been a biggish chap, but now he was fat, his muscles going soft, dimply. Hair was going and all. Unless she was very much mistaken, he'd took to looking at her in a new way, too, a way she couldn't place, just knew she weren't comfortable with.

Out of the bleeding blue, it was. Plenty round there done it, but she never dreamed she'd be one of them. Bumped into an old schoolfriend once, down the Roman, who had four littlies to worry about. Just chatting over the veg stall prices, when all of a sudden, *I have to do what I can, love. Not like it's every night, just now and then when I need to make me rent*. Maggie tried not to judge, but she could hear herself thinking, *Dirty mare*. Mentioned it to Ron when she got home, but he never made no comment, only nodded, and, *Well*. Then.

Pal of mine, Ron said. *Just be nice to him*, he said. *You know I wouldn't ask if we wasn't desperate*. He said. He said. He said. Pal was in the hallway at the time, whole place reeking of booze, sicky and suffocating. Where'd the money been magicked from for that? Horse'd come up, she shouldn't wonder, and bet your sweet life the pal'd staked him. For a sec, she couldn't breathe, the booze fumes and the half-pleading, half-angry look in Ron's eyes clogging up her throat. But shocked as she was, Maggie wondered even at the time why she weren't more outraged. Suppose in some deep part of her, she'd see it coming in that nod. Her man, her big, clumsy old Ron, was asking her to drop her drawers for some other man. For money. For him. For them, he said. Garry was in the bedroom, asleep in his cot. *I can't take the fella in there*. Like she'd spoke them words an hundred times. *You can, princess, baby's fasto*. Princess. *Don't you mean whore?*

Oh, she done it, all right, couldn't of said why. Feeling nothing at the time, not even shame, not then, though she couldn't stop shaking. Didn't even give a monkey's that she recognized the pal, had see him about with their Dolly. But every scrap of love and respect for Ron'd gone and all. Inside a week, she'd slung him out on his ear, and course, after a bit he disappeared out the East End altogether. She never did know how much she'd cost. Not till years later, when McGowan had told her. She'd sworn then always to set her own price after that, but at fifty-nine shouldn't be surprised when she got stitched up again. Somehow, though, always come from the one place you didn't expect it.

Jacob felt as though he'd betrayed her. That was ridiculous: betrayal implied a relationship, and one where loyalty was due, but despite knowing that logically, he couldn't shake the feelings of shame, even of guilt. *Got both of us with that kiss,*

59

Mitzvah. Make a Christian of you yet. Fuck off, Angel. Bad enough, admitting Angel's last wish had been that Jacob look her up, yet at least he'd been able to soften that, even to make it seem a good thing. Jacob was almost certain she didn't know he knew about her videos. She'd been suspicious, sure, yet he'd seen that she'd been moved, too. All because Jacob had kissed her. Bastard.

Rain in the air. Summer night rain, that probably wouldn't fall, the kind of damp that makes you feel sticky rather than refreshed. After putting Lulu into the cab and meantime somehow promising the cinema next week, Jacob had started walking; normally, he took the Northern Line home from Camden, but couldn't be more than two or three miles, how lost could he get? Pretty bloody lost, as it turned out. Wherever this was, it wasn't Gospel Oak, and by Jacob's reckoning, it ought to be. Screw this, he'd look for a cab himself. Throwing money around as if he were loaded, tonight. That meal had been a mistake; Lulu should have gone home after his second set, she needed time to absorb what he'd told her, surely. But if he hadn't repeated his offer of food, that would have made him seem a real traitor.

She was nice. If he'd met her in other circumstances, say at a gig, he'd have been attracted to her. Nothing like the type he usually went out with, of course, although he'd always had a weakness for slightly plump, slightly bruised, totally feminine women. Voluptuous, that's what she was. And vulnerable. You couldn't automatically despise people for their past actions; Angel had been in one of those videos, and Jacob would always love him. God knows why. Or maybe knowing a person's flaws made you care more, as though they'd found themselves wanting, needed you to fill their lack. For Angel's sake, Jacob had to carry on, to see this through to the real end . . . whatever it was. His legacy. *I just want you to meet her, for all our sakes.* Jacob stopped at a main road, lit a cigarette.

'Give us a fag, mate.' The man was black. Jacob knew that should make no difference to how unsure he felt, but it did.

He handed over his packet, saying nothing, making no eye contact. 'Cheers,' the man said, taking one out, tossing the box back to Jacob and moving away. Jacob smiled at his own stupidity, but even so he'd get walking again, looking out for a cab meantime, rather than stand here waiting to be mugged.

All the way down the road, Jacob felt as though he were being followed. Even once he was safely in a black cab, couldn't shake the thought that it hadn't been straightforwardly his imagination. And back at the flat, when eventually he slept, it was only to wake several times from dreams more terrifying than any hallucinatory excess Angel with his absinthe could have conceived.

Chapter Four

Bathsheba knew from the first few minutes that she'd need to be down the line with this Hopkins bloke. The usual wouldn't work – he so was gay. Not many would pick up on it (he wasn't the teeniest bit camp), though Bathsheba knew enough gay men from the circuit to have her receptors finely tuned. She transferred to purest business mode.

'Do you think you'll convince them, Stephen?' she asked. Getting a sudden vision of him in a stock market, yelling, *Sell, sell, sell* at the McGowans in that deep voice. His failure to hide his amusement at her act had been the real homo clue – most men were busy hiding their hard-ons. 'Without putting something else into the equation, that is,' she added.

'Your family knows its business sites are prime.' Linking his hands. 'Technically. By keeping hold of them, they seem to think they'll be able to compete on a level with us. That's not realistic, but I can see their reasoning.' His tone just this side of contempt. 'I don't get the sense they're bluffing to force a bigger offer, do you?'

'No.' Lifting one shoulder. 'It's a tad more . . . complicated.' And she'd so *bet* that was a bespoke suit, few straight men dressed as well, not even Daddy. Pity in some ways (face it, Stephen Hopkins was bloody attractive, with that combination of being very, very black and yet terribly English), but of course, since the age of twelve, Bathsheba had been terrific at adapting to circumstances. Besides, she'd never chance her relationship with Garry, you couldn't be sure where serious flirting would take you. Away from marriage, possibly, and she'd never allow that.

'So what do you suggest, Ms McGowan? I take it you *are* suggesting something.'

'That all depends.' She watched him watching her. Unnerving, the way his replies took such an age (no doubt it was meant to be), so she'd just *keep* her bloody nerve. After all, she could keep the scissor points deep in the top of her thigh for five whole minutes now.

'On what's in it for you.' Shaking his head at a man who tried to approach him.

'Well, any risk needs to be worth it.' Best to spell out the credentials. She waited until the bloke Hopkins had blanked moved further away. 'My family's hardly . . . Mickey McGowan you know about. And whatever you think you know, double it. Then Stan worships his daddy, natch. Even Del, that pretty face's been known to work miracles.' Going for arch. He didn't bite. 'The two boys have got thirty-six per cent of the business between them,' she told him. 'Daddy could have gone for fifty-one himself, but he didn't. My maths make forty-nine an unlucky number.' *Get her, playing the big accountant.*

'The third brother was an intellectual, wasn't he?' he said. 'Amongst other things.'

'Mm, an academic. And a ten per cent shareholder, till he *secretly* sold up, of course. I countersigned the transfer for him, some time before. But you know that.' Bathsheba thought she detected a nanosecond of surprise then, even of respect. Angel's needing her had come late, and he'd so taken a nasty pleasure in it (for reasons of his own), but she was grateful now she'd seen him one last time. She raised her eyebrows at Hopkins, laid her hand on his forearm. Put a laugh into her voice. 'Don't underestimate my family, or me.'

'So one hears.' Sliding his arm out from under her grasp. 'I believe Angel left a will?' he said. Interesting – that was someone trying a tad too hard to sound disinterested.

'Did he?' *Well, did I?* 'Think that's my family's concern, don't you?'

'How do I know you're not working for them?' Polite. Formal, even.

'You don't.' Bathsheba was desperate to know why Hopkins wasn't using Angel's 10 per cent as a bargaining chip with the other McGowans. If they knew ISU owned his shares now, it would at least rattle them. Hopkins must be handcuffed in some way. *You might want to keep it to yourself, B. Knowledge is power.* Fine, Angel was right that it made sense for her to keep Daddy and co. in the deepest dark, yet how on earth could that reasoning apply to the ebony prince here?

Someone brought Hopkins over another mineral water. He nodded his thanks but kept his eyes on Bathsheba, stretching out his legs, casually rubbing his thigh. If he didn't go regularly to the gym (four or five times a week?), then Bathsheba was a lard mountain. Mid-thirties? She felt uncomfortable, as though Stephen Hopkins was a pop star, herself a poxy tongue-tied teenager. Hard to credit he was a key player in (admit it) a *scandalously* dodgy campaign. ISU seemed determined to dominate Soho, without any sign they cared how they achieved that. 'Bring Ms McGowan one of these as well, will you?' Hopkins said. Like he was talking to the air. Suddenly, Bathsheba's flesh went goosey, and she knew exactly what she wanted – to be able to produce drinks in a crowded hotel ballroom, without moving a single toned muscle.

'I've got a partner,' said Bathsheba, when her water was in front of her. 'He works with my brothers, has for three years, knows the business inside out. *Everything.*' She shook her head. 'But they'll never make him a full part of it.'

'Again, so one hears.' Flashing his perfect teeth. Bathsheba wasn't going to stand for Hopkins dissing Garry. Not out loud.

'You'll know then that they're short-sighted and greedy,' she said. Coldly. 'And Daddy wouldn't *hear* of a girl getting more from the business than as many frocks as she can eat,' she went on. That came over as unapologetic as she'd rehearsed it, even with the sex winkled out. 'Afraid the Catholic guilt so skipped a generation in me. Don't owe them a bloody thing.'

She sipped her water, taking her anger down. When Mama died, it was fine for Stan and bloody Angel, they'd had their educations. Even Del, after he ditched his A-levels (poor delicate diddums), of course it was made sure he had something to do. But she'd been left to shift for herself. And to try to keep out of Daddy's way. Bathsheba took another sip of her drink, forced a smile across the table. Look at him, weighing her up. All men were the same, straight, gay, or like Angel. Thought they had you taped by sight.

'Okay,' Hopkins said. After what seemed a *very* long time. 'Are you saying you want your partner to have something with more prospects?'

'That's right.' *Little B, thinking she can cut it. Hopkins must be pissing himself.*

'Technically, it wouldn't be too delusional to expect a position for him somewhere.' Stephen nodded, as though to his own thoughts. 'We've got a lot of interests, as I'm sure you know.'

'And what do I get in my own right?' Insurance never hurt.

'I imagine you'd want money. But we have to be talking at least controlling shares in the whole outfit, all three shops, distribution of course, the Holly Blue, even the desk-top. ISU wants the lot, we're only interested in you if you can help us achieve that. And provide information on the extra-curricular.' He sniffed, touched his nose. All right, he didn't have to over-egg the pudding. She did know he meant the drugs. 'Okay?' Drawing in his legs.

'Possibly,' she replied. 'Though you should remember, Stephen, the McGowans can hold out for a good while yet, and I'm so not somebody you can stitch up. My *frocks* make up the missing five per cent. How else do you think I could countersign?' Instinctively, Bathsheba knew she ought to get that said. Hopkins might be powerful, but he was only one of many faces in ISU Holdings. She wasn't going to let him use her in order to move up the company. 'I'm a silent partner in the firm,' she added.

'You mean you're not your father's daughter for nothing.' He smiled properly then, gorgeous eyes and everything. 'Good. So what do you have in mind?'

'Surprised you haven't thought of it, sweetie.' Bathsheba let a mocking note in. 'Divide and conquer.'

'Turn them from a family business into three individuals.' He laughed. 'Very Shakespearean. And how do you propose to do that?'

'Patiently,' she said. Even Daddy had his weak spots. Angel's death, for one. Maggie Dawson, for another. His temper, for a third. But Bathsheba was giving away nothing else, not until they'd drawn up a proper deal.

How the hell had he got into this? Couldn't even blame Angel for that one; Jacob had suggested it all by himself. Three dates, if you could call them dates, with Lulu, and meantime, he'd decided it would be a good idea to meet her son. Weird. Even if he'd been straightforwardly interested in her, Jacob didn't think he'd be ready to play happy families. Had to be the guilt he was still feeling, there was no other explanation. Just as well he hadn't kissed her again when they'd gone to the cinema, else he might have asked her to marry him. Knackered suddenly, Jacob straightened the display of the new hardback about Hadrian, went to check the till receipts. Wasn't a bad part-time number this, better than being a waiter or something, but after a late one at the club, the Hampstead Bookstore could seem a very long day job. The engendered shame could be a bastard, as well: he almost never read these days, the books he loved living for him only as memories. Oh, screw it, he'd leave the locking up to Michelle, she owed him for last week.

Shrugging on his leather, Jacob called a goodbye and ducked out of the shop. He was going for his *tea* at Lulu's; somehow, he didn't think that meant a few sandwiches, cakes and a pot of Earl Grey. It'd be something and chips, just as well he was hungry. Tubes were packed this time of day, Jacob practically never had to use them in rush hour. Change at Moorgate for the Hammersmith and City, get out at Stepney. From there, Lulu had said it was only a five-minute walk, if that, so he hoped he could understand her directions. Didn't seem to have understood much else since getting Angel's letter.

By the time Jacob had found her flat, he was twenty minutes late. The block was smaller than he'd anticipated, in quite a well-kept garden. Pity about the crisp packets, but someone obviously cared for it; this, you could see, in the splurge of colour. Standing outside Lulu's door, Jacob felt nervous, as though meeting Fred mattered. *Got to you has she, Foxy?* No, he just didn't know why he was here, what she'd expect from him. God, the doorbell played 'Greensleeves', or rather it rattled out an approximation.

'You found us, then.' Lulu beamed at him. She looked good, Jacob couldn't help noticing that: like, yeah, a Wagnerian set-piece whose curves had somehow acquired pliancy, softness, corporeality. *Who's a clever muso, then. Tell that one to her, could you?* No, okay, but those weird short trousers women wore emphasized her long legs, her tee-shirt in a paler blue went with her eyes, clung to her breasts, to the flesh beneath. He could smell her perfume, something flowery. There was a smudge of lipstick on her teeth; Jacob found that sweet. *Get a grip, Mitzvah.* Look, it reminded him she was human, not merely one of Angel's experiments. And it made the guilt worse. Awkwardly, he kissed her cheek, handed her the bottle he'd nearly left behind on the Tube. 'I made pasta salad,' she told him, as she led him down the hall, into the lounge. 'Was my day off, I had the time to do something proper. It's got shell-fish in, but you eat bacon, so . . . That okay?' Sounding anxious.

'Great, sure.' He looked round. Pink dralon three-piece, self-assembly furniture, clean enough but kind of shabby. One of those carpets that did your eyes in if you stared too long. 'Where's Fred?'

'In his room, he'll be out in a minute. Don't often bring men home, he's throwing a bit of a moody.' She laughed. 'I told him to get washed and changed, he told me to *take a chill pill.* Jesus, if I'd of spoken to Auntie Maggie like that, would of been knocked into the middle of next week. Sit down, Jacob, can I take your jacket? Oh, and feel free to smoke. Fred'll kick off, but he's got to learn he doesn't make all the rules. There's an ashtray on the side, see?' So Lulu was nervous too; Jacob hadn't heard her say as many words in one go before. He smiled at her, fished out his cigarettes. Bloody needed one.

Lulu fetched them both a glass of the Merlot, sat next to him on the settee. He could feel the warmth of her thigh, smell her shampoo underneath her perfume.

'We can eat whenever,' she said. 'Don't need to yet awhile, if you—'

Fred came in, unsmiling, though he did manage a mumbled greeting. Angel used to say that language carries the past, that it knows more than we can; there was something in Fred's *All right?* which spoke to Jacob on a level he couldn't get hold of, the meaning slipping from him. The boy was nothing like his mother, except that both were tall: almond-shaped eyes, deep and watchful; thin lips, the bottom one slighter fuller than the top; dark hair; snub nose. A beautiful child, though skinny in the way young boys often were. Even the forehead was familiar, broad and high. Was Jacob imagining things? Surely he must be. Obviously feeling awkward, Fred brought his bony hand up to fiddle with his ear; Jacob noticed the lobes then, fat and too long. Oh, God. This was no illusion. Why the *fucking* hell hadn't she told him?

Mum had brung home a right saddo this time. Gawping at Fred like a gorm, really pongy smoke coming from the fag in his hand. Rank. And look at that conk. More like Conc-orde. Fred waited to see if the bloke would say anything. Jacob, his name was. Way snobbo. Not that Fred didn't want his mum to have a boyfriend, but did she have to be such a rubbish picker? Still, Jacob probably had a good job, didn't look like the *spongers* Nan went on about. His trainers were Reeboks, could say one good thing about him.

'You must be Fred,' Jacob said. About time.

'Yeah. You're Jacob, in it.' Couldn't think of anything else to say to him. Fred sat on an armchair. 'Can I put the telly on, Mum?'

'No, you can't, we got company.' She smiled though. Been in a good mood all day, she had. Right laugh, them cooking together, hadn't done that since he was little, not to remember. She'd let him pick out the afters and all. 'Why don't you put a CD on?' she said. 'Not one of them hip-hop things, fat tunes, is it? Something nice. One of mine.'

'God, Mum.' Like hip-hop was phat. 'Robbie Williams okay? I don't mind him?'

'Nor do I,' said Jacob. Sticking his fag butt in the ashtray. 'The swing album, that, I do like. There's a rumour his voice might be digitally enhanced, but I don't buy that. Have you got it?' He spoke funny, sort of posh but as if he was trying not to be. Opposite of Mum. Fred found the CD – wasn't hard, Mum only had about twenty, Fred had as many as that in his room. She still played records, when there wasn't anyone but them in.

'Jacob's a musician, Fred,' said Mum.

'What, for real?' Fred pressed the start button. 'For a job?'

'Sure, I play piano.' He wiggled his fingers, like Fred didn't know what a piano was. 'And guitar a bit, but that's just for fun.'

'You made any CDs?' Bet he couldn't even play really.

'I have, yeah, a few.' He smiled. Seemed more friendly then. 'But you wouldn't have heard of me, I do what's called session work. Where a band needs an extra person.'

'And he does gigs,' Mum put in. 'In a club. Three nights a week, isn't it, Jake?'

'Mostly there, that's my regular slot, though I do get a fair bit of other live work meantime. I'm about to play a few shows with The Jellies. You won't have heard of them either, but they had a couple of hits in the sixties.'

'Wicked.' Fred hoped this was true, yeah. Else Jacob was

making him and Mum both look tits. Like that one who said he'd been in goal for Chelsea reserves.

'What about you?' Jacob asked. 'What are you good at?' He lit another fag. Typical grown up question, blatantly didn't think they could talk normal to you. 'Reading, do you like that?' Bloke wasn't giving up.

'Yeah, it's all right.'

'He's got a thing about the dictionary, haven't you, chicken?'

'And I like computer games?' Mum was *such* a show up. 'You know.'

'You're clever, then?'

'Well, precisely,' said Mum. 'His reports say he's really clever. But he's a lazy sod when he thinks he'll be.' Why'd she always talk about him like he was invisible? 'Too easy distracted, for some strange reason.'

'Sounds familiar,' Jacob said. 'I knew someone else like that.' He turned to Mum. 'Very much like that. A long, long time back.'

'Jacob . . .' Her face had gone all funny. Sort of worried.

'What about this pasta salad, then?' Jacob put out his fag. 'I'm starving.'

'Thank you,' said Mum. Why was she thanking him for being a gannet? Jacob stood up – shit, was some sort of giant – reached out his hand to her. She took hold of it. If they were going to start all that, Fred'd be straight round Nana's after tea. If he was let.

But, course, he wasn't let. And even the next morning, when Mum chucked a sickie from work, it was her, not him, went round there. Told him straight he couldn't come, the selfish cow, though Jacob knocked for Mum, so the snobbo must of been going and all. Secrets together already, leaving Fred out. Knew her good mood was *too* good to last.

Lovely summer mornings were still mornings, how could anyone really and truly like them? Not that it was early, gone eleven, but even here on the street, Lulu still felt she'd only

70

just fallen out of bed. *Always loved your bed, you did.* She rubbed her eyes – bet taking today off sick seemed bloody justified. Must look scutters, as Fred would say.

'Told Maggie you're my new boyfriend,' she admitted. Knowing she sounded slightly accusing. 'Seemed best.'

'Living in a fantasy world, aren't you?' Narrowly saving her treading in dog shit. She stumbled, from his words much as him pulling her out the way. Total *bastard*. She'd never asked him to come this morning to Maggie's, he'd gently insisted, persuaded her to ring Mags last night, everything. What did he think it was going to achieve? He'd promised not to bring up anything particular round there, but Lulu couldn't make out why he wanted to go then. He just kept saying family was important, as if he wanted to get serious with her, and now he comes out with that nasty thing. Not like Lulu had invited him into her life at all. Never asked him to come near any of them. Angel had. She'd been trying not to think about the whys involved, but with Jacob being . . . this, this *git*, she had to ask herself what the hell was going on. Some sort of evil joke? Like in Seniors, when the good looking sporty boy would ask the boffin out, for a laugh. Lulu would rather fillet her own feet with a blunt knife than be made to look a prat by Angel again. Be made to feel that . . . inadequate. When she'd heard he was dead, course she'd cried, but after, couldn't help thinking that at least she wouldn't have to see him at Garry and Bathsheba's wedding now, that he wouldn't get another chance to despise her. Maybe she *was* kidding herself – could hardly blame Jacob if he didn't want people to think someone like her was with him.

'Only a couple of minutes from here,' she said. 'You're that keen to go, you can go on your bloody own.'

'God, I'm sorry.' Touching her arm to make her stop. She turned to face him, not giving a stuff if he saw her eyes were full of tears. Hoped he felt really horrible. 'Bloody hell, Lu, only tossers disrespect women.'

'Well, precisely.' Getting her voice sarky as possible.

'I'm so sorry.' Reaching out to tuck her hair behind her ear. 'Believe me, I'm not like that, and it was crap anyway. I mean, I should be so lucky. Since Angel died, I've not been myself,' he added. 'But I promise, if we'd met in any other way, I'd still like you. A lot.' He smiled. She kept looking right at him. 'You're great, Lulu. You're lovely.' Kissing her cheek. Her mouth. What was this supposed to be? Never knew where you were with him. He mean it, about liking her a lot? Either way, don't go there before he definitely does, girl, that's asking for trouble. You've done that too many times, and you always end up sitting on your fat bum indoors. On your tod. Jacob put his arms round her, held her close, his lips against her hair. 'I'm really glad I met you,' he said.

'Really?' She pulled away, looked back into his eyes. 'Sure about that, are you?'

'I am, yeah.' Stroking her face with his thumb. 'Don't be cross with me, please don't.' Then he glanced at his watch. 'You say we're nearly there? Didn't realize you meant literally she lives ten minutes from you, we'll be way too early.'

'Told you.' Had tried to explain you had to keep to exact arrangements where Mags was concerned, but men didn't go in for listening to what was underneath your words.

'Fancy popping into that pub for a bit of Dutch courage, then? If you're still talking to me, that is.' Shaking his head. 'A pint, get this over with now I've forced us into it, have a nice day afterwards. All right?' Even calling the shots on nice days. Like his mate Angel. 'Anything I should know first?' he asked.

'Not that I can think of,' said Lulu. Feeling herself smiling, faintly. How much can you cope with, Jacob Fox? Let's see whether you want to be a part of this life. This *family*. You run a mile now, you can keep right on running. 'No, there is, as it goes,' she said. 'Yeah. Maggie's a tart, Jacob.' Putting a challenge in her eyes, best she could. 'A whore.'

This was getting beyond it. Maggie'd swore she'd never, ever let a client tie her up again – had to be a few pennies short to do anything so risky of your own free will – but it was getting so's she had no choice. Mind, being tied naked to a chair just to be stared at, was ridiculous much as anything. Not that she felt like laughing. Skin damp with sweat, heart going too fast. She'd known him getting on half her life, but she never trusted him now.

He weren't even trying to wank. Seemed it really was just looking, his face all soft with admiration, like she was in one of them art galleries he'd always tried to get her to come to. This chair was too hard, didn't do her knee no good, sitting so long. Lamp was behind him, what give him a spooky halo effect, but she must look really old with that light on her. Bright sunshine outside. What the flaming hell was he getting out of this, staring at some nervy, past-it pro? Wig was bound to be crooked, as well. She didn't have *time* for this. Thank heavens he hadn't gagged her and all, having a job getting her breath as it was. Not that he'd done the ropes tight, but one round your chest, another round your legs, you was definitely at a massive disadvantage.

'Clifford, dear—'

'I said, no talking.' His voice pleasant. She felt her legs start to shake, her eyebrows itching with the sweat. 'You look lovely,' he whispered. Bli, he have cataracts? But even in her head, Maggie weren't comforted by her feeble jokes. Normally, she managed to keep her thoughts separated off from her work, more or less, but now they was coming so close together as to be nearly one thing. Clifford was making all of her be a whore.

'I need a wee.' Trying to say it without no apology there.

'Then have one.' He shrugged. Bleeding *have one*? Just sit here and do it? She should bloody cocoa. Weren't even like he was into water sports . . . least, he never had been. Used to be a reliable bloke. Worst you could say was he was a bit sad. Then, this weren't the same man she known all them years, the one what brought her kitchen gadgets and power tools and glittery tops, who liked her to be firm but fair. She'd always thought of him as her Rent-a-Punter, though even that couldn't raise the normal invisible smile today. He'd been . . . text-book, did they call it? You could of read him that easy, was ridiculous. But the mad bleeder he'd turned into reckoned he'd give the law, worse, Social Services, twenty-six years' worth of presents if she never sat here, tied up, nearly wetting herself. A sticky, silent burp. Maggie almost believed today he thought he meant the threats. Daren't call him on it anyway, what come to the same thing. Damage limitation.

'Time's up, dear,' she tried. Blimey, she had Lulu and her fella coming round in twenty minutes – what if Clifford was still here then, and she was like this? Lu'd murder her.

'I think that's for me to decide, don't you?' But he sounded a lot less sure.

'No, dear, I don't.' Something'd told her this was her one chance of getting rid – by having a go at sounding normal. 'You know the rules,' she added. Firmer. Sweat running from under her nose on to her mouth, salting the cracks.

'All right,' Clifford said. 'Don't want to outstay my welcome.' He got to his feet, come over to untie her. 'But we must do this again.' He stopped, his hand on the top rope. 'I mean we really must, Maggie.' A surge of total panic suffocated her relief. Short of digging out the shooter, how the bleeding hell was she ever going to make this stop?

'Oh, I thought you'd of brung Fred with.' Maggie smiled at them. 'Never mind, come in. I got the kettle on.' She was tiny. A pixie person. Jacob hadn't had time to think clearly about what he'd expected, but he knew it wasn't this bustling, smart blonde whose pink stiletto sandals matched her skirt. *They're a family. That's the point, Mitzvah.* That bloody letter was getting worn out in his head, more than ever since meeting Fred last night. So this was the *linchpin*? When he'd had to reach right down to shake Maggie's hand, she'd openly laughed, her expression intelligent, relaxed; he couldn't recognize the *hard-faced old bird* Angel had offered him. Surely prostitutes didn't look like this, not when they were in their late fifties, early sixties. She wasn't exactly stunning now, but it didn't take a great leap of imagination to see she'd been pretty special. And though the lounge was what his grandmother would call *Ech, oysgeputst*, all frills, ornaments, too much furniture, it was immaculate, the kind of clean that was habitual. Jacob had always believed long-term prostitutes didn't have any self-respect, yet as Maggie brought the tea things through on a flowery tray, biscuits arranged on a plate, he could see that she respected herself in spades.

'Lulu tells me you play the piano?' Maggie lit a menthol cigarette, patted her hair; her hands were liver-spotted, the one token of her real age. Jacob nodded, took out his own packet. Desperately didn't want to get into a discussion about occupations, screw that. If Tourette's kicked in now, he'd be mortified. 'Sorry, should of offered,' Maggie said. 'But no doubt you prefer your own, know I do.'

'Yeah. Uh . . . thanks.' Jacob took a mouthful of the strong tea. Lulu was nibbling a bourbon, dropping crumbs on her skirt, her hand trembling. Looked like a child. No wonder she'd got into porn, with a *prostitute* as a mother figure. His heart filled with pity, which meantime threatened to spill out into the room. 'Never thought to ask,' he said. 'Why Lulu? Is it after the singer?'

'Started off Louise,' Maggie replied. 'But when she was a little girl, she couldn't say it, called herself Lulu, so we all did. Name's hern, now.' She laughed. 'Funny bugger, she was. Always doing handstands and backbends, never still for a second.'

'Am these days,' said Lulu. 'Idle mare, me.' But Maggie threw her a disapproving look. Tutted, loudly.

'You work hard enough, unless I'm very much mistaken,' Maggie said. Then, turning to Jacob, 'Lu didn't mention you was that tall. What are you, six-three?'

'Six-four.' Jacob grinned, put his cigarette out, took a pink wafer biscuit. Tea, biscuits, chat; so ordinary it was surreal.

75

'My mother says it's my own fault I find it hard to get trousers to fit, I didn't ought to be ridiculously long-legged.'

'Make her right,' said Maggie. Smiling. 'If you *will* be a freak of nature, on your own head be it.'

'Maggie!' Lulu exclaimed. But Jacob found he liked this woman, this prostitute. Maggie was . . . comfortable with herself, wasn't trying too hard to please the posh bastard. Who was he to judge her? She'd had two children to bring up on her own. How much difference from what the girls in the club on the prowl for rich blokes were prepared to do? There was a kind of autonomy in Maggie's version, at least; more bloody honest, too. *Fucking bleeding-heart liberal.* Jacob had never understood why that was an insult.

'Penny for them,' said Maggie.

'God, sorry, that was rude.' Jacob shook his head. 'Spaced out there for a minute. Think I'm a touch nervous, made my brain shut down.'

'Lu hasn't brung hardly any men home before,' Maggie said. 'She's most probably nervous and all, aren't you, love?'

'Suppose.' Lulu shrugged. 'Don't really know each other all that well, do we?'

'Not yet. But we will.' As he spoke, Jacob had a strong sense this was true.

A phone rang then. Maggie reached into her bag, took out her mobile, looked at it.

'Scuse me a sec,' she said, standing up. 'Hang on, Mr Piozzi dear,' into the receiver. She disappeared out to the kitchen.

'Told you,' Lulu whispered. 'That's a punter.'

'How do you know?' Jacob felt his neck grow warm.

'Mobile.' But Maggie came back in then. If it had been a punter, she couldn't have wanted much to talk to him. 'Oh, Mags, before I forget,' said Lulu. 'Had Bathsheba on the phone first thing. Bit previous, I thought, but she presumed I'd be going to work. Said to tell you Mickey McGowan's been asking after you.' Lu pulled a face. 'B seemed to think that was good, what with the wedding being next year.'

'Did she, now?' Maggie's expression closed off. 'Well, she can stick it up her bleeding backside. Scuse me, Jacob.' She picked up her cigarette packet again.

'All right, don't shoot the bloody messenger.' Lulu took another biscuit. The two women glared at each other.

'Any chance of some more tea?' Jacob said.

Bethnal Green, 1975, no, '76. Heatwave, plague of ladybirds as though London was in Bible times, tarmac melting, sticking to your sandals. When the kids was easy, before the days of stealing out her purse, before sex, before they'd broke her heart. Maggie'd been on the game for ten years by then, moving from casual blokes found in the boozer, to advertising and the place off Wardour Street, to regular contacts she see at home. Same year she'd met Clifford.

She'd known Mickey McGowan for ever, of course. After all, he'd been there at the beginning, though she hadn't known his name then. Not that she bore him no grudges – he was just a man, and Ron'd brung him into their home. True, she'd never much liked him after he'd messed their Dolly about, but you just knew he was going places – if you'd been to China, he'd been twice, spoke the lingo. By '76, had his finger in loads of pies, including a dozen or so girls working for him, dirty street brasses, *Fiver for a plate, love* types, hardly legal some of them. Everyone knew, though he played the respectable card – wife, kiddies, snooker hall. Yet he was bleeding lethal when he was crossed, she made no mistake about that. His men called him the Commandant or Red Hot Poker. Not that he was a known villain, not strictly speaking, but he had an in with a lot of naughty sorts, most probably because of the rumours about the way he'd finished off that nancy bloke. Nasty business.

Maggie couldn't remember quite how they'd first started having the occasional drink. She'd still drunk then, only the odd Martini and lemonade, mostly because in them days weren't so acceptable to sit in a pub with an orange juice, but even that bit took the edge off. Changed your judgement. She weren't no naïve youngster, early thirties, yet he made her believe he could make life simple, and with the kids growing up, she didn't want the risk of them realizing. If she had protection, that might cover her with Garry and Lu and all.

He was an heavy man, tall, well built. Ugly bleeder really, but his personality was a mask for his face. Blimey, been a long old while since she'd even glimpsed him, leave alone give him lodgings in her head. Though in '76, she'd let him well and truly in her life, and for months it'd seemed a clever decision. Was both making fair enough money, he was weeding out the funny bunnies, she'd felt more secure than she had since the early days with Ron. They'd even become mates, after a fashion. He was her pussycat. Weren't no question of nothing else – neither of them was interested – and that made it perfect. But.

When would it of been? Heatwave was more or less over, kids back at school. An afternoon, it was. She had a feeling it was a Wednesday. Funny, things you remembered.

This one's a bit special, Maggie. He's paying over the odds, play nice, so.

Brung his toy box with him, the *special* bloke had, all the better to play her with. Chains, handcuffs, whips, a knife. And a cine camera. Mickey offered her a couple of Valium. See the look in his eyes, brooking no arguments, thought she'd better take them.

But they never helped. She'd not known you could feel pain like that and come out of it, make the kids' teas when they got home from school, watch the news, even sleep at night. Pain that felt you was being eaten, but you couldn't tell if it was that causing the agony or if you was being eat by the pain itself. The flaming helplessness, the sick lonely certainty that you had no control over what was happening to you. To her.

And all the while, Mickey McGowan, the flaming Red Hot Poker, her pussycat, was filming it, getting off on it. His bag was torture.

So she'd got rid of him.

If that little madam Bathsheba thought Maggie would let him back into her life, she had another think coming. But what was nagging was why McGowan would want to *play nice* after all them years. Could it really be he'd decided to go to Garry's wedding after all? Though she couldn't believe he'd forgive her, so what *did* he flaming want? He'd already had everything – she'd not done a man for the sake of it since Ron, but she hadn't so much as touched herself after that Wednesday, except for washing. Fantasies was too bleeding dangerous. Hurt too much. That lump of skin, nerves, weren't hern, not in her private self. Perhaps McGowan had a terminal disease, needed to make peace with his enemies before meeting his Maker. About time the old bastard took a leaf out his crazy son's book and died.

Fred was Angel's son. No matter how often Jacob rehearsed that, he couldn't divorce its meaning from the way he'd been led to find it out. Over twenty years of manipulation; should have realized before now that his emotions and not just his actions were being written for him. With love and three fucking kisses. God. Jacob shouldn't have kept that Angel video; maybe he'd destroy it, get it out of his life. But even as he thought it, he knew that wasn't a possibility. *Fancy me, do you, Jakey boy?* No. He was sure of that now, at least.

Jacob took his brandy through to the lounge, lit a cigarette. Only two more left in the packet; maybe he'd try again with giving up when those were gone, Angel shouldn't have control over Jacob's bloody health as well. Getting dark, but he didn't want to put on the light, though he did close the curtains, turn on the television.

Every single person he'd ever met shovelled on a load of bullshit, apparently, took for granted meantime that he'd wallow in it. Obviously been right to start living so much alone. But even with the thought, Jacob knew he'd never been any good at sustaining anger. *Peace and love, Mitzvah.* Angel

79

relied on Jacob's fear of letting go. Though of course it hadn't been fair to get pissed off with Lulu: sure, she'd lied by omission, but come on, it had been Jacob's choice not to ignore his instructions, she'd had very few options. Realistically, he'd courted her for Angel; all she'd straightforwardly done was to comply. Since last night, Jacob had a horrible suspicion he knew exactly what that letter had been: an invitation to build some kind of relationship with his friend's son. That was the legacy. Though why not just say so? Even for Angel, playing chance with his own flesh was a bit much, especially for something he easily could have ensured. *I know you, better than anyone has ever known you.* Jacob put out his cigarette, lit another before he became aware what he was doing.

Yet . . . how bad was it turning out, really? Hardly dreadful. Might be down to luck rather than to Angel's arrogant bastard predictions, but today had been, well . . . Touching, how Lulu had cheered up as soon as Jacob had, forgiving him totally when he didn't deserve it. That resignation aging her face this morning had been replaced by simple pleasure; you seldom encountered people that transparent. Musos certainly weren't. Women like Susie weren't. Even Fred wasn't. And Vicky Park was a revelation, Jacob hadn't known there were such pretty places in that part of London. Fred was obviously suspicious of Jacob, but then so far, Jacob hadn't entirely fallen for Fred either. Meantime, he could fake it; this, he could live with. Wished he knew, though, why Lulu made him promise Angel shouldn't be mentioned to Maggie. *Don't mention my name.* From Maggie's reaction to Bathsheba's message this morning, seemed any dislike didn't end there; *McGowan* the brand name of a product she couldn't stand. All he could get from Lu was Angel leaving before Fred was born, and bloody typical, that the occasional grand had mysteriously appeared. Maybe she wasn't so transparent after all. Yet why should she trust Jacob with her whole life, before he'd proved himself? In her position, he wouldn't. As for what he'd learned about Maggie, it wasn't anything like the shock he'd have anticipated, meeting a hooker. Maybe those videos had inured him, prepared him or something.

Bollocks. Of course they'd bloody prepared him, that's exactly what Angel intended. *They're a family. That's the point.* Hadn't even been obscure. In the middle of all that elliptical crap, Angel had explicitly, straightforwardly, told him the score: if you took one member of that family, you had to take them all. *That* was the point. By forging a relationship with Fred, Jacob would be making one with Lulu, even with Maggie. With pornography and with prostitution. Okay, Maggie was surprisingly nice, good fun, and Lulu . . . actually, Jacob did think she was great. And lovely. Uncorrupted somehow, trusting, looking at him as though he of all people could protect her. But what about Angel's contorting sister, Lulu's sort-of-brother, anyone else who comprised the family, did Jacob want to involve himself with them? They could be any kind of weird, for all he knew. He glanced over at the television screen, without registering what it was showing. *Kvetch, kvetch, kvetch. Go with the flow, Jake.* He'd have to try, sure, or be a serious bastard, but it meant accepting that once again Angel had decided who Jacob had to care about.

Now he was restless, his brain itching, as if there was something else he should be doing, just out of sight, wormwood on the periphery of his imaginative vision. But sometimes he did feel like that on nights when he wasn't playing. Maybe . . . maybe if he took one last look at that video, it would lay a few ghosts for him. *Funny, man.* Jacob smiled into his brandy, had a final drag of his cigarette. Oh, screw it, what harm? Wasn't as though he'd be seeing anything he hadn't seen before.

He fumbled with the drawer under the table, found the video, put it into the machine. Some dreadful quiz show morphed into the opening credits of the film; Jacob fast-forwarded until he found the Angel scene. He froze the frame on the opening shot, swallowed the rest of his drink. With his heart beating a touch faster, he pressed the play button.

Lulu, being opened by Angel's long fingers, and entered

from behind, her face twisted into what Jacob was sure was real pleasure. The shadowy third, tossing himself off by Lulu's face. A close up of her being fucked, hard; a wider shot of her loving it. Oh, God. God. Jacob had spoken to that face, kissed the mouth that was screaming. His cock was hard, about as hard as he could remember it being. There was no question about what he was going to do: freezing the picture again a few seconds before Lulu came, Jacob took off all his clothes, tangling his feet in the legs of his jeans in his hurry. Then he sat back down, rewound the film to the start of the scene, and surrendered to an act borne not out of boredom or frustration or habit, nor even of shock, but out of a terrible desire.

Part II

Erotema

Birth, and copulation, and death.
That's all the facts when you come to brass tacks:
Birth, and copulation, and death.

T.S. Eliot

Chapter Five

According to Garry (who'd got it from Maggie), Lulu was seeing someone. Bathsheba would make sure she was introduced to him – you never knew who would come in useful. She touched her coffee to her lips. Wished she'd got a cold drink (August was for abroad, not for being trapped in London), but Del always bizarrely wanted masses of caffeine no matter what the weather. Look at her brother now, slurping away as though coffee wasn't even a tad warm. Anyway, she'd had other things on her mind when she'd ordered. Like how to keep Stephen Hopkins convinced she knew how to weaken the McGowans.

'I *said*, we been turned down.' Del had that tone of voice on he'd inherited from Mama – injured piety. 'That's what's wrong with me, since you ask.'

'Sorry.' Bathsheba patted his hand across the table. 'Turned down for what, darling?' She glanced round the hotel bar. Apart from her and Del, there were only three other customers, well-dressed older women (unsurprisingly enough at this time of day), six over-made-up eyes gazing towards her brother.

'The new licence,' lowering his voice, 'for Chicks 'n' Flicks.' He rubbed his face, hard. Mm, let's face it, if he didn't get into something less stressful, he'd so lose those looks that attracted all this attention. She was doing him a favour. 'Stan's in a meet with that councillor bloke, getting the full SP. Not that it'll do no fucking good. Cunts.'

'Less of the language in here.' Loud enough for that passing member of staff to overhear. Then, softly, 'I come in whenever

I'm working in Aldwych.' Okay, Hopkins had managed to sort that one. Rather looked like putting paid to Stan's idiotic plan of getting fully legit by themselves. 'Can you make sure Stan fills Garry in properly?' she asked.

'Yeah, no sweat. Though Garry won't be able to do nothing, will he?' He stared into his empty cup. 'Don't get me wrong, he's a nice enough bloke, blinding really—'

'Just want to make sure he's got the picture.' Bathsheba pushed aside her coffee. 'Think I'll have a water instead,' she said. 'Fancy a little refill?' Buying some thinking time within the *Anything else I can get you, Miss Bathsheba?* faffing that the staff at the York Hotel went in for. Hopkins scuppering the licence, she so ought to be able to capitalize on. Daddy wasn't going to be too chuffed that the boys had cocked up the application, and even they weren't immune from his rages. Plus every droplet of dissent helped send the Commandant a little further round the twist. Though she hoped Daddy wouldn't do anything massively awful to Del, he was too fragile. You had to build up all your resources to cope with this world – plunge your hand into freezing water for longer than you could bear, press pins into your thumbs – anything to make you stronger than the next person, more resilient. It would never even occur to Del that things like that were necessary. Would probably think she was madder than Daddy.

'Del, mind your arm, you nearly had coffee down your back. Sorry,' she added to the waiter. *Reckon the wrong brother copped it, don't you?* No, she bloody didn't. Del was a poppet, at least he'd tried (ineptly) to protect her when they were young, which was more than the other two could be bothered to manage. Gave her that sex education book, too, blushing, saying his girlfriend thought it a good idea as Ma wasn't here. Until then, her body had been what she could make its skeleton do. After that, she'd fallen in love with her *labia*, her *clitoris*, the inside of her head. If it weren't for Del (admit it), her relationship with Garry wouldn't be what it was. All Angel ever did for her was to remind her she wasn't anybody's little princess.

'Shit, I need this.' Del piled in the sugar lumps again, greedy pig. Terribly rash – he was lucky with his figure now, but he was only thirty-four. 'Sorry, B,' Del said, 'better shoot in a minute, got a chemist to see.' Right, while he was still here, she ought to try to get the real gen on that synthetic coke (whatever it was). Garry was always antsy if she asked *him*, like a teenager caught in his bedroom with a dirty mag. He seemed even less keen than Del was on the McGowans diversifying any further into that market.

'You're going to see him about the new . . . ?' Fab, that sounded as though Bathsheba had only left out the name because this was a public place. She added a smile.

'Yeah. But it's bad news, that chemist's an headcase.' Wiping the coffee from round his mouth, bloody yob. 'Having his shit in the Holly Blue, I can wear. But not the—'

'Stan wants to *street* it?' Though street what was the real question.

'No. No, he's not silly. But . . . ' He tilted his head upwards. Must mean selling the gear to Daddy's cronies. Sweet Jesus. Though no one forced them to take the stuff, and someone was going to supply it. No point in getting all Mother Superior. But would a respectable business want to take over that line too, or know enough just to end production? Suddenly, Del laughed, making her focus on him again. 'Stan's talking about gratis comps with the' mouthing the word '*hardcore* as well,' he said. 'Buy two thousand vids, get a nose job free. Even you can see that's not on, I bet.'

'Even me, sweetie.' ISU *couldn't* want dodgy shit on their potential patch. Face it, she could do without Hopkins getting impatient, if it meant her losing out.

'Stan'll have the final word, though, won't he?' Del said. 'The old man don't want to know since Ange.' Finishing his coffee. Suddenly, Bathsheba remembered that holiday to Dublin after Angel's PhD graduation. Not that the memories were her own. *Dad says you three would only spoil the craic.* Mama had been barely cold in her grave, and Del had really minded Daddy leaving them behind, sensitive idiot. Bathsheba was convinced he ought to be in something more creative these days, anyway. *Soul of an artist*, Mama used to say.

'By the way, what's happening with Angel's shares?' she said. Daddy was so deep in mourning, surprised he wasn't wearing bloody weeds. Probably hadn't even spoken to his legal yet. But Stan might be getting impatient by now, hoping for a bigger cut maybe. Hoping one day he really would be the man his father was, certainly.

'Reckon they'll revert to Dad.' Del raised one shoulder. 'AGM's November, he'll have to sort it then. Stan reckons probate's a bastard, don't think they've even applied yet. Sorry, really better split, meant to be seeing a bird later as well.'

'Yeah, course. And Fidelio . . . I'm sorry about the licence.'

'We'll survive, *cara*.' He stood, put a tenner on the table, bent to peck her on the cheek. 'Don't go worrying about it. I shouldn't . . . Well, no point you even knowing.'

'Knowing what?' She smiled. 'Haven't been to confession in years.'

Bathsheba gave him a few minutes, then (making sure she said goodbye to her little waiter) walked out into the street herself. She turned left rather than right, chancing that she'd still get to rehearsal on time in spite of the detour, walked past the marble and glass building fronts over to Waterloo Bridge, where she stopped, looking out at the river. No waves today, not one. There were butterflies in Bathsheba's stomach, the kind that can only be got rid of by achieving what you'd planned, or by suffocating them in chocolate and buns. Bathsheba was so a long way from being ready to be a porkette. She opened her bag, took out her mobile. First Hopkins, then Lulu, then she'd check in with work. You had to get your priorities right, or you might as well give up the game, fling yourself off the bridge, and be drowned in the poxy calm that far too many seemed to settle for.

* * *

'I've *got* to get to work later, Lu.' Jacob stopped, searched his pockets again. 'Won't be able to if I can't find it. Must be somewhere.'

'Sure you didn't leave it in the offy?'

'Yeah, I'm sure.' This, he could do without. 'Fifty quid in it, and my cards, even my travel card. Shit.'

'Eureka.' Lulu was rummaging in the Victoria Wine bag. 'You're always doing things like that,' she added, handing him his wallet.

'Thanks.' Jacob stuffed it in his back pocket. God, she was starting to sound like an indulgent wife. Wasn't as though they were even straightforwardly seeing each other; a few kisses over a month or so didn't make a relationship, and definitely not the years-old marriage she seemed to think she was in. But then she smiled, and his irritation moved into fade-out. Screw it, of course she was allowed to sound fond, anyone should be flattered by that; he was just nervous at the thought of her seeing his flat. Too much like letting her see his life. 'Come on,' he said, 'if we don't get to my place soon, be time to turn round again.'

'Got a few hours yet,' she reminded him. 'I'll make sure we get you out for your gig.' As they passed the Indian, she laced her fingers in his. He stroked her palm with his thumb; her hands always felt so soft, like she hadn't done a day's work in her life. *Believe me, she's worked those hands plenty.* Shit, Angel never left them alone for one minute. Even though the game had been over for a couple of weeks now, Jacob had a lingering sense of unfinished business; maybe it'd be different once he'd really got to know Fred, created a shape for a child in his life. Routine, familiarity, making it normal: those were what Jacob needed. Meantime, he'd have to start by calculating exactly where Fred's mother fitted in, instead of going with the flow, the way he'd been doing up till now.

'We're here,' he said. Releasing her hand, taking off his shades, leading the way up the stairs to his flat. 'Just let me find my keys . . . '

Weird. It was so weird to have Lulu actually there, standing with her wild hair, in that gypsy-style summer dress, in the middle of his lounge. Watching her taking it all in, clocking up a list of definite articles: the old settee, the low coffee table, the keyboard, the black ash shelves, the Huddersfield Festival poster, the television and, oh God, the video.

'It's nice, Jake,' she said at last. 'Can tell it's a bloke's place, but you keep it tidy, don't you? Makes me feel a right slob.'

'I'll put the wine in the fridge. There's one already open, I'll get us some.'

When he came back into the room, Lulu was sitting on the floor with her sandals off, her back against the wall underneath the open window, head against the curtains Susie had chosen. Her face was damp with the heat, make-up blurring, a few strands of hair sticking to her forehead. Jacob felt as though a film star had stepped out of his television screen, that any second she'd disappear back into his fantasies. Get a grip, you idiot. It's just Lulu, a friend, a real person. She held out her hand for the glass of wine, took a big gulp, smiled.

'I love pink drinks,' she said. 'You not going to sit down?'

'Sure.' Jacob hesitated, then knelt next to her. Couldn't stay long like this, his back would never take it. She was right, the flat had gradually turned back into a bloke's place, without any of the unnecessary extras women leave around, without much evidence of past coupledom. The smell was male now: the most functional polish, ingrained cigarette smoke, plain soap. An economy scent. Bloody hell, until today no woman had even been in here since Susie left. Come to think of it, there hadn't been *anyone* here since then. At one time, the place had been over-stuffed with people, but then those were mostly Susie's friends, right-on types with glossy hair, trainers. Could just imagine what they'd say about Lulu. Jacob ripped the cellophane from a new packet of Gitanes, leaned over to get the ashtray from the low table. His lighter was in the drawer, but he couldn't bring himself to open it; just as well he'd bought a box of matches. 'Do you want some sounds on?' he asked.

'Not bothered. Nice change to get a bit of peace.' Lulu put her glass down beside her, stretched out one arm, as though sinking into the luxury of not being at home. A glimpse, a trace of stubble in her armpit, coated by white deodorant. Jacob found himself staring at the hollow at the base of her throat, his gaze drifting to her breasts in their low-cut dress. She'd hardly caught the sun at all, a faint blush barely tinting her pallor. Oh bollocks, don't start thinking about her skin. 'What you thinking about?' Lulu smiled. 'Spaciest person I've ever met, you are.'

'Why are you on your own?' He was used now to his blurted questions surprising himself.

'Why are *you*?' Looking hurt. Maybe she did believe they were in a relationship; to be fair, he could see how she might think they were at least starting to be.

'I only meant . . . It's hard to credit how you're not married or something.'

'Well, I'm not, am I?' Lulu picked up her glass again, sipped from it. 'And thirty-six . . . doubt I ever will be. Married, that is.'

'You hardly look thirty.' No need for soft soap: it was true. Comparatively.

'Not the point, mate.' She shook her head. 'It's not about looking all right, it's about being young enough in here.' Touching her amazing chest. 'Look, be truthful, I'd like to get married. But I'm presuming it won't happen. Far from it.'

'It might.' How many women would admit they wanted marriage, in a situation like this? You had to admire her chutzpah. Or her innocence.

'Might it?' Raising her eyebrows. Jacob laughed.

'I like you such a lot,' he said.

'Yeah, I know.' She shrugged. 'Watch your fag there, you'll get ash on your clean carpet.' He couldn't tell if she was being sarcastic, but he put his cigarette out, smiled.

'Would it disturb your peace too much if I played something for you?'

'What, on that, you mean?' Gesturing to the keyboard. 'For me? No, I'd *love* it. That'd be great.' Transparently delighted. 'What you going to play?'

Good question. Jacob swilled some wine round his mouth, got to his feet, rubbing the base of his spine. Trouble with being a muso, you couldn't bash out something casually to impress, people expected you to produce a tune that sounded better than their Aunt Violet's party piece. On the other hand, Lulu wasn't exactly Simon Cowell; that look in her eyes suggested he could play three dissonant chords and she'd think it was marvellous. That he was marvellous. He switched on the keyboard, flicked it to the preset piano combi to keep it sweet and simple, sat on the stool.

'Do you know "You Were Always On My Mind"?' he asked, turning round to glance at her. She shook her head. Was she blushing? It was so bloody easy to make her feel special; handed Jacob a touch of guilt, forcing him to think that not too many men had been kind to her. Then, that he could do. He swivelled back to the instrument, gave himself a quick keynote on the sly to check he'd be comfortably in his range. *Going to sing for her as well, Jakey? Nice one, slave for life you'll have there, boy.* Yet Jacob couldn't help going for it; not that he had the best voice in the world, but his schtick was he understood how to put a song across for a woman. Worked with most, the only advantage he had in the game.

Though he found himself changing the words.

You've no one else lined up tonight,
It's in your interests to be blind . . .

And he knew she wouldn't get it, would be as moved as if he'd kept to the book. His voice sounded sincere, tender, even to his own ears. Bastard. Although, come to think of it, which of them was he having a dig at with the new lyrics? The second he finished the song, he turned the keyboard off, meantime stopping her praises almost before she'd started them. Shit, she brought out the worst in him, things he really hadn't known were there.

'How's Fred?' he asked. Moving to kneel by her again.

'That why I'm here?' Lulu finished her wine. 'Jesus Christ, Jake. Be truthful, I'm getting a bit confused about precisely what's going on. You take me out a couple of times a week, and sometimes it seems to have to do with me, but then other times . . . Well, it's for him. Angel, not Fred. Or it switches over, understand what I'm saying? Like just now, the way you stopped playing.'

Kept disconcerting him, Lulu dragging out stuff that seemed brighter than she was. *You always did think Oxbridge was the only fucking measure, Mitzvah. How come you're still playing two-bit dives, then?*

Lulu was running her finger round the rim of her empty glass, her expression watchful. Jacob too was watching his motives: had he been trying straightforwardly to seduce her with that song, or simply to avoid the difficult conversation he'd started?

'It's not you,' he said. 'Need to work out more about how I feel, that's all. One minute I'm living my little life with just me in it, and the next Angel's filled it with a lot of other people who could be anything.' Trying to be honest felt bloody dreadful. 'You all scare the crap out of me.'

'And you reckon we're used to someone like you?' Lulu banged her glass on the carpet. 'Leave off, Jacob.' She tapped a crimson fingernail against her teeth. 'Don't give me that waffle, give me something real. Angel might of been a lot of things,' she added, 'but he didn't talk out of his bum.'

'Right. Fine. Keep comparing me with him, that'll get us really far.' Knowing he sounded a petulant git.

'Best you can do?' Lulu said. Laughing. Jacob had to grin.

'Shit, sorry.' He eased himself from kneeling to sitting cross-legged, reached out for her hand. 'I'm not that great at relationships, Lu, as you've probably noticed.'

'Now you come to mention it . . . ' She squeezed his fingers and winked.

'Yeah.' Jacob drained the last of his wine. 'I've had three

serious partners and got dumped three times, and a few short things that were just pointless crap. That's it.' He picked up his cigarette packet, put it down again. 'Not like I've spent the rest of the time screwing around, even. Sure, I was a total slut at college, but after that only ever had . . . about five one-night-stands, and they all had to be women I already knew a bit. Had to be, I don't know, some hope in there it'd go further or whatever? Even if it was me who decided after not to go with it. I'm such a bloody romantic. But there's something always gets messed up, where I'm concerned.' Rubbing his finger under his nose to give himself time to consider his words, wanting to offer her something to make up for that song. 'Starting things going isn't a problem for me, it's keeping them.'

'Why?' God, Lu got straight in there.

'I think . . . what I do is, I kind of get involved with who I want the person to be, not who they are,' he said. Was that right? 'That's always a recipe for disaster, of course it is.' Wondering why he could never have said anything like that to Susie. 'I'm forty-one going on fourteen, my history's a lot of bollocks.' He kissed her palm. 'That doesn't make me Mr Confident, when it comes to someone like you.'

'What's someone like me?' Suspicious.

'That's just it. I'm not sure, and I don't want to invent you.' *For all our sakes.*

'People always do that, don't they?' Lulu said. So quiet, it was as though she were talking to herself. 'Spent my whole life trying to be what blokes thought they wanted.' She smiled. 'Never got it right though. Evidently.'

'It's not a possibility,' he said. 'For anyone.' Jacob couldn't be sure, but he had a feeling she was close to telling him about her past career. And suddenly, he knew he didn't want to hear it, at least until . . . until he'd made love to her. If she said something now, he'd never be able to do it; while he was still in apparent ignorance, he could pretend, maybe even to himself, that he wasn't worried about how he'd measure up to all those hundreds, perhaps thousands, of men. About her professional expertise. And holding her hand, looking at her anxious face, the movement of her rich plump body as it turned towards him, Jacob knew absolutely that he wanted her. Not watching her in a video, masturbating over the observable history she had with his friend, but Lulu, in the flesh. If he kissed her now, that would happen: he'd close the gap, move from voyeur to performer, but without having – exactly – to acknowledge that was what he was doing, further than he was admitting it to himself at this moment, anyway. Intimidated or not, his hard-on was certain what it wanted; even so, wasn't too late to back out, he'd done nothing yet. His heart was seriously pounding, Jacob felt for a second that he might throw up. Then he kissed her.

Clifford would be kissing Maggie tonight. A frisson of excitement, as though he were still a young man counting the minutes till he saw his sweetheart. Potty. Clifford hadn't had a proper sweetheart as a young man. Life had never treated him fairly, he'd been subject to a series of petty injunctions because no one knew how to deal with his intellect. *They're only jealous*. That ought to be *envious*, Mother. He should have made partner, the full significance had only come home once any chance of achievement was lost. Should have been like his cousin, whose practice might be seedy but was his own. Clifford had even sent work that way. Chump. All his life, he'd felt he had been a *what* not a *who*, and he was starting to realize that even the what didn't add up to much. The sick truth was, with his medical complaints, he stayed alive now only for QVC and for Maggie: the shopping channel was a perfect way to buy her gifts. Clifford went to his sock drawer, took out the little box. A diamonique ring, that she'd never know from the real thing. Over the past weeks, she'd got the wrong idea about him; her fear and suspicion wounded him badly: he'd *never* hurt her. Unless she gave him no choice.

A fit of coughing came on then; Clifford returned the ring to its box quick smart, sat on the bed until he recovered. He looked across at himself in the mirror: never been what you'd call a handsome man, always too short and sandy and portly to be considered in that light, but his sixties weren't being kind to such looks as he'd had. Clifford pulled out his handkerchief, spat into it. No blood, thank the Lord. He knew, though, that one day there would be. He'd die, and there'd be only Maggie and his cousin to care. Sixty-five, what had he to show for it? A dismal retirement do where even the fizz had been fake. Clients were never stinted, oh no; just the week before Clifford had retired, he'd been present at the out-of-court settlement for ISU, where they'd had that decent Stolly. That had spoiled even his innocent pleasure in their Pussy Parlour; whenever he went in now, he couldn't help thinking of it as he sipped his watered-down drink. Clifford wouldn't trouble himself to return if it weren't one of the few places where the pretty waitresses very properly called him *sir*, something he could tease Maggie about. If he'd had the courage to stay in Classics, he might have been carried home on his shield. Metaphorically, of course. Instead, all he had to look forward to was the slow descent into tubercular fade-out.

No good sitting around getting morbid. He might be dying, but he didn't have to be a misery about it. Better brace up, galvanize, there was still a job to be done . . . The picture; whenever he was low, that was guaranteed to raise the old spirits. Slowly, he got to his feet, crossed the room to the wardrobe, pushed aside the overcoats, suits. He pulled out the carrier bag, carefully eased the wee painting out, set it down on the bed.

All his vast experience as an art lover had never shown him anything as beautiful. Maggie as a young woman. Not literally she, but someone so like it was as though this woman had been reincarnated as Margaret Dawson. The curves of soft flesh, the tiny but proportionate limbs, the big generous smile. In miniature. A woman who bit great chunks from existence, made your own cautious nibbles seem anorectic. Over two hundred years ago, the painter had captured the erotic force of those chubby buttocks, spread those perfect legs, expressing a feeling which didn't change with the centuries. The painting was morally Clifford's, he made no doubt of that. Sometimes, he could even achieve a full erection for it, as he hadn't been able to for flesh since he was a very young man indeed. He *wouldn't* lose Maggie: she was his, his own love, his family, and his one consolation for a life not lived.

Lulu was falling in love with Jacob, she knew that even before he kissed her this time. *Love don't belong to you, it always belongs to them. Remember that, my girl.* Maggie had drummed that into her since Lulu was little, but it'd never made any difference. Lulu fell for men too easy, always had, that's all there was to it, and Jacob wasn't the usual loser she went for and that only made it worse. Now, with her clothes scattered over Jacob's living room, his cock inside her, his hands guiding her hips as she gave him the best ride she knew how to give, she could see there wasn't any going back. The only person she'd ever fallen for harder than this was Angel, and that was different where she'd been so young at the time. Even seemed, if she could just stop thinking, that she might perhaps get to like having sex with Jacob, was obvious he was really keen to make her feel good. That once, doing the video with Angel, it had nearly happened for her then. *Never knew you could let yourself go like that, baby.* Well, she hadn't, not precisely, but if he'd stayed, she knew she would of done. And if Jacob stayed, maybe he'd finish what Angel had started. He wasn't nearly as dangerous, which had to be good, though he wasn't as beautiful either, but had Angel kept all his looks into his forties? Lulu didn't scrub up so well as she used to, that was for certain – her tummy touched Jacob's skin as she moved, her tits pointed down to face him, the sun through the window lighting the liney map of her carrying Fred. Not that Jacob seemed to care. He was about to come, she could feel it – and she'd let him. No one much expected first times to go on for long, he shouldn't be too disappointed. He could have her again, when she'd had the cuddle. Jacob would be a cuddler, she could tell, and that thought made her fall for him even more. Couple more seconds. Couple of deep groans right from her chest, tightening her cunt. Timing the inside shudders for five elephants. And.

'Oh God, that was great,' she said, leaning down to kiss him. His face was soaking wet, all them curls stuck down on his head, and his eyes so grateful. She collapsed on him, then rolled off, helped him get free of the condom. He put his arms round her, held her tight. For a minute, Lulu was totally happy. This must be similar to how people felt when they'd come with someone else, not alone in their bedroom. None of Lulu's sexual fantasies had her in them, even. Not since she was a teenager.

'You okay, Lu?' Jacob said at last. 'Was that really . . . '

'Yeah.' She kissed his chest. His body was in good shape for his age, definitely, though his neck was older than he was, like he was wearing something he'd bought in too baggy a size. Hadn't really noticed that before. 'You?' Positive what he'd answer.

'Feel I know now what everyone makes such a fuss about,' he said. 'Always been a serious fan of sex, but that . . . Shit, that was something else, Luniu.'

'Good.' Kissing him again. 'So does that mean you'll want to do it another time?'

'God, yeah.' He laughed, hugged her harder. 'Think we should make it, you know, official. Tell everyone we're seeing each other. What do you reckon?'

'Maggie and Fred already think we are,' she pointed out. But it was so hard keeping the grin off her face. Jacob was her boyfriend. They were *seeing each other*. Bloody Christ.

'I'll have to meet the others.' Jacob reached over to get his fags. 'To be honest, I'm curious to see Angel's little sister, anyway. What's she like?'

'Hard.' Terrific – they'd just made love and he wanted to talk about Bathsheba. No, that was paranoid, he was bound to be interested because of Angel. 'Something peculiar about her, be truthful, though you can't put your finger on it,' she made herself go on. 'But she's pretty, and she's quick, loses me half the time. Fred loves her.' She sat up to pass him the ashtray, then snuggled back in. 'Not a lot like Angel to look at, she's small and dead skinny, lucky cow. Stan and Del of both got a bit of him, though.'

'Who?' Jacob drew on his fag.

'His brothers, you know? Specially Del. Spit of my Freddie, as it happens.' For the first time, talking about this stuff didn't feel like an interview. They were having a proper chat, and it was lovely. Been silly to get a bit worried.

'How have they got such . . . prosaic names?' he asked. 'When you straightforwardly compare them with Angel and Bathsheba. *Stan. Del.* Sound like a couple of barrow boys.'

'Didn't he say?' Lulu laughed. 'They're really Constantine and . . . oh, something else funny, forget what. Their mum was foreign and a bit of snob, I think.'

'I met her once, didn't notice. Maybe I didn't know him at all.' After another drag, Jacob put out his fag. 'It's really weird, the way you know all this stuff about him that doesn't mean anything to me.' He sounded sad. Must of cared a lot about Angel. Lu wasn't convinced it hadn't been a bit sexual, but whatever it was, it was in the past. And showing he cared was good. A good sign.

'You must have things you know about him and I don't,' she said.

'Well, sure, but . . . ' Stroking her back. 'You've got the loveliest skin I've ever touched,' he said. 'Their family business is something dodgy, isn't it?'

'If you call running blue video shops and a strip club and porn distribution dodgy, then yeah.' She could have his hand on her back for ever. 'Didn't you know that, either?'

'Not really. No, fuck it, I didn't.' Kneading her flesh. 'Should have, the clues were there. Let's forget about him, Lu. Shit, your skin. Makes me want to bury myself in it.'

She guessed what he was about to do, and though part of

her was flattered, pleased, she knew she'd never properly relax, with worrying about what she smelled like down there. Wasn't so easy to fake with that, either. Before he could go for it, she had his cock already getting hard again in her mouth. But she presumed maybe she'd get more comfortable in time, and it wasn't like he was complaining for now. If she wanted him to stay being her boyfriend, for the phone to keep ringing with offers to go somewhere, for the kisses and cuddles to carry on, she'd be best off keeping him happy.

Phone. Doorbell. Fire. Happened so quick, Maggie could hardly register it. Rushed to the bathroom, soaked a towel fast as she could, flung it over the flames. Out in a second, only smoking steam left behind to say anything'd been wrong. First instinct was to open the door, but her better one said that weren't the best idea she'd ever had. Instead, she stamped a few times on the towel to make sure, then lifted it up. A charred and smoking wig. Flaming *wig*.

Maggie moved back through to the living room, lit a cig to calm her nerves. Kept her finger on the button of her lighter for a couple of seconds, watching the flame. What the bleeding hell had gone on here? First she picks up the phone and no answer. Then the doorbell goes, but before she can get to it, something burning comes through the letterbox. That wig was personal, way too thought-out for kids. Vigilantes, maybe. Poor slags over Tower Hotel'd been getting a lot of trouble with that. Streams of punters, they had – from the City, and tourists, loads of local Pakis – but they seemed to have near as many people not quite so happy with them, and course it was only a mile or two off. Then, Maggie weren't like them girls, she paid rent for a kick-off, and hardly no one knew what she done. Even the neighbours just thought she had a few gentlemen friends, for a wonder. Far as she was aware. Come to that, how many people knew her hair weren't her own?

Opened another window to get rid of the smoke – least it

weren't real hair like her wigs, else the stench'd be unbearable. Whoever it was hadn't really meant to harm her, or even her flat, else why check she was in with the phone and then warn her with the doorbell? And she was sure there weren't no petrol on it, would most likely of burned out on its own. Didn't make no sense. Unless . . . If this had to do with a client, she'd bleeding murder them. Peter B was peculiar enough . . . no, he was too full of nerves and what he thought was called *hinhibitions*. But, it could, for an instance, be Clifford's twisted way of telling her she needed his protection. Who'd he think he was, her fairy godmother?

Lu best be told, because of Fred being here so much. Maybe Garry could ask round, see if anyone knew anything. Not that they was likely to, hardly crime of the century. If Maggie'd been coloured, she'd be getting this on a regular basis, leave alone if she worked somewhere like the Tower Hotel.

She put out her cig. Knees suddenly didn't feel too steady. Peter A would be here in just under the hour, then Clifford a couple of hour later – she'd have to get the mess cleared up, nip out get a bottle of sherry, see to her face, comb out the work wig. Thought of doing that . . . Just have a little sit first. Was really aggravating, but if Clifford was behind this, it'd worked, in a way – wouldn't be sorry to see Peter A or even Clifford hisself, despite she'd get one of his disgusting wet kisses and declarations of love.

Didn't want to be alone though. Not tonight.

This was no way to work, no way to live. Whoever'd done it, Maggie couldn't believe it weren't connected with her job, one way or another. Other kinds of work didn't have all this. Lulu's Jacob never got his piano set fire to, did he? But if you'd got something to do with sex, the world hated you. Shops got bombed, kids could of got killed, pensioners got lighted wigs pushed through their letterboxes, women got cut up, terrified. She'd have to get that locked box out, should never of put it right away. Thank God she'd kept it, though. Because when sex was your living, the flaming world wanted you dead. Funny to think that after all them years, Maggie was finally grateful to McGowan for something.

'I'm going to be late for work at this rate.'

'No you're not, Tube'll be here in a couple of minutes. You know what Fred says—'

'Take a chill pill. Yeah, okay.' Jacob put his arm across Lulu's shoulders. 'Got a mint?' he asked. No air down here, must be even worse for people who had to travel in rush hour, soaked in summer sweat before they started. The platform was empty now, apart from that old wino on the bench. Jacob took the Trebor that Lu found in her bag. 'Thanks.'

'It's great for me you being so tall,' she said. 'Can wear heels and still be shorter than you.' She peered along the platform.

'Yeah.' Every woman Jacob had slept with made a similar comment about his height, and it always happened after the first time. Except for Susie, though that was only because she never wore heels. But Jacob was having a seriously hard time getting hold of the fact that he'd actually slept with Lulu, that they were really seeing each other.

'You all right, mate? Spacing out again?'

'Just going over a few numbers in my head,' he replied. She smiled up at him, clearly loving that he was a muso. Another thing she had in common with other women that he'd gone to bed with. But she wasn't really like them, was she? The woman in that video, this woman on the platform, they were the same. Only somehow not. God, the sex had been amazing, but then how could it have avoided having greatness thrust upon it? She knew exactly which buttons to press, a professionally developed instinct. Knew how to prevent him disgracing himself, too. And he hadn't been able to stop the feeling that he was making love to one woman, screwing another. Never known excitement as intense. Wasn't just that: Jacob loved Lulu's body, the softness, its infinitely accommodating generosity. Shit, those strong, certain thighs, those breasts, heavy with dark nipples. Even her stretch marks seemed

102

womanly, fecund, juxtaposing the now with the unmarked girl of his video. *Think you're fucking with the grown ups, Foxy? Rather you than me.* The last woman Jacob had known Angel sleep with had barely counted as one: a beautiful, hard-bodied seventeen-year-old with a death wish in her face. Maybe past thirty-five there was more flesh, more hair than there ought ideally to be, less suppleness, even less straightforward passion, but right now, Jacob wouldn't have swapped Lulu for the most nubile young girl on the planet. And yet.

This was a bloody relationship. He was officially seeing an ex-porn actress, for God's sake. Everything was schonky about this, even Angel's bloody family business; how could Jacob not have guessed that? And if anything went wrong mean-time, he might jeopardize his chance to be what Angel wanted of him in relation to Fred. For the buzz of being adored, the thrill of fucking his fantasy, Jacob was laying a hell of a lot on the line. Playing with Fred's life as well as his own. This was a dangerous situation Jacob was getting himself into; if he didn't watch out, he'd mess everything up. As usual. Or maybe he was building a self-fulfilling prophecy. Oh, screw it, let's just see what happens.

'Who's sitting with Fred?' he said.

'He's a big boy, he'll be all right till I get back.' Against the sound of the Tube finally turning up. 'Besides, he knows to ring Maggie if he needs anything.'

Disappointment in Lulu so immediate, Jacob almost hated her for a second. He'd have to do something about her casual approach to childcare; a phone was no substitute for a live body. That, he'd have somehow to provide.

'Jesus.' Such a great time yesterday with Jacob, then today she had to get landed with this. Lulu slipped off one sandal, ran her bare foot along the length of the steel. Felt smooth, cool against her skin, as if she was giving herself a treat. 'Was just a wig, for Christ's sake.' She looked down at Maggie. 'Presume a sick joke. Aren't you overreacting?'

'Fred spends a lot of time here, love.' Shrugging. 'Just in case.'

'Was that bloody thing here when we were kids?' Gesturing to it.

'Kept it in the back of . . . well, me work cupboard for years. In a locked box thing.'

'Terrific.' Lulu leaned over, picked it up. Guns always felt colder than you expected them to be. Heavier and all, at least the old side-by-sides were. Lulu didn't know about shooters you got now – had an idea Garry might have something she could take a look at, but she didn't want to make certain. Was bad enough being faced with her auntie owning one. *What you don't know can't hurt you.* Bloody well could do though, when it came to a gun. This had to be her punishment for trying to have an ordinary life. She laid the sawn-off back on its baby blanket, rubbed the grease from her fingers with a tissue. Maggie seemed even tinier kneeling on the carpet beside the gun, as if she was worshipping it.

'Shove up.' Maggie heaved herself from the floor to the settee, lit a fag. They both stared down at the horrible black metal against the pale blue wool. 'Nanny Wedge crocheted that blanket for Garry, soon as he was born,' Maggie told Lulu. 'About the last thing she done before she went doolally. Time you come along, I had to rely on the market.'

All of a sudden, it came over Lulu that she'd pick up the loaded gun, point it at her heart, pull the trigger, she wouldn't be able to help herself, like that feeling you got sometimes at the Tube that you'd throw yourself on to the line, even though it was the last thing you wanted. Quick as that, she used her toe to flick the edge of the blanket over the bloody thing, waited for her heart to slow down.

'Don't want Fred seeing this,' she said. 'I mean it, Maggie.'

'What d'you take me for? Though bit late for you to turn earth mother, ain't it?'

'Leave off, don't start on about being a good parent.' Lulu glared at her auntie. Bloody cheek of the woman. All right, hadn't been a bad childhood, Maggie had always done her best, but if she wanted a competition on mothering, Lulu would give her one.

Late-afternoon sun must of moved bit more towards night then, catching the little piece of steel that was still showing, glinting it like a knife. August in London was shit, the air too sticky to breathe whatever hour of day or night, sickly-sweet, the sun showing up all the things it shouldn't well into the evening. Wished her and Jacob could take Fred to the seaside, sort of thing you did with your *boyfriend* and your son, but course money was too tight. Not to mention getting time off. She squinted out the window at the sky. A giant baby blanket over London, without any of the grubbiness of the one at her feet. Lulu would give anything to see a grey cloud up there, something to break the heaviness of the day. Maggie stubbed out her fag, leaned over, lifted the gun in its wrap, held it on her lap.

'Least I knew how to clean it up, oil it and that,' she said. 'That's one blessing.'

'Christ.' Why was Maggie so mental over this? Had to be something she wasn't saying. 'You taught us shooters were about the worst things you could get involved with.'

'Tell you, I'll be bleeding sure it's the worst thing for the other fella, not for me.'

'You know what, Mags?' Lulu ran her hand over her tired eyes. 'No one ever rings up in this family with normal news. Nice stuff. Get what I'm saying? No one ever tells you so and so's pregnant, or got married, or a great new job, or moved house. It's all so and so's dead, or inside, or . . . or nearly got blown up. Or just bloody miserable.'

'Don't exaggerate. Bli, only wanted you to know what happened because of Fred. Flaming sure this won't be necessary.'

'Better not be.' Maybe Fred shouldn't come round here for a bit. But how would they explain that? One thing his nan controlling when he visited, quite another Lulu having to say don't go at all. Precisely when everything was coming on so well. All right, was true that Lulu always thought it was so nice of a bloke to want her, least she could do was love them, but this time, for most probably the first time since Angel, felt she was loving on her own account, too. Because it was right for her. And for Fred, come to that. 'You ever been in love, Auntie?' she asked. Never, not after being a little girl, said anything like that to her.

'With Ron – you know, Garry's dad – suppose I was.' Maggie stroked the blanket. 'But like I always told you, it's never real. Like the men what come here.' Calm.

'What?' Bloody Christ, this was an even bigger first. Lulu more or less held her breath. Was she going to get some sort of explanation, after thirty-six years?

'They don't have to please a woman, do they? Don't have to worry about performance. It's all pretend. And that suits them fine, if I'm not much mistaken.'

'I . . . um, I've heard men boast that some . . . ' Out with it, girl. Might be your one chance to hear honesty in this place. 'You know, some working girls love it with them.'

'Right.' Maggie put on a macho voice. '*Yeah, I sorted her out.* Men are fools, love.' Placing the gun carefully on the cushion. 'Don't forget that, if you can be off of it.'

'Jacob's really decent. I mean, I really like him.'

'Know you do. Think he might be a bit of a clever dick on the quiet, but he's all right, for a bloke.' She laughed. 'Nice not to have to worry about you, for a change. Pity he does such an hand-to-mouth job, though.'

'He does okay.' Lulu was desperate for a drink, but no point asking the teetotal queen for one, even when they were talking like they hardly ever had – as if Maggie saw a grown up sitting by her, instead of a stupid girl who always messed up. Felt she could ask her auntie almost anything though, right this minute. 'Why d'you do it, Maggie?'

'Money. Righteo, better show you where I'm going to keep this thing from now on.'

Being brought right to the sweetie-shop counter, still not

allowed to buy anything. Never been taken seriously in this family. That's why Lulu loved Jake, he was real nearly all the time if you asked him to be, not in tiny doses. You might not always like what you heard, but least he didn't shut up before he started. Something he had in common with Angel, funny enough. Whatever the reason Angel had brought Jacob to her, or most likely out of guilt brought him to Fred, she was bloody grateful. Jake's world didn't have guns and nasty practical jokes in, it had music and cuddling and . . . life. It had life. Somehow, Maggie's world seemed like it was dying, that even in summer there was a hint of autumn. Decay. That's what it had. But Lulu wasn't forty yet, she didn't want to catch the cynical shit that killed you off slowly, eating you up from inside. She wanted a bit of cheerful living. Wanted someone to think she deserved them sweets.

Chapter Six

'Nice to meet you.'

'Yeah.' Looking at his hand before holding it out. They barely touched palms before each of them backed off, as though they were in the ring. Bathsheba had seldom seen Garry look so uncomfortable at meeting someone new.

'Shall we get a table?' Bathsheba asked, tapping Jacob's arm.

'There's one in the corner, look,' said Lulu, and raised her eyebrows – clearly she'd noticed something a teeny bit odd as well. Bathsheba shrugged at her, led the way through the crowd. Insisting they come here was a smart move. Garry actually suggested they meet over at the Holly Blue, how inappropriate was that? He'd meant well, bless him, thinking it would bond the men, but . . . Watching Garry and Jacob watching boobs and fanny all night – very productive that would have been. Yes, Bathsheba normally loathed pubs (nasty smoky places full of overweight boozers), but not as much as lap-dancing joints, for goodness' sake. At least this pub did serve a proper choice of wine, and her little City suit made her blend in rather than stand out, which was more than she could say for Lulu's too-tight red shift (telephone boxes were desperately last century). Menu was pretty classy, too – masses of olivey nibbles and seafood. She could so imagine Stephen Hopkins in here.

'Sit next to me, Jacob,' she said. 'I want to see what our Lulu's been hiding.'

'Right.' He glanced at Lulu, then at Garry. Bathsheba was going to have to separate those boys. She put Jacob on her left, with Lulu opposite him and Garry next to Lu. That would have to do.

'What you been up to?' Lulu said to Garry. 'Not seen you in weeks.'

'Working.' Garry took a cigar out of his top pocket. Immediately, Jacob produced a packet of cigarettes – Bathsheba wouldn't have taped him for a smoker. She'd just have to grin and bear it passively. 'Mum looking all right?' Garry asked.

'You'd know if you went round.' Lulu picked up her glass. 'Could ask if anyone minded you lighting that thing. Stinks.' Silly cow waved the cigar smoke away. Right over to Bathsheba. 'As it goes, Maggie's not been herself this week.'

'Yeah, she rung me for a nag. Ain't nothing to get your knickers in a knot about.' He looked over at Jacob. 'How'd you meet this one, mate?' Nodding his head towards Lulu. 'At a gig of yourn, is it?'

'Our first proper date was, yeah.' Jacob tapped his cigarette on the side of the ashtray. He turned to Bathsheba. 'Lulu tells me you're a contortionist. That must be—'

'Mm, for the moment, sweetie.' She smiled. Although he was stupidly tall, he was surprisingly attractive (in a Jewish sort of way). One of those lived-in faces you expect in a musician, eyes that seemed focused on the middle distance. He so had to be a dreamer (God help him). And he was lean, which was nice for Lu, might encourage her to do something about herself. But the real shock was how well-spoken he was. Lulu normally sold herself to the lowest, roughest bidder. 'Suppose we're both entertainers, Jacob,' Bathsheba added. 'Nice, to have something already in common.'

'Isn't it?' Jacob touched Bathsheba's hand, but looked again at Garry.

'Not me, mate. Never been one for showing meself off.' Garry hoovered up half his pint. A tad naughty, he'd *promised* he'd stick to wine since she'd decided he needed to lose a few pounds, but she could hardly blame him for wanting beer when meeting Lu's boyfriend. A macho thing. Quite sweet, really.

'Takes a certain kind of person to perform in front of others,' Bathsheba said.

'Not sure it's as straightforward as that,' Jacob replied. He smiled, making a concertina of his face. Lulu was dipping her finger into her wine, sucking it. Looked bloody miserable. No doubt curly-top here didn't know about the stag films – that might be a useful cardlette for another day. 'Though I kidded myself I was training to be an academic at one stage, started my PhD and everything,' Jacob went on. Laughing. 'Suppose there must have been a good reason for me not sticking to libraries. Must have wanted something you only get from working with an audience.'

'Didn't tell you, did I?' Lulu said. Her face shiny. You'd think she'd use powder on top of that thick foundation. 'Turns out Jacob was at university with one of your brothers.'

'With *Stan*?'

'No.' Lulu moved her gaze from Bathsheba to Jacob and back. 'Angel,' she said.

'Uh . . . Yeah, I'm very sorry for your loss,' Jacob added. Putting out his cigarette, taking a long drink from his pint.

'Good God. I mean, thank you.' Could this truly be a coincidence? Angel himself claimed they didn't exist, that we always make things happen. 'Well, I couldn't be more . . . ' Oh sweet Jesus, of course it wasn't a coincidence.

'Fuck me,' Garry said. Almost under his breath. He shook his head at Jacob.

'This is *amazing*,' Bathsheba said. 'Bizarre.' Jacob had to be the one Angel meant, there was no other explanation. *Might just pass on the burden of responsibility, B. If something happens to me, and I can't get the money to Luscious, then I know a pawnbroker who will.* 'Wow, I can't get over this.' She'd thought Angel had been making a word-play on porn . . . but he so must have meant a Jew.

'No, well.' Jacob looked terribly embarrassed.

'I'd never have guessed you'd be pals,' Bathsheba said. She could use this. Maybe . . . *Yes*. Jacob knowing Angel could open a different channel for Lu to discover about Daddy. Had to be better for Bathsheba to be distanced from the direct line of information, at least initially. 'Why didn't you say some-thing before, Loopy-Lu?' Treating her to a beam.

'Forgot.' Lulu finished her wine. 'Can you get me another one, Jake?'

'Let Garry go,' said Bathsheba. If she knew anything about men (and she so did), then the boyfriend wouldn't be able to resist offering Lulu her own poxy past, gift-wrapped. Especially if he knew another key player. 'I'm dying to hear all about it.'

'No shit, Sherlock,' Garry said. 'Me and all.' But he balanced his cigar in the ashtray, stood up. 'Same again?'

'Just a water for me.' Bathsheba shot him a warning look. Probably Lu would end up grateful to Bathsheba for bringing everything out into the open, giving that relationship a chance of being based on honesty. Giving the whole family a second chance.

'There's nothing to tell, anyway.' Jacob handed Garry his empty pint glass. 'We read English together, shared digs, then lost touch years ago, more or less. But we were good friends, once,' he added to Bathsheba. 'He was a big influence on me.'

'Yeah, I reckoned that,' said Garry. And made his way to the bar.

You bastard, Angel. Jacob lit another cigarette, trying to seem calm. *Trouble with you, Jakey, you're too easy a target.* The game would never be over. Cumulative. There'd be thing after thing for Jacob to discover, crowding his brain until there was no room left for his real life; meantime, he'd forget every scale he'd ever learned, every detail of his own history, in an effort to keep up with all this fucking dreadful stuff Angel was laying on him. Why Lulu had to go and mention Angel . . . Screw her. No, God, Jacob could be a bastard himself, was hardly Lulu's fault. Her silence wouldn't have helped with Garry, anyway: they'd recognized each other from the video place straight off. But how Jacob hadn't seen it then, he'd never understand. Of course,

Garry hadn't had the crop when Jacob had taken in the films, he'd been comparatively fatter in the face; Jacob had only seen the Angel video once at that stage and not night after night after night as he had since, but even so.

'You all right, love?' Lulu sounded anxious. She must know she'd said the wrong thing. In fact, had seemed she'd mentioned Angel deliberately, in a futile attempt to get one over on Bathsheba. How could you not feel for Lu, needing such a pitiful triumph?

'Yeah, fine.' Of course, Garry worked for the McGowans; how stupid was Jacob?

'Do you think I look like Angel?' asked Bathsheba. 'If you ignore my size, that is.' Preening, idiot woman. Apparently modelled herself on how she thought a twenty-something successful type should appear, regardless of circumstances. Who the hell wore an office uniform for a night in a pub? Especially if they didn't work in a bloody office.

'Not a bit,' he said. 'Except for the colouring.' To think he'd been worried in case from some reflex response, he'd fancy her. Selfish, affected, way too scrawny, loved herself; sure, that was very attractive.

'Well, precisely,' said Lulu. 'Told you she didn't.' How could Lu sit in the same pub as someone who was practically her brother, after . . . It was nearly incest. The skin on Jacob's forehead prickled. Was he disgusted? Weirded out, for sure. And with Garry looking like he did now, he was a dead ringer for the way he'd been on the video. The shadowy third had acquired substance, with a vengeance; though who Angel was avenging was another question. If Jacob hadn't decided to keep that video, he'd have handed across a tape with Garry in the credits: for sucking the breasts of someone who was almost his sister, for wanking over her face. Too fucking weird for words. And what if Garry let on that Jacob had been in the shop, had owned the films, how would Lu feel? Oh crap, this was getting miles too complicated. Jacob should just walk away. Though, of course, there was still Fred.

112

'Jacob? B's talking to you. He's always going off in his own world, for some strange reason,' Lulu added.

'Sorry.'

But before Jacob could ask what had been said, Garry was back with a tray of drinks. Jacob stared right into Garry's eyes, saw a sickness in there, as visible as the liver disease had been in Grandpa's. Or maybe that was projection. Either way, Jacob couldn't imagine how he'd ever look again into Lu's and not see the same sick lust giving a sepia tint to the eyeballs. This, he was terrified of; it would mean an end to all he'd started with her.

'Yourn was a London Pride, weren't it?' said Garry. Putting the tray on the table.

'Uh, yeah.' Jacob looked away as Garry sat, tried desperately to think of something to say to Lulu, something that would make his feelings for her settle down.

'See any good films, lately?' Garry asked. To his own surprise, Jacob laughed. Garry shook his head, grinned. 'Struth, you got some front,' he said. 'Call you Dolly Parton, you don't watch it.' A complicit cover-up, must be; thank God.

'You know what?' Jacob reached across the table, took Lulu's hand. 'This woman's the best thing that's happened to me in a long time.' *Bloody hell, Mitzvah, steady boy.* Yet whatever she'd done, it had to be miles stranger that she'd look twice at him, for sure. Lulu flushed, even her nose turning crimson.

'Is that the menopause, Lulu?' Bathsheba said. Giggling. 'Look, you clash with your hair and your dress. Pink and red so don't go.' But even that bit of disguised spite didn't stop Lu looking happy, not a trace of the sickness anywhere. Candyfloss flesh, as though nothing bad had happened to harden her. If Jacob couldn't sort out his own emotional state at the moment, he could at least make hers a better place to live in.

So when, must have been about an hour later, Bathsheba got him on his own for a *little word*, he made a solemn covenant with himself that anything she told him wouldn't be allowed to spoil Lulu's night.

'I'm not lying, Nan.'

'Didn't say you was, love, but–'

'You said I might of got it wrong?' Wasn't *fair*. Grown ups were always on at you to tell them stuff, then they didn't believe you. Ran all the way here to say it, and all.

'Explain it me again.' Nan patted the settee, and he went across, sat next to her. She lit a horrible fag. Fred could see her hands were shaking. Perhaps she was only making out not to believe him – another thing grown ups had a habit of. Stupid. Like you couldn't see what was going on. Though you had to act as if you never. Being twelve was like being in prison. A specially pants prison.

'Was indoors,' he said. Slow. 'Looking up some words in the dictionary, out that Jacob's newspaper. Then I heard something. So I goes to the living room window. You know, the big one, yeah, where Mum's got that rubbish spiky plant.'

'What sort of something?'

'*Told* you, I don't know. Something. Really loud, like a bang. Probably nothing to do with it.' Fred tried not to get wound up, but Nan thought she was going for a job on *The Bill*. 'Then the doorbell went, so I had to go out the hall? Though when I opened the door–'

'You look through the spyhole first?' Fiddling with her wig.

'Course. Looked through, then I opened the door, and there wasn't no one there, just the box. Like a wrapped shoebox size, with a bow.' It'd really, really looked like the kind of thing that saddo Jacob would send Mum, didn't think about them being out together tonight. Otherwise, Fred wouldn't of touched it, no way. 'Was only light, like it was chocolates or something?' Thought he'd scoff them before Mum got back, serve her right. Shit, could just think what Uncle Garry'd say about being such a tit. Fred's throat went tight. 'And . . . know I shouldn't of opened it, but it never said who it was to. So I did.'

'And?'

'*Wasn't* a toy, Nana. I didn't get it wrong. Was *dead*.' He did cry then. Nan put out her fag, and her arms went round him much as they could, giving the biggest cuddle he could remember. Poor dead kitten. Just lying there all dead. No blood, no stink, but well dead. Eyes staring open. Poor dead mouth screaming with no sound coming out. Fred cried for ages and ages, till Nan's blouse was all wet and snotty. He waited till he'd calmed right down, then pulled away. 'Can I have a Coke?' he said. Voice shuddery.

'Much as you like, my love.' Nan went to get him a can. She was gone a few minutes, could hear her mumbling on the other side of the wall. Talking on the phone, probably to one of her blokes, when Fred really didn't need to be on his own. Why was what he wanted *never* the most important thing? But she did come back in with a Mars as well. 'Try and eat that, Fred. Sugar's good for shock.'

'Feel pukey.' But he managed to get it down him, taking big swigs of the Coke to help. 'You believe me now?'

'Yeah, course I do.' She sat back next to him, patted his knee. 'Fred, love, what d'you do with . . . the box?'

'Left it. Shouldn't I of?'

'Course you should. Tell you what, you stop here the night.'

'What about Mum?' Shouldn't he go home to look after her when she got there? But he wasn't going to say, case Nan suddenly thought he should.

'Bleeding tempted to let . . . ' She shook her head. 'Don't fret, I'll ring your mummy's mobile, let her know what's what.'

'My mate was meant to be staying, but he wasn't allowed. Mum doesn't know.' Hoped Mum wouldn't chuck a mental – she'd been funny lately about him being by himself at night. 'She's out with B and Uncle Garry and her *boy*friend, in it.'

'Look, if she's got to go home to that, much better for her if Jacob's with, unless I'm very much mistaken,' Nan pointed out. Took Fred's drink off him, had a sip, handed it back. But she *hated* Coke.

'Why'd it happen, Nan?' Fred rattled the can. She didn't have an answer to that one, course not. Why'd this sort of thing always have to . . . Never did to his mates, they just had their tea, played out, watched telly, went to bed. Was a pile of crap, being him.

'I'm out of ciggies,' she said. 'You be okay if I just nip down–'

'No.' Shitty old *bag*, how could she think about more fags when . . . *Way* selfish.

'Well, you'll just have to bleeding come with.' That tone said she meant it. She stroked his head. 'When we get back, promise you, we'll ring Mummy, double lock the door and do some sausage sarnies. Bit of a nosh-up. How's that?' She turned his face towards her. He could see her wrinkles close to, specially round the eyes and mouth.

'Yeah, whatever,' he said. In a real prison, bet you wouldn't get screws as short as her, but if you did, was blatant they'd be the hardest ones there were.

Those dreadful descending notes you heard everywhere, a quasi-musical tinnitus; Jacob wouldn't have the intrusion of a mobile if you paid him. Instantly, the atmosphere shifted up a notch, palpably tightened, as though a long-distance conversation was always going to be more important than any carried on face-to-face. Without missing a beat, Lulu and Bathsheba both opened their bags, Garry turned to fish in his jacket that he'd hung on the back of his chair. Didn't any of them ever turn the bloody things off? Wished he hadn't got the last round, then he could escape to the bar. Lu pushed back her hair, clamped her tiny gold phone to one ear, pressing the other with her finger.

'Can't hear you, Mags. I'll just take it outside, okay? Ring you back.'

'Everything all right?' Jacob watched Lulu's face for trouble. 'Is it Fred?'

'Most likely.' She smiled. 'Though I presume it's not an

116

emergency, Maggie wasn't hysterical. He's probably ditched the mate, gone round there. Find out in a sec, need to go and do a wee anyway.' Rummaging in her bag, producing a lipstick. 'Won't be a tic.'

'I'll get them in while you're nagging,' said Garry. He moved off, followed by Lu, who winked at Jacob as she went. She must have picked up some vibe that he wasn't remotely interested in Bathsheba; women could often tell that stuff, God knows how.

'Good. I wanted to have a little word with you.' Bathsheba took a green olive from the dish, nibbled it, rolled the other half in her fingers. 'You don't mind, do you, darling?'

'No.' But he didn't like the sound of this. He shifted in his seat, so he was facing Bathsheba. Her gaze kept flicking past him; whatever she wanted to say was obviously meant for his ears alone.

'Now, you have to understand, I adore Lulu,' she said. Bringing her mouth too close to his. 'I'm so only telling you this out of concern, sweetie.' Ridiculously ostentatiously, she glanced round the pub then, as though Lulu might be hiding behind a fat man or a pillar, eavesdropping. Bet he was about to hear about Lu's career; well, he could probably tell Bathsheba more than she could him: positions, expressions, the exact sound of her orgasm. That almost-brother, Bathsheba's partner, coming on Lulu's face. But no one, and for sure not this child-bodied woman, was going to lead Jacob into ruining Lulu's evening. He'd go for nonchalance, whatever he heard. 'Look, Lu doesn't know this.' Bathsheba put the half-eaten olive into the ashtray. 'And Garry and I've only known for a while. Hardly anyone does, not even the man involved.'

'So why are you telling me?' Not the porn, then? What bloody man?

'Think you should know, that's all. I've always thought Lu should, but it's so not *my* place to say anything to her.' She took his hand. Her fingers were hard, bony. 'There's Fred to consider, as well.' Widening her eyes. Lu was right, there was

117

something intangible but definitely strange about this woman. Something all too familiar. 'You know, until recently I didn't realize Fred was my nephew?' she said. Poisonous.

'Meantime, if you don't come out with it, they'll be back.' Jacob pulled his hand away, shook a cigarette from the packet. She wasn't going to faze him with that one.

'Well, it's a teeny bit delicate. It's . . . about who Lulu's father is.'

'Her *father*?' Last thing Jacob expected. He lit his cigarette.

'I'm what most people call double-jointed,' Bathsheba said. 'But it's really hypermobility, to do with faulty collagen. That's how come my skin's so smooth.' She stroked her cheek. 'It's genetic, sweetie.'

'Genetic.'

'Mm.' Bathsheba's eyes two evil wishing stones set in deep hollows.

'Hypermobility.'

'That's right.' She nodded.

Lulu and Garry arrived back at the table almost in the same second; Lulu's smooth, white face was pinched, Garry's expression half-cut and cheerful.

'We'll have to go, Jake,' Lulu said. 'It's Fred . . . Oh shit, some people are sick.'

Jacob's breath wouldn't leave his lungs. God, what now?

'Is he all right?' Bathsheba asked. Concern oozing from her mouth like pus.

'Yeah, no, he's fine, he's okay, it's not that. Tell you both later.' She picked up the wine Garry had brought over for her, took a huge mouthful. Jacob exhaled.

'You'd better scuttle off quickly, to make sure,' Bathsheba said. 'Oh, and Lu, tell Maggie my daddy was asking after her again.' Looking innocently at Jacob; man, she was cool, how did she know he wouldn't challenge her, say something to Lulu straight away, cause a scene? But.

'Come *on*, Jacob.'

And so he followed Lulu out through the crowded pub,

apologizing for her as she crashed into suited bodies on the way. Clearly, her evening was ruined without him having to do a thing.

Somewhere in another summer, Maggie'd tried to retire before. Must of been 1989, couple of month before Fred was born. That would of made Maggie, what? Forty-six. Bli, Clifford must of been around for a good thirteen year by that time. Thirteen year of him making excuses for his dick – if it hadn't been for all the women what'd laughed at him, if it hadn't been for his poor health, if it hadn't been for her seeing other gentlemen – when he didn't realize it was all the same to her. Held his dick over her like a sword, he did, even if it would be hard put to cut margarine. But she'd been determined to end things with him, to end all her *relationships*, to get herself a life that belonged just to her.

Maggie pulled her dressing gown round her more, though it was still muggy out, close even gone midnight, and course Fred'd made her shut all the windows. She'd wait till she was sure he'd be asleep, then open a couple. Reached down beside her for her tea – lukewarm, but least it was wet. Lit a cig, the smoke hanging in the airless room like a ghost. Who'd kill a baby animal? Weren't youngsters, she'd lay money. And if whoever'd sent it had been watching Lu's place, they'd of known Fred would get the box. Make no mistake, it was Lulu or Maggie who was being got at.

Have to get some air in here. Maggie balanced her cig in the ashtray, pushed herself out the chair, went over to the windows, reached up to open the smallest one. Bit of an effort, though she managed without having to fetch the stool. She pulled the curtains to, just leaving a gap for the breath of fresh to get in. But none come.

Was going to be a fresh start, she'd thought back in '89. Even before Lu'd fell pregnant and that'd forced Dolly to tell Maggie the truth about who Lulu's own dad was – *Bit late now, ain't it?* – Maggie hadn't been happy with her niece seeing Angel McGowan. Not just because of his family, neither. One time, he'd been stood in here, and she'd glanced at that mirror over the mantelpiece, see just herself and Lu reflected there. No Angel where his reflection should be. Course, it must of been the position he was standing in, but it'd creeped her all the same. Like he never had a soul.

Something evil rooted in him, the sort what'd pinch a girl, hard, just for the fun of it. Not beat her, that'd be too easy, but find a million little ways to hurt and torment and wear her down. He had his looks, education, a good job, money off the firm, what'd he want with someone like Lu? Too interested in her films, you asked Maggie now. Liked the idea of her being sold under the counter to other men, she shouldn't wonder. Addicted to risks, same as his old man, right contemptuous of anyone what weren't. Difference was, Angel didn't have McGowan's self-control, even his dad realized that well early on – *That boy's a loose cannon* – though course it'd been said too proud. Poor Lu'd tried to keep up, but she was led by bleeding *love*, Angel was led by the wickedness in hisself.

Little toad had flaming well laughed when Maggie'd told him what she knew. Maggie was still recovering from the shock of it herself, and *he* laughed. *Can't wait to tell Luscious.* But Maggie weren't having that, made sure she give it him straight about what she'd done to his daddy. Oh, and Angel took it serious all right, despite the laugh was still in his eyes – he must of known she'd do anything in this world to make him stay away from Lu and the littlie she was carrying. Could almost say he seemed to respect Maggie for daring him. Was most likely relieved and all – saved him a job, passed the responsibility on to her. Though even then, for years she'd thought Angel might come back, take one more bleeding risk with his own flesh and blood. And Maggie'd wanted out of that world, away from the Angels and McGowans and even the Cliffords – the kinds of people what'd deliver dead things to kids. Lu'd got herself a quick exit. But somehow, Maggie hadn't quite made the shift. Was always going to be tomorrow, till the idea just faded away.

So flaming hot in here. She'd hear Fred, surely, if he got up. Maggie eased off her wig, took the clips out, pulled away the net. She scratched her head, run her hand through the short, fine hair, her fingers feeling for the bald spot. Years ago, she'd had pretty hair, though it'd never been what you'd call thick. Now, her scalp felt like a dried-up old coconut. But dear oh dear, if you couldn't let it go in the middle of the night, in your own living room, you'd be stuck with your head sweating for your looks for ever.

Garry pulled off his tee-shirt, slung it over the back of the settee. No air in here. Could do with a bigger place, some-where you could breathe, out of London even. Bathsheba had their flat lovely now with all them pale colours – though he still thought it was a bit bare, to speak true. Be magic to see what she could do with an whole house, after they got married. He wanted to start their proper life in a real home, not just a building. Maybe Kent way. She come back through then with his glass of white, and one of her bottles of water. Seemed crazy to him, paying for the Thames, but if she liked it, had to be fair enough.

'Cheers, beautiful,' he said, pulling her on to the settee with him.

'Don't, Garry, it's too hot.' She unscrewed the cap off her water.

'Hope Fred's all right.' Bound to be something and nothing. 'You forget what it's like being a kid, don't you? Shit seems bigger'n it is. Think I should give Lu a bell?'

'Leave it till morning, sweetie.'

'Fucking funny, it being that Jacob brung the bastard vids in.'

'Mm, so you keep saying.'

'Reckon we should tell Lu?' Didn't like the thought of hurting the poor cow.

'Suppose she might know already.' Stuck the tip of her tongue into the bottle, then licked her lips. 'I tell you this much,' she added, 'Angel was right about there being no coincidences. Let's face it, there's got to be some bizarre connections here we're not seeing.' She held out her arm. 'Look, it's made me go goosey thinking about it.'

'Gets in everywhere, don't he? Angel.' What if they wasn't the only videos Jacob had? Angel must of had a copy of theirn. It'd had some distribution and all – well limited, but fifty wankers must of had copies at one time. If B found out, how'd she look at Garry then? Once you knew shit about people, changed your view of them for ever. As if your actual eyes was suddenly a different shape. Like his had went with Mum, years ago. With Angel and all, come to that. And in his own fucking mirror. Garry wouldn't handle it, if Bathsheba's trust in him was destroyed from out *her* eyes. She'd saved him, give him a belief in hisself, in them. Knocked his despair on the head. Someone like her loved him, he weren't a piece of dog shit. She was the gentle part of hisself, the beat of his heart. Garry gulped his wine. 'You reckon lover-boy'll pass on about the Commandant, is it?' Still made him feel well sick, fronting that. Weren't natural. Specially the way Angel never give a toss about it. Fucking junkie pervert.

'Mm, should imagine.' She smiled, rubbed her neck. 'Jacob so sees himself as the knight in shining armour type. Wonder how Angel managed it, getting him and Lulu together? Hey, maybe Jacob's *saving* her.' Little giggle, naughty mare. 'Yeah, he'll tell her for her own good.'

'Can't see why it'll help you.' He put his glass on the floor. 'What if Lu decides she wants to know your dad, they get close or something? Might want to play happy families.'

'They won't.' Shaking her head. 'Besides, it wouldn't stop the bastard losing the plot even more, *that's* the point. How's he going to react when he hears Angel fathered Fred? If I were Lu, I'd so want to see Daddy, tell him. And I'll be out of the firing line.'

He knew the plan really was to send her old man barking. If Mickey McGowan lost it, would be easier to make the boys sell to that Hopkins geezer. To stop the rot, like. But though Garry understood the thinking, was hard to make it square with his girl. Seemed so fucking cold. She weren't like most people, to speak true, see the world as if the air was nuclear fallout, but she was never cold. Mickey'd been a right cunt, couldn't take that away from him. Beat her black and fucking blue when she was a teenager. Wouldn't let her stay on at school. Didn't see how brainy she was, how sussed. Worst of it was, he never done that making up for it stuff – backhander, then a cuddle. She never even had that much.

But . . . right pity Lu had to be involved just cos Angel couldn't keep it in his trousers, though there'd be murders if Garry said that out loud. Lulu was a good girl really, just well over-emotional, could imagine her wanting a piece of her old man. Could see how she'd take the blame on herself, and all. When she was younger, she was always giving it, *Not my fault*, cos she was pretty sure everything was. Mum made her right, be fair. Not that nothing bad'd happen to Lu now – B wouldn't let it. No fucking way.

Bathsheba rested her head on his shoulder. Always, always felt nice when she done that, though she'd been doing it most nights for over three year. Made him feel like home, like he was her home and she was his, no matter where they lived. That he mattered most in the world to someone, that she weren't afraid to take the same back from him. Even sex, great as it was with her, weren't as natural in his heart as this. He took hold her hand. Wished he could magic up some Bob Marley from here, nice and romantic, but he couldn't be arsed to move. Must be well nice to have a quiet life, go out, do your thing, come home to your wife and forget it. Have a couple of sprogs running round, just like her.

'Got a gig at eight tomorrow,' she told him. 'Though I should be home before you, it's only in the City.'

'Didn't think you was going to do much more of that.' Still hated the way punters got off on it. Sick fuckers.

'No, I'm not.' Snuggling into him. 'Not exactly doing masses,

123

am I?' She was so light, he could hardly feel her weight against him, even though she was pressing herself right in. Amazing, way her body was that thin but that strong. *She* was amazing, without a shadow. Might be his goldfish, but no one could say she couldn't half swim.

'B? You want to go up?' A deaf man could hear how much he loved her.

'Yeah, in a minute.' She stroked down his stomach, making his cock stir. 'Garry, sweetie . . . Can you do me a teeny favour?'

'Depends what's in it for me.' He give a laugh.

'I'll make it worth your while,' she said. Her special sex voice.

'Go on, then. What?' Weren't easy to concentrate, with her moving her fingers down to the waistband of his jeans.

'Need to know about the synthetic coke.' Pressure getting harder. 'I *know* you hate talking about it, sweetheart, but . . . wouldn't ask otherwise, but I really do need the full SP.'

'Aw, *ma*te, why?' Though at this moment, felt he'd tell her any fucking thing, even that new type of crystal meth – Super-Crank as Stan called it – the lot. Would of made shit up if he'd of got nothing to give.

'This job's so about information, darling.' Her lips touching his belly-button. 'I'll be careful with it, promise promise. Only, Hopkins is getting pretty insistent.'

'You sure he's a poof?' Fucking better be, amount of time she spent nagging to the black cunt. Anyone touched his B, he'd tumble it straight off. And kill them.

'Positive, silly.' Biting his stomach. 'Come on, you've got to give me what I need.'

'That go both ways?' he managed to ask. Even if she took it that he only meant a shag, it'd still be a result. But then that fucking video popped in his head, and his hard-on turned straight into a soft-on. 'Just give Lu that ring first, yeah?' he said.

It was too much knowledge to bear alone; Jacob desperately wanted to talk to Angel about it, but what answers would he achieve there? *Course I knew, that was part of the thrill.* And,

Course I didn't know – who gave you the right to lay this on me now? Either way, the assurance came only through the Ouija of Jacob's own mind, he knew that, he wasn't crazy. At least, not yet. Pulling the sheet over his shoulder, he turned away from Lulu, from the face that even in sleep was still swollen with tears for the kitten, for the fear of why it had been delivered. The way the thing had stared at them: so far from the almost iconic innocence you attribute to young animals, as to seem as though it had . . . *einhoreh*, would his grandmother have called it? Evil eye, anyway. Nearly impossible to imagine who'd do such a dreadful thing. And dead men can't kill.

What must it have been like for Fred to see that? At twelve years old Jacob, despite the squaddie invasion of Guildford and the IRA bombings he hadn't known were consequent, had been taking grade eight piano, climbing trees, drinking Tizer, discovering pop music, having a prescripted suburban childhood. Could remember laughing when Babu told him sunflowers possessed *einhoreh* or whatever, explaining to her there was no such thing. Worst that had happened to Jacob when he was a child was his father leaving, yet Dad hadn't left Jacob's life, just his home. Wasn't until Jacob was well into his teens that he'd discovered Dad's thing for attractive young women, and by then it had seemed explicable.

Lulu rolled over but shuffled closer to Jacob, still softly snoring, her back pressing too hot into his. He didn't have the heart to move further away. If Bathsheba was to be believed, then Lu knew nothing about who her father was . . . Though how did Jacob know that Bathsheba was to be believed about anything? No. No, as soon as she'd said the word *genetic*, Jacob had known she was telling the truth. Lulu and Bathsheba both had that weirdly white, unblemished skin, *faulty collagen*; both could twist their bodies into strange and wonderful positions, *hypermobility*. Now he knew, he could even see a look of Angel in Lulu: not in her features, but in the width of her shoulders, the way she moved, even the length of her earlobes. Lulu was Angel's half-sister. Fred was the product of an incestuous union, of one of the few still powerful taboos. All those jokes about inbreeding . . . Nothing about this was funny. And why had Bathsheba told him? Why the hell did anyone need to know that? *It is a wise father that knows his own child.* A happier child, perhaps, who remains in ignorance. *Still the pseudo-intellectual, Foxy? Love the fact there's some things you can rely on, even in death.* Fuck off, Angel. This is all your fault, anyway.

'Jacob?' Lulu didn't really sound awake.

'It's all right, I'm here,' he said. Reaching behind him to pat her side. Immediately, the snoring began again.

An overdose, contaminated heroin, organized vice, porn, bombs, whores, incest, a dead creature in a shoebox: in less than two months, Jacob had gone from living an *Independent* life to walking around inside a tabloid. Even down to the cliché of an insane refusal to involve the police, *They won't do anything. I just spoke to Garry, better leave it at that.* But these people . . . Lu wasn't just Lulu Dawson (36) From Stepney, London, or Single Mother Porn Star; Jacob had the inside story, the raw material. The woman. He liked her, cared about her, was incredibly attracted to her. Could maybe even imagine straightforwardly loving her. And yet nothing was straightforward, in the circumstances. Lulu didn't know she was Angel's sister; given what Jacob had seen Garry do to her in the video, would she care? And Fred didn't even know who his father was, let alone that it was his uncle. So much of the story was funded by the sex industry, as well; Jacob might not be a high flyer, but he was used to an honest foundation. For a second, he felt a terrible compulsion to jump out of this bed, leave this flat, get as far away as he could and never come back. *Thing is, Mitzvah, I'd be right there with you, man.* The one person you couldn't run away from was yourself; clearly, that was bollocks.

So as Lulu half-woke for the second time, Jacob felt for her, began to make love to her. After all, if your world was shit, you might as well demand from it meantime some sort of pleasure.

Chapter Seven

It wasn't really much more full-on than some mainstream films, even those on television; this, dispassionately, Jacob could see. But from the first time he'd watched this video, it had been imbued with all the passion he'd ever experienced. And now, it was invested with how he felt about her, the woman he was seeing. Or maybe he'd invested Lu with the video. Weird, that two or three weeks of having sex with her hadn't stopped the need for, the pleasure in, this crappy old film; like tonight, with Lulu asleep in his bedroom, he was out here, watching the bloody thing as though he were Fred's age, had never had a real woman. What if she came through, caught him, how would he ever straightforwardly explain? A week or so ago, after meeting Garry and Bathsheba, Jacob had totally believed he'd never want to see the video again, yet how long had it taken, a day, two days, before he was slipping it into the machine, compulsively watching the same scene. *Welcome to my world, Mitzvah.* Jacob ran his hand over his sore eyes as Lulu offered her breasts to Garry and Angel simultaneously, before Angel pushed the other man away, relegated him to masturbation. Trouble was, Jacob couldn't see how he'd ever escape this world: caught like the farmer who wants a wife in that circle of incest. Shit, leaving that aside, he was actually the kind of man who got off on porn. Even the kind of man who, like now, watched it without desire, waiting for it to motivate him. He'd never have believed it of himself. Takeaway sexual responses, kept warm until his appetite was manufactured. Oh, God.

He froze the frame at the point where Angel opened Lu with his fingers, Garry briefly out-of-shot; leaned forward to peer through the juddery fuzz the pause button created. DVDs were meant to be far better quality, maybe he should buy a player, see whether he could get the video transferred on to a disc. Bet Garry would have a shrewd idea if that were possible. The thought made Jacob smile. He moved off the settee, went over to kneel by the screen, pulling his dressing gown open. Angel's thumb and forefinger had made a gaping hole of Lulu's cunt, that long cock was poised to enter. God, how many people could say they had intimate knowledge of an adult, consensual family fuck? Wasn't a proxy experience, either; Jacob never had to imagine himself in Angel's place. *You're my brother, man.* Jacob's hand went to his own cock, coaxing its semi-erection into a full hard-on. The scene jumped into life. Yeah, this was the best half-second of the whole video, that moment when Angel made her cry out with the suddenness. Your sister, but my woman now, mate.

The lounge door. In one movement, Jacob rose to shield the screen with his body, pressed the stop button, the porn transmogrifying into some music show. His heart seemed to have risen into his head. Shit. *Shit.* How the hell was he going to get out of this one?

'What you doing, Jake?' Lulu's voice was thick with sleep.

'Sorry, did I wake you?' he managed to say. Odd, to sound so normal.

'Don't know, I suppose. You watching something?'

'Just checking what's on. Couldn't sleep.' He pulled his dressing gown round him, got to his feet, turned to face her. She was standing in the doorway, her breasts hanging low, heavy under his old blue tee-shirt, her hair tangled from the sex they'd had earlier. Could she really not have seen? Her eyes were screwed up, although the only light came from the television and the fibre optic, but then his eyes would have adjusted where hers probably wouldn't have yet. Maybe all she'd noticed when she came in was his back.

'And what is on, then?' she asked. Still not moving from the door. Was that a pointed question? Jacob had to make a decision here; meantime, one thing he knew was he was *not* ready to lose her.

'Wasn't concentrating on the programme, to be honest,' he said. Trying a grin. Screw this: women always looked as though they were blaming you at some level for the sin of being male, a constant mental *kvetch* at your gender. Though, to be fair, maybe he deserved it. Sometimes felt it was actually down to him, her family being a bunch of freaks and deviants, or at least that he'd become one of them. 'You want tea?' he went with.

'Not yet awhile.' She did smile then. Just. Her eyes fully open now. 'Presumed you were looking at Channel 5, love,' she added. 'Precisely what it seemed.'

'Please don't get upset with me, Lu.' Jacob took a couple of steps nearer to her. 'Wasn't really doing anything, just . . . '

'Yeah.' She pushed back her hair, shifted her weight on to one leg. Stood there with her hip thrust out, framed by the doorway, she looked as though she were touting for trade. 'It's not that I'm funny about . . . well,' she said. 'But you can't help feeling it's because you're, I mean I'm, not enough, get what I'm saying?'

'That's crap, Lu.' Jacob held out his arms; she stepped forward into them, and he hugged her, hard. 'On my grandmother's grave, it's only you I'm interested in.' He kissed the top of her head, smelling sour female, hair that needed washing. Felt her body relax, her pillowy flesh squashed against him, as though it were that tree trunk fungus Grandpa used to point out. *You can't ever tell without really looking what's beautiful, Jacobniu.* 'What makes you think you wouldn't be enough?'

'Bloody hell, Jake, look at me.' Lulu pulled away from him, ran her hands down the air on either side of her body. 'Not going to win any prizes, am I?'

'You're the sexiest woman I've ever been with,' he said. Truthfully. But he'd noticed she had selective deafness when it came to hearing she was special.

'If that's true . . . ' She twisted a strand of her hair round one perfect finger. Piano-player's fingers; from the way she hummed along to tunes, he suspected her of having perfect pitch, as well. Though if he mentioned that now, it would look like deflection. 'If that's true,' she started again, 'and . . . Look, I hope you don't mind me saying this. But . . . Well, what *were* you thinking about when I came in?'

'Here.' Jacob sat on the settee, held his hand out to her. Lulu moved round to join him, barking her shin on the coffee table.

'Shit.' She flopped down beside Jacob, rubbed her leg, setting his teeth on edge with the same scratchy sound as when she filed her nails.

'Lu . . . ' Taking her hand, he kissed it. 'There's something I've got to tell you. Been thinking about it for a while, and I've decided you've got a right to know.' He turned to look at Lulu; her face was glossy with fear. 'Don't worry,' he said. 'This has nothing to do with how I feel about you. Just, well, it's got to do with both of us, in a way. I think . . . I've put it off too long already.' From the way she clutched at his fingers, Jacob imagined that whatever he said next would be a relief compared with what, clearly, she expected to hear.

'Mr Hopkins?'

'What? Oh, thanks.' Stephen took their drinks from the topless waitress, whose improbable breasts, ten years younger than the sagging skin that surrounded them, were unfortunately at his eye level. He gave her a couple of random coins from his loose change. Sensed Bathsheba stand, watched her uptight walk to the lavatory; *her* figure was fairly attractive from the back, boyish in those trousers, but search as he might, there was nothing of Angel to be seen in her. Each time Stephen looked for it, the loss arrived fresh and crisp. Dead. He'd give much to discover that Angel had remembered him in his will, even if only with a token. *What, of my love?* That money he'd paid Angel had gone somewhere, to someone. If the family had got it after all, the implications were enormous; if they hadn't, that didn't necessarily negate culpability, they could have myriad other reasons. Right, it seemed the McGowans *were* involved with crystal meth, and specifically that bloody Super-Crank: bit of a damn coincidence, exactly what had been cut with the gear that had killed Angel; it wasn't a standard drug in England yet, by any means. Nor remotely standardized, it could contain anything. Those hints Angel had thrown out before . . . Stephen was prepared to lay a lot on the line to be sure the McGowans had supplied their brother. Bathsheba and her Machiavellian fantasy were bringing him every day closer to the truth. That's all Stephen was waiting for now: proof.

Fratricide. The kind of word Angel had loved, let linger in his mouth, used most around those who would never understand. Had liked it best on the rare occasions he'd caught Stephen out, taunting him with his failure. For the entire five years, pain had been the dominant emotion for Stephen, but now, there was no chance of redemption; even if – when – the feeling faded, there would be no pleasure to take its place, or none that came from Angel. *Big black batty-boy crying, then? Won't do your image much good, mate.* Not that Stephen had cried. *So fucking English, that's your trouble.* If Stephen hadn't been so fucking English, perhaps Angel would have loved him. *You reckon?* Perhaps.

He took a mouthful of his Peroni; loathed drinking straight from the bottle, but it was politic to create the whole picture. Sometimes, when Angel had been sniffing round one of the young dancers, Stephen had told himself that was the same thing: Angel protecting his persona. But of course he'd known, knew, that was utter balls. Angel hadn't given a flying fuck what anyone thought, had liked sex more than he'd liked people; he'd never cared about gender, colour, character, he'd simply needed constant access to fresh meat. That had been his real addiction, dope was a sideline. Had even tolerated men with a Hobby. But then Angel had hardly ever judged anyone, not by standards Stephen or most of the world would recognize. And as though in acknowledgement of that *laissez-faire*, it wasn't sex that had ended everything, as it could so easily have done. It was family. Probably.

Stephen glanced round the club, taking in the punters as they watched the woman on the stage, which was so small she seemed in danger of falling off. Several of the men he recognized as having been here before, yet technically they were so much of a piece, he'd be hard pressed to say why he could pick them out. Except for that rather handsome Asian boy, of course, who probably came in desperation to assert his heterosexuality. A short, oldish punter in a pinstripe turned and caught Stephen's gaze, as familiar as his bank teller. Yet how could one utterly despise him: Stephen himself was becoming a regular, and with very little reason, less excuse. The Pussy Parlour was hardly one of his classier purchases for the company; you could still, more than a year on, see its battle scars, displayed as though they were something of which to be proud. How had he ever allowed himself to be moved from industrial holdings to this? It wasn't as though the fringe benefits on most of the properties were of any interest whatsoever. Like someone tone deaf in charge of a symphony orchestra. Or, as Angel had once said, an atheist martyr.

Now Angel was dead, Stephen could admit one thing: in an important sense, his association with Angel had procured the necessary qualifications for the job; all those years of building a rep for solid share sense had been nothing compared with the edge insider trading had given him. And that was discounting Angel's 10 McGowan per cent, his one loving gesture. *Well, you didn't like my other gift. This one'll only cost you three hundred grand.* Eyes kinder than his words. Pity wasn't always utterly harsh. Even the necessary condition of temporary secrecy was an erotic bondage, a period of engagement before the final consummation. Something they could have enjoyed together, had Angel not pumped a lot of shit shit into his weak veins. *I'd have enjoyed you struggling with it, anyway.* But Angel couldn't take back either of his gifts now. Though maybe he *had* left Stephen another.

'Sorry, where were we?' Bathsheba sat back down at the table. 'Think you were trying to blow me out.' She smiled. 'Perhaps I should be grateful, it's better than being blown *up*.' Before going to powder her nose or whatever women did, she'd looked nervous, unsure; now she was back to being the professional performer. Stephen rather admired that, certainly more than he did her disgusting contortions.

'Not at all,' he said. Her qualifications as his eyes and ears in her family were too good for either fate, though she was deluded if she believed he'd ever give Garry Dawson a job. 'I was pleased about the drugs, I merely expressed concern at the delay in dismantling the firm. Of course, you'd be compensated for your contributions to date—'

'You can so be a pompous sod.' Bathsheba laughed, as though it were a joke. But Stephen had heard similar sentiments from Angel many times. Bathsheba nodded over her shoulder at the dancer. 'Thirty-five if she's a day, sweetie. The Holly Blue's are all under thirty.' Smiling again. 'Talking of which, your girls liking it at our club?' she asked. 'Thing is, Stephen . . . ' Picking up her drink. 'We've got *masses* of talent working for us. Let's face it, we have to think about the recession.' The first person plural was a shrewd detail, but she had no real power in that family. *Knowledge is power, Stevie baby.* Well yes, and she wasn't muzzled as Stephen was by Angel's demands for secrecy around the McGowan men. Maybe a potentially free tongue on his side would be an advantage. Bathsheba's value was complex.

'I don't have any particular agenda there.' He shrugged. 'We want the properties and the good will, we're not bothered about placing girls.' Difficult to keep ISU's interest in the McGowans to the front of his mind: justice for Angel was always going to be the greater concern. The only moral concern. He had to be careful never to let Bathsheba guess that; she wasn't yet above suspicion herself. Her position as countersignatory could make her Angel's ally, but equally it could make her interested in the profits of his death. She must never know it was important to him how and why her brother was gone.

'I've put several more things in place this last fortnight,' she said. Touching her water to her lips. 'I can unplace them as easy as winking.'

'Unplace?' *Ignorant bint. Told you, Steve, those nuns didn't teach her a thing.* Only one conversation ever about his sister, and Angel had disparaged her. What, if anything, had he told people about Stephen? 'Is that a threat to withdraw?' he asked. However ignorant she was, Stephen wasn't going to ditch the potential of her bringing him at worst a further 36 per cent from her brothers' shares; with her own and Angel's, that would make 51. Delivering Angel's killers, of course, would be an incalculable gain.

'Stephen Hopkins?' The bloody bank teller man was standing by their table. Stephen ought to have expected this: every single time he tried to have a civilized exchange in one of the clubs, some delusional twat thought they'd a right to a piece of him.

'Do I know you?' Stephen said.

'Clifford Black?'

'The name rings a bell,' he admitted. Grudgingly.

'Late of Alighieri, Foxcroft and Gibbins. My former colleagues deal with ISU. I'm never sure whether to come over to you, but today I thought I would.'

'Oh, of course.' Balls, balls, balls, it was that chap Foxcroft laughed at: the one who undoubtedly kept his bog-roll under a crocheted Spanish lady. This was just what Stephen needed, an interloper to whom he couldn't be rude. 'Good to see you again, Mr Black.' Holding out his hand, which swallowed the other man's whole. 'Can I get you a drink?'

'That's very kind. A small whiskey, if I may.' He pulled out a chair as Stephen half-rose to get the attention of that topless waitress, sat down next to Bathsheba. 'I don't believe I've had the pleasure?' Clifford said to her.

'No.' For a moment, Stephen thought she wasn't going to

offer anything else; she'd even turned her head away. But, 'I'm Bathsheba McGowan,' she added, finally. Even *her* hand was barely smaller than Clifford Black's, Stephen noticed. They all three sat looking at each other, an uneasy triumvirate of conversational responsibility. *Where's Mr Manners, then? They wouldn't think much of that at Rugby, boy.*

'*Bath*sheba,' Clifford said eventually as his drink arrived. 'Unusual name, if you take my point.' Leering, his face a hundred broken veins.

'Mm, bizarre.' Bathsheba sipped her water, her face cross.

'This was one of the first places we got hold of round here,' Stephen told her. 'A, F and G handled it.'

'I knew one of your brothers, slightly,' said Clifford. 'Through my cousin, amongst other things. A very small world.' Chuckling. 'He was a character, Angel. I take it I'm right, you're related? Seem to remember your name written down next to his somewhere.'

'So how are Foxcroft and his son?' asked Stephen. The thought of this creep knowing Angel made Stephen want to rip Clifford's heart out, toss it, then him, from the club. *Worried he's disrespecting me? Want to watch that sentimental streak, Stevie.*

'Haven't seen much of the old firm since I retired.' Clifford swallowed his whiskey.

'Better things to do, I suppose,' Stephen said. Like come here and slaver, and take Angel's name in vain. In a *refrained* voice, of course.

'Absolutely.' Clifford smiled at Bathsheba. 'Your brother wasn't one for all work and no play either, was he? With all that money he eventually accrued, seems rather a pity he didn't get more chance to enjoy his leisure. Oh yes, he loved a good time, I believe. You must take after him in that respect. Here for the evening?'

'That's right.' You had to admire her cool; Stephen could barely remain civil. He pressed his palms together to stop himself reaching across the table for the chap's throat. Was Black

135

implying something about Angel's estate? Man was an utter fool if he thought Stephen wouldn't find out for certain. Soon.

'Well, I'll leave you to it.' Clifford rose. 'Nice to see you, Stephen.'

'You too, *Clifford*.' They'd be exchanging telephone numbers next. Nodding goodbye to Bathsheba, Clifford walked towards the exit, glanced back over his shoulder at their table. Stephen raised his arm in farewell. 'Right then,' he said. Keeping his voice low, as though Clifford would spring up behind them again. 'My company isn't used to the softly-softly approach. They're on my back, frankly.' Or they soon would be, which was never his favourite position. 'There's a range of other methods we can employ, as you well know. I'm starting to think you're stalling me out of some misguided family sentiment.'

'No.' She tapped her fingers on the table; her veins were clearly visible through the back of her hands, the skin almost translucent. And suddenly, he could see Angel after all.

'You came to me,' he reminded her. Forcing himself to look away. *Yeah, though who set up her gig, man? She might look back and realize it wasn't entirely her own plan. Know I would.* It was all Stephen could do not to open his mouth, let Angel out; Bathsheba's gullibility was so irritating, so female. Ambition truly was blind in her case. But he bit the inside of his cheek. She was disposable income; nevertheless, he couldn't afford to fritter her away just yet. 'I'd like to see some real friction in the outfit within a couple of weeks,' he said. 'With at least your brothers' shares coming soon after. We're technically aiming for a quarter of the territory by 2006, we can't hang about waiting for a few premises and some distribution. The Internet's a real threat to that sort of business, especially with bloody webcams. If we wait too long, what your family has will be obsolete.'

'Make it a month.' Bathsheba fixed her gaze on his. Her thin lips moving slightly.

'All right, a month.' The woman seemed to believe she'd end up controlling legitimate Soho; frankly, even ISU didn't have the smallest chance of that, against the established competition. Looked at baldly, a modest quarter seemed an overestimate, at least in the next four years. 'But I want progress reports.' He was tired now of tormenting her, had done enough to keep her keen. 'If you'll excuse me, there's somewhere I need to be.' Important not to say goodbye, to leave her alone in this place with his silence. Another technique he'd learned from Angel. To her credit, Bathsheba didn't say another word either.

'What the fuck are you saying?' Lulu snatched her hand back, sat nursing it as though he'd damaged it in some way. 'You're one sick bastard you know, mate. Fancy bloody well believing that scheming bitch – she'd say anything, make me look bad. You saw how she was with me that night.' Panting, audibly, her cheeks and nose bright red. Jacob tightened the cord on his dressing gown, reached over to get his cigarettes.

'Really think it's true, my love,' he told her. Soft, as if the timbre of his voice could hurt her as much as what he said. He was having trouble making his lighter work; Lulu took it from him, sparked it, held it to his cigarette. 'Thanks.'

'Just couldn't handle you fart-arsing about with the stupid thing,' she said. Standing up, walking round the table. 'So you really think it's true, do you? D'you know, *I* really thought it was true you cared about me. Yeah, right. Bloody Christ, Jake – you telling me Fred's related to Saddam Hussein or something?' Flinging her arm wide, knocking her hand on the television screen.

'No, course not. What's that got to do—'

'You might as well be saying it. It feels nearly that bad, can promise you.' Her eyes mad with illogicality; suddenly, Jacob was pretty frightened. 'You're telling me my own son . . . I mean, if Mickey McGowan's my old man, then Fred . . . Oh shit.' She shook her head. 'No, it's not happening, mate. No way. Can't believe you were stupid enough to believe it.'

'But—'

'What the fuck d'you know about any of us, anyway? We

some sort of experiment for you? Bet you're loving this.' Lulu shot evils at him, stopping his words in a ball in his throat. 'Suppose B swarmed over all sweet, butter wouldn't melt. Blokes are *so* predictable. And thick.' Abruptly, she came back, sat down again. Sounded like the air had been pushed from her body in the movement. '*Why*'d you believe it?' she asked. Almost a whine. 'I wouldn't of, but you had to, didn't you?'

'Uh . . . ' Jacob hawked up what he needed to say. 'I think you do, too.' He'd thought that a serious risk, but she looked at him as though he'd simply stated the obvious.

'Feel sick, Jake,' she said.

'You weren't to know.' Jacob put a finger on her leg, then removed it before she could tell him to. 'Sounds to me like no one much does, not even Mickey McGowan.'

'Well, precisely, Bathsheba's a stirring little tart,' said Lulu. 'Most probably *is* a pack of lies.' The palpable hope made Jacob wince; her anger had been far easier to hear.

'Maybe, Lu.' Resting his cigarette in the ashtray, he took her hand again; she let him, watched as, gently, he pulled her thumb back so it touched her wrist. 'That's genetic,' he said. Letting go. 'Angel could do it too, couldn't he?'

'Yeah.' She nodded, her eyes filling with tears. 'Presumed it was like . . . some people can curl their tongue up or whatever. Didn't seem a big deal.'

'It doesn't have to be.'

'Then why'd you tell me, Jacob? Leave off. If you reckon it's not a big deal, you never had to . . . ' Covering her face with her hands. 'What the hell would I be meant to do with knowing?' Her voice muffled. Jacob drew heavily on his cigarette, stubbed it out, stroked her hair, slightly greasy under his palm.

'I'm sorry,' he said. 'Thought it'd be better coming from me. If Bathsheba and Garry know now, your guess is as good as mine how, then it wouldn't be long before—'

'*Garry* knows?' Lulu raised her head. 'Since when?'

'Not sure. Not long, I think.'

'It's got to be crap.' She was shaking now, visibly.

'Let me make you a cup of tea,' Jacob said. Getting to his feet.

'Yeah.' She looked up at him, her huge eyes green with pain. 'Stick a brandy in it.'

He bent to kiss her head, and went out to the kitchen. What on earth had he done? *Saved your own skin by showing Lulu hers, boy. Don't kid yourself.* Jacob tested the weight of the kettle, switched it on. *Proud of you.* Screw it, was exactly how Angel would have handled the situation; Jacob knew that, as surely as if he'd seen it happen. But it wasn't as though he hadn't planned to tell her, he'd been waiting for the right moment all week, and comparatively, this had been it. Couldn't have kept quiet for much longer, not without feeling he was lying to her.

Jacob took two mugs from the tree: his old Queens' one and her favourite, the Winnie-the-Pooh she didn't know Susie had given him. Popped three sugar lumps into Lulu's, then added another. Why did he have lumps rather than . . . That's right, the absinthe. Still sitting in the cupboard, barely touched. How long for? Two months? A life ago. *Remember, I know you, better than anyone has ever known you.* For sure, better than Jacob could claim to know himself now. The kettle clicked; Jacob started to pour the water into the mugs, remembering just in time about the teabags. He added milk to both, brandy to hers, then changed his mind and sloshed some into his as well. Heard the toilet flush. What was Lu going to do once the shock had worn off? Confront Bathsheba, have it out with Maggie, lay it on Fred? Perhaps Angel had been fully clued up about Mickey McGowan, realized it was going to come out, had sent Jacob to Lulu for that as much as any other reason. *Leave off, Foxy, I'm not that deep.* Angel had always pretended to be irredeemably frivolous; Jacob sometimes wondered if that explained the heroin: a need to block the depths with easy shallows, a way to prevent any access to his pain. Or maybe that was apologist bollocks.

He picked up the mugs, took them through to the lounge. Lulu had switched on the small lamp. Clearly she'd been crying, but she was blowing her nose on a piece of loo-roll, then managed a weak smile.

'Wish I bloody smoked,' she said. Taking her drink. 'Shit, you're saying I slept with my *brother*. Enough to put anyone on the fags.'

'Angel wasn't your brother, sweetheart.' Jacob sat beside her, lit a cigarette. Thank God, she seemed to be accepting it now. 'Only by blood,' he went on, 'and sure that's heavy, but it's not the same as straightforward . . . uh, incest.' Morally, what she'd done with Garry had to be closer to that.

'Piss off. Social Services got enough workers, they don't need you.' So like Angel. 'Just can't help being a nice Jewish boy, can you? If this isn't bullshit, then course he was my bloody brother.'

'Sorry.' Jacob touched her arm. She shrugged him off.

'What about Mags?' Lulu rubbed one eyelid, hard. 'She know?'

'No idea, sorry.' He grabbed her wrist; if she didn't stop that, her poor lid would be really sore. 'That was stupid of me, I should have asked.'

'She'll know.' Lulu pulled away, put her free hand between her legs. 'Not much happens in our family, she doesn't know about. Oh Jesus – Fred . . . '

'What will you do?' he asked. 'Not that you have to do anything, of course, but—'

'For *Christ's* sake, stop being so frigging careful. Not got a clue yet what to do, be truthful.' She sipped her tea. 'Bloody hell, Jake, I only take one sugar.'

'Yeah, I know. Sorry.' Choked, as though he'd over-sweetened his emotions, too.

'But I tell you this much for nothing,' she said. 'I'm not going to leave it.' Putting her mug down, curling her legs under her. They sat in silence for a couple of heavy minutes. Jacob felt totally impotent: why the hell couldn't he think of something to make it even a little better? Lulu yawned, so hard he heard her jaw click. 'Thing is, makes you look at your life differently, you get me?' she said at last. 'Right away, just like that.' Smacking her palms together. 'Jesus, bloody Bathsheba knows more about me than I do. Seems I've got a clever little sister, isn't that nice? You start feeling like . . . what can you trust?'

'In what way?' Desperate to avoid saying Lu hadn't told him about her past.

'You know who my real mum was? Maybe we should ring up some random person out the phone book, ask them. Far as *I* know, it was this woman called Dolly, Maggie's younger sister,' Lulu went on. 'She dumped me on Mags when I was . . . Christ, not a year old. Might not get Mother of the Year, but I'd never of done that.' She shook her head, as though the idea were so dreadful she had to force it out of there. 'Suppose on average only saw her about every six months after that, she moved away. Basildon, so not far, but . . . How do I know really what went on? I mean, really and truly?'

'You were there.'

'Jesus, Jake, you went to *Cam*bridge. Should see it's not that simple, not after . . .' Lulu examined her nails. 'To be fair, I did go back to live with Dolly. Twice. Once when I was four or five, just for a couple of months. Remember not getting why I'd been sent away there, thought it had to be my fault, so suppose I cried a lot. Reckon her new bloke didn't like wailing kids. She can't of done, neither, she never had any more to replace me.'

'Shit.' His father leaving was nothing comparative to this.

'Yeah, well. Then she made me go to her when I was eight and the bloke had scarpered, though I was sent home again inside the year. Anyway, she's dead now. December '99. Know what?' Taking a mouthful of her drink. 'I hardly cared when she died. All she gave me was my name, and I soon changed that, didn't I?'

'You don't even look like a Louise.' He didn't know if that were true, but in some obscure way he felt he had to defend her against her real mother.

'No, most likely not. Anyway, Maggie was, *is*, my mum, far as I'm concerned.' She smiled, wiped her nose. 'Not that I didn't spend loads of time when I was a teenager telling her she wasn't. Little moo, I was. But I know one true thing, mate – she couldn't think any more of me if she'd given me birth. No matter how much we get on each other's nerves, or how tough she was on me. Promise you that much.'

'See? In the same way, Angel's *not* your brother.' Jacob pushed her hair away from her eyes, tapped out his cigarette. 'But didn't you ever wonder who your dad might be?'

'Yeah, *course* I bloody did do.' Twisting her fingers together. 'Just said, I had a mum. But I never had a dad. Used to spend hours wondering what he was like, understand what I'm saying? Used to decide he was like this bloke on telly, that bloke down the road. Made up whole lives for him, loads of lives.' Lulu held out her hand; he took it, stroked her palm. 'They told me he was just someone Dolly had met in a pub, never saw after. Maybe Maggie believed that, don't know. Somehow doubt it now.' Her eyes teary again. 'And I've done the same bloody thing to Fred, haven't I? He must wonder about his dad. Funny thing is,' she added, 'never had a good excuse not to tell him before. Have now.'

'Unless you use it as an excuse to tell him.'

'Yeah, unless I do that.' She turned, so that her body leaned against Jacob's; he put his tea on the table, and both his arms around her, holding her tight.

'Luniu.' There was nothing more he could say to her now; all he had left was to offer her such comfort as he could. Almost under his breath, Jacob started to sing the only lullaby he knew.

'Shut the fuck up, Jake.'

Maggie drew back the curtains. Going to be quite hot again today, unless she was very much mistaken. Fred was crash-banging about in the kitchen. Shouldn't let him stop over so much, but since that bleeding kitten he hated being left, and it weren't fair if Lulu hardly got to see her Jacob. End of the day, didn't want Lu to have a lonely life like hern, although that's what Maggie'd chose.

She lit a cig, checked her wig, called through for Fred to do her a coffee. Tea weren't going to be enough this morning, not after the night she'd had. Must of been about midnight, feeling under her bed for her secret biscuit tin – a Rich Tea would of been just the thing to settle her tummy – when her hands'd touched it. For a second, she'd not been able to think what something so hard, cold, was doing there, where her biccies should be. Then she realized what it was. Fear'd rushed through her, from legs to her head. And yet the gun was hern – most probably faint clean away faced with someone else's. Nothing was certain in this life, even a locked bedroom door. Like McGowan sending over all them little *How are you* messages, as if it was the most normal thing in the world. And Clifford saying more'n once, shocked, it weren't him sent Fred the box, just like he reckoned he had nothing to do with the wig, but how could she be sure? *Just sit there for me, my darling.* Not even certain about wanting a good night's sleep – couldn't do much shooting if you was soundo. Mind, knowing her luck she'd wake up, offer the bastard a bleeding custard cream.

Fred come through with a mug. The chipped one, should of chucked that.

'Want me to make you pancakes, Nana?' Had sugar all round his mush, dirty ha'porth. 'Wicked at flipping them now.'

'No, not for me.'

'Bummer. Can I have breakfast telly on, then? It's got the news?' Crafty beggar.

'I should cocoa,' she said. But smiled, so he'd know she was joking. 'Give us me glasses off the sideboard.'

Crikey, other people had no idea of what time reasonable human beings got up. Who was that, this time of the morning? Weren't eight, yet. Postie, maybe. Though even if it was, who's to say what he'd brung?

Maggie went out the hall, slower than she'd move of a rule – maybe whoever it was would of got fed up, gone away. But when she looked through the spyhole, he was very much there. Every plug-ugly inch of him. Flaming *cheek*. Had a good mind not to answer.

'What you doing here?' Glancing over her shoulder. 'You can't come in, dearie, got me grandson staying.'

'That's nice for you.' Mad old buzzard sounded like he meant it.

'So sling your hook, there's a dear.'

He looked right puzzled, for real. Marvellous. Déjà bleeding vu.

They'd of been about twelve and thirteen. Lulu'd just begun to look smashing now she was coming out the puppy fat stage. Had that craze for wearing them pretty flouncy skirts with bits of petticoat sewed in the hem. Lovely fashion for the youngsters, that was.

'But . . . I'd like to meet him,' he said. Pulling her back to today. 'I've seen him on the stairs once or twice. Seems a nice boy.'

'Meet him?' What'd he have, rocks in his head?

'Why not?' Watery eyes peering at her face.

'Blow that, course you can't meet him. Do me a flaming favour.'

Seemed to remember that was the year Lu's bust first started showing and all, though it'd been before that was the only thing boys noticed about her.

'No?' Looking a bit umpy now. 'I think you'll find I can.' Clifford took a step forward. His nose was nearly touching hern. Don't move back, Maggie girl, he'll come in quicker'n a virgin's willy.

'Fred's never, not once, met a client.' Speaking practically into Clifford's mouth. 'Ain't making the mistakes with him I made with me own two.'

Garry'd been a flipping skinhead, God help him, but they wasn't bad kids at all then.

'Lulu isn't legally your child. So Fred's not your grandson, strictly speaking.'

'Bugger off.' Her sudden anger startled her, made Clifford take a step away, his expression hurt. 'They're mine, and it ain't nothing to do with you, mate.'

Hardly the Waltons, though not a disaster. Maggie was making enough money to give them most things they wanted, and everything they needed. Even their Dolly was sending the odd twenty at that time, for a wonder – guilt money, what'd never come when it'd of really been appreciated, but still. Nice for Lu, and more'n Ron ever done for Garry.

'Maggie, I'm sorry. Make no doubt, I know I shouldn't have said that.'

'Believe me, no, you shouldn't of.' If he thought he was getting in now, he had another think coming.

How she could of been so stupid, Maggie'd never know. A school night, Lu was meant to be having tea with one mate, Garry with another. But they'd all forgot it was some strike afternoon for the teachers, lazy blighters, and both kids'd took it in their heads to come home first.

'Nan? You okay?' Fred was at her elbow.

One bloke leaving as Clifford and the kids all pitched up together.

'Yeah, fine, love.' Maggie half shut the front door. 'Go on back to your programme, there's a good boy.'

Clifford weren't early or nothing, Maggie'd squeezed the other bloke in for a quick appointment, weren't even a regular, and she hadn't give it a thought about how punctual Clifford always was. Just not like her.

'And who's this little chap?' said Clifford. Pushing the door back open. Idea of that gnome calling anyone, leave alone Fred, little . . .

'This is an old friend of mine,' she told Fred. 'He was just passing.'

'At eight o'clock? Well keen, in it.'

'Don't be rude, Fred.' Had to talk normal to him.

145

The other man was flaming paying her at the time . . . And they knew. Lulu and Garry both knew. Most probably had their suspicions for a while, but children only see what they want or expect to see.

You whore!

Don't speak to your mother like that.

I don't want any trouble.

Auntie . . .

Everyone talking at once. Everyone except Maggie. Her flesh'd crawled with it, like maggots was feeding on the shame.

'I came to ask your grandmother if she'd marry me.' Clifford give a sickly smile. 'What do you think of that then?'

Maggie and Fred both stared at him. Fred clutched at Maggie's arm.

'Don't worry, Fred love. Ain't going to marry nobody.' Yet the way Clifford looked at her, could see he never agreed.

Do your bleeding best to keep the family together, to hold off the rest of the world, but it was too late to stop the knowing. You could keep out the Old Bill, the pimps, the villains, the past, but you couldn't make something what was known unknown. When Maggie'd first held Fred, she'd swore then she wouldn't let the same thing happen with him.

And now she had, or nearly had. Hours later, she was still thinking about it.

That was it, then. Fred was playing out with his mates, she didn't have an appointment till Socks-on Sam tonight, and he could go whistle and all. No time like the present. For the last time, she'd dial Clifford's number. Just let him bleeding try anything – she'd make it clear Garry'd be told if Clifford much as said the words Old Bill or Social Services. Enough was enough. Should of done this the first time he'd threatened her, that's what families was for. Just come right out with it. *Clifford? It's me. Don't bother coming round no more. It's finished.*

Wasn't Angel's face looking down at her. Funny, she'd presumed it would be, even though she'd seen him around several times before, so she should of known better. Her face in the mirror wasn't Angel's, either. She'd made a child with her own brother, and you couldn't see it anywhere on her. Even her heart was having a job recognizing it, though her tummy did, must of lost pounds, number of times she'd run to the loo since the other night. Jacob could of made her stop loving Fred – if he realized what he'd been risking, that was unforgivable. But no, Jacob was decent, and anyway, Lulu couldn't make herself believe Fred was damaged by who his father was. Couldn't see him as anything other than Fred, thank Christ. Why'd Angel have to be dead? Never wanted to talk to him this bad, not even when he'd left her. Had so much to ask him. Fred's lifetime to ask him. Now all she could do was look at this other man, this stranger, hoping he'd be able to make it something less shit.

On the train out from Waterloo to Richmond, squashed in the tail end of evening rush hour, she'd been trying through the crowd to spot faces that might be similar to his, to remember what he looked like, but all she'd been able to see was a bald head. In the cab from the station, even that picture had got blurry, till she wasn't sure if he had a bloody Afro. Now, with him standing in front of her, still she wasn't certain precisely what she was seeing. Christ, don't let her throw up, not here. Hadn't realized he was so big – not many men apart from Jacob were still taller than her when she had these shoes on. And he made Jacob look like Cleopatra's Needle compared to Big Ben.

'Can I help you?' he said. The thing she said to so many people every day at work.

'I'm Lulu Dawson,' she managed to reply. Smoothing the skirt of her dress.

'So you are, girl.' He nodded, not smiling. Coming into focus more. Bloody hell, Boris Karloff – all he needed was the bolt through the neck, though his clothes were fancy enough for any Hollywood actor. Is that what *she* looked like? Shoot herself, that was true. Still couldn't see anything of Angel or

Fred in him, not in the bulbous nose, the pock-marked skin, the pouches under his eyes. Though suppose the eyes were precisely the same shape, just looked totally different on him. Different shade of brown, too – hadn't occurred to Lulu that brown eyes weren't all exactly the same colour. Hang on, her eyes were blue, so . . . No, so were Dolly's and Maggie's and Nan's and Garry's. Other side of the family. They stood looking at each other for long seconds. What was she doing here?

'Can I come in?' she said at last.

'Maggie send you?'

'Jesus, no.' Why would he presume Maggie had sent her, unless everyone knew the truth but Lulu. Should of gone to Mags first, but for some strange reason, she couldn't of. Would of been . . . like delivering a dead kitten herself. Or asking for one. Don't start thinking about that again, really will make yourself sick.

'All right.' He moved aside, let her step across the doormat. Then he led the way – she'd forgot every word about his limp – down the hall, into a long, airy kitchen, done up with smart pine units. Hardly anybody Lulu knew lived in a whole house. Angel had always had access to all this. She could of had, too – if they'd got married, Angel would of had to of told his dad then they were together, she'd hated the way he'd kept her secret from . . . Don't be mental, you couldn't of married your own brother. How nasty was it, to love Angel like she had? Maybe some part of her had always known the truth, maybe she was just a sick bitch. 'Will we have coffee?' Mickey asked. 'Just made a pot.'

'Thanks. Milk, one sugar.' She watched as he poured coffee into two proper cups from one of them flash silver things you put straight on the stove. They both sat at the scrubbed kitchen table. He lit a small cigar. 'Imagine this ain't a social call,' he said.

'No.' Did he know, did he know, did he know? Blocking out any other thought. 'Mickey McGowan,' she said. Testing how the name felt in her mouth. Tasted of blood. Then she realized

148

she'd bitten her lip. 'You knew my real mum.' Attempting to pick up her cup, only managing to rattle it against the saucer. 'Dorothy Dawson. Dolly.'

'That's right, so.' Looking genuinely curious. Puffing away on his cigar, calm.

'I'm thirty-six,' Lulu tried, pressing her finger to her bloody lip. Suddenly, she was dying to do a wee. 'Didn't you realize that?' Watching his battered face. The expression changed, was sure it did. His eyes came to life.

'What you saying, love?' Mickey drank half his coffee in one hit.

'I think . . . Look, I don't know how to put this.'

'Find the best way normally's just to come out with it.' His tone almost kind. Was this really the bloke Maggie said was a vicious git? Maybe Mags hated him only for being Lulu's father.

'Been told . . . ' Lulu cleared her throat. 'No, I mean I'm sure it's true now. You're my dad, Mickey.'

'Fuck me.' Unless he was up for the first Ugly Man Oscar, no way in this world he'd even suspected he had another daughter. But least he wasn't denying it either. Yet. 'Sorry, that's a facer, girl.' He peered across at her, as if he was short-sighted. 'Fuck.' Shaking his head. 'You sure about this?'

'Yeah.'

'Why didn't Maggie tell me? Why didn't Dolly, come to that.'

'That's not the worst of it.' Don't cry, Lulu, whatever you do.

'No?' A peculiar laugh. She got a whiff of his aftershave. Feminine, somehow. Lulu breathed out, hard. Let go of her fantasies. All them lives she'd made up weren't lived by this man, them dark brown eyes had seen stuff she couldn't begin to imagine. What had she thought, he was going to open his arms to her? *He's probably seen your films, Lush. Keeping it in the family.*

'Sorry to spring this one on you,' she heard herself say, 'but you've got a grandson.'

'I've got a what?' Getting slowly to his feet. 'This better not be a fucking wind up, lady, I tell you.'

'It's not.' Oh Jesus, why wouldn't he sit back down.

'What age has the little bastard?' Balling his fist into his other palm.

'Twelve.'

'Yeah, I did know you had a boy. Fuck.' Walking to the worktop, smacking his hand down on the marble, turning back to her. 'Sorry, I'm being—'

'Not just mine.' Best way was normally just to come out with it? *One elephant, two elephants, three elephants . . .* 'He's Angel's boy as well.' Head pounding.

No one, not even when she'd been an actress, had ever looked at her like that. As if she'd spat on his mother's grave. She didn't have to imagine what he was seeing now, still, staring. She might as well of took her clothes off, asked him to fuck her. Christ, she *was,* she was just a dirty, disgusting bitch. Sick to her stomach, Lulu put her head in her hands. All she could hear was the bubbling sound of that fancy pot of coffee keeping hot.

Chapter Eight

Was never really dark along here. September nights'd always been Maggie's favourite, way the last of the natural light was exaggerated by the artificial even as late as nine o'clock, yet there was still more of a difference between day and evening than you got July, August time. Shored you up, a night like this, made you feel life weren't so terrible. A week into retirement nearly – still felt like only an holiday, but she was breathing more easy, had to be said. That rusting paranoia, what'd been eating into her flesh, was getting less with every day, as if retiring'd took a wire brush to it. Even Clifford, who course was still bleeding ringing up all the time, hadn't said no more about threats or proposals. Much the same thing, when you come to think about it – fact, seemed to Maggie both had been a way of saying out loud his desperation. The other stuff . . . if that *was* him, it'd been temper shots in the dark, a littlie stamping his foot. Maggie'd overreacted, unless she was very much mistaken, where she'd had so much on her mind, coming to terms with stopping work for real. Gun under her flaming bed – Lu was right, what was she thinking? Felt a bit of a fool, truthfully.

She walked slow, wondering about stopping for a kebab. Was one of her secret vices, that – would never of admitted it to Fred, was always telling him he eat too much junk food. Still, least kebabs had a bit of salad in them. No, maybe she'd wait till she got home, do herself some nice tomato soup. Had to remember she didn't have a lot coming in no more. Mind, Clifford would still help out from time to time, wouldn't be able to stop hisself, and she couldn't see Mr Piozzi not sending over the odd joint of meat, Dennis changing her fuses, Sockson Sam slipping her milk and butter, popping in for a chat. Loads of marriages ended up having no sex in them – maybe little marriages was no different.

Maggie stepped into the road for a sec, save treading in a big pile of dog dirt on top of an hamburger box. Filthy beggars round here. Been a *smashing* evening, so lovely seeing Pat. Had forgot how good it could be, jawing to a woman her own age, to someone she'd known all her life. Not much time for mates in Maggie's game, it'd always felt too dangerous to be close to outsiders. Be different from now on. Crikey, she could still picture Pat way she'd been in Infants, hardly seemed to of changed. Wonder if Pat thought the same about Maggie? See her with plaits tied with strips of rag, gap in her teeth, scabby knees? Nanny Wedge could never get over how often Maggie'd hurt herself – *Stockings don't grow on trees, my girl.* Maggie'd never thought they did do, and told Nanny Wedge that. Got a clump for it, often as not, but not hard. Never that. Was a nice childhood, even after Daddy passed away. Sort she wanted Fred to have, before he got too old to have one at all.

Them kebabs did smell tempting, all oniony and burny flesh – she'd be at the takeaway in a few tics. No, come on Maggie girl, have some flipping willpower. She picked up her feet more, went by the shops, turned down into Church End. Bit darker round here, off of the main street, though you had to be truthful, Council weren't doing a bad job of keeping the lampposts in good working order, for a wonder. More impressive than a few year ago, anyway. Sometimes, did seem the world was getting better, not worse.

'Only a crappy PC game, Jake. See, the Druid can turn into a Werebear. Well easy.'

'I'm too old.' Jacob pushed the chair away from the computer screen, stood up, rubbing his sore back. 'We didn't have stuff like this when I was young.'

'In the Stone Ages.' Fred looked at Jacob over his shoulder, laughed. 'What d'you have, one of them hoops and sticks?'

'Sure, and we only ate gruel.' Self-consciously, Jacob ruffled the funny cockerel's plume at Fred's crown. 'Know you hate it, but after that I need a cigarette.'

'Open a window then, minger.' Fred moved the mouse, made the screen go dark. 'What time d'you reckon Mum'll be back?'

'Don't know. I've rung Padley's, told them I won't be in.' First time since the night of Angel's letter that he'd missed a gig. 'Managed to get cover, was only an extra shift, anyway.' Why did he feel the need to justify his actions? Way the child was opening that Twix, as though it needed total concentration, suggested Jacob had bored away a few of Fred's braincells already.

'Want a bit?' Fred held out one of the chocolate sticks.

'No thanks. I'm going to get that cigarette, when I remember where I've put them.' Where the *hell* was Lulu? First time she'd ever asked him to babysit, but she'd sounded so insistent on the phone, so anxious, Jacob hadn't liked to question it. Sod, really couldn't think what he'd done with his cigarettes, but mislaying his girlfriend was more worrying. Twice Lu had gone AWOL now in less than a week; until the night he'd told her, he'd been under the impression she'd spend every spare second with him if she could. Since then, she'd been distant, secretive. Absent. Wouldn't be surprised if she were in some pub tonight, getting slaughtered on her own. Or maybe even picking up a bloke. No, don't go with that thought. Meantime, he was stuck with a twelve-year-old running rings round him.

'You think Mum's still at the shop, yeah?'

'Probably.' Checking his watch. Almost ten. Never known her finish later than nine, pretty much be back by this sort of time. Jacob spotted his jacket behind the settee, fished hopefully in the pocket for his Gitanes. 'Your granny might know.'

'Some bloke asked Nan to marry him the other day,' said Fred. Stuffing the end of his Twix into his mouth.

'What bloke?' Jacob couldn't imagine a prostitute getting married, though he shouldn't be so prejudiced. *Right on, man.*

'One of her boyfriends – Dwarf Man.' Fred twisted his body into a hunchback, pulled a dim-witted face. 'Looked well upset, when she wouldn't,' he said, straightening. Fred lifted his knees to his chest, spun his computer chair round. 'Help me take all this lot back to my room?' he asked.

'But we only brought it all through the other day.' Tempering his exasperation.

'Yeah, well one time, with my old computer, I had it in here and when I came home from school, it was gone.' Holding his arms out, then letting them drop to his sides. 'Didn't get a new one for ages, right, till Nan sorted it. Don't care, this one's way better, got wicked graphics.' Spinning on the chair again. 'Holidays finish not tomorrow the next day, so I want it back in my room. You going to marry my mum?'

'Uh . . . Early days yet.' Mustn't seem embarrassed under Fred's stare. 'How would you feel if your mum did get married some time?' Shit, as though it were a possibility.

'Don't know.' Fred shrugged. 'Mum's mostly loads more cheerful. That's well crunk.' Another shrug. *Crunk?* Jacob felt at least a hundred. 'You're all right,' Fred added. 'Seen worse.' He stood up, moved over to the window. 'But if she got married, he couldn't start ever making out like he's my dad.'

'No.'

'Get enough of that from Uncle Garry.'

'Sure.' Jacob hadn't seen any evidence of Garry doing anything remotely paternal, but now wasn't the time to say so. He watched the ghost of Angel's face made flesh, tried to imagine how Fred would look as an adult; what if the child had inherited some weird defect from his parents being siblings? Jacob was no closer to loving the boy, but, for sure, was involved enough to wish him no harm, nothing but good.

'D'you reckon you should ring Mum's mobile?'

'Give it another half-hour, okay?' Jacob spotted his cigarettes on the windowsill. Thank God. 'Don't suppose you've got a chessboard?'

'Yeah, course.' Scornfully. *Middle-class assumptions again, Mitzvah. Nice hit of guilt for you.* 'It's cerebral, in it? I looked that up. Sure you don't want to play it on the computer?'

Halfway through the game, Jacob realized Fred was going to win. Back to all those long nights in Cambridge, after the pub: getting stoned, eating Smarties, playing chess or backgammon, Jacob losing two-thirds of the time despite Angel's constant restlessness. And Jacob had been in the chess club at school, whereas Angel wouldn't have been seen dead . . . Could still catch him out, how sad he was, how their history mattered more than their weirdly shared present.

'Mate in two,' said Fred. 'Here, Jake, right, Jake.' Suddenly, Fred looked excited. 'Can you bring your guitar over next time? Show me some stuff?'

'Yeah, sure.' Jacob found himself grinning. 'Tell you what, you don't moan about my smoking and I'll teach you guitar. Haven't played in months myself, as it happens.'

'Can we start tomorrow night?' Fred tapped the black king against the board.

'Got a gig. Saturday afternoon, when your mum's at work?'

'Wicked.' Fred banged the king hard on the carpet. 'Mum's still not back,' he said.

'No.' Almost eleven now, she had to be in a pub. 'Let's give it a bit longer.'

'You said that ages ago.' He got up, went to the kitchen, came back eating a slice of their leftover pizza. '*Please* ring her,' he said, with his mouth full. 'Couple of months ago, I nearly got blown up near her work.'

'You did?' Took every one of his years not to say, *Me too.* God, if the explosion had something to do with Angel, the potential wickedness was unbearable. No, how could the dead predict the movements of the living? That one had to be coincidence. Still.

Her mobile was turned off. Crap, she almost always kept it on. They'd have to try Maggie; Jacob prayed she didn't have a client with her. Maggie's phone rang and rang, not switching to a machine, not doing anything except squeezing its sound tight into Jacob's ear. Clearly wasn't rousing Maggie, anyway. Screw this, didn't anybody but him give a toss about the kid? Just assuming Jacob would cope; did they think he was some sort of *balnes*, capable of performing miracles, including knowing how to be the perfect guardian? Best he could manage was to agree to watch a video of *Buffy the Vampire Slayer*.

'Anyone want a coffee? Tea?'

'No, swimming, mate.'

'Another hot chocolate. Least that's sort of what it's meant to be.'

'Black coffee, thanks, sweetie.'

Jacob walked down the corridor to the machine, fished in his pocket for change. Maybe he'd pop out for a quick smoke first, but would that be dreadful? None of what the doctor had told them made sense, he wanted time on his own to absorb it. *A vicious attack.*

'Oh right, an attack can be gentle, then, is it?' Garry had said. *Several severe blows to the head and face.*

'Definitely wasn't an accident?' Jacob had heard himself ask. The others had looked at him as though he'd recited a nursery rhyme or something equally inappropriate. *Police want to question her, sir.* Though only Jacob thought to ask about brain damage. *The vital signs are good.* Odd expression, as though signs could gain an urgency, even an agency, that had nothing to do with the person. *Unconscious, but not in a coma.*

'Difference, is there?' Garry's wet-eyed sarcasm had made the doctor seem even younger as she clearly struggled to answer in ways each could understand; thankfully, *She's awake* had come soon after. Jacob slid the coins into the slot, pressed the buttons, committed himself meantime: couldn't go outside for a cigarette now, let other people's drinks get cold.

It was that potato sack over the head Jacob couldn't bear to think of; someone actually had been walking the streets, looking for someone else to blind before beating them. Made him feel what his mother called *queasy*. Bloody was going to have that cigarette. But then he thought of Lulu's pale face, her dishevelled appearance comparative to Bathsheba's immaculate unconcern, and decided finally against it. Lu felt guilty, he knew that, although what difference she thought it would have made had she been at home with Fred wasn't clear. For sure, Jacob was slightly hurt about her being with her *father* without telling him, and not for the first time, apparently, but that had nothing to do with Maggie being attacked.

Outside the visitors' room, a policeman and policewoman were having a muted conversation; must be the ones who wanted to talk to Maggie. Jacob nodded at them as he passed, feeling obscurely sheepish, the way he always did in close proximity to the police. God knows how Maggie would feel, confronted with them.

'She's definitely more awake.' Lulu forced herself to smile as she took her hot chocolate. 'Doctor just said she's speaking a bit and everything now.'

'That's great.' Jacob passed Bathsheba her coffee, sat down next to Lulu.

'We're allowed in two at a time, but I presume only for a couple of minutes.'

'Doubt she'll be terribly interested in seeing me, my love,' said Jacob.

'*I* want you there.' For the first time in days, she desperately did want Jake around. 'For some strange reason,' she added. Wasn't his fault about Mickey McGowan, she knew how it felt to get shot as the messenger.

'Garry and I ought to go first,' said Bathsheba. 'She's *his* mother.'

'Wouldn't let me mum hear you make that difference,' Garry said. Winking at Lulu, like Bathsheba had said something cute. 'But yeah, I better see her before the Old Bill do.'

Lulu stared into B's face. Might not be Garry's real sister, but she was Bathsheba's. The bloody witch did have a look of Mickey, something in the flat dark of her eyes, their cocky expression. Lulu turned away, gazed down at her plastic beaker. Jacob put his arm round her. Didn't watch as the nurse came to take Garry and Bathsheba through to the ward.

'You reckon it's too late to ring Fred?' Lulu asked, when the door had swung shut. 'Don't want Mrs Marshall getting the ump with me.'

'How could she mind? Don't be daft.' Jacob gave her a squeeze. He glanced at his watch. 'By the time we've seen Maggie, it'll be morning.'

'Suppose.' Fred had been well embarrassed at Lulu having to contact one of his mate's mums that time of night. But other than a couple of the girls from Heaven Scent, who he'd turned his nose up at, she'd had no choice. When had she stopped having friends? They sat in silence for a bit, Jacob stroking her shoulder. Then,

'Was Mickey McGowan nice to you?' he said. Out of nowhere.

'Fairly.' Lulu sipped her nasty chocolate. 'Not the warmest bloke, but *he* asked to see *me* tonight. Don't think he's sure precisely what to say to me, be truthful.' She put her beaker on the floor, took his hand. 'Christ knows why I didn't tell you before that I'd met him, love. Really sorry.' Bloody Mickey and Angel had made her behave badly towards her one chance. Like when she'd come back from that year at Dolly's, she'd been a total cow to Maggie for months. Jake kissed her finger-tips. 'Went to this place in Islington,' she told him. 'Had grilled skate, cost a bomb.' Sounded bloody pathetic.

'That's good, baby.' Pitying. Lulu wanted to explain to Jacob how she felt, but she hadn't got it sorted yet, not by a long way. Two meetings with a sweet-smelling stranger weren't enough. 'Does he know about Fred?' Jacob asked.

'Yeah. Reckon he's turned over by it, Jake.' Was the worst bit – being with Mickey had started to make her ashamed of Fred after all. Never wanted to be a single mum, but she'd always been proud of her boy, even when he was getting in the way. 'Didn't stop him banging on about how great Angel was, when he talked at all. Be fair, he's grieving.'

'Sure. You'll have to give him time, Fred might end up being his consolation.'

Garry banged through the swing doors then, Bathsheba behind him.

'We're off,' Garry said, grabbing his jacket from the back of a chair. 'You can get in there now.' His face hard, furious. Hadn't seen him like that in donkey's. Jesus, was Maggie that bad? Lulu jumped to her feet, bent to pick up her bag.

'She okay?' Lulu said to Garry's back, as he swung open the door right slap bang into the policewoman's shoulder and waltzed off without saying sorry.

'Maggie's fine,' said Bathsheba. Impatient. 'Gives a whole new meaning to being on the bash,' she added. Lulu wished Garry had smacked the door into that bitch instead.

They had to go down a short, surprisingly dark, corridor that smelt faintly of wee, before getting into the ward. The first bed, curtained off, was Maggie's. Jacob pushed the shiny material aside, let her through first.

Blood rushed from her head.

Never seen anyone look that terrible. Maggie's face just wasn't recognizable, swollen purple, her eyes black and slitty, her mouth split. Instead of hair, she had this white turban of Tubigrip. Even her neck looked different, raw and choked. Only holiday she'd been on with Dolly, to Dorset, Lulu had watched a chicken being killed and plucked – that's what Maggie looked like now. One skinny arm was wired to tubes or drips or something, her fingers twitching, compulsive, precisely the way the chicken's dead feet had. Pull yourself together, don't you dare cry, Maggie needs that like a . . . well, hole in the head. Lulu kissed her, just gentle.

'Fred okay?' Maggie asked. Or something like it.

'Yeah, he's all right. Be seriously relieved to know you are and all, though.' Lulu pulled up a chair, sat by the bed. Jacob didn't seem to be able to move, say anything, evidently much as he could do to look. 'What happened, Auntie?'

Maggie turned her head to one side, breathing noisily through her puffed-up mouth.

'Yeah,' Lulu said, as if she was replying, 'but what *precisely* happened?'

With an obvious effort, Maggie lifted the hand that wasn't wired up, made an angry, kind of dismissive gesture. And again, stronger. This time, was all too clear – *Leave it.*

'Oh, Mags.' Lulu took the hand. Shit, did Maggie actually *know* who'd done this? 'Maybe you'll remember more in time.' But Maggie gave a one-shouldered, resigned shrug.

'It *wasn't* a random attack? That what she means, Lu?' Jacob sat down then, on the chair next to Lulu's.

'No, course she doesn't.' Couldn't lay yet another thing on the poor bloke – he'd think he was in a mad house. This past week of keeping him at arm's length was a big mistake, could of pushed him right away for ever. But protecting him now was different, more like protecting them as a couple. Stop him running. Anyway, just because Lulu presumed Maggie had her suspicions, didn't mean they were the right ones.

A nurse came to tell them they should let their aunt rest for a few minutes before she saw the police. Jacob leaned over to kiss Maggie, just like he was one of the family. That's what mattered, someone caring about the people in your life, for your sake, not some bloke who took no responsibility for making families that bit too close. Lulu was choked.

'We'll be in later,' Jacob said. 'Sleep well, Magniu.'

Clifford switched on the light, the chandelier dwarfing the picture in size, but not in splendour, oh no. He settled into a kneeling position before it; Maggie wouldn't marry him now, but he'd always have this as solace. Nothing would keep her with him on a permanent basis: he'd made a fool of himself with that ham-fisted coercion, spoiled any matrimonial hopes he might have had. As a card up his sleeve it was perfect, but to blurt it out like that, to keep needling away at it . . . Sometimes, he wondered if he deserved her. As for that childish joke with the wig, he was thoroughly ashamed of himself. Maggie must have guessed he was responsible. The joke was on him, now.

Perhaps marriage wouldn't have been his cup of tea anyway; not easy to change your ways at sixty-five. Life had passed him by. As though he'd been given a fancy motor car at seventeen but never learned to drive, left it mouldering in the garage until he'd ceased to see why anyone kept a vehicle at all. Too late now. Not even any little spins around the block for him, not in this rotting carcass. Had things been different, he might have had a grandson by this time, some boy like young Fred. Handsome fellow, that.

He kissed the floor underneath the painting. It felt like kissing her feet. Put his hand on himself; if he could just achieve an erection, it would prove how he worshipped her. She was too good for the life she led, was right to want to leave it behind; his mistake had been in not attempting to procure her solely for himself earlier. But he had this, his shrine to her, until the diseases got him anyway and he made an exit from this world.

Burglars.

He froze, one hand still on Little Clifford, who inexplicably sprung to attention.

'You dirty fucking cunt.'

Garry could see exactly what that nonce was up to – wanking in front of a little bastard porno picture that, shit, looked a bit like Mum even from here. Sick. Was exactly like being a kid again, walking in on a punter. Exactly. How'd the tosser have the front, after what he done? Garry's blood was pumping round so hard, thought it'd burst out the top of his head. Clifford turned round then, keeping his hand on his dick, like he was shielding it.

'Garry? It *is* you, Garry, isn't it?'

'And you'd be the dirty fucking cunt. Know your name, then.'

'Clifford Black,' the prat said. 'Remember me? We met several times when you were a child.' Pulling his dressing gown closed at last, tying the cord. Garry fucking remembered him, all right.

What'd the bastard think, forgot your bloody life, is it? Forgot cunts what walked all over it? Name was one Garry'd hated since he was thirteen years of age. He eyeballed the perve. Like B reckoned, *had* to be this cunt after the wig bollocks, if Mum was right about that much. Had to be. Mum virtually said she'd tumbled that and all.

Clifford stuck out his hand, the one what'd been on his rank dick, as if he expected Garry'd take it. Like Garry wearing gloves'd make it all right.

'Fuck off, mate.' Voice none too clever.

'What do you want, Garry?' Clifford got to his feet. Not that it made much difference, with that stunted body.

'Someone said her name. Her fucking name, a second before.' Trying to control his breathing. 'Was you, weren't it? Got to be.' If it weren't, Garry was making a right idiot of hisself. But no, course it was.

'Has to be what? I simply asked her to marry me.' Sweat on his forehead.

'You'll be lucky, you perve.' Fucking marriage, is it? Give him marriage down his throat, Clifford weren't careful. 'I'll ask you this for once – what d'you do to me mum?'

'Do to her?' asked Clifford. 'Nothing. I'd never harm one hair of Maggie Dawson's head.'

'What about of her *wig*?' Get out of that one, then.

'Oh Lord.' Clifford rubbed his wet bonce. 'I . . . That would never have hurt her, I . . . took precautions. It was a stupid thing to do, I can't tell you how sorry I am. I've regretted it ever since. Believe me, I'm not the kind of man–'

'And the rest?' B and Mum was right. Knew it. Though hard to imagine this runt beating anybody. Yeah, maybe he hadn't done the damage hisself, most likely paid someone. A brief was going to have a lot of naughty contacts.

'I never meant . . . Garry, I assure you, I'd never have gone to the police, make no doubt.' Opening his hands. What the fuck was he on about, police?

'You're lucky she don't want to press charges, pal.'

'I realize that.' Least he was admitting it, finally. 'It wasn't . . . um, blackmail as such, though, not in the strictest sense.' Words all quavery, like they was coming out a much older bloke. 'A man like yourself should see that. But I can't tell you how ashamed—'

'She's told me what you been up to.' So Clifford'd been blackmailing her and all – why hadn't Mum said about that? Too bastard fucked up from the beating. Even the words she'd got out had been a job. 'What about that dead kitten went to me sister's place?' Fifteen year ago, could of been Garry opening that, seeing what Fred'd see. Garry felt in his jacket for the shooter. Cunt deserved the fright of his life. 'Fred's just a fucking *kid*. I should of come round here then.'

'I assure you, Garry, that had nothing to do with me.' He was shaking well bad now. Wanker. 'I thought it was *disgraceful*.'

'Oh, right. So the wig was you, and you blackmailed her, but you don't know nothing about the kitten or the GBH. Yeah, well likely.'

'GBH?' Clifford shook his head. 'What . . . Has something happened to Maggie?'

'Like you don't know.' Shifting his weight to the other leg.

'I *said*, has something happened to her?' Face'd gone right stiff, as if Clifford weren't scared all of a sudden. Jesus H Christ, bloke was only getting stroppy with him.

'She's in the London, mate.' Watching a pretty clever impersonation of shock come over the toe-rag. 'Beat to frigging Kingdom Come, case you never noticed.'

'Beaten? *No*.' Clifford walked right past Garry, sat down on one of the two tatty leather armchairs. For an ex-brief, his flat weren't all that, didn't look like he'd have the money to pay an hitter. Unless he was into someone for the dosh. Probably spent most of his wedge on prozzies. Though that chandelier must of cost a few bob, couldn't be that skint. Funny smell in here, like someone'd peeled a couple of pound of oranges and left the skins lying about. 'Is she all right?' Clifford asked. Speaking true, Garry felt wrong-footed. Geezer was behaving like he genuinely didn't know nothing about it.

'No thanks to you.' But what if Mum'd been wrong? Did say she weren't 100 per cent certain. Though *someone*'d got her looking like a bowl of rotten fruit. Someone what'd said her name, what labelled the fucking attack – pro job or not, weren't just a chancer, even though her bag was nicked. And B said firm the wig must of been a rehearsal, definite, she reckoned the kitten looked like one and all. And Clifford'd admitted blackmail. And this was one of the cunts what'd ruined all their lives. And was a sick bastard.

'I do appreciate you coming here to tell me,' Clifford said. He round the twist?

'Come here to show you this.' Garry pulled out the shooter, what slipped a bit against the leather of his gloves till he got a proper grip, shoved it up to the bloke's face for a split second. 'Think of it as a warning. Don't do second chances.'

'You really think it was me?' His eyes full of tears. 'It wasn't.'

'Then who was it?' Bouncing on the balls of his feet.

'Let the police find him. And they'll get every co-operation from me, I–'

'Less of the earache, right?' Feeling some of his anger run off out of here, leaving Garry behind. Weren't that he never cared about Mum, but she didn't half bring shit on herself, living like a dirty tart. On all of them. If Clifford Black *hadn't* jumped her or paid someone to, she'd dropped Garry right in it. Not like Bathsheba would of put in her two pennies' worth, if Maggie hadn't reckoned the wig was down to this bastard. Since Garry was a fucking kid, he'd kept tangled in Mum's grubby working life. Sick of it. Bone sick.

'But . . . ' Clifford's eyes was all panicky. 'Please, listen to me. Listen. I think I've got something you might be interested in. It'll prove we're on the same team.'

'Oh, we are, are we? Never in a million.'

'I put bread on your table.' Tapping his fingers together.

Garry's anger rushed back through the room, jumped into his brain.

'You what?' he said. Soft as soft.

'I . . . I . . . just meant, I'm on your side.' Clifford's terror had legged it back in after Garry's fury, for definite. 'Please, don't hurt me.'

'Me *mum* put bread on our table, pal. You could of been any fucker.'

'Please, just listen.' His eyes wet.

'Why the fuck should I?' Sooner of fucking starved. Breathing too hard again. Best buy hisself a space. 'You got thirty seconds. Shoot,' Garry said, sitting in the other chair, waving the gun. *Same* fucking *team*. Though might as well hear this out while Garry sorted his breathing, had a think.

'I met your girlfriend the other day,' Clifford told him. 'Well, there's hardly likely to be two Bathsheba McGowans, is there?' he went on, in that high, nervy voice. 'She was very cosy with a man called Stephen Hopkins. He's quite big in ISU. Its . . . less savoury side, shall we say.'

'So?' Yeah, B told Mum tonight that Clifford'd turned up and been fucking rude when she was trying to have a business meeting. *Not that I made the connection then.*

'Maybe I'm not telling you anything you don't know. Okey dokey.' He cleared his throat, tapped his hand against his leg. 'What you might *not* know is that Mr Hopkins is HIV positive. The strong rumour in the legal world is Angel McGowan had been infected himself for several years, and gave the virus to Mr Hopkins. Along with information about the best way to purchase properties of a certain nature, if you take my point.'

'You saying Angel was batting for the other side?' Sweet. Bathsheba'd want this.

'Angel McGowan held ten per cent of his family firm's shares.' Clifford smiled, sort of demented turtle. 'He sold them to Mr Hopkins. Who's recently been in touch with me.'

'*What?*' Had to be a wind-up. B would of said about it. 'So where's the dosh? Ange died whatsname. Aw, what is it again? Struth. Intestate.'

'Are you quite sure about that? Is Bathsheba sure? Because

I assure you, she shouldn't be. And need I remind you that in order to transfer his shares, Angel McGowan needed another director to countersign. Strikes me, if his sister's taken up the mantle . . . '

Bloke. Was Dissing. His Bathsheba. Bad. After hanging round home like a pedestrian kerb crawler for fucking ever, he has the front, the *front*, to start on B. Words cracking open Garry's skull, bits flying round the rotting smelling room.

'Shut the fuck up.' Garry rises to his feet, slow, goes over to Clifford, pins him to the chair by his throat. Presses the gun into Clifford's temple with his free hand. 'That's the last word you say about her, to anyone. Got it?' Thought of even her name in this evil old perve's mouth makes him want to spew. 'Fucking more blackmail, is it? Bet you was the school grass, bet your sweet life. You're not on, pal, won't get a touch out of me.'

'Ssss . . . ' Bloke never has enough air even to say sorry. Good job. Garry squeezes that bit harder. Trouble is, he squeezes the trigger, same time.

Bathsheba thought she ought to run Garry a bath and get him to bed, even though it was twenty past nine in the morning. Face it, state he was in, a day off was so a risk worth taking. He might be able to get in this afternoon (with masses of TLC) but if not, they could explain it away through Maggie being in the hospital and them having been up all night.

'Let's get you out of those bloody clothes, sugar plum.' Turning on the taps.

'Me shoulder's killing me.' Garry was having trouble taking off his shirt.

'It's the impact,' Bathsheba told him. Keeping her voice neutral. 'It travels up your arm, darling. You'll feel better after a nice soaklette.'

'Can't stop fucking shaking.' Trying to unbutton his jeans. 'Bang in trouble here.'

'Ssh. Let me help you. That's it.' As Bathsheba undressed

166

him, she could smell the blood, butchery, like Smithfield's (Daddy so loved it there). How bizarre, it was actually making her feel ravenous, though she hadn't eaten red meat in over ten years. Once Garry was in the bath, perhaps she'd do herself a couple of crackers with jam. 'We'll have to burn these clothes,' she said. 'And decide what to do about the gun.'

She'd known he'd make her proud one day. They weren't lookers-on in life any more, they were the people who made things happen. He'd do anything for her now.

That creep deserved all he'd got, after those insinuations he'd made in the Pussy Parlour. Even though Garry claimed the shooting was an accident, he'd had the guts to wash (as much as he could), to wear the man's overcoat, to drive home without cracking. And bringing that painting with him was fabulous – looked valuable, but even if it wasn't, a thief wouldn't necessarily have known that. Still, they'd have to get rid of it sharpish. Wonder if Jacob liked erotic art?

'What the fuck's funny?'

'Nothing.' Bathsheba checked the temperature of the water.

'What if Mum changes her mind, fingers him? Old Bill be straight round there.'

'She won't, she wasn't sure enough.'

'Literally blew his fucking brains out, babe,' Garry said.

'I know. Have your bath now, sweetie.'

'Thing is, B . . . ' Garry winced as he climbed into the water. 'I ain't sure enough, neither. Like, when I said about the kitten, he was sick about it. Really reckon he was and all.' He looked up at her. The water was turning a pretty shade of pink. 'Though I said to you about the blackmail, didn't I? And you was right, he admitted that wig shit, so—'

'The cat wasn't Black.' Her heart was thumping loudly, but it was now or never. In a state of shock another one might get absorbed into the first.

'What . . . Who gives a fuck what colour it was?'

'No, *Clifford* Black. The cat wasn't him.' Bathsheba smiled, touched his shoulder. 'It *so* doesn't matter about his guilt, sweets, he wasn't worth saving. He made your childhood hell, him and people like him.' No one ought to be allowed to get away with that.

'Yeah, make you right there. But how'd you know he never—'

'Well, it was for practice. Silly, really.' Sitting on the edge of the bath. If he loved her, he'd take her side. Absolute loyalty. 'Not practice for the beating,' she added. 'I had nothing to do with that.' Though hard to believe it had just been her good fortune. Kismet. 'Truly did think that *was* Black. Probably was.'

'You?' His expression (to put it mildly) disbelieving. 'What, you seriously telling me you killed the thing and put it—'

'Not me exactly.' Wetting her fingers in the pink bath water, she stroked his fuzzy head. 'Well, I did kill it and wrap it. But then Big Phil, who used to be on the door—'

'Know who he is, B. *Why?* Shit, that's horrible, girl. You got to know that.'

'It needed to be.' Had to make him see with her vision how their human future was more important than an animal's life. If a veggie could understand that, he should too.

'Jesus fucking Christ.' Garry pulled away from her hand. 'Fred's me nephew. Yourn and all, come to think. Stroll on. *Shit.*' Eyes horrified. Damn him. What was a poxy kitten compared with shooting a man? 'What am I meant . . . ?' He shook his head. 'Just don't get it, darling. *You?* No, you said to Mum it was most probably him.'

'What I *said* was it could look the same as the wig thing.' Touching him again. 'You gave me the idea in the first place, actually, telling me about Maggie's fire.'

'Fucking marvellous. I'm an hero.' But he hadn't moved away from her this time. Please, please, don't let her have been wrong about him, she couldn't bear that. 'You know your mate Hopkins's got Angel's shares?' he said.

'Well, yeah, I do.' She rubbed his earlobe. Him changing the subject had to be positive, didn't it? 'Though God knows what's happened to the money. The boys haven't a clue there was even a sale, okay? You know I don't feed you absolutely every detail, for your own sake. It's you who has to see them every day.'

'You countersigned for him.'

'Mm, absolutely weeks before he eventually got rid of them.' Damn. She'd known Black's jibe, about her name being *written down* next to Angel's, must have meant he'd seen her signature on the transfer. After all, he'd worked for ISU's solicitors. Well, this would teach him to keep his bloody nose out. Wished though she'd told Garry to find out if Black knew where the will was, she'd missed a trick there. 'But—'

'Anything else to fucking lay on me? Any babies you slung in the river?' His teeth literally chattering. 'You knew about Angel's shares,' he said. 'Slaughtering a cat and fucking lying about it fits in there, is it?'

'Sort of.' Why couldn't he accept she *always* gave him as much as he needed to know? 'But I didn't *lie* to you. Look, there's a long history with Daddy and Maggie,' she said. 'He's got a cat tattoo on his bum that had something to do with her, according to Angel.' Bathsheba sighed. This so was tedious. 'Thought because of a couple of messages I sent across, supposedly from Daddy to her, she might believe it was him. Maybe she'd confront him, send him closer to la-la land.' Mm, especially given the implication it was Maggie told Angel who Lulu's father was. That woman being in Daddy's face again might be too much for him after that. 'It was a punt, sweetheart. An extra.'

'That's all right then, is it?' Barely above a whisper. 'Fred's *twelve*. Poor bastard.'

'Even if Maggie didn't think it was Daddy . . . ' *Just tell him you've finally lost it, B.* 'Needed to be sure I was capable,' she tried again. 'Probably sounds tragic, but I had Angel in my head telling me I wasn't tough enough. Always.' Moving her hand to the back of his neck. 'I have to send my own father loopy, sweetie. If I couldn't kill a pussycat and frighten a kid, then I'd never manage. With Daddy out of the equation—'

'You can handle the boys. I know. You said.'

'I so can.' Shock must be wearing off. 'My shares are more significant if they sell—'

'But you had nothing to do with last night?'

'No.' Bathsheba watched him watching her. 'Though if I had, would it make any difference to how you feel about me?' she asked.

Garry's pale eyes seemed to grow paler then (though that must be an illusion), his shaking getting even worse.

'She's me mum, for fuck's sake,' he said. Making Bathsheba's heart fall to her stomach. 'It bother you, killing that thing?'

'No.' Not like she'd spun it out, it had been quick, clean. Merciful. 'And Fred's fine, knew he would be.'

'Yeah, well, I fucking did a man in, darling. Physically. Me there, him there, bosh.' Pressing his hands together. 'You never seen nothing like it, bits of brain . . . fuck, so much blood.' Gagging. 'Was the worst thing ever happened to me, and if you was responsible . . . ' Rubbing his eyes. Bathsheba held her breath (*please*, don't let him reject her). 'But . . . Yeah, I'd feel different. Shit scared, most probably.'

Silence seemed to go on for minutes. Bathsheba mustn't be the one to break it.

'Come on, B, how'd I know you're not fibbing again?' As though he hadn't noticed the long gap. 'Don't, do I, except in me heart. But, shit,' he said. '*Nothing* could ever make me not love you. Aw, *m*ate, I hate this. But . . . not, not the kitten, not what I done, not even seeing me mum lying there, and I fucking hated that and all, promise you. Nothing.'

'I love you, too.' Bathsheba felt like screaming with the relief.

'Yeah, but what's that make me, *pussy*-whipped?' Tears in his words, now. He put his arms around her waist. His wetness seeped through her nightshirt 'You don't see life the way most people do, mate,' he said. 'Used to think I was like that, but I ain't. You're the real thing, and it's bastard terrifying.' *You do know he's saying you're not right in the head?* 'Can't live without you, though,' Garry added. Shouting Angel down. Protecting her mind. 'Wouldn't want to. Used to reckon I felt

. . . less than other people, you know? No bastard got to me, till you. Shit, you might be me own goldfish—'

'But no one can say I can't half swim.' She burst out laughing. If she hadn't won, then Bathsheba was a cripple. Even though *he* was sobbing, it was because he loved her. Adored her, for ever and ever Amen. Thank God, thank God. Now all she'd to do was concentrate even harder on making sure her family fell apart. Keep an eye on Hopkins. And to discover what Jacob had done with the money, of course. But first things first – she'd make love to her darling. That was what they both needed most.

Probably a dreadful thing for Jacob to have done, going to his gig, telling them at the bookshop that he'd be in tomorrow morning for sure, but he couldn't handle spending every minute at the hospital. Maggie would be home in a day or two, anyway; now he'd apparently become part of the family, Jacob needed space, distance, a semblance of his own life. At least he was getting that at some cost to himself: coming all the way here from bloody Camden in a cab after playing, planning his rush-hour journey back to Hampstead tomorrow meantime, those weren't the acts of a straightforwardly selfish man. But.

Lu was asleep at last. For the past hour, he knew she'd been pretending, breathing the way people thought they did when sleeping, which was far more regular than any dream would allow. Jacob moved further away, eased himself upright, careful not to disturb her. God, she'd been hurt. Last thing he wanted. *Not a sadist, then, boy? Give it time.* No, wasn't a possibility. He wanted to protect her, to keep her safe from all the crap in her world. Shit, Maggie could have been killed, Angel *was* dead, Lu was trying to cope with her son being her nephew; Jacob didn't want to be the cause of more pain. Screw this, he couldn't just sit here, watching her sleep. He slipped out of Lulu's bed, pulled on his boxers, made his way into the lounge. Switched on the lamp, poured the last of that rough Shiraz into a glass, lit a cigarette. Her glass not his; you could see faint traces of lipstick on the rim.

Wouldn't have been so bad if he'd simply not wanted her: no one was in the mood for sex all the time, and last night they'd had no sleep, and he'd been at the club until twelve tonight. He was knackered. That, they could have coped with. But of course, when he'd tried to offer those excuses, she'd heard he was lying. Not that she'd said as much, but this, he could see. God, even yesterday, had she taken her hand, placed it on her cunt with her typical generosity of spirit, his response would have been instant. Well, it had been tonight, but his instinct then was to snatch it away. Why the hell had she persisted? Taken his hand again, sucked his fingers, put them back on her? He'd tried; not touching her after that would have caused too much of a problem. But he could hardly move his fingers, as if they were filled with helium, he'd to fight to keep them on her. Then, shit, replaying it now was almost worse than the moment itself, he'd half-fallen asleep, his fingers still. But he'd been awake enough to be desperate for the point he could roll over, belong to himself again. And that woman knew about sex, which was why she'd understood his feeling as revulsion.

His sexy, sharp Lulu. Remembered two weeks ago at the club, the crowded night when that female vet shared their table and told them she'd been on work experience abroad, tossing off boars. *Girl*, Lulu had said, *we've all done that*. Confident. Making him want to take her home that instant and fuck her. But now. Perhaps seeing Maggie so badly beaten had affected him. Or maybe Lulu's own reality had been shown to him in that hospital bed. Wasn't as though Jacob had stopped thinking Lulu was gorgeous, had stopped liking her, feeling grateful to know her. If he was honest with himself, wasn't even that he'd been turned off, for whatever reason. The thing Jacob was having trouble getting hold of was he'd suddenly needed more. He'd needed that video. *Want to fuck her in front of me fucking her, do you, Mitz?* God, yeah, that's exactly what he wanted.

For those few minutes, he couldn't have stood to touch her without that video playing. Nothing would have stopped him, had he had the opportunity, not Fred asleep in the next room, not Lulu's feelings, nothing.

Even the thought of it now, amongst all this guilt, was giving him a raging hard-on. Had he been in his own flat, with access, the temptation would have been too much.

Getting light out. A few raggedly bird calls, sounding as though they were imitating mobile phones, crept in through the open window. How the bloody hell was he supposed to get to work after this? And meantime, he'd sit here, probably smoking cigarette after cigarette until the packet was gone, trying with everything he had left not to masturbate. That, he felt would be too big a betrayal right now.

Part III

The Money Shot

Then, Isabel, live chaste, and brother, die.
More than our brother is our chastity.
I'll tell him yet of Angelo's request
And fit his mind to death, for his soul's rest.

Measure for Measure

Chapter Nine

'How come you both knew?' Lu was running her finger over the sticky table.

'How d'you think?' This was all he needed. 'Angel told B.'

'When?' Pulling in her chair to let some bird get past. Couldn't she sit still?

'Eight, nine month back?' Picking at his cold sore. 'Angel took her that River Café, told her loads of shit, out the blue.' Doing his nut in, this place. Probably tourists'd feel stitched up if the pub was halfway decent. Wouldn't surprise Garry if there was a warehouse somewhere flogging splintery bars, fucked carpet. Minting it. Loads of nice pubs in Soho, why'd she have to pick here? 'Stop bastard fidgeting, driving me mental,' he said.

'And how did Angel know?'

'Mum.' Like being in an interview room.

'That why he left me, because Maggie told him?' Lulu had a big mouthful of her G and T. 'Well?'

'Aw, *ma*te, *I* don't know.' Right this minute, Garry couldn't of give a toss if her dad was Archbishop of Canterbury and Angel had run off with a nun. What was Mum going to say, when it come out Clifford Black'd had it? Seven whole days with nothing happening. Course, B's advice was act ignorant, but he hadn't got away with that since he was five. 'To speak true,' he said, 'B reckoned Angel didn't seem bothered you was related. Know what he was like. Nut-nut. Sick cunt.' Gulp of his wine. 'So no, weren't to do with Mum.' Couldn't get used to being in a pub without a pint. Not like Bathsheba's health kick was doing him much good, knew he weren't looking none too clever, all flaky skin, dark shadows. As if he was the dead one. 'You see Mickey McGowan then, is it?' he asked.

'Mind your own.'

'Suit yourself.' Head felt like Keith Moon was bashing away in there.

'Made a real effort to look nice for him,' she blurted out, all upset. Tell her, nothing seemed important after you'd been covered in some cunt's brains. Fuck, the power of it, like you was being shot back, and the stink. Enough to turn anyone's stomach, no wonder Garry couldn't hardly keep any bastard thing down. Like B said, had to be thankful Black was such a waster, else they might start to feel bad. 'I hated it, mate,' Lu nagged on. Twisting her hair back into one of them ponytail things. 'He took me out to dinner the second time, and I showed him pictures of Fred, but . . . Was like he'd forgot to put on the inside of him.' She fucking know about people's insides, is it? If she'd see what Garry had, she'd be freaking well out. 'Get what I'm saying?' she added. Couldn't give a shit, speaking true. 'He wasn't . . . *there*, Garry. You reckon it was the shock? Not that he's horrible as such, but . . . he smells funny. Like Parma violets. Them little purple sweets, you know?'

'What you on about?' Maybe if Mum had a pop, he should just say, straight, it weren't him done Clifford. Hoped he wouldn't have to say even that much to the Old Bill. None of their friendlies was Murder Squad, all Vice, that was the bastard.

'Why'd Bathsheba tell Jacob?' Pulling her thumb back to touch her wrist.

'She thought it'd be better coming from him.' Garry scratched at the sore patch on his cheek. B told Jacob same night as the kitten was. Same night.

'Well, precisely. Course, she's always got my best interests at heart.' Lulu looked at her watch. 'Got to get back in ten minutes. Won't get any lunch, now.'

'Why you got such a down on her?' Garry asked. B was the one thing holding him together, the one person who could explain him why his shit feelings was wrong. She hadn't lied, it was he hadn't understood properly. Weren't unusual, though she'd never say *that* to him. She'd never hurt his feelings. 'B's not done nothing to you.'

'No.' Lu turned up her palms. 'Just kept who my father was to her bloody self.'

'I did that and all,' he pointed out. Lighting his cigar.

'If she told you to wear a tutu and stilettos in the middle of Peter Street, you'd do it.'

'Piss off.' Getting *right* on his wick now. Weren't no one's slave.

'There's too many secrets in this family,' she said. 'Maggie was petrified after that wig stunt. Seen her gun, have you? And I really do reckon she knows who attacked her.'

'She says no, mate.' Had to be Black, fucking had to be.

'Jesus, you forgot what it was like, growing up around all them lies?'

'No, I ain't. Struth, you reckon it was better, once it come out?' Tell her one thing for nothing, some shit you didn't need in your mind.

'Oh, I don't know.' She crunched an ice cube. Went right through his bloody bonce. 'For me, it made sense of loads of stuff. Like . . . why I felt different from my mates.'

'Still wish sometimes I never knew.' He closed his eyes. Bad move. 'Fuck,' he said, opening them again. 'When I first met B, took me ages to say about Mum. Had to make *me* look a cunt, you know? Course, turned out she'd heard already.'

'Bathsheba's a user, far as I'm concerned,' said Lulu. 'Doesn't even care what happened to Maggie, not really. She been round there since Mags has been home? No.'

'Steady, mate.' Holding up a warning hand.

'Well, she bloody hasn't, thinks she's the business just for ringing up. A million pound says she had her own sly little reasons for letting Jake tell me. Poor sod–'

'*Poor sod*, is it? You're having a laugh.' Garry balanced his cigar in the ashtray. 'Too many secrets? Yeah, make you right,

Lu.' If he didn't end this, he'd go off his fucking head. Fuck her. Stupid cunt. Wrapped up in her fucking self. Well, he'd tumbled her. 'Far too fucking many,' he went on. 'Put a stop to that, shall we? What you reckon?'

'Come on, settle down.' Patting his hand, condescending bitch. 'I've got to get back to work. So should you.'

'Ain't Fred, darling, can't talk to me like that.' Garry downed the rest of his wine. 'Your *poor sod*'s got a secret of his own.' He turned to the geezer at the next table, who looked away, quick, at the wall. Most likely hadn't expected the warehouse to deliver agg and all. 'Here, mate, let me introduce you. *This* is Lucinda Luscious.' Moving his body round slow to face her again, checking in with her eyes that she got it. Oh yeah, without a shadow. 'The old ones are the best,' he said. She was shaking her head, even though he nodded his. 'Never knew he knew, did you? Thought not.' But she just kept on with the head shaking. 'Be fair to the poor sod, can't say you never done it, can you?'

'Bastards.'

Did you do it, Mitzvah? This time, it really was a letter from a dead man; the first one, although it had arrived six weeks after the death, had also been its announcement, as if Angel had been telling Jacob personally about the overdose. But now, holding the paper that was covered with too-familiar hand-writing, Jacob was stunned. Angel must be some kind of *dybbuk*, compelled for past sins to wander the world looking for a body to enter, one where the demons couldn't get in. Tough shit: plenty of demons clawing their way into Jacob's head these days. And those sins didn't straightforwardly seem to be in the past, either.

Jacob put out his cigarette and laid the letter carefully on the coffee table, separating the pages, smoothing the paper as though he were about to iron it, blowing off a fleck of ash. Would it have killed Angel to have begun, *Dear Jacob*? Well, clearly not, but the abruptness of the opening seemed bloody harsh, given what a shock the rest was bound to be. Probably the point. *You think you've lived your whole life dealing with moral dilemmas. Bollocks. Here's a real one for you.* Three hundred grand. A fortune. Made out to Jacob Samuel Fox.

The brandy was almost gone; Jacob poured the last of it into his glass. He must have done half a bottle, but his brain was so fucked with the dreadful burden Angel had forced on him, the booze didn't seem to be adding anything. Just as well, he had to play in a couple of hours. For ninety bloody quid. He'd only taken the gig because seeing Lulu was proving so much more expensive than sitting on his own listening to CDs; ages since he'd had to be this unfussy about work. All day yesterday in some dire recording studio in Essex for a couple of hundred, straight on to the club last night, shop today, crap depping tonight, Fred's guitar lesson tomorrow while Lulu went over to Maggie's . . . Jacob might as well be married to Lu. And in the middle of all that, Angel's legacy. This, he could live without.

It was hard to follow. Angel's name wasn't on Fred's birth certificate, otherwise had Angel died intestate, Fred would have inherited; that part was easy enough. Angel wanted Lulu to have the money, to support Fred. Sure, made sense. And seemed sensible to make Jacob some kind of executor. But the cheque wasn't even signed by Angel: who the hell was Ian Silverman? Maybe the thing wasn't kosher, was some elaborate joke to get Jacob in schtuck. A backdated cheque signed by some mysterious bloke, a secret will . . . Had Angel written his own bloody Victorian melodrama? *You see, Jakey, I've had to make provision in case you didn't do what I asked; the cheque will lead you to her, if my first letter didn't. Bet it did, though. Remember, I know you, better than anyone has ever known you.* Maybe, but what if Jacob simply pissed off with the money? Had to be a possibility. He checked the copy of the will yet again. Yeah, it definitely said only that Angel would *prefer* it if the cheque were invested for Lulu as Fred's guardian, not that Jacob *had* to do that. It was his own, made over *to*

181

Jacob and *by* someone else before the death, rather than willed to him. Meantime, Angel was obviously gambling on Jacob having a relationship with Fred by now, but why chance it, why not straightforwardly leave his estate to Lulu or Fred? And wouldn't there be inheritance tax? Or maybe this was a way to avoid that. *One, two, three four five, Once I caught a fish alive.* The single time Jacob had taken him fishing, Angel repeated that stupid rhyme all night, making the same joke about lines every time he snorted one; small wonder neither of them had caught a sodding thing.

Shit, couldn't sit here all evening trying to make sense of stuff; he had work to do. Responsibilities. Putting the letter back together, he caught odd phrases, *Assume you took my message to Garry Dawson . . . Lulu still a looker, is she? . . . Fred worth anything?* as though Jacob were creating a differently ordered narrative, one that might make the truth more available. *Why not go the whole hog, read it right to left? Fucking hell, it's not your bloody bar mitzvah, Mitzvah.* But that's exactly how it felt: a rite of passage, composed largely of incomprehensible words.

Chilly tonight, better put his thick jacket on. Screw this, all the way over to the Holloway Road, two Tube changes and then a longish walk in a dodgy area with what had happened to Maggie following him round. Later, the rush to get back, praying that he'd catch the last Tube, that he wouldn't have to mess around with night buses full of slaughtered teenagers. And in between, a greasy-aired club, where the rest of the band would be off key and their heads. *Always say you should leave no turn unstoned. Cool.* Great, now Angel lived only in Jacob's head, there was no chance of either of them growing up.

But three hundred grand was a grown up amount of money, for sure.

She'd wanted to be a beautician when she grew up. Actually, what she'd really of liked was to be famous, though that was impossible. People did say she had a nice singing voice, bit like Debbie Harry, but course that wasn't going to come to anything. When she was about sixteen, she'd considered sending her picture in to a Page Three competition – her tits were definitely her best features – except Auntie Maggie would of gone mad. Mags didn't even reckon you should go topless on the beach. *It's not natural.* Job in Selfridges wasn't bad though, least it was on the perfume counter and a hell of a lot better than her mates were doing with their YTS rubbish. Lulu had always spoke quite nice, which helped at the interview, and she'd got the five CSEs at grade one, so she'd been lucky. *Proud of you.* Lulu had loved hearing Auntie Maggie say that. Even Garry managed a, *Done all right there, mate*, and bought her a cider and black. He was killing time in a warehouse then, *Just till something better turns up*, but to be fair, he'd never had one day's unemployment since leaving school the year before, totally the opposite to the rest of his crowd. If Mags knew there were odd bits of hooky gear *turning up* at the flat, she never said.

Had been at Selfridges nearly two years when Douggie did it. Sent their private pics to the Readers' Girlfriends section of *Barely 18*. Just soft stuff, boobs and bum, but. First she knew about it was when some bloke contacted her to arrange a proper newcomer photo-shoot. She should of been angry, only Douggie was so pleased she didn't have the heart. Though course, once he'd seen the pictures, he'd packed her in. And that's when the photographer had told her he could make her a star. That'd show her bastard ex.

What a silly, silly tart she'd been.

First off, it was just a few more pics. Non-commissioned, flat fee. Lulu'd tried to tell herself it wasn't any different from Page Three, but it bloody well was. Baby faces, big tits and bald money shots, for the British and Japanese markets. *Well, they don't want to look at someone of thirty, do they?* Men were peculiar – even at the time, Lulu'd thought no girl would pay to see a bloke in a school cap and shorts. Must of got something to do with power. Looking back, was hard to think precisely why she'd gone along with it. Not fear, the photographer was a sleaze but he was no hard case. Besides, thought of Maggie finding out was way more scary than any bloke. Not being skint, she was earning and didn't have a habit or kids to support, like some of the girls she met on shoots. Not even, after a few times, the hope of getting famous, she soon wised up to that one. Turned out she didn't appreciate showing off her body, either, made her feel she was covered in slime. Had never much liked being touched by anyone else in her private parts, and the first time she'd ever seen her you-know-what was in the newcomer spread. Looked like chopped liver.

But deep as she'd hated it, it had felt . . . more like her than the perfume counter did, for some strange reason. More as if she was in the place she was meant to be. Didn't have to pretend, to try and fit in, for once. She fitted perfectly, made to bloody measure. That's what Angel had spotted in her and all, soon as she met him. *You be Eve, I'll be God.*

Bastard, hypocrite, bastard, shit-head, bastard. Why couldn't Jacob of been different? Jesus, what if he was another of them who thought, *Got to be young to be sexy.* Bet they'd been having a good old laugh at her . . . or would of done, if Angel hadn't been dead. Most likely Jacob wished she still shaved herself nearly bare down there, was turned on by her past self, not by her now. Was like she'd slept with Jacob before she'd known she had, was like, like *rape* almost. Bloody Christ, thought with Jacob she'd finally come home. Still a silly tart. Just grateful she'd never told him she loved him . . . Maggie was right, love was a made-up feeling, based on what men wanted you to be. Well, he could stick it. No way was Lulu going to stay with a man who was only after one thing – Lucinda Luscious.

Mobile was silent. Like it was dead. Proper phone rung several times a day, Lu and Fred and Garry and even Bathsheba, for a wonder, checking she was still breathing. Never the mobile, though, as if it'd been pinched with her bag. Maggie hadn't realized how quiet her life'd seem without it. How all the not ringing got louder in your head, till you thought you'd go round the bend. And the new locks on her door just kept her inside the silence. Not that she could of got out anyway, with her still looking like she'd give Muhammad Ali the ump. Course, Lulu popped round of an evening, and that Jacob a couple of times, but Fred'd only come the once, for five seconds flat. Hated the look of her beaten, if she weren't much mistaken – though seemed queer, going from trying to get him out of here, to trying to get him in. Mind, he did have school again now, and with him not around, was easier to keep the gun in the living room. Bleeding daytime telly. News many times as Maggie wanted . . . what was a lot less often than she used to want, be honest. Cooking programmes, when she'd be hard pushed to eat beans on toast, leave alone salmon mousse with chocolate sauce and ants eggs or what-have-you.

So much for little marriages. They belonged to the men and all, in the finish. Minute blokes wasn't getting something off you, they didn't want to know. Even Socks-on Sam, even Adrian, and they'd been coming round, what, nineteen, twenty year? Suddenly got too far for their poor old legs? Though mustn't start confusing the professional with the personal – that way bleeding madness lies. But what she really couldn't make out was why Clifford of all people'd give up. Even if it had been him what done this to her, you'd of thought he'd of covered his back by behaving normal. For the first time he evidently didn't *want* to see her. Guilt, maybe. Assuming he even knew what'd happened, that was.

She sipped her lemonade, turned over to ITV. *Maggie.* No, that wasn't on the telly, it was in her head. Again. A low whisper before the world went dark. Truthfully, could of been anyone. Anyone male and not young. Just wished she never kept hearing it, through the silence of the not ringing. Dying for a ciggie, but four days in the hospital and four indoors without one, didn't want to go back on them, not if she could be off of it. Fred'd be pleased, she kept it up. Bugger, she shouldn't of talked to Garry and Bathsheba about her suspicions, but she hadn't been exactly with it. Garry might well of warned Clifford off – that was most probably why she'd not heard, come to think. Loyalty'd always been Garry's strongest and weakest point.

Maggie touched the bandage round her head, tugging at the front to straighten it. Pressed the remote, back to B1. *Tony Blair has today made a statement in the* . . . She'd took to doing that, changing channels for no reason like the boys done. Like she could switch over from fear to some other feeling. Weren't only being frightened of it happening again, she was petrified of the nightmares, way she'd wake up not knowing if this was home or hospital or hell. Was like losing yourself. Even the thought of it brung on them pains in her chest. *Anxiety attacks*, the doctor'd said. Give that man a coconut.

The body has been discovered of a sixty-five-year-old man in a flat in Bromley. He has been identified as Clifford Black, a former solicitor with a large City firm. Mr Black had been shot through the head, his estimated time of death more than a week ago. There were signs of a forced entry, but none of a struggle. Police are appealing for witnesses . . .

'Had the Old Bill on me mobile.' Maggie sipped her tea and, over the rim of the cup, eyed Garry and that Bathsheba, who was sat too close together on the settee. The skinny twins. 'They're coming round first thing tomorrow.'

'Why?' Garry pulled at the scab of his cold sore. Bit of blood appeared on his lip.

'Why d'you think? Clifford had me number programmed in his. About the only one he did have in there what wasn't work.'

'Well, you can *so* not be a suspect,' said Bathsheba. 'Look at you.'

'Course *I* can't, no. Even they know that.' Maggie straightened her bandage and reached for her cigs. 'Funny though, ain't it? Could of been the butcher, the baker, the candlestick

186

maker what died, even one of me other gentlemen, but it weren't. Was Clifford.'

'Yeah,' said Garry.

'Yeah. And he could of fell down the stairs, had heart attack . . . but he never. He stopped a bullet. What d'you think about that, son?' Hated doing this to him, but had to make sure he weren't going to fall apart. Only a couple of month ago he'd been verging on the plump, now he looked like a famine victim.

'I was at home, with B,' Garry said. Eventually. His voice had no tone to it.

'But we don't know yet what day he was done in, do we?' Maggie pointed out. 'So unless you turned into an hermit, that won't do.' Inside, she was shaking.

'He means he hasn't been out and about,' Bathsheba said. All sour. Never noticed that look of her old man before. 'Just work, the hospital, here, home.' Crossing her legs, fussing about with her skirt, case she showed a bit of her stick thigh. Wouldn't of dreamt Garry'd end up with a girl that prissy. 'Let's face it, someone's always been with him, and that someone has been me, masses of the time,' the McGowan bitch went on.

'Garry always wants to take care of his mum, I know that.' Maggie drew on her ciggie, the smoke hurting her poor lungs. 'But there's ways and ways.'

'Never done it, Mum.' Garry crashed his teacup against his teeth. 'Shit.' Bli, if he was going to be like this with the Old Bill, they'd have him banged up before you could say Not Guilty. Maggie badly wanted to think he hadn't done it, but the way he'd stormed out the hospital . . . If it *was* him, Maggie was partly to blame. And Bathsheba'd been keen enough to wind Garry up that night, going on about the kitten and that. Even she must feel bad now. They had to get this sorted, before they all went down. Mentally and literal.

'If you never done it, then believe you never,' Maggie said. Way she had all them years ago about the nicked Wagon Wheel biscuits. 'Don't know about look at me, look at you.'

'Your mum's right,' Bathsheba put in. '*We* know you're innocent, sweetie, but you're so sure they'll pick you up, you look as though you're waiting for it.'

'They ain't got *no reason* to finger you, son.' Trying to grab his look.

'Might fit me up.' Sticking his nail in his lip.

'What happened to me was just some mugger, unless I'm very much mistaken.' Though she hoped with every scrap of her that weren't true. 'Lucky I never mentioned the name bit to the police. Must of been hearing things, I reckon.'

'No circumstantial, is it?' Garry ripped the scab right off, blood running down his chin. Bathsheba got a tissue out her bag, give it him with a little kiss on the cheek.

'Go careful, petal,' she said. Soft. 'Easy.' Like he was a bleeding greyhound.

'This has *got* to stop, you hear me?' Maggie put out her cig, leaned forward. 'You're thirty-seven years of age, pull yourself together, boy.' Was an horrible, horrible thought, her son most probably having killed, but weren't no sense nor reason in it wrecking all their lives. Course, she felt for Clifford, she'd even miss the mad old bugger, yet the Dawsons was what mattered. Besides, none of *them* would frighten an old woman. Had a bad couple of hour herself, make no bleeding mistake, after seeing it on the news, though she'd cleared her head now. You had to. If you was sick at the idea your own flesh and blood might blow someone's brains out, you threw it up and that was that. Maggie had a suspicion she'd be even more reluctant to face her dreams tonight, but that was just too bad. Anything, facing anything, was better'n Garry . . . End of the day, Clifford'd been making her life a flaming misery, they mustn't let him keep on. Mind, she'd warned the kids about playing with guns – made her think twice about hern.

'Mum?' Garry'd finished mopping his face, scrunched the bloody tissue in his hand. 'You sure I'll be all right? Speak true.'

'I'm sure.' Firm. Touched her deep, way he'd gone back to how he was in the Wagon Wheel days and all. 'Just be strong, love,' she added. 'Remember, you never done it.'

'That's what I keep telling him,' said Bathsheba. Bit contemptuous?

'What the . . . what's that?' Garry's head jerked up.

'Door. Will you get that for me, Bathsheba?' Maggie asked. 'It'll only be Lu this time of evening, but look through the spyhole first, check.'

'Fab, that so saves me a trip.' Bathsheba pointed to the carrier she had with her. Posh, one of them made out of heavy plastic and with string handles. 'That's for her.'

'Bed.' Lulu leaned the flash carrier bag she'd brought in with her against the cabinet.

'But it's only half-nine?'

'It's a school night, won't hurt you to get an early one for once. Go on, off you go, you can have the telly on in your room for a bit. Say bye to Jacob.'

'I'll leave the guitar here, Fred.' That carrier was from Moschino, he'd heard of it; funny, seemed more Bathsheba's style than Lu's. 'You can practise before next time.'

'For real? Wicked.' Fred went off quite happily then, as far as Jacob could tell, only stopping to pick up his dictionary. 'Homework.'

Jacob lit a cigarette. Maybe they should do something about getting the boy a guitar of his own: three lessons in, and already Fred was remembering chords, sequences, not bothered that the strings were cutting deep into his still-soft fingers. A good ear, like his mother. One thing he certainly hadn't inherited from Angel.

'You putting the kettle on, Lu?' Jacob settled back into the settee, watching her bum as she walked to the lounge door.

'Nope.' Lulu went out to the kitchen, came back with a half bottle of vodka and a carton of orange juice. She got two glasses from the cabinet.

'Uh . . . not for me,' Jacob said. 'Don't much like white spirits.'

'Oh, imagine you'll want one, mate.' She made two heavy-handed drinks, shoved a glass in Jacob's direction. Crap, maybe she'd had a letter from Angel as well, knew about the money before Jacob had been able meantime to decide how to play it. That might explain the shopping, even he knew Moschino stuff was expensive. He should just tell her now, get it over with. Pre-emptive strike. Eat your heart out, George Bush.

'Can I talk to you?' he started.

'As it goes, thought we might watch a film,' she said, sitting beside him. 'What sort of thing d'you like?' Taking a huge mouthful of her barely diluted vodka. 'We never watch films together, do we?'

'A film?' Jacob had a long drag of his cigarette. 'But—'

'Yeah, you know, people pretending to be other people, we sit and look at them.' Another gulp of her drink. 'Amazing what they can do nowadays, with technology.'

'You're in a weird mood.' He tasted his own drink: hair lacquer laced with sugar. Didn't like the sound of this, but had it been a real question about watching a film, he'd seem a prize prick if he made a big deal of it. Lulu had on that look of hers that shadowed you, a third-rate private eye.

'Don't you like it weird, then?' she said. 'Was beginning to wonder. One thing I do know, you don't seem to want me of late, and I'm pretty normal.'

'That's not true. No, obviously you're normal, didn't mean it like that.' Jacob put his glass on the floor, tried to take her hand. She pulled away. 'Think a lot of you, you know that,' he added. 'What's this about, Lu?'

'Me being the world's biggest prat,' she said. Softly. 'Jake, I know you know. About . . . what I used to do.'

'Oh, God.' Jacob put out his cigarette, picked his drink up again, swallowed half of it. Panic was rising in his stomach, as though his body was getting ready to run. What should he . . . No point denying it: that, he knew would be a disaster.

Garry. Bet that wide-boy had told her about Jacob coming into the shop. Or maybe Bathsheba had stuck her oar in again. Shit, if Jacob had got in there first, he could have made it sound different. Better.

'Well?' Lulu grabbed his face, hard, forced him to look at her. Her eyes had turned practically navy; bollocks, she seemed so furious. 'Jesus, Jake, thought you'd least be man enough to give me some sort of explanation. Course, it'd be a load of rubbish—'

'Didn't say I knew in case it hurt you.' Which was true. 'How did you find out?'

'Garry told me. How'd *he* know, babe? He was vague there. You boast about it?'

'No, God. He knew Angel left me a few films, that's all. A legacy.' Legacy of a few films and a lot of dough; if Jacob mentioned that, would it deflect her?

'Right, and I presume you fancied fucking the star of the show, did you?'

'Once I'd met you, got to know you, sure.' Going with honesty was his only hope now. 'Course I did, I'm not mad.' But crap, from that look on her face, honesty was the worst policy. He *couldn't* lose her before he'd even worked out what they were to each other. 'Lu, baby . . . that came out all wrong. I wanted you, yeah, a lot, but that would have been just as true if I'd never seen a single frame of those films.'

'Meant to believe that, am I?'

'You should.' Jacob forced down the rest of his drink, coughed. 'But you can't see how fantastic you are.' Overdo the angst now, and he wouldn't have a prayer. 'To be honest, most of them I hardly watched. Found them . . . a bit silly.'

'Most? So you did what with them, then?'

'Got rid.' Praying Garry really hadn't told her how. 'All except one.' He'd never been this upfront, not with anyone. The panic was still there, but he could do this, was sure he could. He had to make her follow him. 'One, I've kept,' he went on. 'One, I love.'

191

'Angel.' Out of nowhere, Lulu pinched his arm, twisting the skin. *Shit*, that really hurt. 'Should of known you were queer,' she added.

'I'm not. It's . . . ' *How you going to explain this one, Jakey? Can't wait to hear.* 'Look, I'm not a psychologist. But . . . think it's got to do with knowing . . . '

'Your bloody times tables?'

'Knowing both of you. Like . . . a threesome, with none of the emotional risks. Could do without, uh, Garry being in there, but even that can't spoil . . . I *love* watching my friend screwing you, and you loving it. I'm so, so sorry he's your . . . you know, your brother, for your sake, but how I feel about the film . . . It's getting stronger, not weaker.' God, even telling her was seriously turning him on; if he could persuade her to let him make love to her in front of the video . . . Stop getting carried away, you *nebbish*. You could lose her, and all you can think about is getting your rocks off. Pathetic. 'Might even have to do with him being dead, and me being alive, and . . . All I know for sure is it's the most exciting thing in the world, because you're the most exciting woman in my world. Ever.'

'Fuck off.'

'What?'

'You deaf? I said, you like fucking so much, you can fuck right off.'

'But . . . Lu, I'm trying to tell you something.'

'And I'm trying to tell *you* something. Fuck off.'

'But . . . ' So this was what you got for laying yourself on the line. Wonderful.

'You reckon you can just say a lot of, of, of *shit*, and the more you say the more all right it'll be.' She laughed. 'Wrong.' Pushing her hand through her hair. 'Fuck off.'

'I can't.' Jacob moved further forward on the settee. 'Not unless I really believe you mean it. And I don't, Luniu.'

'Jesus, that's right, come over all Jewish.' Lu slapped the cushion. 'You only do that when you feel cornered.'

'No, I don't. It's not something you can switch on and off—'

'*You* do, mate.' She pushed her back into the arm of the settee, crossed her legs. Jacob wanted to hold her tight, to make this stop, but the way she was sitting made even attempting that not a possibility.

'I should have told you,' he tried.

'Yep.'

'You don't know how much I've wanted to.' Especially the last week or so. 'Look, you making those films doesn't turn me on *per se*. That, I promise.'

'Words, Jacob.'

'*No*. We're building a life here. You, me, Fred, even Maggie. Sex is just one part of that.' He lit another cigarette. *Tell her to go on, fuck you off, you've got the finances.* 'I'll burn the bloody film, if you want me to,' he said. Giving Angel the mental evils. 'Just . . . don't punish me for liking it. For not telling you, sure, I deserve it for that.' Though she'd hardly been open with him. 'But I can't help how I feel.'

'*Really* thought you'd mind, when you found out. Thought you'd hate it.'

'Part of me does,' he admitted. 'I hate what might have made you feel that's what you had to do. I'm definitely not keen on . . . well, the way men will have looked at you—'

'Wanking.' Making the hand gesture.

'Sure. But I don't think any the less of you for it.' Touching her knee. 'And that's *not* why I'm with you, either. I'd never even properly watched that sort of film before.'

'Porn.'

'Well, yeah. Porn.' He managed a smile. 'Thing with that one film, it's very . . . specific, how I feel.' Tapping his cigarette. 'How I feel about you is, too.'

'And how's that, then?'

Could you measure something like that? Or even begin straightforwardly to define it. Jacob had been sent to her, to her child, and now he held the financial key to her having a real future. And yet, he was powerless before her, weak in the face of her sexuality, past and present; there was a part of him excited by that, another part wanting to turn it around. She was waiting for an answer, for *the* answer; if he gave the wrong one, Jacob felt sure she'd tell him again to go. And mean it this time. *It's only words, Mitzvah. Like the lady said, you know a lot of them, boy.* Wasn't as if he'd even have to choose them himself.

'Lu, I love you,' he said.

'That film, Jake – it was when I conceived Fred.'

'I love you.'

I love you. That's all Angel had needed to say, for her to agree to it. Wasn't like she'd believed him with all her heart, though with enough of it to give him the power. *Something to show our grandchildren,* but even he couldn't of meant that. First actual film was a shock, she'd been ill for a week after with what felt like flu, but when she'd watched it back, she knew. He was right. She looked natural, happy up there, had the art of faking even a life off to a tee. Perhaps, somehow, her being so crazy about Angel had come over when she was with other men. There was even the advantage that in the films back then, shaving *totally* bare wasn't the fashion, so she could cover her bits more. And it did all make her nearly famous, sort of, for a little while.

'You want another drink?' she asked Jacob now.

'No, thanks.' His eyes even bigger with being anxious. Lulu uncrossed her legs, stood up, the left one nearly buckling where it'd gone numb. She poured herself a miles weaker drink this time. Slowly, buying herself some time.

You stupid bleeding whore.

Maggie's voice, full of something that was practically spite. All the comebacks Lulu could of said when Maggie found out about the so-called film career had gone liquid in her throat. Part of her made her auntie right, only a stupid bleeding whore would do porn. Why the bloody hell had Lulu protected Angel

194

over it then? Maybe she wouldn't of said he wasn't involved if he hadn't been a McGowan, but if Lulu was ever going to change Dawson for that, she had to keep everybody sweet with each other. Mags knowing had one good side, though, with Garry becoming her manager. *Someone's got to keep you safe.* Before, she'd signed away her exploitation rights, everything, and Angel was too busy with his proper job at the college to get involved in all that.

'Any chance we've got something different in to drink?' Jacob asked.

'Couple of cans of Stella in the fridge. Help yourself.' Too busy putting shit into his veins more like but she didn't know that then, not with the front bit of her brain. Jesus, for a while she'd thought he was bloody diabetic. He was too busy screwing around as well, men and women both and for all she knew, fucking parrots, but every time, she'd forgive him. *As if it means anything. You know better than that, Dawson.* Christ, she'd been a mug.

Jacob came back into the living room, chugging his can. She knew she owed Jake something for what he'd said, some sort of reply at least, but she couldn't think what to say. He gave her a tentative smile, she even smiled back, but then she turned away, fiddling with the bits on the cabinet. Suddenly, she remembered B's carrier. Something from Angel's estate – no way had Lulu been going to open that in front of Maggie, and B specifically hadn't wanted her to neither. How could Mags of kept the truth about their father secret from Lulu? Tell Angel, not her? Could hardly bring herself to kiss her auntie tonight. One day, Lulu *would* ask her about it. Promised herself. Looking inside the bag now, she took out the little brown paper parcel, tugged at the string. Oh, that's really appropriate. Thanks, mate. So *her* legacy was a nudy painting, most likely worth a few shillings, but even so.

'What's that?' Jacob asked. Maybe he'd bloody like it.

'Nothing.' And the woman looked like a young Maggie. That was just nasty. Yeah, this had Angel's stamp all right. Wonderful couple of days she was having. She stuffed the picture back in the bag, stuck the whole lot in the bottom cupboard of the cabinet.

Twenty-two she'd been, when Angel had his big idea. *Then I'll be part of every part of you, darling.* Come off the pill, do one last film, only not with actors, with him, and make a baby. Tried to tell him it wasn't likely she'd get pregnant just like that, but same as always turned out he'd been right and she'd been wrong. *Come on, everyone has affairs at work, why not with your own bloke?* Even when he was treating his plan that bit too lightly, she'd still been bloody thrilled – they were going to have a real life at last. A real home, with a mummy and a daddy and kids, where they'd make their own rules, so she wouldn't be able to feel all wrong inside, wouldn't have to humiliate herself to feel right.

'Lu, you seen my other cigarette packet?' Bet Jacob knew where to find it, was just trying to get her to speak again. Without turning round, she shook her head.

Should of known better – who invites their mate to a conception? Angel was most probably on some incest kick, in more ways than she could of known about then. And they *were* good mates by that time. *Call it . . . a testament to friendship.* And, *It'll sell better that way.* And, *Do it because you love me, Lush.* Total loyalty was the one thing Angel really cared about. The one thing he wasn't capable of, she knew that later. Still a mystery to this day why Garry, who for certain sure didn't fancy either of them, had gone along with it. For some strange reason people always did, with Angel. But then Garry hadn't really spoken to her again till Fred was born, and never, never, never about that.

Yet . . . maybe Jacob did love her. He'd loved Angel, he'd said so, why not her as well? Him liking one film didn't make him a punter, it was miles more personal than that. Wasn't as if he'd tried to wriggle out of it, not like he'd had to admit he had a thing about that video. He was trying to get everything out in the open. Lulu wasn't the same person she'd been in them Angel days, wasn't some naïve young girl any more. And that kitten, how would she of faced that on her own? He'd even made Fred feel better about it, by being around if nothing else. She owed it to herself, to Fred, to give this another chance. Anyway, Angel would of won, else – that film would of ruined her life. Again.

'Didn't you find your fags, love?' she said.

Chapter Ten

'I've got something for you.'

'It's about time, quite frankly. Your month's expired.'

'Let's face it, sweetie, you so couldn't have got this one on your own.' Bathsheba sipped her coffee, glanced round the hotel bar, caught that little waiter staring. Difficult to keep the triumph off her face, smiling at the staff was as good a cover as any. If Stephen Hopkins seemed to have had his hands tied by Angel, she certainly hadn't. To be fair, perhaps Hopkins had thought of that (maybe even counted on it). She forced herself to silence, the verbal equivalent, Angel always said, of staring someone out. Yet she *so* wanted to detail to Hopkins what she'd done with Del. Unfortunately, hurting her brother had simply had to be in the equation, but otherwise it had been perfect.

You can't say anything to Stan or Daddy, Del.

What, don't tell them you're a back-stabbing bitch? Or that Angel was?

But everyone could be bought with an appeal to their emotions.

He said that about me?

Yesterday. Said he'd given you too much responsibility, that you were no Angel.

Especially when you could tell them what their father really thought of them,

Why's he keep going on about Lulu Dawson?

And how that same father had betrayed their sainted Mama. And produce, if necessary, eleven stone of evidence.

'All right, Bathsheba, you can stop playing with me now.' Hopkins leaned back in his chair. Clearly trying to look relaxed (and not making a bad fistlette of it), his eyes couldn't hide his keenness. Bathsheba signalled to her smitten waiter for a refill.

'Fabulous, thanks. Alfred, isn't it? You're a poppet, saved my life. Need another drink, Stephen? No?'

'Get on with it, for God's sake.' Mm, a touch rattled?

'What would you say if I told you Fidelio was prepared to negotiate?' Picking up her fresh coffee. 'He's got sixteen per cent, and an active interest. That makes thirty-one between ISU and me.'

'Is Stan aware of Del's thinking?' Brushing at the knee of his trousers.

'No.' Bathsheba smiled at another admirer as he passed behind Hopkins.

'You're actually trying to convince me Del McGowan won't say anything to his brother? To his business partner?' Hopkins laughed. 'Utter balls.'

'A few weeks ago, I'd have agreed with you,' Bathsheba said. '*Will you come into my parlour, said the spider to the fly.*'

'Angel used to quote that.' Bathsheba put her elbows on the table. 'Then, you knew him a weeny bit better than you led me to believe.' One thing Angel hadn't told her, but the information she *had* got from him was profiting her in ways he'd never have foreseen.

'Did I?' Hopkins reached for his vodka tonic, took a gulp.

'Oh, sweetie, forgot to say, sorry to hear you're ill.'

'I'm not.' Sounding puzzled.

'You will be though, won't you? Sorry to hear *that*, then.' Looking at this fit, beautiful man, was hard to believe that if that sad act Clifford Black had been right, Stephen would probably get AIDS and die. But everyone was going to die of something, ridiculous to get sentimental about it. You could use bad gear and OD (if you were stupid), or you could (let's say) get shot through the head. Hopkins might well outlive her.

'You can be a foul woman,' he said. Calmly. Bathsheba forced herself not to react, though she could feel her cheeks get a tad hot. Still, for such a very black man, *he* suddenly looked masses paler. 'But I'm not going to discuss Angel with you,' he added.

'Bit of a coincidence. After all, he *so* never mentioned you.' Maybe that was going too far. 'Del probably will sell to you, Stephen. But if Daddy or Stan find out before I've finished putting extra . . . divisions into the equation, then we'll all be in trouble.'

'Really go for the scatter-bomb approach, don't you?' Hopkins shrugged. 'The stakes have always been high, you're delusional if you don't realize that.'

'Mm, Del told me one of the smaller clubs near the Holly Blue got busted two nights ago.' Had ISU's footprints all over it – close the place down, then buy it for a steal. She'd have to move faster if she didn't want Hopkins to start down that road with the McGowans. Few benefits for her and Garry in that one. 'All I'm asking is you keep this quiet until the end of November, when we're all due our pay-outs,' she said. 'Including *Angel*.'

'I'd say he's had his.' Shifting forward in his seat. 'Will Del meet me personally?'

'Eventually, with me there.' The triumph tugged at her lips, lifting them into another grin. This *so* felt good. Thank God for Angel's death. 'I'd have to countersign, of course.'

'Of course,' Hopkins agreed. 'Just how much has he got on the Super-Crank?' His voice different now. Urgent. Even angry. ISU obviously didn't like the drugs one bit. 'The chemist, for instance?' Tapping the table with a clenched fist. A big clenched fist, face it.

'He's more involved with that side than Garry is,' she told him.

'Good, I've wanted to make Del's acquaintance.' Eyes smiling, although his lips weren't. 'I hear he's a pretty boy.' For the first time, bizarrely camp.

'A pretty *straight* boy.'

'I'm not prejudiced,' he said. The first joke she'd heard him make, too.

'Sorry, sweetie, *he* is.'

'We'll see. And Bathsheba, I'm closer to other information myself.'

Hopkins rose when she did, and (another first) kissed her on the cheek. She so hadn't expected that. Perhaps he was starting to view her as an equal, even if he did think her *foul*. An acknowledgement, even, that she had more power than he did. That would show Angel, and Daddy. Though what *other information* was he close to? But as she walked out into the drizzly September afternoon, Bathsheba's heart suddenly felt a tad heavy. How much longer was she going to be forced to be brave? Always fighting her own corner. Women have the only body part designed just for pleasure – that *had* to mean God intended her to be happier than her brothers. She walked along to Waterloo Bridge to hail a cab before the greedy rush-hour crowd nabbed them all, but stopped to look over at the London Eye. Garry had always fancied trying that (bless him). Perhaps she'd suggest it, to cheer him up. Face it, she had to do something. Daddy was desperate now to make someone the villain in Angel's death. Last time she'd seen him, he couldn't shut up about Lulu and Maggie – Angel not being able to bear the incest was his latest theory, senile git. But as Daddy became more obsessed with the past, Garry was getting more upset by the shooting. If she weren't careful, Bathsheba would end up visiting the wrong man in the poxy loony bin. Being brave was one thing, losing despite that would be too hard.

The Thames was getting rough, they might be in for some proper rain. She pulled up her coat collar, but couldn't bring herself to move. Okay, right. Now she *had* to work on Jacob, find out where the inheritance was – whatever it took. No one was indispensable, certainly not some third-rate musician attached to that slapper. Then she could get Garry out of London, force him to have a rest before he went to work with ISU. If you loved someone, you'd do anything for them (admit it, anything was easier to do with real money). Well, at least she was starting to use Angel, rather than the other way around.

It almost certainly will be contested, pardon the pun.
Jacob hadn't noticed any pun, had to work it out. He'd been tempted to tell the solicitor that it was more precisely described as *paronomasia*, but even as he'd nearly said that, he'd realized it was just an hysterical reaction. Solicitor was bent, that was obvious, and no *macher*; this, you could see by that tatty old office. *Of course, there's a strong argument to suggest the cheque was legally yours before the death. Particularly as it didn't come directly from Mr McGowan.* Sure, whoever had bought Angel's shares would come into conflict with the McGowans sooner or later, but meantime Jacob could be in Puerto Rico with the money for all that slimy solicitor cared.

Pulling his jacket closer against the wind, Jacob started to walk towards Brent Cross Tube. Few mulchy leaves on the ground, though North London in September was, comparatively, hardly Cambridge. Vividly remembered Angel kicking, scattering, great piles of leaves along Sidgewick Avenue, on the rare occasions they'd gone to lectures in Michaelmas term. Stopping suddenly, Jacob took the postcard from his inside pocket. A sepia picture of the Backs, focusing on King's College Chapel; nothing bloody changed in Cambridge, nobody's memory ever made a difference to the view. Across the top, Angel had printed, *The last word.* The solicitor had repeated that as he'd handed the card across the desk, but until this moment, looking again, it hadn't registered: this was the final written communication Jacob would ever get from Angel. Ever.

Never smile at a crocodile, Mitzvah. Never keep gear you know is bad. Never take sweets from brothers-in-law. Death's full of crystals, but all that glistens is not jewels. Never accept anything from Garry Dawson. And Jakey, look out for my boy. Do it because.

With love, Angel xxx

How the bloody hell was he supposed to interpret that? No wonder Angel had gone into the more esoteric branches of lit. theory: he was incapable of saying anything straightforward, had to create the elliptical from what, for anyone else, would be a plain line. *Linear structures are falsely imposed, mate.* Not by Angel, that was for sure.

But . . . hang on. In the first letter, Angel had predicted his own death from bad heroin; that was, apparently, exactly what had then happened. Did that mean it was an effective suicide, or had he been going for the law of probability? Jacob glanced up the street. There was a pub at the other end, looked a bit dodgy, but how bad could it be at twenty to twelve on a Tuesday? Needed somewhere to sit and think and have a cigarette. Pint wouldn't hurt, either. Tucking the postcard back in his jacket, he started moving again.

The place stank, of stale booze, evil breath. But there were only a few other people in there, all men, all old, each alone, and no one so much as looked at Jacob. He bought his John Smith's, found a table in the corner. Why was Garry Dawson important? The second letter had asked if Jacob had delivered Angel's message to Garry; that must have been the videos, but of course there should have been six. Made sense that the one kept back was probably the real message. Or maybe Jacob was making it more complex than it needed to be. *You, Foxy? You'd cut a thirty-piece jigsaw into sixty and sling out the picture on the box.* What would have happened if he hadn't followed Angel's initial instructions? Perhaps the money would have felt like Jacob's own, had he never met Lulu. He could be sitting in this pub now, not knowing who the hell Garry Dawson was, nor caring. *Dream on, mate.*

Jacob lit a cigarette; so much bloody smoke in here already, despite the small number of customers, was almost pointless. Forget the crap about crocodiles and crystals. Did Garry count as Angel's brother-in-law? Bad gear, don't accept anything from Garry Dawson . . . No, *that* couldn't be right. Garry was living with Angel's sister, was Fred's uncle more or less, Angel couldn't mean *Garry* had given him bad gear. Anyway, how would Angel know it was dodgy before trying it? Or if he did, then why not throw it away?

Start again. Jacob took a long swallow of his bitter, pulled out the postcard, laid it picture-down on the table. Pub door opened, a youngish woman came in. Legs that for sure didn't justify that tiny denim skirt; her top miles too low for this weather, far too glittery for daytime. A brass, had to be. None of the other punters paid her attention, nor did she look as though she expected any, making straight for the bar. Her back bulged fat over the fastening of her bra; Jacob found himself fascinated by that. But she might turn round, think he was looking for business. He forced his eyes back to the card. Okay. Angel had kept some drugs he knew were bad; the implication might be he'd got them from Garry. Jacob had been sent to Garry with a film he'd never delivered: Angel had intended it . . . okay, to tell Garry he knew. But then why, when Jacob had met him in that pub, hadn't Garry been more chary once he realized the connection with Angel? Yet no matter how much Jacob re-read the thing, there was no other fucking explanation. Garry. Had killed. Angel. And Angel had let him. Colluded, even. Jacob crushed out his cigarette.

Outrage hit him like a sudden migraine. Angel was dead. Garry had fucking murdered him. And so Angel was dead. If Garry had been in this pub right now, Jacob would have smashed this glass, stuck it right into those cheekbones, into those pale blue eyes. Would have murdered Angel as well, for that sick complicity. Arrogant bastard, so sure Jacob's loyalty would make him ignore that part. Shit, shit, fuck, wasn't even any point going to the police: a cryptic postcard from a dead man? Sure, really strong evidence. Crap, or maybe it *was* just Angel playing with them all again. Jacob couldn't keep still in his chair, perched on the edge as though Garry might actually pitch up; couldn't do anything about Angel's death wish, but Garry Dawson wasn't going to get away with having granted it. If he had granted it, of course. Promise you, Angelniu.

Fred mashed the teabag hard against the mug. Wasn't that he minded making Mum a cup of tea, did it all the time for Nan, but what he hated was having to take it through to her when she was in the bath, right. He'd be thirteen in a couple of weeks, was way embarrassing seeing your mum in the nuddy when you weren't a little kid any more. Mum said it was her one luxury, having tea in the bath, but why couldn't he make it for her before she went in? She reckoned it went cold, if he did that, reckoned he was turning into *A right little prude*, but that was better than having to look at her fat old body.

He took the tea through the hall, knocked on the bathroom door.

'Leave it out here, yeah?' he tried.

'Don't be daft, Freddie, I'll get the carpet soaked. Bring it in.'

Knew that wouldn't work. Trying not to look straight ahead, Fred opened the door.

'There are,' he said.

'How am I meant to reach that? Give it here.'

Couldn't do anything about it, then. Fred crept over to the bath, keeping his eyes up, at the tiles near the ceiling. Mum burst out laughing, splashed him hard with her bubbly water. He giggled like a girl for a second, forgot he wasn't meant to be looking, then she got him. Took her great big boobies in her hands, jiggled them at him.

'Scared are you?' she said. Killing herself. 'Don't blame you, mate.'

'Bet I'm bloody adopted.' Trying not to laugh again. Wasn't funny. Wasn't.

'Excuse me, less of that bloody language.' Mum was *well* in a good mood. 'Course you're not adopted – with these stretch marks? Leave off.' Holding out her hand for the tea.

'What you going to do if I don't give it to you?' Putting

205

his arm up high, but careful, case he spilled hot liquid on his head.

'Answer the door to your mates like this?'

'You wouldn't?' he said. Or more screeched.

'Like B might say, I *so* would.' Hadn't seen her mess about like this in ages. Not a bad bloke, Jacob – bit of a stiff, but he was safe.

'Here.' Fred gave her the mug. 'If you ever show me up, I'll—'

'Yeah, you'll what?' She winked. Started singing. 'Heads and shoulders, knees and toes, knees and toes . . .' Doing the actions.

'Nooooooo!' Had enough of this now. Backed out the bathroom with his hands over his ears, exaggerated, so's she'd know he wasn't leaving with the ump. Might have half-hour in the living room on Jake's guitar before she came out, wanting her programme.

Fred opened the case, found the plectrums, *pleckies*, though where was that book of old songs? Obscure songs. Ob-scure, he'd looked that up. Under the settee? Nope. Mum reckoned Jacob would well lose his head if it wasn't screwed on. Tried both the drawers in the cabinet, no luck. Tugged at the bottom door – that was trapped for some reason. Then he saw a bit of thick plastic bag was poking out the side, yeah, wedging it well tight. He took a chance on busting the thing, pulled harder. Door opened, and there was that bag Mum had brought home from Nan's the other night. Must be a secret, in it – she usually left stuff about. Not like Nan, who always had her bedroom door locked from the outside, even when it was just the two of them in her flat. Mum was rubbish at keeping things to herself, must be something way interesting if she could be arsed to hide it.

She'd be in the bath ages yet, singing her crappy *obscure* songs, adding loads more hot water till she ended up a wrinkly prune. Anyway, how was he meant to know it was private? Best thing was take it right out the cupboard, blatantly, else he'd seem well sly. The bag was from a posh clothes shop, but there weren't clothes inside. A parcel, that had been opened then half-wrapped back up. Fred lifted it out the bag, took off the paper.

A small, old-looking painting of a naked lady with her legs up and apart. You could see her bum and her minge and her tits, and it wasn't like looking at a dirty book or pictures on the Net, sort of seemed more real than that, even though it wasn't a photo. Fred felt funny, hot and red. Was getting a boner, wanted to touch it, but say Mum came back out? He looked hard at the painting, trying to fix it in his mind. There was something about the lady's face, now he could concentrate on that and all. Something . . . familiar. Suddenly, Fred dropped the painting. Shit. Shit. It was *Nan* when she was young. And it had given Fred *an hard-on.* Rank. He was, was, was a dirty perve, should well have his willy chopped off. But . . . why had it been painted in the first place? And why did Mum have it here? Another fucking way his life was crap compared with everyone else's. Bet no one from school had to look at sexy pictures of their nan. Some of them weren't even allowed to watch 18s.

They wouldn't do it if they didn't enjoy it. Jacob had spent two nights' money on this stash, watched them in a spirit of research, and decided. Wasn't that he believed every orgasm: most of the women's looked and sounded dreadful fakes, whether they were from sculpted Americans or the slightly more plausible figures of Eastern Europeans and Brits. But none of the actors seemed poor or unhappy, clearly they liked flaunting their bodies; given their acting was so crap, Jacob didn't see how they could fake that. After all, what harm? Angel had often accused Jacob of prostituting his talent. Was probably worse, and not so straightforward, to flesh out some has-been or never-was band when you could have put your skills on the line working the jazz circuit. Worse than having sex in comfortable surroundings, making more money than you ever would in a conventional job. And God, yeah, most of the films were quite exciting when you got used to the format. Not in the heart-deep way of the Angel–Lu video, but they were easy, comforting, simple; anyone who was part of creating that must have some sort of job satisfaction.

Though he had to admit, he wasn't exactly thinking with optimal clarity. Since yesterday lunchtime, when he'd realized the possible extent of Garry's depravity, Jacob's brain kept getting confused by sudden attacks of pure indignation, of disbelief, of murderous rage. The sense of violation was acute, but he couldn't properly get hold of it; only thing he was sure of was that the women in these films were comparatively violated far less than Jacob had been by his new knowledge of Angel's death. That's if it was knowledge. Sometimes, he doubted what otherwise he felt he knew, but then Garry's face always came back into his mind. *Nothing sounds strange to me, mate.* Fucking bet it doesn't, you bastard. Poor Lulu, she'd be devastated, if it turned out to be true. Not that Jacob was planning on telling her: however upset she was, she might still want to protect her brother. And Jacob wasn't having that. Once he'd decided what to do, he didn't intend to be stopped, and certainly not before he'd come to a decision. *Hey, Mitzy, you're a wild man!* Not even Angel taking the piss was going to stop him. Especially given that Angel might as well have held his own arm out to Garry Dawson. Selfish bastard. Unless Jacob really had read the bloody riddle all wrong. Great use of that academic brain, Angel mate: a part-time job in a crap ex-poly, leaving you plenty of time to expend your energies doing other people's brains in. Neither of them had exactly fulfilled their promise.

Better get those videos put away before Lu arrived. Couldn't believe she'd understand his motivation for buying porn that didn't even have her in it. Hadn't seen her for a couple of days, and despite everything, was really looking forward to it, had missed her, wanted it to be a good evening. Maybe tonight he'd tell her about the money; trouble was, he'd been so caught up in what to think about Garry, it was hard to keep anything else straight. At least he'd managed to deposit the cheque at last, and so far no one official had come knocking at his door, though that was a lot of money to stick in a current account, according to the letter he'd had from the bank this morning. An unreal amount, as far as Jacob was concerned. Until July, he'd spent forty-one years getting to a pared place where small pleasures and pains were big enough, the only way anyone could be in charge of their own existence. Screw Angel, Jacob had never wanted a complicated life.

Twenty minutes late. Jacob was getting twitchy, bloody determined to keep Garry away from their evening, worried that every extra minute alone made that less likely. Then, suddenly, she was there. Walking into his flat, she shoved her brother out of it. She'd come straight from work; Jacob was glad, he'd always liked the clothes she wore for Heaven Scent: a formal dress tonight, tight and plunging, low but sharp heels, part of her hair caught back in a velvet bow. Slightly old-fashioned look, which suited her curves, made her seem like a forties' movie starlet. Now, after her third glass of wine, she was sitting on the settee, her legs crossed and angled away from her body, as though she were playing into his fantasy, about to take dictation for . . . who was it? Joan Crawford.

'You look great,' he said. Sod, should have mentioned that when she arrived.

'Do I?' Sounding surprised. 'Thanks.'

'Forgot to ask, heard any more about that murder?' Hating the feel of the word.

'No, not precisely. Maggie's a bit stressed about it, but then coming on top of what happened to her . . . '

'You don't think they're related?' Nothing would bloody surprise him now. The Dawsons could well have had Monroe killed and hid Elvis, even set up September 11th. 'It wasn't him who she thought attacked her?' he asked.

'Doubt it.' Lulu started on her fourth drink. 'Might sound callous, love, but shit happens all the time.' Putting her glass back on the coffee table. 'I mean, think of Angel.'

'Yeah.' Jacob lit a cigarette, to try to regulate his breathing. Really didn't want to think about Angel. He got up to put on another Sinatra CD, went to sit back on the chair, but changing his mind, moved over to the settee. Lulu finished her wine. He hadn't seen her drink like this before, not so quickly. She laid her head on his shoulder; that wasn't characteristic, either. Made it awkward for him to reach the ashtray.

'I love you,' she said. Must have taken a lot for her not to say that days ago, when he had. Even where it wasn't true, though he was certain that for her it was, the natural response to *I love you* was surely *I love you, too*; anything less seemed harsh, ungenerous. Two things Lulu wasn't for sure.

'Good,' he said. 'That's nice.'

'Hope so, mate.' Taking his cigarette from his hand, she leaned forward and half across him to put it out. He could see right down the front of her dress, to where her lacy black bra barely restrained her breasts. She had an amazing body, yet Jacob was still having a problem straightforwardly touching her; even after their row, when they'd made love, he'd had to think of the video meantime to get it up. 'Can I have another wine?' she asked.

'Sure.' He went to the kitchen to open a new bottle, freshening his own drink while he was there. So she loved him; he wasn't surprised. Lu would worship anyone who treated her like a human. But he wasn't going to beat himself up over it: she eased some kind of lack in him, and that meant he did value her. Love was just a word. *Fuck off, Mitz. Saying something's just semantics is like saying rain's wet. Love exists because it's a word, you dick.* Really? Say that about death as well, can you?

Jacob took the drinks into the lounge, sat back down next to Lu. She downed half hers in a couple of gulps.

'You okay, Lu?'

'Yeah, fine.' She'd taken her shoes off, was rubbing one stockinged foot against the other, her hand resting on his stomach. 'Jake . . . you know that film?'

'Yeah.' God, don't let her start going on about that again.

'You still got it?'

'I have, yeah.' Why did he admit that?

'It's a strictly limited edition, you know,' she said. 'Only fifty copies were ever made. Yours is most probably one of the only ones left.'

'Really?' Angel had it right, then: it was rare, valuable even.

'Have you watched it since . . . '

'What do you want me to say, Lulu?' Felt she was trying to trap him. Could hardly tell her the truth: the row hadn't stopped him, but Garry had. After that postcard yesterday, the fucking thing hadn't had the same appeal. 'I'm sorry you don't like it, but—'

'No, I wasn't getting at that.' Stroking his stomach, his chest. 'I mean . . . I want you to be happy. Presumed . . . you might want to, you know, watch it together. D'you get me?' Her tone uncertain.

'See it with you?' Shit, why did this have to happen now? And yet, 'Yeah, I'd love to, course I would,' he found himself saying. His hard-on automatic. 'But, why have you come round to that?'

'Not precisely sure.' Lulu kissed his chest. 'Just want to make this work, love.'

'You mean, uh, tonight? Watch it tonight? Do you?' Words running to catch up with his heart. He couldn't turn this down. Couldn't. No matter what the emotional difficulty, he might never get a chance like this again.

'Easy, boy.' She laughed. Running her hand lightly over his cock. 'Can see you're keen,' she said. 'Yeah, okay, why not?' Finishing her wine. Jacob swallowed his brandy. Pulled away from her to take the video from the drawer.

For a fraction of a second, the anger was back: he was about to see that bastard get his rocks off with Lu, with Angel, in a situation that would have been close to Jacob's ideal a week ago. Garry had killed a dream. But God, Jacob had wanted this, wasn't going to let anything spoil it, he'd never taken much notice of Garry's role in the video anyway, was seconds away from something most men would . . . well, kill for. He got up to turn off one of the lamps, slipped the tape into the machine. Suddenly, he was nervous, as though he were about to take an exam. Or watch Lulu take one. Weird.

'You sure about this?' he asked.

'Yeah. But I feel a bit . . . funny.' She took the bow out of her hair, put it on the floor.

'Me too.' Jacob smiled at her. 'Like being a virgin, isn't it?'

'Suppose.'

'Ready?' He sat close to her, the remote in his hand.

'Okay, go for it.' Her fingers on his thigh.

Jacob pressed play, forcing himself not to fast forward to the scene that mattered. The bog-standard plot crawled along, the young Lu flashing her knickers, alone, then at Angel, then at Angel and Garry. Stop thinking, stop bloody thinking.

'All right?' he said.

'Well . . . yeah. But Jake, look how young and slim I am there.' Phlegmy.

'Sure, but you're sexier now. Promise.' The scene wasn't far away, a few minutes. Jacob's balls ached, his cock almost painful with anticipation. He slid his arm round Lu, his fingers finding a hard nipple. Shit, was she excited? Could he get more out of this? 'Are you wet, baby?' he asked. 'Are you?' Running his free hand up her leg, to where her flesh came over her stocking tops, as though no clothes could contain her sexuality. Surely they weren't just going straightforwardly to watch the film. He couldn't bear it. Her younger self was naked now, holding her breasts out to Angel, to fucking bastard Garry. And suddenly, Jacob paused the tape. 'Get undressed,' he said. With someone else's voice.

'Jacob . . . ' Lu pulled away, looked into his face. 'You know what you're asking?'

'For sure. Get undressed.' Stroking her face. 'Do it because you love me.'

Lulu closed her eyes.

'Okay,' she said. Flat. But Jacob knew she'd get into it, if she gave them both this chance. 'You'll notice the difference,' she warned.

She turned around for Jacob to unzip her; his fingers fumbled, nearly ripping the material. Then she stood, stepped out of the dress. All flesh, black underwear. Get rid of the rest, baby, please. Jacob pulled off his tee-shirt, his jeans. Lu reached behind her to undo her bra. Her breasts, oh shit, hanging low, their astonishing nipples really hard for him now. She unclipped her suspender belt, rolled off her stockings, slowly, suddenly Lucinda Luscious again. Slipping a finger into the crotch of her pants, she rubbed there for a couple of seconds, then put the finger into her mouth. Jacob thought he was going to explode, heart and cock first. He tugged off his own pants. She bent to run her hand over him, her breasts brushing his face. Then she turned, taking off her briefs, her bum right by his mouth.

'God, you're something else,' he said. Getting up, he pushed the coffee table to the side of the room. Pulled her on to the floor with him, ran his tongue over her nipples. 'Ready, baby?' he asked. She nodded. Jacob pressed the button; they watched as Angel and Garry sucked Lulu's breasts, played with her cunt. Then Angel pushed Garry away. Jacob rewound. Angel pushed Garry away. Angel pushed Garry away.

And then. Angel opening Lu with his fingers. Jacob froze the frame. Turned Lulu on to her knees. Opened her. And started the film moving again. Angel entered her; Jacob entered her. Two female cries. Never felt her so wet.

'You dirty bitch, you're loving it,' he said. Please God, don't let him come before Angel. 'Who are you feeling, baby, him or me? Him or me? *Him* or me?' Grabbing her hair, forcing her head up to look at the screen. 'Tell me, him or me?'

'Both,' she said. 'Both. Oh shit, Jake, it's . . . '

'No dialogue at this bit.' Timing his thrusts, so they matched Angel's. Last, last. Her cunt was tightening round his cock. The young Lu was screaming now; the older, softer one whimpering. So Angel was better, was he? Jacob thrust harder, pulling her

213

hips back into his groin. *Come on, you dirty little bitch. You do love it.* 'Come on, you dirty little bitch. You do love it.' Last, boy, last. Tighter and tighter, holding him in.

He'd never come like that, felt her come like that. And all Garry had was some thin spunk over her face.

Maggie was bleeding worried sick about Garry. Boy was a bag of bones, bundle of nerves, any other flipping collection of bad things you cared to mention. Now she was feeling that bit better in herself, she had time to think about what Clifford's death might mean for all of them. Not that the Old Bill was showing any interest in Garry, but that weren't to say he was safe. And Maggie couldn't keep on kidding herself there was a small chance he might not of done it – else why would he be such a wreck? Flaming marvellous. Not so much as a parking ticket his whole thirty-seven year, and now he could well have the threat of a murder charge over his head. Well, she wouldn't let that happen, not if she could be off of it.

She poured herself another cup. Nice, to be able to make tea in the pot and be able to lift it yourself. Last couple of days'd made all the difference. Bandage off tomorrow, please God. She lit a ciggie, settled back into the settee. Bet McGowan would know what to do. Tempting, to arrange a meeting, ask his advice, but could she really go back all them years, cancel out what they done to each other? If she never had no other choice when it come down to it, then course she'd go to him, but till then, best sit tight. Maybe if she got another message asking after her, all right. Yet he'd only ever been a pussycat in her head, she'd been well wrong about that. Seemed funny that he'd give a monkey's how she was, now – something about that still didn't wash.

You wouldn't dare, so.

Bleeding well would, and all, you don't leave me alone. And don't come that Irish rubbish with me, your daddy swum over before the War.

He hadn't believed her at that point, unless she'd been very much mistaken – she'd see the laugh in his eyes, that expression of contempt on his ugly mug. And be fair, there was the film he'd took of her with that evil bugger, he most probably thought she wouldn't say nothing to Mrs McGowan while he had that to do what he liked with. She'd met the missus once. Pretty woman, but sort of faded. Half-Italian, half-Greek, give her an unusual look about her. Snobby mare she'd been, but if you was married to a man like McGowan, suppose you had to take your pride where you could find it.

Mickey Finn for Mickey McGowan. Sounded like one of them posh meetings you see on telly about lawyers and things. For once, Maggie had turned herself into a player. Been almost too easy, excepting for getting Sid the Pin to do his stuff.

What if he wakes up?

He won't. Got enough dope in him to keep an elephant soundo all night.

Not Sid's finest work, had to be said. But McGowan should of been grateful – all gain with no pain. The outline of a pussycat, no colour, on his backside. Nice little surprise for the missus. And all it'd cost him was his gun, half his little toe, and a piece of paper left with Clifford Black, to be delivered to the Old Bill and to Mrs McGowan if anything happened to Maggie. Bli, she'd been petrified when he come round, his groans sounding like the start of something, not the end, his eyes a lunatic's. But then he held his hands up, quite literal. Big as he was, he was messing with something bigger. With her bleeding pain. Like he said, wounded animals was dangerous, specially when they had their young to consider. *No more chances though, lady, not even you can get me twice. But let me tell you this – you're not the great mother you think you are.* The Red Hot Poker was letting it go, for a wonder. Actually thanked her for getting that quack from down the road in to dress his flaming toe, squeezed her hand while the bloke did his stuff. And as he'd left the next day, he'd kissed her goodbye, a proper kiss, on the mouth. Maggie'd never understood that.

She'd never understood neither why she'd cried.

Putting out her cig, she looked out the window now. Piggy night out there. Wonder what Garry was up to? Poor, stupid bleeder. Maggie's throat was tight. Turning into a right wet weekend since her accident. With that thought, the tears come.

He'd felt shamed when she'd cried. *You always thought fucking was dirty, Jake. Want your mummy to smack your bot-bot for it?* No, for once Angel was wrong: Jacob had never thought sex was in any way bad, quite the opposite; his bloody problems with it had mostly been to do with sustaining a relationship, or sometimes with suspecting he might not be skilled enough. *You're not.* Oh, piss off. Yet when he'd held Lulu sobbing in his arms, he felt he'd made sex with her about just him. And surely that was what masturbation was for. *You should know, wanker.* But then he'd kissed her, told her he loved her, and now that she'd managed a smile, shit, maybe it wasn't so terrible. After all, no one had been exploited: it had really mattered, this, you had to say was the whole point, that it was Lu he'd made love to in front of that video. No one else would have done.

'I conceived Fred doing that film,' she said. Wiping her nose on her hand.

'Yeah, I know.' With his free arm, he reached for his cigarettes, lit one. 'You warm enough?' he asked.

'Bit chilly.' She sat up, pulled on his tee-shirt. 'Smells of you.' Curling her arms round her knees. 'Mickey McGowan wants to meet Fred,' she told him.

'Thought he hadn't been in touch since your dinner?'

'Yesterday. He rung the shop.' She ran her hand through her messy hair. 'State of me,' she said. 'I don't know, Jake – not like Fred even knows he's got a grandad.'

'Don't rush into anything, sweetheart.' God, what would she say when she knew how much dough there was up for grabs? She'd had too many shocks lately. Jacob wasn't about to rush into anything, either.

'No. D'you think I'm a slag?'

216

'*What?*' Jacob choked on his cigarette. 'No, course I don't.'

'Was *my* idea, though. About . . . you know.'

'It was a gift, baby.' Lifting her hand from her thigh, he kissed her palm. 'I'll be grateful all my life for that.'

'Well, precisely.' She hugged her legs again. 'Knew you were fixated on it. But what's it going to make you think of me?'

'That you're brave, and beautiful, and generous.' He smiled. 'All the things I already straightforwardly thought.' Stroking her hair off her face.

'Wonder what my dad would think?'

'Hardly the sort of thing you tell your dad, is it?' Jacob drew on his cigarette. No, he didn't feel shame; he felt almost saved, as though all the crap he'd had to deal with lately he was being protected from. Even thinking about it now couldn't hurt him. Lulu had fought off his dragons, at least for a while. 'Sex and parents should be in separate categories, no matter how old you are,' he added.

'Feel bloody ancient, at the minute.'

'I want a woman, not a girl.'

'Blokes always say that if they're with someone over thirty,' she claimed. Sharply. 'Well, course they would do, if that's all they can get.'

'You're not all I can get.' *Bet she's really flattered, Jakey.* 'No, I mean—'

'Still can't get my head around Angel being my brother,' she said.

'You probably won't, not exactly.'

'Can't bring myself to talk to B about it.' Running a strand of hair along her lips. 'She never mentions it, neither – like we agreed not to. Funny, don't you reckon? Think we're both . . . embarrassed of being sisters or something,' she said in one of those falsely light, snarky tones. Jacob made a non-committal murmur come out with his exhaled smoke. Shit, don't let the woman spoil things with that angsty stuff. But she kissed his shoulder as he stubbed his cigarette. 'Jake . . . am I ever going to meet *your* family?'

'Uh, I guess. Sure.' Jacob lit another cigarette.

'You just put one out.'

'Yeah, big night,' he said. God, fuck, shit. Why hadn't he seen this coming? *They're a family. That's the point, Mitzvah.* Of course she'd expect to be introduced to his mother, his father, his father's latest girlfriend. Hardly unreasonable. Well, tough shit, it wasn't a possibility. Though what could he say to her? My mother would think you were a common *shikseh*; my father would probably want to shag you. Bloody hell, what would Mum make of Maggie, Bathsheba, that bastard Garry? Even Fred would be a problem. Lulu would dress up for the meeting, getting it ever-so-slightly wrong: too bright, too tight, too . . . much. Like that brass in the Brent Cross pub. All the things Jacob adored in Lulu would sign her death warrant with the Foxes. Good-time girls focused on feelings, not aesthetics, in a straightforward way; look at the difference between Lu and Bathsheba, and there was no question which Jacob preferred. But Mum would think that was dreadful. And she'd let Lulu know. Screw it, he wasn't going to expose Lu to that, mustn't put any of them through it but least of all her. 'Do you want a cup of tea or something?' he asked.

'Not yet awhile. In a bit, maybe.' She picked at the perfect gold polish on her toenails. 'How about you meeting *my* dad, then?' she said.

Chapter Eleven

'Make us a pot of coffee, love.' That wasn't a request.

'*Da*ddy, you and Del both drink far too much caffeine. What happened to the herbal teabags I bought you?'

'Tasted like piss. Binned them. Go on, I'm parched here.' Half-cut, more like. Bathsheba so knew he'd been drinking on his own. She'd just spent two bloody hours at the gym, while he'd been soaking (good job he didn't have any looks to lose). Still, there was one bright side – she could at least judge how his obsession was coming along, without him putting on some sober veneer of sanity.

'Won't be two ticks,' Bathsheba said, making her way out to the kitchen. She took a peeklette in the fridge before filling the pot. Gross, just a few dead animal parts, a pint of full-fat milk and three eggs. If he had a heart attack, he needn't come to Bathsheba for sympathy. The contrast with what Stephen Hopkins had eaten at lunch today was fabulous. Caesar salad dressing might have about ten squillion calories, but at least the man was prepared to eat *rabbit food* in public.

Three hundred thousand pounds. Bathsheba simply couldn't believe it. She'd assumed Angel must have had debts, that there wouldn't be anything like that much left, but she had no reason to doubt Hopkins. With Del about set to sell up, they had to have all their financial cards on the table. Scandalous, that Angel hadn't thought the money ought to go to the family, but obviously she wouldn't have had a prayer of seeing any of it if it had gone back into the firm. Hopkins so *had* to find out the exact terms of the will and confirm where it was, otherwise the money would go to Daddy anyway, unless Lulu put in a claim for Fred. And paternity wouldn't be easy to prove (more than a tad on the posthumous side).

Coffee was nearly done, might as well have a cup herself, though she'd water hers down, unofficially. Suddenly, Bathsheba went goosey. That was *so* it – there was something official that made Jacob an executor. *I know a pawnbroker who will.* Angel wouldn't have left that to chance, even his behaviour wasn't that bizarre. This was going to be trickier than she'd anticipated. Any vague idea she'd had of seducing Jacob (not literally, natch) out of his commission was complicated if his poxy position was legal.

'There you are, Daddy.' Bathsheba sat on one of the armchairs. Daddy swallowed his coffee down, lit a cigar. 'So Lulu's coming over tomorrow, then?' she asked.

'Yeah. No doubt done up like a dog's dinner, so.'

'Well, she's like her auntie there, isn't she? Loves the flash.'

'Believe you me, girl, they ain't got a thing in common, them two.' Snorting. 'The aunt'd come out in her pelt, and shame the devil.'

'Lulu's more her father's daughter, is she?'

'Watch your fucking mouth.' Daddy raised the back of his hand to her, though she was too far away for him to smack.

'Sorry, I'm being silly. Suppose I'm a tad jealous.' She smiled at him.

'No, you ain't.' Balancing his cigar in the ashtray. 'Weren't for Lulu, our Angel might be here now. Do you know?'

'How do you work that one out, Dads?'

'Don't you ever fecking listen? Just like your mother, Dolly Daydream.' The man didn't know her at all, did he? 'Told you before, reckon he couldn't handle what Maggie Dawson bloody said to him.' Daddy leaned over to scratch his foot. 'You found it hard enough yourself. Lulu's all right, but she ain't no substitute. For him, that is.'

'No.' Anyone would think Angel had been some sort of

220

paragon. Go on, admit it, Daddy – he was a selfish pig, just like his father. No wonder Daddy had loved him so much.

'Ought to have one of them DNA tests.' He shook his head. 'Wonder what me grandson's like? She won't let me near him, love. Me own grandson, if she's not been feeding me shit. He like Angel? Couldn't tell from them blurry old photos she showed me.'

'Not the weeniest bit like.' This was new. Flash of panic. No way was Bathsheba going to let him get sentimental about Fred. Jesus, what if Fred's existence made Daddy get his mental act together? 'He's all Lu,' she insisted. Lifting one shoulder. 'Wouldn't surprise me if she didn't know *whose* he was. She did used to be a porn actress.'

'Yeah, there was talk of her being the British Lovelace,' he said. 'Not that she had what it took, was all hype.' Laughing. 'Now I got to meet the bloody boyfriend. She reckons he's a bit of class. That right?'

'You mean *Jacob*'s pitching up here as well?' Bathsheba so hadn't predicted this, for Jacob to come smarming round Daddy. She didn't want them on the same side, not with them both having a thing for poxy Angel. Sod, damn, what if Jacob waxed on about Fred?

'Met him, have you?' Daddy asked.

'He's all right.' Sound casual. 'Not the sharpest knife in the drawer. He's a pianist – only in horrible dives, though. Has to work in a shop, as well.' But Jacob *had* turned out to be useful in getting information across, maybe Bathsheba would find a way to use him in the Daddy–Maggie equation. 'Though guess what? He knew Angel, years ago,' she added.

'*What?*'

'Oh yeah.' She sipped her coffee. 'At Cambridge. Big mates, apparently.'

'And now he's with Lulu.' Daddy's face had closed down, as though someone had turned off the TV in his head. 'Bit funny, ain't it?'

'Mm, suppose.'

'Bloke what makes his living playing piano, who was Angel's mate . . . How long?'

'Three or four months? They got together shortly after Angel, well. After he died.'

'After he died. Right.' He pushed the ashtray away from him, pulled it close again. 'The boys know he knew him?'

'I've no idea.' Mustn't overdo it. 'Talking of the boys, Del hasn't been in work for days, according to Garry.' She crossed her legs. 'They're getting fed up with him.'

'That boy's a waste of it,' he replied.

'Constantine had to oversee last week's distribution himself.'

'Never thought we should of took on a Dawson.'

'Fed up with *Del*, Daddy.' Bloody nasty git.

'Ah.' Re-lighting his cigar. 'ISU's put another offer in,' he said. Unexpectedly. She tried to look as surprised by the information as she so was by the sharing. 'Just for the shops first off, and a better price. Stan told them to stick it, but Del weren't that sure.'

'What about you?'

'Stan represents me.' He shrugged. 'Garry see much of Maggie, since her accident?' Dear God, his brain was like one of those puzzle-book mazes these days, that curled round and round but always led you back to the same point. Angel.

'He's very busy,' she said. 'Hardly even sleeps.' That much was true, poor lamb.

'She was lucky that never done for her. Very lucky lady.' Daddy watched Bathsheba's face. She kept it still.

'Mm.' But she went that goosey she actually shuddered, the hairs on her arms standing up until she could see the roots needed doing. Was Daddy saying what she thought he was saying? He'd been having dinner with the prodigal Lulu that night (but then of course he wouldn't have done the deed himself). Bathsheba had so *known* it couldn't have been just a random piece of fortune.

'She wants to be more careful,' he added.

'Let's face it, most people do.' Carefully. She stood, picked up his coffee cup. 'Little refill?' she asked. Not waiting for an answer.

In the kitchen, on the dresser, was Mama's collection of plates. Delicate, hand-painted, nothing vulgar like the rubbish Daddy insisted on. For a poor immigrant woman, she'd had a real love of the beautiful. Though that was all she'd had, that and her dreams for her children. Dolly Daydream. Except admit it, she'd made a lot of them come true. Stan getting into UCL had been amazing enough to Mama, but of course, then bloody Angel had to be steered towards Cambridge. *He's nearly genius.* Sweet Jesus, those awful holidays to Halkidiki to visit their great aunt, every year the tourist hotels at Cassandra getting bigger (the girls in ever teenier bikinis), when in the poxy village everything stayed shabby and hopeless, and you never even saw a woman outside, except on Sundays. Bathsheba so wasn't going to get shut away like that, behind the dust and the scarves, knowing there were plenty of other things to be had just down the road. Was a bigger nightmare than the one she'd had all the time when she was really little – of getting a call from God saying she had a vocation to be a nun. Why those women let the even worse thing happen to them, she'd never know. If they were happy, then Bathsheba was a six-foot man.

She picked up one of the plates, held it to her cheek. Cold. Inanimate. Had to make certain Daddy didn't get too involved with Fred, had to keep the poison flowing. The two weapons that would really have helped her (face it), one was bloody dead, and the other she was deliberately sending madder. *Un*fair. *Unfair.* If it wasn't for Fred, maybe everything would have been sorted by this time, even Angel's will. *Linear structures are false.* That's what Angel said. But time had to go in a line, didn't it? If it didn't, she'd bloody well arrange not to be thirty next month, and Fred would never have been born.

'You grinding the fucking beans out there, or what? Want a bullet up your arse, B.' Mm, someone did, anyway, if things were going to move on.

'Coming, Daddy,' she called back. That plate didn't look exactly right when she replaced it. Maybe she hadn't put it quite straight.

Now Fred was gone, Lulu could look at it. Course, Jacob hadn't wanted to borrow it to her, but she had a bloody right to watch it on her own, to try and get her head round it. Been four days since that night, and Lulu was still having a job sorting out what she thought about what they'd done. It wasn't right, but she couldn't put her finger on precisely what was wrong. Wasn't just the brother thing, though that might have to do with it. *She*'d been the one to suggest watching the film, for some strange reason. *She*'d agreed to take her clothes off, let him do what he liked to her. There'd even been something exciting about being wanted that much, about an old love and a new one coming together, but she'd still had to fake her orgasm. Had felt it was nearly going to happen, even presumed for a couple of minutes it was, but it didn't, not precisely. Wasn't the same as faking it was as a rule, it was more like being back there, acting again. Yet she felt funny about what Jacob might of been getting off on – had a bit of it been Angel? But she couldn't of asked him, that wasn't the role she'd been cast for, she knew that much. If she wanted Jacob to stay her boyfriend, she had to be – what's the word? – passive, sexually speaking, even when she was appearing aggressive. Giving. From that point of view, he wasn't any different from any other man. From Angel.

Lulu tried to concentrate on the pictures, but they didn't seem to make sense at all tonight. Just lumps of flesh, ridiculous, a record of something that didn't really happen. Bits going in other bits like people were machines, not even getting her embarrassed for herself, where it seemed so distant. She'd thought the other night might of made it belong to her, but it hadn't changed a thing. Angel wasn't any more alive there than he was now. Could of been one of them foreign films, for all the sense she was getting out of it, except for she kept being brought up short seeing Lucinda Luscious looking so pretty. Why hadn't she known at the time she'd been a babe? But most of it . . . sort of sick making, if anything. How could anyone get off on this? Was as if she was peering in some stranger's bedroom window. Couldn't link it to what she'd felt a few nights back at all. Might just as well give up, stick it at the back of the toot drawer where it most probably belonged, get ready for Jacob's gig.

Thank Christ she'd been able to make Fred get over being squeamish about seeing Mags – wouldn't be so easy to get out on a Saturday night else, not with Jacob so sodding fussy about Fred being on his own. Fred'd kicked off, but for once Lulu had been firm with him, told him it was hardly Maggie's fault she'd been hurt, that she was much better now and he should see for himself, so he soon shut his noise. He was a good boy, really. Funny, after Angel had left, she'd started to hate being pregnant, resenting being kept prisoner by her own body for the sake of someone who hadn't even stayed around for the sentence. Yet soon as Fred was born, she knew she'd die for him. By the time he started school, she'd even begun to enjoy him. Babies drank your blood, but after they'd turned into people, the wounds had healed, and you forgot. Mostly. And yet, her baby came out of her being with her brother . . . *Stop* it. Had promised herself not to keep thinking about that.

She took herself off to the bathroom, went to the loo while her bath was running. Was she being a mug again, here? Maybe Jake was another one going to leave her with a head full of bad shit. What about the other night, when Jacob said he'd never much liked opera, and she'd told him Maggie and her always called it *bellyache music*. Evidently, his last ex said it was *screeching* – he thought that was sooo funny, a *perfect description*. But Lulu's was funnier, sharper, she knew that. He didn't seem to see it. Only a stupid thing, though it made her feel she'd never be clever enough in his eyes, not compared with the women he'd been with previous. Something else he had in common with Angel.

Turned off the taps so's she could flush the loo. Wasn't that much water in the bath, but she only had time for a quick splish anyway. Most likely his ex was one of them women who did the things Lulu had read about in Jacob's newspaper, like that pole dancing to keep fit. What did the paper call it? *Faux porn*, whatever that meant. But she did know they were playing at lives like hers, just to get a perfect body. Trying something on for size that they could leave behind in the gym. Though bet your sweet life their men got the benefit in the bedroom, and not just from their tight bums. No matter how clever or posh or rich or beautiful a woman was, she still had to keep her man happy. If you couldn't, it said loads about you, next to nothing about the man. But then Jacob had been dumped, not the other way round. Whoever the ex was, she must be dead picky.

Lulu ran the razor over her legs. Should get some more of that home wax stuff, though it was hard to let the hair grow long enough, if you were seeing a bloke. Used to get a profes-sional wax regular when she was acting. Bloody Christ, she'd looked so *young* on that video, almost like a different person. Even if Jacob's last girlfriend was really the same age as Lulu now, they'd split up well over a year ago, so the other woman would always be thirty-five in Jacob's head. That meant Lulu was already older than her, and would keep piling on the years and the pounds where the ex never would. That film was like competing with herself, and all. She couldn't win. Then again, how many other women could keep hold of the younger version of themselves, offer that to their boyfriends as well as what they had on offer now? Maybe Lulu should think herself lucky.

A mirror. That's it. She'd save up, buy one of them big mirrors from the Portobello Road. She'd noticed that reflec-tions of having sex were sort of triggers for men who got off on porn, a way of avoiding getting too intimate, too real. Funny, she hadn't seen Jacob as a *Me* man, and in loads of ways he wasn't. He did being close. But anyone she'd ever heard talk about porn mostly used *I* not *We*, course they did, and the trick was to get the *We* back by taking advantage of what made the *I* tick. End of the day, wasn't as if he was into all porn, this was about his relationship with one film, and least it did involve her.

Anyway, he loved her, he'd said so. Twice. And he was coming to meet Mickey McGowan tomorrow. Course, she knew she had Brownie points with Jacob for fucking in front of the video, but he wouldn't of agreed just for that. Truth was, he wanted to please her, and that felt nice. Drying herself off on a towel that really should of been in the wash, Lulu had a big think about what to wear down the club tonight, what colour she should do her nails. He was fond of traditional red. From now on, she'd make sure she always looked her best when they were together. Love deserved special treatment.

He was looking as smart as he could when his wardrobe mostly comprised jeans and tee-shirts, plus one good suit and a couple of shirts for weddings, funerals, bar mitzvahs, particular kinds of gigs. Luckily, he'd found these cords in his wardrobe, and Lulu had helped him buy this casual shirt; nothing he could do about his trainers, it was these or his stupidly formal shoes, couldn't afford to spend more money on something he'd never wear again. Did have his hair trimmed meantime, though, made sure his shave was extra close. Weird, never made this sort of effort when he'd met Susie's family, but then her father was a Labour councillor, rather than a vice merchant who'd fathered both of Fred's parents. Rather than a man who, quite possibly, Jacob legally owed a hell of a lot of money. Yet what contribution had Mickey McGowan made to Lulu's growing up? You could call it back pay, even debt collection. *Or you could call it theft, Jakey. Just semantics, remember?* Crap, wasn't even Angel's name on that cheque; maybe semantic fields *were* significant.

Richmond wasn't so very different from where Jacob had grown up, of course. Surrey seemed to him full of places without an identity, with nothing straightforwardly to tell you where you'd come from, although Guildford did at least have those great hills, views, the world's ugliest cathedral that from the outside was more tool box than chocolate box. As the train pulled out of Clapham Junction, Jacob squeezed Lu's hand. Would Angel's dad recognize him from graduation? Not that Jacob could do anything about it, but he'd prefer not to be linked to Angel: that, Jacob felt might look inexplicable, appearing again after twenty years. *This is my best mate, Jacob Fox. He's got to go and see to his parents now.* Hardly a memorable meeting. It was so vivid to Jacob only because of that *best mate*, the first and last time Angel had ever called him that. Had made his day more than his high 2.1, almost negating Angel's unearned First. God, how naïve had Jacob been? Angel doling out sweeties, knowing exactly how few to keep your loyalty. *Didn't need many for you, did I, best mate?* Not then, maybe, but that cheque could buy a hell of a lot of sweets.

'The house is dead posh, Jake,' Lulu said.

'Sure I'll cope.' He smiled. 'Your hair looks really nice, up like that.'

'So you said – I told you it's a French pleat, remember? Nervous, are you?'

'Must be, if I'm repeating myself.' Kissing her fingertips. Looking in the mirror this morning, there had been more lines than ever round his mouth; he was observably turning into a middle-aged, careworn neurotic. So many times, he'd been on the verge of showing Angel's postcard to Lu, of asking her if she thought Garry really could have supplied Angel, but he'd resisted. This far. Still couldn't think clearly about it: was as if he had a barbed wire fence in his head, stopping him from going over into that territory without serious difficulty.

Jacob held her hand in both of his on the taxi ride out to the house; her palm was sticky, he could hear her breathing too fast. When she got out of the cab, he noticed dark patches had appeared under the arms of her pretty blue dress. She must have realized, because she slipped her jacket on before walking up the path. God, this would be only the third time she'd knowingly seen her father, no wonder she was wound up.

'Pleased to meet you.' Mickey McGowan had lost the little hair he'd had when Jacob had last seen him, and his face seemed to have melted; maybe it was Jacob having more knowledge than he'd had then, but his eyes looked harder. A mystery, how the good-looking McGowans had come from this man's seed. 'Come in, will we have a little drink to celebrate?' His limp was more pronounced than Jacob remembered, too. Weird, that Mickey hadn't shaken Jacob's hand or kissed Lulu, yet his manner was comparatively friendly enough. Or maybe he was assuming a cordiality he didn't really feel.

There was a champagne bucket in the lounge. Sure he had enough gilt in here? But at least there were several marble ashtrays, one of which had a couple of cigar butts in it; Jacob pulled out his Gitanes.

'Sit down, both. You like bubbly, mate?'

'Sure.' Easing himself gingerly into one of the soft leather sofas.

'Know my little Lulu does,' Mickey said. 'We had it at dinner, didn't we, love?' Maybe he simply couldn't see his daughter. She was a lot of things, but *little* wasn't one of them. 'How's Maggie getting on?'

'Oh, she's much better, thanks,' Lulu told him. He wasn't looking at her.

'Good to hear. You're a musician, then, Jacob?'

'I am, yeah.'

'Why you still playing shit clubs? Not good enough or not hungry enough?'

'Mickey!' Lulu sounded horrified. Jacob had almost heard Angel in those words.

'Not hungry enough,' he admitted. Taking his glass of champagne, lighting a cigarette. Susie had banged on about his lack of ambition; hoped Mickey wasn't going to start down that path, might infect Lu.

'Private school, university?' Was obvious he had no recollection of having met Jacob before, anyway.

'He went to Cambridge . . . with Angel,' said Lulu. Jacob slightly wished she hadn't, but you couldn't censor people.

'Ah.' Mickey sat on the other sofa, next to her. 'Another one who weren't hungry enough, with less bloody excuse.' You couldn't tell what he was feeling from his voice; somehow, Jacob didn't think it was surprise. Then why pretend not to know? Screw it, that was strange. 'Still, his mother wanted him to go there, set her heart on it, do you know?' Mickey told them. The Irish expressions sat oddly in that Cockney accent, rendering both weirdly false. Untrustworthy. 'Least me boy done that for her, and I had a little weep at his graduation, don't mind telling you. Well, cheers. Down the hatch.' He emptied his glass.

'Brought another picture of Fred,' Lulu said, fishing in her bag. 'It's only from the other week. Jake took it.' She passed over the photograph of Fred posing with a bar chord; he'd insisted on wearing his baseball cap, *I've run out of gel, my hair'll look pants, all sticking up,* and refused to smile, eyes as mean and moody as a twelve-year-old's could get. Mickey glanced at it, laid it face-down on the nearest coffee table.

'Getting big,' he said. 'Plays guitar then, does he? You teaching him, Jacob?'

'I am, yeah. He's already pretty good.' Drawing on his cigarette, he gestured to the photo. 'Like Angel there, isn't he?' What had possessed him to say that? Lulu was blushing, but Mickey's face didn't change.

'The very image,' he said. Softly. 'Anyone need another drink? Sure, it's bloody Sunday, no one should work on the Lord's day, as me missus – God rest her – used to say. Less you got to, Jacob? At a *club*?'

'Not tonight, no.' Probably not a good time to mention it wasn't Jacob's *Shabbat*.

'Right then, we'll get locked.' Mickey refilled their glasses, lit a cigar. 'You miss him, mate?' he asked. Jacob swallowed his mouthful the wrong way, had to put out his cigarette to cover his fight for breath. Mickey wasn't talking about Fred, that was for sure.

'Every day,' Jacob said at last. Shit, maybe the bloke knew about the money; keeping Angel in the frame might be a trap.

'Me and all.' Mickey chewed his cigar. 'He was the best of them. And the bloody worst, don't get me wrong, mate. I knew me son.'

'Wish Fred had known him,' Lulu put in. But Mickey ignored her.

'You was good mates, that right?' he said to Jacob.

'At one time, the best.' He did know. He *must*.

'Closed mouthed, that boy was. Liked to keep all the bits of his life separate.'

'Sure.' Jacob had a lump in his throat; the man's eyes might be empty, but he was suffering meantime, this, anyone could see. Or maybe he was faking, lulling Jacob into a false sense of security.

'Got that from me, he did.' Mickey nodded. 'But when it comes down to it, can't be done. Everything catches up with you in the end, don't it, Lulu love? God help us.'

'Well, precisely,' she said. Still pink in the face.

'Want a real drink, boy?' Again with Angel's voice.

'Brandy, thanks.' No need to ask whether he had any; you could probably say you wanted Finnish vodka with freshly squeezed kiwi fruit and a twist of organic lemon, and Mickey McGowan wouldn't blink. You could even ask for absinthe.

'I'll stick with the champagne, please,' Lulu said. 'If there's any more.'

Mickey went over to the vast wooden cabinet, opened it to reveal several rows of bottles and a small fridge. Angel certainly hadn't inherited his taste from his father. But the whiskey Mickey poured for himself was Black Bush, Lu's champagne a Krug, the brandy Remy Martin; three hundred thou was probably loose change to him.

'*He* was too fond of the hard stuff,' Mickey said, handing Jacob his drink.

'For sure.' Jacob smiled, raised his glass.

'Didn't think he'd die like that, though. Thought he had more nous, do you know?'

'Excuse me, d'you mind if I use your toilet? I remember where it is.' Lulu put her drink down, got to her feet. Jacob wanted to tell her that her dress was scrunched up, but obviously he couldn't. She moved out of the room more slowly than she usually did, giving the coffee tables a wide berth.

'Does she not like talking about him?' Mickey asked.

'No, she does. He's part of our lives.' Trying not to look conscious.

'But not about his death.' A dull-eyed grin. '*I* like talking about it.'

'Sorry?' Oh God, here it comes.

'Going to find out why, and who was responsible, boy.' As though he were talking about a lost shoe. 'And when I do . . . ' Pointing to his own chest, mad-eyed.

Then suddenly, Jacob saw: this wasn't about the money, it was about the way Angel had died. *Dad reckons he can fucking retain the name and all th'addition to a king, mate.* Though this bloke was such a weird mixture of barely suppressed viciousness and open sentimentality, Jacob could totally believe someone was going to suffer. Maybe here was a possibility of finding the truth about Garry. But screw it, Garry was practically Lulu's brother. And Angel *was* her brother; who did Mickey blame for the incest? Certainly wasn't warm to his *little Lulu*, no doubt would far rather it were she who'd been killed. Was starting to seem as though there wasn't a great deal of difference between being dead and being alive, it was more a case of how you got there, how lives and deaths were constructed. From that point of view, maybe Angel *should* be looked at as a suicide, one planned to incriminate Garry; an act of violence, aggression. Confused, Jacob stared into his brandy.

'If I hear anything, I'll let you know,' he said.

*   *   *

Torn heart. Maggie picked it off the table where Fred'd left it, fingered the stiff paper. Sort of thing what she would of suspected Clifford'd send, if he'd still been here. But he hadn't sent it, had he. Clifford'd died for being too fond, not for nothing worse. How horrible was that? For Garry and all. Though you could say Clifford'd brung it on hisself, none of her other men'd ever got all silly over her. Even when she'd packed it up, there'd been a couple of tries at getting her to change her mind, like with Welsh Adrian's bribe that he'd pay to get that new bridge for her teeth, but nothing serious. No way would any of them of bothered to beat her up over it – and Clifford would of gone straight to the Old Bill if any of them had. Could see that now. Felt like going round to Garry's with this, but still hadn't been no further than the bins since the attack. Perhaps she was getting that whatsname. That phobia thing where you couldn't leave the house. See about it on one of them talk shows they had in the afternoons. Mummy's friend Mrs Twidle had that once, unless Maggie was very much mistaken, but they didn't have a name for it then so she'd had to get better.

Anyway, couldn't of took it to Garry, even if she could of got out. Flaming hell, every time she see him, he'd got more worse. His eyes never seemed still, glance bouncing from one thing to another till it made you dizzy. Top lip was a mass of permanent cold sores now, right up to his nose, all cracked, yellowy, flecked with blood. Like some of the kids round Maggie's way when she'd been a little girl. Even his crop needed doing, you'd of thought Bathsheba would of seen to that. Made Maggie wild, him letting hisself fall apart. He should be a man about it. Even though he'd done it for nothing, evidently.

Felt restless. Not just from what'd happened though, to her or to Clifford or to Garry. Maggie'd felt less normal in general since she'd laid herself off – maybe the beating'd made her go funny in the head. Mind, you wasn't safe even in your own home. You got torn paper hearts delivered by courier. Or you got wigs, kittens, nothings. And pain, of course. Worry, heartbreak, too many flipping regrets.

Should never of let Fred go home after Sunday dinner, not with Lu and Jacob out till eightish tonight, but it'd been doing her head in, him not looking her in the eye since he'd got here yesterday evening. Attack must be still making him feel funny round her. Getting that heart'd been her last straw – what if she was putting him in danger? Had to be honest, with the men around nothing held the same amount of threat. She went down her new bag for her mobile. Bli, only one pip on it – was a time when she'd never of let the charge get that low. Sat looking at it in her hand. Rubbed the display, what'd gone smeary. Really should get that charged up, you know. Didn't do to let things slide.

Jacob couldn't help himself, he had to put both arms round her while she was looking for her key, pressed himself into her back, her arse.

'Do you think Fred's back from Maggie's yet?' he asked.

'Meeting my bloody father turn you on, did it?' But she was giggling. Clearly, she loved champagne. Money could buy a lot of that kind of love.

'Come on, let's get inside.'

'Give us a chance.' Fumbling a little as she put the key in the lock. The hall light was on, bollocks, Fred *must* be home. Still, Jacob squeezed her bum as they went through to the lounge. Perhaps Fred would go early to bed. 'Oh, Jesus, state of this place.' Lulu swept her arm out, knocking a video off the top of the television. Looked as though every cassette had been pulled from the cabinet shelves, involved in some complicated card-like trick, boxes and films everywhere. Couldn't be a burglary, could it?

'Maybe he's had some mates round for a video fest,' Jacob said. Were all boys this messy? Jacob didn't remember being like that; his mother would never have allowed it.

'Frigging hell, Jake – what if this is like the, you know. The kitten.'

'It isn't.' But how was he meant to be sure?

234

'Fred!' Lu went through to his bedroom. Two seconds later, she was back. 'He's not here,' she said.

'Still at Maggie's?'

'Then how'd them videos get all over the . . . oh shit, Jake. *Shit.*' She pointed to the table. A cassette with all its tape hanging out, torn. Lulu picked it up, examined it, passed it over to Jacob, her expression appalled. 'That's me,' she said. Whispered.

'You?' It couldn't be . . . She wouldn't have been so casual as to leave it where Fred could find it, would she? He turned it over, his fingers getting tangled in the loose tape. Read the label: *Last.* God, it was, it was the Angel video, for sure.

'How the *hell* did he get hold of this? Lu?'

'It was in the toot drawer. He never looks in there.'

'Well, this time he did.' Jacob was close to hyperventilating with anger.

'But I presumed . . . I never meant–'

'Tough shit, doesn't matter what you bloody meant.' He waved the destroyed film under her nose. 'Look at this, Lulu. Look at it. How do you think he must be feeling? He was watching his own fucking *conception*, for God's sake.'

'He doesn't know that.' Watery.

'Right, that makes it okay then.' Throwing the video on to the settee. 'Where would he have gone?'

'Maggie's, I suppose.' She rubbed her eyes. 'What we going to do?'

'Suggest you ring her, *dear*.' Jacob sat on one of the armchairs, lit a cigarette. 'Go on, what are you waiting for?'

'You sound so . . . cold,' she said. He eyed her. Blotchy, even her nose was red, but the tears hadn't fallen yet. Her hair was escaping from that stupid French pleat thing; if she kept tugging at it like that, she'd only make it worse. Bloody hell, why had she been so careless? Meantime, she'd wrecked everything: the cosy family life they'd been building, any chance of telling Fred who Angel was, even the fucking film. *You promised you'd look out for my boy.*

Never could see anything through, could you? Useless cunt.
Everything.

'Believe me, cold is the last thing I feel,' he told her. 'Just ring Maggie.'

'Right.' Nodding, she went over to the phone. She held it to her ear for a couple of minutes. 'Machine's not on, that's funny,' Lulu said. 'But Maggie's not left the house in over three weeks, far as I know.'

'Mobile?'

'We don't have that number. Was just for . . . work.'

'One of us better get round there, then.' Jacob put out his cigarette, got to his feet. 'I'll go, you ring his mates. Let me take your mobile, so you can tell me if he turns up.'

'Jake . . . ' Lu moved closer. 'What if something's happened to him?'

'Something *has*.' But seeing her appalled face, suddenly he felt a bastard. Relented. 'He'll be okay, baby. He's had a big shock, probably wants to be on his own for a bit.'

'I love him so much,' she said. Touching his arm.

'Know you do. Come on, get your address book out. I'll be quick as I can.'

'Don't lose the mobile, Fred knows my number.'

'Why would I lose it?' Slipping it into his pocket. 'And yeah, I do know how it works, thanks.'

'Please say we'll find him, Jacob.' Pulling at her pleat again.

'We'll find him,' he repeated. Kissing her forehead. But that might be another promise he wasn't going to be able to keep.

Chapter Twelve

'Keep your bleeding hair on.'

'It's me, Nan!'

'Heard you the first twenty times. I'm coming.'

Bolts being pulled back went right through his teeth. Door opened, and she was stood there in her dressing gown though it wasn't late, not even half-seven yet, and she reeked of perfume. She sort of smiled, but she never stood aside to let him come in.

'Want to talk to you,' he said.

'Can't it wait, Fred? Got company, love.'

'But you're not dressed.' Fred wiped his nose on his sleeve. Why didn't she want him in there? She'd let him make the custard dinnertime, though afterwards was blatant she'd wanted him to go home. He hadn't given a shit then. 'It's important, Nan,' he added.

'Face like a smacked bum.' Mixture of worried and pissed off. 'You been crying?' She put her fingers on his cheek. 'Give us a minute,' she said. 'Wait there.' And shut the door in his face. Fred couldn't believe it, but looking at that lump of wood, all closed and . . . definite . . . Selfish cow, she could see he was way upset? He hadn't said anything about that rank picture of her, just put it straight back, but might as well of told *News at Ten*. She wouldn't care. Nan was just some old tart, who had *company* when she was in her dressing gown. People her age shouldn't be having sex, but bet that's what she'd been doing. Ever since Fred could remember, she'd had *men friends*, though she must be well embarrassed of them, you never got to meet any properly. Shit, she was scutters, a total skank, with her scraggy old neck and her false hair and her knee bulging out of that knotty leg. She most probably knew all about what Fred'd seen tonight, and thought it was fine. It wasn't.

The door opened again, and some greasy old bloke ran out, pushing past Fred on his way to the stairs. Fred could see the top of his head as he went down, all oiled hair with a big bald patch in the middle, like he was wearing an onion ring. Was *that* saddo Nan's new boyfriend? She must be desperate, it was worse than that dead Dwarf Man, even. Nan reappeared then – was her turn not to look Fred in the face.

'Do them bolts behind you for me, love.' Sounding right awkward. Good job.

He followed her down the hall, into the living room. She sat on the settee, lit a bloody fag, patted the cushion. But Fred went over to the armchair.

'Why doesn't anyone tell me stuff?' he said. Had promised in his head he'd get straight to the point, but when it came to it, wasn't that easy.

'What you on about? Fancy a little Coke?'

'No. What I want is to know why this family isn't normal.' Felt his eyes filling up again. He squeezed them tight shut for a sec, stop the tears coming.

'Course we're normal.' Fiddling with her stupid wig.

'Yeah, well what'd be normal for us would be the worst thing in the world for normal people.'

'What's happened, my love?' Soft. Making out like she cared.

'I . . . ' Fred looked at his hands. All of a sudden, they seemed too big for his body. He pulled his thumb back so's it touched his wrist, held it there till it hurt.

'Take your time,' said Nan.

He'd been well bored, though hard to imagine that at the minute. Give anything to be fucking bored now. He'd got home from here before five, had ages till Mum and Jake reckoned they'd be back. Jake had brought him over the book version of *Lord of the Rings* after Fred talked about the film, but he

238

couldn't get into it written down – *The Hobbit* was way better. Could of gone and knocked for someone, though it was getting on for teatime, and you never knew if people's nans were visiting of a Sunday? Fed up of his computer games, he needed PlayStation 2 . . . no chance. Nothing on telly, cos Mum was too tight to go digital. And everyone had a DVD except them.

'Was Mum,' he said. 'In a video. Wrong sort of video.' Forcing her with his eyes to look right back at him. Hers full of something Fred didn't get.

'Oh, Fred.' See, was *obvious* Nan knew straight away what Fred meant. Her face was collapsed in, her mouth had stayed open after the words had come out. 'Flaming hell, I'm so sorry,' she added.

'She's the one should be sorry. Was . . . How come you *let* her?'

'Your mum always know what you're up to?' Snappy.

'*I'm* not up to stuff like that.' Right, so Nan was putting all the blame on Mum. Made Fred feel really churny in his guts.

'Lovey, that was a long time ago,' Nan said.

'Not for me, it wasn't.'

'No.' Nan put out her fag, come over to him. Sat on the arm of his chair, but didn't try and touch him. Good. He'd of legged it out of here. 'What happened?' she asked.

Trouble was, seen all their bought videos a million times, and the stuff they'd recorded off the telly they never stuck labels on. That's it, play a few minutes of every tape, then write on them what the film is. Something to do, in it. So he pulls all the boxes off the shelf, must be least thirty of them, sticks the first one in the machine. What shitty crap's this? One of Mum's, *Terms of Endearment*. Right, where's the label thing? Course, no one's stuck it to the tape, and it's not loose in the box. Tips out a couple of the other videos – exactly the same. Why's Mum have to be so rubbish, chucking out useful stuff? But then, Fred never kept labels neither, can't really have a pop. Maybe she's put a few away somewhere. On the off-chance, Fred goes over to the toot drawer, has a rummage.

Nope, but there's another video. This one's labelled – *Last*. Nice one, very useful. Not Mum's handwriting, though. Maybe it's Jake's. Might be all right, then.

'I found it,' he said. 'And . . . Uncle Garry was on there, and some bloke who looked like Del McGowan, and . . . she's a dirty *whore*.' He sniffed, hard, so's the tears went back up his nose. 'I'm thick, Nana. When it started, I thought she must of been an actress once. Thought that was wicked, but I didn't know why she never said. Now I know.'

'Uncle Garry?' That funny look back in her eyes. 'You sure?'

'I'm not lying, you *know* I'm not.' Rubbing his forehead.

'Your Uncle *Garry*?' Yeah, like she didn't know.

'Say B'd seen it? What'd Garry do then?' If B left, Fred would never forgive any of them. 'Or say Jacob did, he'd of packed Mum in straight away. Serve her right, disgusting cow. She's not my mum, she's a slag.'

'That's enough of that, Fred. Grown ups sometimes do things—'

'Stop it!' Fred jumped out the chair, nearly knocking Nan flying. 'You . . . everyone . . . I'm not a kid. Mum was in a dirty film with Uncle Garry. You can't make that all right, yeah? You can't, Nan.'

'No, I can't.' She stood up, went to get her fags. 'But unless I'm very much mistaken, your mummy would go back and change it, if she could. You'll see that one day.'

'Yeah, right, when I'm grown up like you lot.' Fred felt his head was going to burst open. 'You're *all* fucking minging.'

'Pack it in this instant, you don't want a backhander.' But was like she'd read about being cross in the dictionary, was trying it out. 'Won't have language, you know that.'

'Words don't matter, Nan.' If she tried to turn this round on him, he'd never come back here, never. He'd run off some-where, none of them would ever see him again. 'Who was that man, the one that left just now?' he asked. 'Why'd you pose for some painting?'

'I *never* did.' Nan shook her head so hard, you'd think her wig would of went crooked. She tugged at it.

'What's Uncle Garry have in them shops, and, and in the Holly Blue? Not words.'

'So sharp you'll cut your bleeding self.'

'Everyone in this family's a perve.'

'Don't be so silly.' Yeah, trying to make it all ordinary. Small.

'Silly?' Fred nearly laughed. 'Silly's when . . . when you muck about.'

'Yeah, course. Sorry.' Her voice all tight. 'What d'you want me to say?'

'Nothing.' Wanted her to say it wasn't true, none of it, and that Mum was just a mum, Nan was just a nan, Uncle Garry hadn't done dirty stuff with Mum, nothing was shitty, it was all gravy. But she couldn't, could she? Wasn't one person in his family he could go to, who didn't have to do with crap. Except for Bathsheba, and he couldn't go to her, cos then she'd be upset. Fred wished they were all dead.

Great, that was probably Nan's *company* back again. But might be Mum, come looking for him. Then he heard Jacob call through, saying he was on his own. Shit, Fred left that ripped up tape in the living room, Jake was bound to of seen it. And if he sussed it, that could mean he'd go away, and there'd be no one normal. Somehow, Fred would have to fix things. But like they kept telling him, he wasn't a grown up. Was too hard.

'What you want me to do about the door?' asked Nan.

'Get it,' he said. Whatever happened, couldn't be worse than what already had. Nan's face said she thought so and all.

Jacob bent to kiss Maggie on the cheek. One look at her face told him Fred was here, and had said something; this, he'd been expecting but somehow still trying to tell himself wasn't that likely.

'How is he?' he whispered.

'Not so clever.' She gazed up at him, her eyes searching his.

241

Jacob wanted to tell her it was all right, he knew everything, but until he was totally certain how much she knew, he had to keep schtum. Not as if Jacob was sure how much of the film Fred had got through.

'Let me see him, Maggie.' He touched her shoulder. 'It's okay.' Then, in her ear again, 'Ring Lu, let her know he's safe.' Pressing Lulu's mobile into Maggie's hand.

'She's the last person I want to talk to. Give her murders.'

'Don't, Maggie. She needs to know Fred's safe.'

Fred was sitting on the edge of a chair, picking at a hang-nail. He didn't raise his head as Jacob came into the room.

'So this is where you've got to,' Jacob said. He moved slowly towards the boy, rested his hand on Fred's double crown. 'You want to tell me about it?' *Get you, Mitzvah. Been looking in the child psychology section at work, have you?*

'It's nothing.' Fred sucked at a drop of blood on his finger.

'Sure.' He could hear Maggie in another room; she must be speaking to Lulu.

'It's not.'

'I've been home, Fred, to your flat. I saw, mate. What you did to that film.' Squeezing between the crowd of furniture, Jacob knelt by the side of Fred's chair. 'You must have hated it.' Cautious. After all, Fred might just have watched the opening scenes, Lu flashing her knickers as she made a cup of tea alone.

'You know about it?' Fred looked up. 'You and all? Jake?' His expression gutted, his feelings lying bloody in Jacob's hands. For a second, Jacob wanted to deny it. Or tell Fred how gutted *he'd* been to have the film destroyed. Shit, or maybe he could make everything all right by producing his bank statement, saying that the man Fred might have seen fucking his mother was actually his father, who'd provided for him. But nothing was going to turn Jacob into the hero in Fred's accusing eyes. Not even the truth.

'I love your mum,' Jacob told him. *You do, do you?* 'What's important to me is what she does now, not when she was a very young girl.'

242

'With my *uncle.*'

'She regrets it, you must know that.' His stomach hollow. Bollocks, Fred had definitely watched more than the first scenes, then. Yet had he got as far as the sex? Bloody Dawsons everywhere Jacob turned; none of this would be quite so bad without Garry's involvement. Deviant bastard.

'Yeah, well, right, she didn't have to keep the thing, did she?'

'No.' *This how you look after my boy? Nice one.* Oh God, it was mostly Jacob's fault; he'd been blaming Lulu for leaving the video where Fred could find it, yet she hadn't had a copy in the place for years. 'But there might be a good reason,' he added.

'People always say that.' Shaking his head. 'She had it off with *two* men at the same time, and one was my *uncle.*' Spit flecking out of his mouth as he spoke.

'Don't be too harsh with her, Fred.' So he *had* seen the worst. Poor kid. 'Sure, it's dreadful for you, I know that, but she's not having a laugh over it, believe me.'

'You going to dump her?' Aggressive.

'No, course I'm not.' Jacob wasn't equipped to deal with this; nothing had prepared him for these past three months. He stared at his aging hands, the knuckles slightly swollen in fearful intimation of his father's rheumatism. Didn't even have a pension; how was he going to cope financially when he couldn't play any more? He'd acquired this pseudo-family, but without Angel's contribution, he couldn't provide for them. Even emotionally.

For a few minutes, neither of them said anything, though Fred reached out, tapped Jacob's arm, rhythmically, as if trying to communicate in Morse code. It was mind-numbingly irritating, oddly moving. Jacob found himself fitting a tune to it; pretty much went with 'Hound Dog'.

'Listen,' he managed at last. The tapping stopped. 'Your mum's not proud of what she did, but that's no reason for us to make her feel more ashamed, is it?'

243

Fred was crying now; screw that, what was Jacob meant to do? *Give him a hug, you uptight bastard.* As gently as he could, Jacob leaned forward and took Fred in his arms. He'd thought the boy might pull away, fight him, but Fred pushed his face into Jacob's chest. Jacob wasn't particularly strong, yet he felt if he squeezed too hard meantime, Fred's bones would snap. It was as though Jacob could sense them growing against his own bones, which were so much harder, denser, far more rigid than those in Fred's unformed body. Or maybe that was just sentimental crap. Either way, Jacob had a lump in his throat.

'Forgive her,' he said into Fred's hair. 'Soon as you can. You'll make yourself too unhappy if you don't.' *If he's anything like his daddy, forgiveness won't be his strong point, Mitz. What's he going to think when he knows you haven't handed over that money? Always knew you were dying to be a bad boy.* 'Forgive her, Fredniu. Just do it. For you.'

'Hello, darling.' Lulu was standing just inside the lounge door, Maggie behind her. Didn't the woman have any brain cells? Once Maggie had told her Fred was all right, she should have sat tight, waited for Jacob to bring him home. Instead, she was out of breath where, clearly, she hadn't stopped even to think. One of the many dangers of her living a five-minute run from her aunt. Fred struggled free from Jacob, turned to look at his mother.

'Go away,' he said. Still gulping. Snot trickling down his chin.

'I'm not going to do that.' But she didn't come any closer.

'I'll stick that kettle on,' said Maggie. Moving past Lu, throwing her a dirty look as she went, going through to the kitchen. Jacob got to his feet, massaging the dull ache in his back. He felt in his pocket for his cigarettes, went over to sit on the settee.

'I'm so sorry, Freddie.' Lulu's face was streaked with make-up, the French pleat now a loose snaky tangle. 'If I could chop my hand off to make it not of happened, I would.' Blowing her nose on a tissue.

244

'Yeah, right.'

'I would.' Scratching her head, the tangles tinted maroon with sweat. 'Doesn't–'

'Feel like I hate you, Mum.' Barely above a whisper.

'You must do.' Taking baby steps nearer to him. Jacob drew on his cigarette; felt he wouldn't be able to get a breath without that help. 'Hate myself, if that's any consolation,' she went on. Scrunching the tissue into a ball, passing it from one hand to the other. 'Christ, I love you more than anything in this world.' Running a finger over her lips. 'My lovely lump of love. Remember I used to call you that, when you were little? And sing to you? Hours and hours you'd have me up of a night–'

'Why'd you have to keep it?'

'Don't know.' She was at Fred's chair now; pushing one of the little tables out of the way, she sat on the floor in front of her son. *My son. Tell him why that video was kept, Jakey. Tell him who I am. Who I was. Because you love me.* 'See much, did you?'

'Too much.' Screwing up his face. Wiping his nose on the back of his hand. 'How come you could do it, Mum?'

'Not the same person I was back then, chicken. Didn't have you, for a start off.'

'Why'd you bother?' Fred muttered. 'Forgot the pill?'

'Don't *ever* presume you were an accident.' Firm. Maybe she was stronger than Jacob had thought. 'You were wanted so, so desperately. Planned. Really and truly.'

'He needs to know,' Jacob said. 'About Angel.'

'*No.*' Lulu turned to look at him. 'Not now.'

'Might make things better.'

'It won't.'

'Who's Angel?' Fred asked. 'B's brother? The one who died?' He clicked his fingers. 'That's the one what looked like Del, isn't it? In the . . . '

'It is, yeah,' said Jacob.

'This isn't your business, Jake.' Lu shook her head at him.

'Maybe not, but it's Fred's.' Maggie had brought through a

tray of tea. 'Sorry, Lu, but it's too flipping late for noes. I'd like to hear this and all.'

'She's right.' Jacob's eyes met Maggie's; she gave him a sad smile. Lulu must feel they were ganging up on her, but what choice was there?

'Well, precisely,' Lulu said. 'Like she told me about my . . . about Mickey McGowan, know what I'm saying?'

'You've all forgot I'm here.' Fred thumped the arm of the chair. 'Remember me?'

'Since when d'you know about McGowan?' Maggie put the tray on a table, her face stricken. Well, that answered any lingering doubt whether Garry was right that she'd been aware of Lu's paternity. Jacob didn't have any energy to waste on pity for Maggie. 'Mind, not the only one been keeping secrets, am I, madam?' Maggie added. Defiantly. Tugging at the bottom of her hair.

'If no one tells me what's happening, I'm off.' Fred stood up.

'That video was private,' Jacob said. 'Special.' *Go on, out with it*. 'Angel was your mum's boyfriend, ages back.'

'Fiancé,' corrected Lulu. Sounding resigned.

'What about Uncle Garry?'

'Yeah,' said Maggie. Under her breath.

'That was just . . . a mistake.' Lulu got to her feet as well, touched Fred's side. 'Sort of thing that happens when you're young and stupid, for some *very* strange reason.'

'Tell him,' Maggie insisted. 'Don't repeat all them mistakes I made. Or yourn, come to that.' Sitting beside Jacob. He put out his cigarette.

'You want me to explain?' he asked.

'No, I bloody don't.' Lulu crossed her arms. Licked her lips. 'Angel . . . Fred, darling, he was your dad.'

Fred stared at her. Then he looked from Maggie to Jacob.

'Going home,' he said.

Bathsheba had nearly invited Jacob to the flat, but she didn't want to take the risk of being interrupted by Garry. Wasn't

246

just that she was working on a need-to-know basis, it was more that Garry's behaviour had become erratic to the point of (let's face it) weirdness. That so wouldn't help her case. She made her way from the street and carefully down the stairs, nodding to the man who sat guarding the restaurant door. Tad anxious, truthfully. Had to keep reminding herself Stephen Hopkins was a 100 per cent sure now there was that solicitor involved (though why he seemed upset about that, she didn't have a clue). Yet seeing Angel's assets had been frozen, there was no guarantee that Jacob had got his paws on the money, even Hopkins claimed still to be clarifying that. No doubt the legal was holding out for a bigger bung. Though fancy him being actually a cousin of Clifford Black (of all people). Bizarre. But that was another reason not to want Garry around at this meeting. Sweet Jesus, Jacob *better* have had the nous to have moved quickly enough. Hoped Garry was all right, at home alone. Maybe he'd manage some of the tuna salad she'd left for him.

This place was so not her, though the portions were grossly huge which Jacob (being a healthy man) was bound to appreciate, and there was little chance of being overheard by anyone who mattered. Even though it was right in the middle of Soho, might as well be in the suburbs for all the notice the McGowans took of it. Mama would have liked it, though – masses of Greek peasant food. She'd have been comfy here yet *desperate* for her children to find it more than a tad unsophisticated. Tragic.

There he was, over in the far corner. She'd have bet her ideal weight he'd make sure he arrived first, even though she was a few minutes early herself. Old-fashioned courtesy. Well, nothing wrong with that.

'Hello, sweetie.' Kissing him on the cheek. 'Have you ordered wine, yet?'

'Hi.' With the green chili he'd been eating, Jacob pointed to his half-full glass. 'Haven't asked for a bottle, didn't know what you'd want.'

'Let's go native, have a Retsina, if you can bear it,' she said.

'Sure.' Finishing his chili, Jacob lit a cigarette. He hunched over the little table, looking too large for the place. Wasn't taking his eyes off her. A teeny crushlette? That would make things a squillion per cent easier.

Although the tables were terribly close together, Bathsheba's calculations had been right (half past six on a Wednesday night, the restaurant was two-thirds empty). Damn, Jacob wanting a starter was a nuisance, though better in terms of prolonging the evening. Good thing all she'd had today was fruit tea and an apple.

'More you eat, more thin you get,' the waiter told them. Patting his massive stomach. Did he recommend the tara-masalata, and could she have another starter as a little main course? Her palms had gone clammy, but the waiter agreed, with a sad shake of his head. Theatre. Bathsheba could recognize a fellow performer at seventy paces.

'Okay, what's this about?' Jacob emptied his glass.

'Just thought it would be nice for us to get to know each other better,' she said.

'Crap.' He put out his cigarette. 'I've had a bloody dreadful week, don't start messing with my head now.'

'Fair enough.' Bloody hell, Jacob, steady on. Perhaps he believed he held a better hand than she did – after all, she'd have to offer to stitch up her own family in order to stop them stitching him up. It was so too early in the meal for this. Luckily, the Retsina arrived then, and the first course (nothing that appeared so quickly could be freshly prepared). 'You met my daddy,' she said. Taking a piece of pitta bread from the basket, smiling.

'As *Lulu*'s father. I did, yeah.' Cutting into his pastry, the spinach spewing on to his plate. 'That what you wanted to talk about?'

'Not really.' She dipped the bread into the taramasalata. 'Though it's relevant. Did he mention Angel?'

'Sure.' A withering glance. 'He didn't mention much else.'

'No, he wouldn't. Does Lulu like him?'

'You'd have to ask her,' he said. Once he'd swallowed his mouthful. Bet he made his mother proud. Except, probably, for his so-called job. 'But no, you'd never talk about him around Lu, course not. Don't really go for the direct approach, do you?'

'Help yourself to some of mine, if you fancy – there's masses of pitta.' She pushed the dip towards him. Why the bloody hell *should* she speak to Lulu about Daddy? Took more than some stray sperm to make a sister. 'It's pretty good.'

'No thanks.' Jacob grinned, nastily, his face creasing, making him seem at least five years older. 'I'm not here to share, Bathsheba. That's not a possibility. Not sure why I *am* here, as it happens.'

'Don't look like that, sweetie, it's nothing too sinister.' *Share.* No doubt he realized she'd invited him because of Angel's money. 'It's all right between you and Lulu, then?'

'Why wouldn't it be?'

'No reason.' She shrugged. 'Must be expensive, seeing her and Fred.'

'She never asks for anything. Nor does he.'

'That so doesn't mean they don't get anything though, does it?' Bathsheba nibbled at a piece of bread. 'Lulu works in a poxy shop, for goodness' sake, hardly got it to burn, darling. You must have to foot a lot of bills. Doubt Daddy's put his hand in his pocket.'

'Why don't you just tell me what you want?' Jacob finished his starter. 'I need to be in Camden by half-nine.'

'All right.' Bathsheba sipped her poxy wine. Yes, it was vile, but at least the taste was familiar, comforting. Would be strict about having just the one glass, though – muddled thinking was never an advantage. 'Angel left three hundred thousand pounds.' Mm, chance it. 'You're the nominal beneficiary and executor.' Keeping her tone even. 'But can't say I've noticed her living it up, not even a teeny bit. Does she know?'

'None of that's your fucking business.' His eyes furious. Clearly, she'd hit a nerve. If she kept hers, this could play out beautifully. After all, if he was holding out on poor Lulu, it would

249

look scandalous. 'That, I think you'll find's non-negotiable,' he added. When Bathsheba first met Jacob, she'd thought he was just a nice Jewish boy, not terribly worldly-wise, who'd always look after his woman. Perhaps she'd underestimated him.

'Everything all right for you?' The waiter tutted over the waste of taramasalata, but how could she be expected to eat with Jacob turning into Mr Angry before her very eyes? Though (damn it) that didn't stop them bringing her halumi cheese as though it were a proper main course, with masses of fat chips. Chips and cheese, were they mad? And Jacob had half a dead sheep on his plate. He started tucking in immediately, even his chewing looking angry. But at least he was still there. Bathsheba picked up her water glass.

'I'm sorry, darling, I put that badly,' she said. 'I'll start again.'

'Won't make any difference.'

'Oh, it might.' Bathsheba forced herself to eat a chip. 'My family doesn't know Angel transferred his shares in the business.' Bathsheba didn't trust Jacob not to pass on that Del did know now, was on the point of selling too. 'But it'll so come out,' she went on. 'Sooner rather than later. We're in October already, Angel died in May. What Daddy still calls the *divvies* are due the end of next month.' Another chip. 'When that happens, how's it going to stay secret? The Register of Members gets updated then, that's the list of the firm's directors, sweetie, and Angel will be missing off it. Believe me, the family will want to know where the money is. Remember, Daddy's officially the next of kin.' Half a piece of cheese. 'Two ways they might go. Either they'll contest the will, or . . . '

'Or what?'

'Don't think for one minute that Lulu being his biological daughter would make any sort of odds, Jacob.' Lowering her voice. 'Daddy plays by his own rules.'

'Fred's his grandson.' Jacob looked round as a boring little family came in.

'So?' Damn, if Jacob could see that danger, it must be a real one. 'He's managed without Fred for twelve years—'

250

'Thirteen years tomorrow. His birthday's tomorrow.'

'Right. And he can manage for the rest of his life.' If she had anything to do with it, he so would have to. Surely even a mother as lousy as Lulu wouldn't let a madman be around Fred. Bathsheba reached across the table, grabbed Jacob's wrist. 'An incestuous dynasty's not what he had in mind,' she said. 'Mickey McGowan . . . ' Letting him go. 'You must have seen he's not exactly . . . stable. Angel's death tipped him over the edge.'

'What are you after?'

'A cut.' For the time being. 'I can help you cover up the truth, Jacob. The solicitor Angel used . . . He's got connections with a close associate of mine.' She'd so suspected Clifford Black knew something. He'd apparently even pointed Angel *to* the cousin.

'What are you saying?' Concentrating on her face as if it had the answer to the world's problems (well, for her world's, it did).

'The legal's bent, sweetie. And no one except you, me, him and my associate know about the will. Making that part of the equation, we can fix this.'

'So where will your father think the money is?' He laughed.

'In Angel's veins.' That wiped the smile off his face.

'Say I did have it. How much would you want?'

'Half. I'm not greedy, but Garry and I—'

'Even if I did, I'd still have to think about it before I went with that.' Jacob pushed away his plate, although he had some meat left. 'For all I know, you and Garry might want to trap me, for your dad maybe.' Swallowing the rest of his glass of wine, he stood up. 'And for all you know, I might not have got it after all.' Smiling. 'I'm off,' he said. 'Meantime, I suppose dinner's on you? I'm skint.'

But that *think about it* was so an admission. Jacob had the money for certain, and (Bathsheba went goosey) it was almost as certain Lulu knew nothing about it. Attractive *and* tough. Lucky old Lulu – if she could manage to hold on to him. A man who'd take the candy out of the baby's mouth wasn't one who'd be first up the aisle. Or wherever Jews got married. It was enough to make Bathsheba ask to look at the dessert menu, almost enough to make her order something. When Jacob came back with his answer – and it was obvious what that answer would have to be – she'd celebrate with the stickiest pastry she could find.

Taking the cake out the box, setting it down on the kitchen table, Lulu had a sudden thought that it was too childish. Fred used to love dinosaurs, but maybe they weren't the thing for your thirteenth birthday. Jacob reckoned thirteen was a massive deal, to do with manhood; perhaps she should of thought more about that when she chose this sponge. Fred was hardly speaking to her since last week, hadn't even asked her any more about Angel, though she'd tried to bring him up. Well, no, not precisely that, but she'd made it clear their son was welcome to ask anything. This birthday was meant to be a new start, that's what she'd hoped – might well of ballsed it up, buying a purple dinosaur cake. Typical her, she always managed to ruin the best things in her life.

Twenty past two. Jacob should be here soon, said he'd leave the shop lunchtime if he could. Might as well open that bottle of wine ready. Have to go careful though, wouldn't want Fred to think she was drunk when he got in from school. Funny about Jacob. She'd of presumed Fred seeing that video would of put Jake off of anything like that, and he'd been seriously sad it was wrecked, properly sad, as if Lulu had hurt him, not pissed off. Then – incredibly – over the last few days had asked her to describe her other films. In detail. Shit, them films were the last thing she wanted to remember. He'd even got off on the story about her choking on one bloke's cock, and she'd meant that to be funny. There wasn't anything to desire about Lulu Dawson, only about Lucinda Luscious. And it was Luscious who'd hurt Fred. Jacob would be getting one of his mates round next, asking her to do a DP. Maybe two of his mates,

252

one for the bumhole, one for the other place, and he'd just watch.

That wasn't fair, she was being a bitch. Loads of blokes liked kinky stuff, wasn't as if he wanted her to do a sheep or something. Suppose she still felt so bad about Fred, she was looking for someone else to take it out on. Most probably why she was going all peculiar about anything to do with porn. How could she ever get Fred and McGowan to meet now? If they did, was bound to come out that her and Angel were . . . *related*, as Garry put it. *Lulu* couldn't get her head round that, leave alone a thirteen-year-old boy. Jesus, what must be going on in Fred's imagination? This could screw him up sexually for life. He'd be one of them sad cases, still living with their mums when they were middle-aged. Getting excited about the boobs on *Eurotrash*. Believing every flirty barmaid was in love with him. Flashing little girls. Stop it, don't go there. Fred would be okay, he'd just have to get on with it. Like they all had to. Have a glass of wine, calm down, that's it. Sit at the table, take five as Jake would say.

Bloody Christ, though if Jacob hadn't got obsessed with that film, she'd never of had it in the flat . . . Leave off, no point in going there, neither. End of the day, wasn't his fault she'd been so careless. She couldn't make out he was responsible for her son, not yet awhile. Least Fred was going to love his present from her and Jacob, he'd wanted PlayStation 2 for ages, much better than Jake's idea of a guitar, though it had skinted them both. Must say something, him chipping in for Fred – no bloke had done that before. And Maggie and Garry had got games for it, wouldn't be the cock-up that other console had been. Nice Indian takeaway, the bloody dinosaur, loads of Coke, even a bottle of sparkling wine for later that Fred could have a bit of. Be fine. Good, even.

Still couldn't get used to Jacob coming in with a key, though he'd had it all week. Lulu ran her hand through her hair, check she was tidy.

'Bloody hell, what's that?'

'Fred's birthday cake.'

'Well, it's certainly purple. Can't take that away from it.' Jacob bent to kiss her. 'You taste of wine,' he said. 'Pour me one, will you?'

'How'd last night go?' she asked. Getting up to fetch his drink.

'What do you mean?' A touch defensive. Had he been with a woman down the club, fancied a bit of strange or something? No, that was mental. Stop being paranoid.

'Your gig,' she said. 'All right, was it?'

'Sure, yeah. The usual.' He pulled out a chair, sat down. 'Fred talking to you, yet?' Lighting a fag.

'Not really.' She handed Jacob the ashtray. 'Said thanks for his card this morning, that's about it.' Sitting opposite him. 'I asked if he wanted me to talk Maggie into leaving the flat, get her to come over tonight. He just said, *Whatever*.'

'Is she coming?'

'No. Reckoned ordinarily she'd get Garry to bring her, but we're not sure Fred—'

'I can collect her, walk her here.'

'That's okay, thanks. Don't think she really wants to go outdoors yet.' Lulu sipped her wine. Wished Maggie would say something proper about Garry being in the film, but she acted like him and Mickey McGowan had never been mentioned that night. Most likely saving them for a rainy day. 'He was adamant he didn't want any mates round. Can't say as I blame him.' Fred must be right ashamed of her. Worse than Garry had been with Maggie, all them years ago.

'He'll get over it, baby.' Jacob smiled. 'He's talking a bit more to me again, that has to be a comparatively good sign.'

'Bully for you.' But that was mean. 'Sorry, love. I'm just . . . you know.'

'Forget it. Well aware a lot of this is down to me.' He picked up his glass. 'Mickey McGowan send Fred a card?'

'Don't be a prat, Fred still doesn't know.' Jacob have rocks in his head? 'Think he's had enough to deal with, don't you?'

'Yeah, course, you're right, I'm a prat.' Swirling the wine round in his glass. 'Heard from him lately? Mickey?'

'No. Not since we went over the other week. Most probably doesn't even realize it's Fred's birthday. Why should he?'

'Does he get on with his other children? Bathsheba and Garry see much of him?'

'Don't think so, since Mickey sort of packed up work. Does it matter?' Why'd she have the feeling Jacob wasn't just making conversation? 'What's it to you?'

'Curious, that's all.' Playing with the dead cigarette butt. 'He *is* your father, Lu. And Angel's, of course.'

'Thanks for reminding me. Jesus, Jake.' Was bad enough, knowing Fred had seen Angel fucking her – if she had to keep hearing about, well, who Angel was and all, that was too much. Recently, Jacob could get that bit odd. Suppose no relationship gave you quite what you thought it would, even the best of them. You always bought one bloke, got delivered another, slightly different. But then, look at everything that had happened to her since knowing Jake, he couldn't of bargained for all that. 'Want more wine?' she said.

'Half a glass.' Dropping his fag into the ashtray. 'Fred be home soon?'

'Yeah, about four.' She glanced at the clock. 'Gives us a good three-quarters of an hour.' Smiling at him. Be lovely to be held. She got up, came round the table, sat on his lap. 'Am I too heavy for you?' she asked.

'Course not.' Putting his arms round her. 'You smell nice,' he said.

'Do I?' She kissed him, and he moved his hand from her neck to her breast. But only for a second. 'What's wrong?'

'Lulu . . . I'm sorry, it's not that simple any more, is it?'

'What d'you mean?' Christ, was he going to tell her he was finishing with her? He fucks up her family life, then fucks off. Marvellous.

'You'll hate me,' he said.

'Hate you more if you leave it like that, mate.' Trying to keep her voice steady.

'Look, I love you.'

'But?'

'No but.' Stroking her cheek. 'I *love* making love to you, you know that, sex has never been so bloody good, but . . . This might sound dreadful, but I want to be honest.'

'Right.' She tried to stand, he held her there on his lap. Knew there had to be a *but*.

'Don't be . . . Just touching you isn't a possibility. Well, no, it is, course it is, you're gorgeous. But it's not the same compared with . . . I've got to say this. Not now I know there's so much more I can have.'

'Meaning?'

'You've got the most amazing breasts in the world,' he said. 'I even dream about them, for God's sake. But now I know I can hear about . . . men touching them for other people to watch, I want to hear it while *I* touch you. Does that make me sound sick? It's the same with the rest of you, as well.' Tears in his eyes. 'If I'm totally out of order, just say. I'll try to forget the other stuff. But shit, baby, if you let me, I'll be devoted to you for ever.'

'Though not without that?'

'Not what I meant.' He squeezed her, tight. 'I'm not someone who straightforwardly gets off on porn,' he said. 'I've told you that. This has got to do with just you. That, I promise.' Kissing her cheek. 'It's not even about Angel any more. Don't get me wrong, I couldn't stand you doing the films now, you're mine, I don't want any other bastard near you in real life. Just, well, I've started to love that you did them back then.'

'Knew this was coming. Was sort of thinking about it before you arrived.' She did manage to get off him then. Went back over to her own seat, finished her wine. He was bloody well admitting what she used to do was *why* he liked fucking her, was practically saying porn was the one place they could meet, sexually. Well, sod him. She could pick up a punter anywhere. Didn't he give a stuff what had happened to Fred?

'You've let me go down this road,' Jacob pointed out. 'You could have stopped me before we ever watched that film together.'

'Yeah, I know that.' It was true. She'd wanted him to want her, so she'd made sure of it, watching his every reaction, following quick wherever he'd started to go, even pushing him along. Night before last, she'd even bought a packet of extra-strong mints, and she'd not done a blow-job using them in years. If she hadn't gone overboard, maybe they wouldn't be having this conversation.

'*Better to murder an infant in its cradle, than to nurse unacted desires.*' Jake shook his head. 'William Blake said that.'

'Obvious William Blake wasn't a mother.'

'God, Lulu.' Jacob cracked up. 'You're great.'

'So they say.' But she laughed too, Christ knows why.

'Pissed off with me?'

'Don't know.' He was lovely, kind, and . . . hers. Yeah, he was leaving her not much choice, but how many choices would there be if she let him go? Sex wasn't a big deal for her, never had been – she couldn't use Fred's experience to punish Jacob. 'You pick your times, mate,' she said. 'If you'd said all this later, we could of done something about it. Fred'll be back, we can't now.' Reaching over the table for his hand. He stroked her palm.

'Loveliest hands ever,' he said. 'Sure you're going to be all right with this?'

'Nope. But I'll try.' She smiled. Knowing that as she did, might as well of cut out her heart, offered him it for his tea. But he'd of fed off it gentle, she did know that much. He loved her. Men couldn't help the way they were made, was God's sick joke that women were so different. All you could do was try to close the gap, even if you had to pretend there was no gap to close. 'Does that cake look really horrible?' she said.

Weirdly, this place wasn't turning him on, not at all; images were becoming increasingly important to him, he was coming to terms with that, but when faced with live naked strangers, who were offering private dances to any manner of punter, all Jacob felt was discomfited. What if the girls thought *he* was a customer? Well, of course they would, there weren't too many other reasons for men to be in here. Jacob's grandmother would have put her hands over her eyes, called it a *heizel*, making no distinction meantime between a club and a brothel; his mother would simply look disgusted, *Men.* A surprise, to see a few women visitors, although they were all young, with male partners. That plump redhead whispering to her boyfriend was trying miles too hard to look lascivious; Jacob would lay money she'd come along to fulfil the bloke's fantasy rather than her own. But there were worse things than wanting to please others. This, Jacob could understand.

The Holly Blue. Such a pretty name, his grandmother would have thought. His mother would say that holly wasn't blue. Her mind was concrete, never totally forgave him for not reading medicine or law or engineering. *Nice one, Mitzvah. In a lap-dancing club and you think about your mother and grand-mother. What do we make of that, then?* Jacob took a mouthful of his Budweiser; one swallow must be fifty pence worth. He looked straight ahead at the stage, determined to avoid eye contact with the girls. That black one was stunning, but her breasts bobbed straight out of her body, as though suspended from invisible wires. Surely they couldn't be real? Lulu might be fifteen years older than the girl, at least two stone heavier, yet her breasts were comparatively breathtaking, and all her own. Wonder what false ones would feel like? Not that Jacob wanted to go further with that thought. Especially not with Babu and Mum and Angel in his head.

A hundred and fifty grand, straight into Garry Dawson's pocket; Jacob was having serious problems getting hold of that as a possibility. No doubt Bathsheba had played up what Mickey might do, but the cheque being backdated to before Angel's death probably wouldn't stand up in court, even with Ian Silverman's signature on it, pretty much the reason Jacob hadn't invested the money for Lu yet. That was bad enough, without recourse to oblique threats of violence. Although the obsession, that schmaltzy suppressed fury, Jacob had seen for himself; maybe that was plenty to cause concern. He had Fred to consider.

'Made it, then.'

'Looks like it.' Jacob tilted his bottle in acknowledgement.

'Speak true, weren't sure you would.' Garry pulled out the other chair. 'What you drinking?' he asked. Hardly resembled the man of the video shop; three months or so had changed him from a slightly overweight, arrogant businessman to a skeletal wreck. Looked like a junkie now, with that pallor, those trembling hands. But by the same token, Angel had never seemed anything other than in the best of health. Or maybe he'd changed too, during his last year when Jacob hadn't seen him. 'Fancy a dance, do you?' Garry said, after the waitress had brought over their drinks. Jacob almost laughed.

'You asking?' he said. To his surprise, Garry grinned.

'I'm asking.'

'Then I'm dancing.' Was he getting *pally* with this bastard? *Never smile at a crocodile.* 'No, not my scene,' Jacob added.

'Prefer videos, is it?'

'I do, yeah.' Staring him out. If Garry thought he was going to get one over on Jacob by weirding him, he was wrong. Why had Jacob been asked here? The most likely explanation was that Bathsheba wanted Garry to mount another attack.

'What d'you make of the place?'

'Nothing to compare it to.'

'One of the classiest joints in London, this, mate.' As he took a swig from the bottle, a trickle of beer went down his chin. 'Most probably definitely the classiest in Soho.' This friendly crap held an undertone of resentment Jacob hadn't earned, couldn't properly find a place for. Well, he might just make sure he *did* earn it, eventually.

'Angel ever come here?' Jacob asked. Nonchalantly.

'Yeah, course. He had a stake in the business.' *Never keep gear you know is bad.* 'Silent partner, like.' Garry eyed him. 'Thought you was big mates?'

'Long time ago.'

'But you knew he was involved.'

'Sure. Though I didn't know till after he died exactly what the business was.' Jacob lit a cigarette. Was this a fish about the money? 'How well did *you* know him?'

'Don't you want a cigar, mate? No? Speaking true, I knew him best a long time ago and all.' Flicking his lighter. 'Though I see him about after, just occasional. Not in the East End – reckon he never wanted to risk bumping into Lu or me mum. Then I met B, joined the firm, so after that we had the odd beer.'

'Right.' Rehearsed that, did you? The East End wasn't the only place Angel should have avoided: if he'd hung around Soho, why had Lulu never seen him? Or maybe she had, perhaps it was Lu who'd kept more stuff back. 'You go to his funeral?' Jacob asked.

'Yeah. Choker.' Not sounding in the least upset. 'Course, Lu never, though.'

'What's your theory, then? Mickey McGowan seems to have a few.'

'His luck run out.' Garry shrugged. 'Had to happen.' Rubbing his crop. 'Aw *ma*te, don't know no more'n you do. Weren't me own goldfish, know what I mean?'

'Sure.' No, didn't have the faintest idea, but he'd tread carefully; a bloke who might have killed one man could kill two. Not that Garry seemed the hands-on type. 'Angel knew that gear was dodgy,' Jacob said. Slowly.

'What?'

'Trust me, he knew.' Jacob scraped his cigarette against the side of the ashtray. 'Suggests to me that means he also knew someone had given it to him deliberately.' *Thank you, Inspector Morse.* Garry looked puzzled.

'You saying he topped hisself?'

'Maybe. With some help.'

260

'No, mate, not him. He got a lot out of life.'

'Can tell that over the odd beer, can you?' Jacob glanced at the stage. A well-built blonde and a tiny Asian were competing on the front poles; *My money's on the little one.* 'Liked him, did you?' Jacob asked. Turning back to Garry.

'One of me best mates, around the time he was seeing Lu.' Garry examined the tip of his cigar. 'But I don't hang about with junkies and poofs. Too much bastard agg.'

'Come off it, even twenty years ago Angel was into smack and anything he could stick his dick in.'

'He got worse,' Garry pointed out.

'True.' Putting out his cigarette.

'Might of been where he weren't well.' Even though to Jacob it felt baking in here, Garry pulled his jacket close round himself. 'If he did do hisself in,' Garry added.

'Not well?' Perhaps the gear *had* corroded Angel, in the end.

'You know, the AIDS.'

'*What?*'

'He was whatsname, weren't he? HIV. Few year, I think.' Garry stared past Jacob, towards the girls. 'Maybe he got AIDS, wanted to finish it fore it finished him.'

'Shit.' Jacob took a long swallow of his drink. This put a whole other complexion on Angel's death: Garry might have been offered as a scapegoat after all, out of some grudge. *They're a family.* Or maybe even from wickedness. *You know me, mate – make my own rules, like the old man.* And what about Lu and Fred, were they infected? No, it was obviously far more recent than that. 'You totally sure?'

'Yeah, about the HIV.'

Jacob was knackered, suddenly. Summonses came from this lot, he jumped to obey. Bollocks, Jacob had a life before, a diary of his own. Any emptiness in it, he'd chosen; family hadn't been on the agenda, that's pretty much how he'd lost Susie, and Maria before her. *Marriage and children can't be practised, can they Jacob? Can't use the headphones with them.* Which of them had ranted about that? *No romance in a screaming kid*. Susie's line, for sure. He raised his eyes to the stage. That girl on the left looked tired, even her tits were starting to droop. Jacob wanted to get back out into the street, go home to bed. Alone.

'Why am I here?' he said. As he had to Bathsheba, more or less.

'Mum asked me,' said Garry. 'Apparently something happened recent with Fred, wanted to be sure you was going to stand by Lu.' Tapping his hand against his mouth. 'Was a bit funny with me, as it goes. Weren't going to make it worse by saying her no.'

'Bloody hell. Thought East End endogamy was a myth.' *Never take sweets from brothers-in-law*. Jacob was too tired to judge whether Garry was being straight, too tired even to decide whether it mattered. Though the confidential tone irritated the balls off him, despite his weariness. Realistically, Jacob was going to give Bathsheba what she wanted, no matter what Garry said or did. Maybe Garry didn't even know about the money: if there was that much concern floating around about Lulu, wouldn't Garry be suspicious, given that she hadn't seen any cash yet? If so, which of them had the advantage, here?

'Well, are you?' Garry said.

'What? God, Lu and I are fine, don't worry about that.' Better than fine, as it happened, Jacob could hardly believe a woman could be so sweet, accommodating, fulfilling fantasies you didn't know you had. How was she related to this schlub? But . . . the schlub had bought films of hers from Jacob; maybe he still had them, hadn't sold them on. Probably tossed himself off over them. 'If you're that close, thought she'd have told you.'

'Mum wanted me to hear it from you. Marriage, is it?'

'That's between us.' Jacob pushed back his chair. 'I need to go,' he said.

'Yeah, sweet. Just so long as you're sure about you and Lulu. Since Angel, she's had disaster after fucking disaster with blokes.' Holding one shaking hand still with the other. 'She never got her head round him fucking off when she was up the duff. Waited for every geezer to leave her since, B says. Reckons Lu feels inferior. Like . . . there's always someone better'n her out there.'

'Yeah.' How bloody touching, family therapy. Are you aware your girlfriend's making deals with other men? 'Well, he can't hurt her now.' Jacob grabbed Garry's gaze. 'Out of curiosity, is it being too pure that makes some heroin bad? Seems a paradox.'

'Can be. You suffocate if it's stronger than you reckoned on. Or you might have something non-reg like crystal meth or shit speed in the cut, and all. Or fucking weedkiller.'

'Crystal meth. Not sure I've heard much about that.' *Death's full of crystals, but all that glistens is not jewels.* Oh shit. Shit. So Garry *was* the one who'd killed Angel? Jacob had just had a drink with the person who probably *had* removed Angel from the world.

'Or weedkiller. Rat poison. Whatever.'

Jacob studied the ruin of Garry's face. Maybe guilt had destroyed his looks, eaten away his flesh, trapped his nerves in permanent palsy. Tough shit, that just wasn't enough retribution. Eye for eye; tooth for tooth; life for life. Until Jacob had made things right with Angel, there was no chance of building something firm with Lulu and Fred meantime. Bury the past, then look to the future. *Hey, psychokiller.* God, that wasn't the answer. But no way was Jacob going to leave Garry to rot in his own remorse.

He stood up. Garry held out an unsteady hand. *Never accept anything from Garry Dawson.* Jacob shook his head.

'Goodnight,' he said.

Part IV

Angels

Intreat me not to leave thee, or to return from following after thee; for whither thou goest, I will go; and where thou lodgest, I will lodge: thy people shall be my people, and thy God my God.

Ruth 1.16

Chapter Thirteen

'What the *bloody* hell d'you think you're doing?' Slinging her work bag against the settee.

'What's it look like?'

'Talk to me like that, and me and you are going to fall out. I mean it.' Lulu was almost too shocked for real anger. She stared down at her son, at the can of Stella in his hand, the lit cigarette in the ashtray. He was sitting cross-legged on the floor as though he was a mini-hippie invasion, his hair sticking up where he hadn't gelled it. Been thirteen for just a week, and already he was behaving like a teenager. Even Garry hadn't started on the booze and fags till he was fourteen. Jesus, only thought in her mind when she'd walked through the door had been to ask Fred if he'd had his tea. 'Give that sodding thing here,' she said. 'And put out that cigarette. Thought you hated smoking?'

'Made me feel pukey?' For a second, his eyes asking for her sympathy, cheeky sod. She tried to keep hers fuming. 'But I don't give a shit,' he added. Looking away.

'Right young man, that's quite enough of that. *Can*, now.' Holding out her hand. Fred hesitated, then reached up to pass her the Stella. Felt nearly full, thank Christ. She put it on the cabinet. 'Fag *out*.' He stubbed it, glaring at her. From the white tip and the smell of it, that was one of Jake's French things. Lulu bent down, clipped Fred round the ear, sudden. 'Do anything like this again, you're dead, you hear me? Understand?'

'Yeah. Not brain surgery.'

'Want another clip, do you?' Raising her voice. 'You can have one, with pleasure.'

'Baby taps. You never hurt me.'

'Always a first time, boy.' But she knew he didn't believe her. Her hand came out, pointing down at him, one long red nail at the end of one long white finger, like it was in an horror film the rest of her had nothing to do with. 'Watch yourself, that's all,' she said.

'You're not the boss of me.'

'Oh yes I bloody am, Freddie.' If she didn't make that clear, then she wouldn't be.

'Freddie, Freddie, Freddie. You used to call me *Angel Face*.'

'Just an expression.' Kicking off her shoes. One of them crashed into her bag.

'Yeah, right. Coincidence, in it.' Sneering. Lulu wouldn't of thought Fred would ever feel he had to sneak a drink – she'd always let him have little tasters, so's it would never be some big mystery. 'Right coincidence,' he said again. *That* was the score, evidently.

'You want to talk about your dad? That it?' Lulu took off her coat, chucked it on to the armchair, eased herself on to the floor next to him. Seemed a bloody long way down when her tummy was right cramped up with her period. Her knees cracked under her as she mirrored Fred's crossed legs. *Angel Face*. Every minute of Fred's getting older, he was turning more and more like, his features hardening into the bloke he'd be. Made her feel peculiar, though loads of kids looked like their parents.

'Haven't got a dad,' Fred mumbled. 'Even Jake's being more one, yeah? A bit.'

'Suppose he is,' she agreed. A mixture of pity and pleasure sloshed around in her sore tummy. She touched Fred's cheek. So soft yet awhile, but most probably he'd be shaving soon. Be even more like Angel then, whose kisses had given her a rash at first. 'What's this all about, mate?'

'Don't know.' Shrugging.

'Yeah, you do.'

'Loads of things. That . . . you know. And all of a sudden

having a dad, like you just made him out of thin air.' He rubbed his head. Christ, Lulu understood his feelings about that one, all right. 'And . . . other stuff, Mum.'

'Like what?' Dreading what she might hear. But least Fred was talking – most he'd said to her in a couple of weeks.

'Remember when that shop exploded?'

'Course.' Wasn't likely ever to forget that.

'Saw a man go in just before. He left his briefcase behind when he came out.' Fred coughed, into his hand. 'Told Nana about it at the time,' he said.

'And?' Lulu chanced stroking his cheek again. He'd hardly let her touch him since finding that bloody film.

'Met B after school today. We had a cup of tea in a cafe.'

'Well, that's nice. Presume it was?' She couldn't see where this was going, but she had to let him take her wherever he wanted. Maggie had never let that happen with her or with Garry, still didn't, that could well be why Garry resented Maggie to this day. Lulu took Fred's hand, and he let her hold it. The ashtray had only had that one burning fag in, he'd most probably lit it when he heard her key in the lock, purposely. Obvious he hadn't been smoking or drinking, not really – he'd wanted her to think he had.

'Was okay with B,' he said. Eventually. 'Felt funny, cos I didn't want to talk about Uncle Garry.' Flicking his gaze over her face. 'But that wasn't . . . She . . . I thought she liked me, Mum. But, I don't know now. She was a bit . . . offish?'

'She can be like that, love. Don't take any notice.' Squeezing his fingers.

'No, I don't care. Can do what she likes.' Biting his lip. Lulu felt like smacking Bathsheba's face for her. Blowing hot and cold, you couldn't *do* that with a kid. Whatever else, Lulu had always tried to make Fred know she loved him, that she'd always love him. None of this, *You don't watch it, I'll send you back to Dolly* shit that Lulu had heard on and off till she was sixteen. Not that Maggie had ever meant it, but it'd still been a slap round the heart. Every time. 'You listening, Mum?

She's my *auntie*. Never thought of her like that before, not properly. But I couldn't say about that to her, neither. Then after the cafe today, B goes off to whatever after, and I sort of . . . went the same way.'

'You followed her?' Oh sod, why did she have to say that? But,

'Yeah. Just a bit, right.' Pressing her hand. 'And I saw her meet up with two blokes. Black dude, *well* smart, and a flash one, white. The white one . . . He was the same man, Mum. I'm not lying. Was the bloke went into that shop in the summer. Think . . . What I reckon is, he had a bomb in his briefcase then. That could happen?'

'You sure about this, Fred?'

'*Yeah.*' Snatching his hand away. 'And then I started thinking, like, you know. None of you's what . . . Like I was a little kid before. Wandered round in a dream world.'

'Maybe the bloke just left his case behind by accident.'

'But he might not of.'

'Suppose.' Lulu felt her eye twitch, like it used to years ago whenever she'd been nervous. One director had nearly sacked her over it, but *Girls Just Want To Have Fun* depended on Lucinda Luscious. That was in the few months where she was almost sort of famous. 'Seems a bit . . . far fetched,' she said. Hoping to God she was right.

'You used to say life's full of big stuff,' he pointed out. Older by the second.

'That wasn't me, not precisely.' Tightening her ponytail. 'I mean, it was your dad used to say that. Only sort of fancier. I was just repeating it.' Never even occurred to her till now that it wasn't what she believed. Life was all about the little, little bits.

'Yeah?' A lopsided smile. 'Like Jake then, was he?'

'Not really.' Massaging her foot, that was starting to get pins and needles. 'They were mates, though. Must of had something in common.'

'Jake knew my dad? For real?'

'Yeah.' Was Fred going to go into one again? But he gave a sort of choked laugh.

'Wicked,' he said. 'Don't know why, though . . . '

'Well, precisely. I feel a bit like that, and all.' Lulu shuffled along the carpet on her bum till she was next to Fred. She put her arm across his shoulders, felt him lean into her. Didn't want to push it, go for a cuddle, but she squeezed the top of his arm.

'Nearly asked B about one thing this afternoon,' he said. 'I thought, right, her dad – Mickey McGowan – he's my grandad.'

'Yep.' Another squeeze.

'Mum, that *hurt*. Your *nail*. Sh . . . sugar.'

'Sorry, love. Want me to kiss it better?' She made kissy noises at him. Even got a giggle. That left beer and fags behind it in the air.

'Get off, you minger.' Fred slapped her thigh. Just that bit too hard. 'Does B's dad know about me?' he asked.

'Only the past little while. Few weeks.'

'But he doesn't want to meet me, yeah?'

'No, he does, as it happens.' Letting that sit between them. Could she trust Mickey not to tell him the whole truth? Yet she couldn't let Fred think even his grandad didn't want to know. Lulu glanced round the living room. They'd have to find something to replace the gap those videos had made – maybe chucking them all had been OTT. Looked as though they'd been burgled, with just a few bits and Fred's dictionary sitting up there.

'What're we going to do?' he asked. 'About the man in the shop.'

'Not sure, love.' She was meant to know the answer to that, she was the mum. When he was first born, all the other new mums said they could tell straight off what their baby's crying meant, if they were hungry or tired or whatever. Lulu could never of been that confident, just hoped for the best. Though she had to try and work it out now – that *we* was the first time in a fortnight that Fred had made them a twosome. But how could she go to Garry with this? Apart from anything else, he hadn't been right since Maggie's attack, was shrinking in front of their eyes, and not only in his body. Besides, Fred's imagination was most likely just working overtime. Maybe she'd talk it over with Jacob on the phone tomorrow. Pity he had that extra gig, she'd sooner say mad stuff like that to his face, let that creasy grin make her *see* it was mad.

'Sorry about the Stella and the fag, Mum.'

'Just make sure it doesn't happen again.' Pulling him closer, she kissed his cheek. 'And I bloody well mean it, Fred.'

'Rank, anyway.'

'There you go, then.' Winking. 'Tell you what, shall I make us a nice hot chocolate? Still got some of them marshmallows Jake bought.'

'No, can't be bothered. I'm going to bed.'

'But it's only . . .' Lulu looked at her watch. 'Not nine yet, mate.'

'So?' He pulled away from her, stood up. 'Night, Mum.' He was gone to his room almost before she could say goodnight to him.

Lulu couldn't work out if she had her son back. Before all this, had never occurred to her they might ever get – what's the word – estranged. That was the sort of thing you had in magazines. The sort of thing she'd had with Dolly, come to think. Even Garry wasn't estranged from Maggie. Lulu ran her hand over the carpet, rolling the dust into little balls. Best hoover round tomorrow, Jacob was uptight about the place being clean. She put her feet flat on the floor, stood up without having to use her hands. Might be getting middle-aged, but some things she could still do, even with period pains and cracking joints. *Genetic* things. Loneliest she'd ever been, Fred not talking to her – you expected it in other people, but not your son. Your kids were meant to love you no matter what, that was the point of having them. Oh shit, what if he was right, Bathsheba knew someone who'd been involved in that bombing? Lulu couldn't make out she liked her brother's

272

girlfriend, but they were still family. *Close* family, when you thought about it – though Lulu tried not to. She went over to the cabinet, took a swig from the can of lager. Warm. Fred's dictionary was lying flat next to where the Stella had been. Lulu traced the title with her finger, left a shadow of the word in the dust. Lungs felt they were full of it. Wiping her hand on the seat of her trousers, she went into the kitchen to see if there was a fresh can in the fridge.

Jacob took the cheque out of the freezer compartment. Why he'd thought it was necessary to hide it there he couldn't imagine: wasn't as though anyone but Bathsheba could cash it. B E McGowan; wonder what the 'E' stood for? Probably something else fanciful like Electra. *More like Eumenides.* Whatever, she wouldn't get her hands on the money unless she brought over the stuff. If that wasn't available, they'd have to think again. Wished now he'd agreed to meet her somewhere else, outside of his territory, but he hadn't wanted to carry the cheque with him in case he lost it. Ridiculous, he could have written it out when he got there; he was behaving as though this piece of paper was the money itself, as though he were some kind of *karger,* as Babu would have said, although Dad had drilled it into him that no one liked a miser. Jacob folded the cheque, slipped it into his back pocket, opened the bottle of Sancerre. That was Lulu's favourite, felt a bastard preparing to drink it with another woman. *So drink something else, Mitz. Won't though, will you?*

Hadn't seen Bathsheba looking so soft before. Pixie-like, as if she were related to Maggie, her face pinched red from the bloody harsh autumn chill. She came into the flat, glanced round the lounge with an approving smile, offered her cheek to be kissed. He had to bend almost double to oblige. Bathsheba turned for him to help her off with her jacket; underneath, she was wearing a powder-blue sweater, incredibly soft to the touch. Cashmere, probably. And her boots and trousers were obviously good suede. Overall, a big improvement on her corporate look, although doubtless it was just another costume. But that big leather bag she had with her was promising. Or maybe she'd brought that along just to tease him. He got them both a drink, *I'll only have the one, Jacob*, and gestured for her to sit on the settee. Jacob took the chair opposite. Bloody hell, how weird was it, having Angel's *sister* in here? Lulu's sister too. How cozy: Lulu's brother lived with her sister. Jerry Springer would have a field day with the Dawson–McGowan clans.

'Did you bring them?' he said.

'Patience, sweetie. Have you got my cheque?'

'Sure.' He lit a cigarette. 'Wouldn't have you in here if I didn't.'

'You know, I so thought you were more polite than that.'

'Right.' Smiling. 'Your drink okay?'

'Mm, fabulous.' Taking a sip. 'Not working tonight?'

'I'm not, no.' Jacob eyed the bag. Was the bloody woman ever going to get to the point? She'd be one of those who insisted on hours of foreplay and only grudgingly let you fuck her in the end. A lot like Susie, come to think of it. That, he found a difficult psychology to handle, but meantime he'd keep his cool, unless she pushed him too far. A hundred and fifty grand was a big block of ice on your irritation. He'd been *this* close to refusing to hand anything over, to quoting Ian Silverman's name and telling her the money had fuck-all to do with Angel whatever the will said, but of course he *had* met Mickey. The risk was too great; even though he didn't totally understand their world, Jacob realized that much. He drew on his cigarette. 'You want to do this exchange, then?' he said. Evenly.

'Okay.' Bathsheba pulled the bag round, so it was in front of her feet. Unzipped it. And one by one took out five videos. 'Expect you'll want to give them a little checklette,' she said. 'You won't mind if I pop to the loo, will you, darling? I'm a tad squeamish about that sort of film.' She stood up. 'I'll give you five mins.'

Jacob didn't want to run a second of the videos with

Bathsheba anywhere in his flat; he told her where the bathroom was, and sat staring at the pile. They must be kosher, else she'd never have said he could make sure. He put out his cigarette, went over to the films, picked one up. Sure, looked comparatively like those he'd given to Garry, but then so might a tape of *Emmerdale*. And why wouldn't Garry have sold them on? *Why do you think?* Better put them by the player, so it would seem as though he'd checked through them.

Five videos. That made each one worth thirty grand of Angel's money; Jacob's grandmother would turn in her grave. For more than one reason. Five videos, for a combined sum that could have bought a Steinway Model A concert grand, nine foot six. And a matching non-adjustable stool. Having that much money in his back pocket didn't feel real, but then he'd spent a lot of the time since Cambridge appearing insubstantial to himself. As though he was always recording what a life should be, playing it back slightly out of time. The connections other people made with ease felt dreadful to him, suffocating, the taking away of possibilities. Angel used to quote something by Thomas Aquinas, about the only thing humans never lacked was privation: being in one state automatically deprives us of being in another. *Hey man, I was some teacher.* Sure, Angel had been a powerful pedagogue of a kind, but sometimes . . . Perhaps Jacob would have had a chance of being made whole by the things others seemed to want, if he'd not made a friend.

'So, are you . . . *satisfied*, sweetie?' Bathsheba touched his back.

'Here.' He took the cheque from his pocket, passed it to her. She unfolded it, stared down at it for a second or two, then returned to the settee. He shouldn't have given her a bloody drink, she'd barely touched it yet and he just wanted her gone. Jacob had used half the legacy to buy Lulu's past; there was something distasteful in that. Yet at least this way he and Lu got something from the deal.

'Lucky, my Garry holding on to those, wasn't it?' Bathsheba

said. Beaming. 'Funny thing, it was my idea not to sell them sooner. *Thought* they might come in handy.'

'Don't want to talk about that, Bathsheba.' What the hell had he done with his cigarettes? Had them before Bathsheba had given him the tapes. 'They're mine now. She's safe.' Not really knowing what he meant.

'That's *sweet*.' She smiled again. 'I so knew Lulu would end up doing all right for herself. And let's face it, not many of her sort do.'

'She's unique.' Holding in his anger. Where did this woman get off, being such a bitch? Less pixie than evil sprite. Bathsheba crossed her legs, adjusted her sweater.

'Mm, *unique*, that's what I meant,' she said. 'Suppose you're going to sort out the rest of the money with her?'

'Sure. When I'm ready.' But Jacob could see time was running out: no way was Bathsheba to be trusted with a secret, not now she had what she wanted.

'When you're ready, of course.' Picking imaginary bits of fluff from her sleeve. 'I was saying that to Garry only this evening.'

'Discuss everything, do you?' God, this fucking miniature clothes-horse probably knew all about the crystal meth. That it adulterated Angel's final hit. That it killed him. Her own brother, probably murdered by her partner, how did she live with that? Jacob couldn't see Garry keeping it from her; there was only one seat of power in that relationship, for sure.

'No couple discusses everything, Jacob. That would be *too* bizarre.' Raising her eyebrows; even they were too thin. 'I'm positive you know that.'

'I do, yeah.' One thing he couldn't believe she knew about was that sixth video; the temptation to tell her made the inside of his skull itch. Each of the many reasons he'd miss that film for the rest of his life faded a little against the regret that he'd never be able to show it to this woman. Bathsheba was weird, no question, but he'd lay the rest of Angel's money that she was sexually straightforward. A prude. This poker-arsed bitch had the front to look down on Lulu's sexual magnanimity, her loving openness. Made him sick. Bathsheba probably thought it was morally better to live with a killer than cheerfully to offer everything you were to your man. 'Well, I won't keep you,' he said. *There* were his cigarettes, under the coffee table. Must have knocked them off. Retrieving them, he shook one from the packet. 'I'm sure you want to get back to Garry.'

'No rush, sweetie.' Bathsheba picked up her glass. 'Finish this first. How's Fred?'

'You saw him recently. And he saw you, apparently.'

'Those generally go together.'

'Changing careers, are you?' He didn't for one second think she'd know what he was talking about, was certain what Lu had told him on the phone earlier was just Fred's fantasy. But he felt like discomfiting the bitch. 'Into bomb disposal now, I hear.'

'Pardon?' Looking blankly at him.

'Private joke. With myself,' he added.

'Very amusing, I'm sure.' Withering. 'By the way, are the films for Lulu's Christmas present? Or don't you do Christmas?'

'No. Anyway, I work most of the holiday.' For God's sake, woman, piss off. Jacob didn't think he could handle much more of her pointless nasty crap.

'Pity. I so think they'd make a good pressie.' Sipping her drink. 'But then a hundred and fifty thousand pounds ought to make a better one. Hardly teeny, is it?'

'Are you going anywhere with this, Bathsheba?'

'Just making conversation.' Flicking her hair back from her face, in that girlish way only actual girls could pull off. In this light, she looked older than Lu. 'But quite honestly, Jacob – and I'm sure you won't mind me being honest – I can't see her being too chuffed about you having the vids. What will our Daddy say?'

'Anti-porn then, is he?' Jacob laughed. 'I find that hard to believe.'

'Different when it's family, darling.'

'It is, yeah. Very different.' The words were scorching the tip of his tongue; if he didn't get them out there, they'd burn right through.

'Well, I'm sure he'd forgive her in time.' She smiled. 'But it wouldn't make their budding . . . *relationship* any easier, would it, Jacob? How would you forget something like that?' Shuddering, theatrically. 'Even I find it tricky, sweetie.'

'Maybe you should ask Garry about that,' he said. Slowly. Feeling the heat of every syllable. A petty revenge. A revenge-lette, as Bathsheba might say. 'I'm sure he's got a lot of stories,' he went on.

'About Lulu?' Bathsheba's mouth was tight.

'About a family outing.' Jacob lit the cigarette he'd been holding. 'God, you really don't know, do you? Lucinda Luscious made one last film. With Angel. And Garry.'

Her face didn't change; Jacob hadn't known what he'd been expecting, but it wasn't this frozen calm, as though his words had been a gentle snowfall rather than the fire he'd experienced. The room was still, except for the soft tick-tick-tick of a clock, which was weird, as Jacob didn't have a clock in here, apart from the digital one on the video. Must be the central heating or something. Bathsheba's dark eyes continued to look into his, not speculatively but steadily, impassive. He remembered how he'd felt when he'd realized who the third man in the video was; something akin to pity rose in him. But this woman had just stolen serious dough from him and Lulu, she was possibly party to a murder, she was a bitch. Comparatively, what Jacob had done to her was nothing. Still she looked at him. A sharp pain in his fingers. His cigarette, he'd let it burn down. Tossing it into the ashtray, he lit another. Bathsheba shook her head.

'Getting a bit smoky for me in here, darling,' she said. 'If you don't mind, I'll take myself off.'

As Bathsheba left the flat, she touched his arm. And smiled.

Jacob wasn't going to waste another second's thought on her. *Yeah, hit and run, boy.* He went back through to the lounge, ground out his cigarette, switched off the overhead light, closed the gap in the curtains. Last time he'd seen these videos, he'd been bored; now he'd lost Angel, they would have to be enough. If he could get it up for impartial porn, surely these five would do more. Jacob's cock stirred slightly.

He settled down in front of one taken randomly from the pile. Lulu wasn't in the first few scenes; he was hard now, but he wasn't about to waste that on the other girl. Then she walked into shot, oh God, looking so sweet, so innocent, as if she'd been raiding her mother's make-up box. And yet those breasts didn't belong to a child. Even through the all-in-one under-wear thing she had on, he could see the luxury of them. Jacob unbuttoned his jeans, took out his cock, holding his balls with the other hand. As Lulu squeezed the Indian guy, Jacob squeezed himself. Then the other girl was back, stroking Lu's bum, undoing the poppers on her lingerie, sticking her tongue deep inside his girl. Fuck, if Fred hadn't been a boy, maybe in a few years Lu's child would have looked like Lucinda Luscious . . . how would Jacob have coped? Lulu had her mouth round the bloke's cock; was it a possibility to take that much of it into her? Or maybe it was just the camera angle. Shit, look at Lulu's face, her eyes closed with pleasure as the girl ate her, as she in turn sucked the man. Go on, baby, show me. Show me what you were made of then. The bloke reached down to pull Lulu's breasts free, pinching hard at the nipples; the girl's tongue appeared and disappeared into Lu's cunt. Jacob began to work himself harder. There were five of these videos, how could he stand that much happiness? Lulu was on her back now, the man fucking her face, the girl sucking at Lu's clitoris. You could see . . . God, Lulu was coming.

It was a peep show, for Christ's sake. What was he doing here? Stephen swallowed the last of his rum and Diet Coke, signalled for another. He'd never been much of a drinker, *Just can't handle the old jungle juice, can you, Stevie baby. Disgrace to your people, you are.* Hadn't touched spirits since the night

Angel died; for those few hours after hearing the news he'd have drunk anything, taken anything, to stop the thinking. Some people said they drank to deaden the pain, but they were, technically, delusional: if you drowned thoughts, then hurt was more diffuse, that was all, and so a little more bearable.

'Thanks.' He took his drink from the pretty mixed-raced waiter, one of those muscle-boy, baby-faced types Angel said were a cross between Action Man and Tiny Tears. The Manacle was a good enough investment for them, but Stephen couldn't raise any interest beyond the professional; all this young male flesh on display, and he might as well be in the Pussy Parlour. Angel had taken too much from him, sucking even his sexuality from beyond the grave.

Utter balls. Half-pissed rubbish. Stephen knew he wasn't letting himself react in case it led to something more than a quick bunk-up, and there was no way he was allowing any further complications into his emotional life. *Really are a repressed public schoolie, aren't you?* Better than being Angel McGowan's lack-of-love interest. He glanced round the room. That air of furtiveness was deeply unpleasant, emitting not from the acts, which were entirely upfront, fun if you looked at them objectively, but from most of the punters, seedy married types with an out of their league yearning in their dreary faces. Frankly, Stephen would sooner die than be associated with one of those twats. If he came to Soho for any reason other than work, it ought to be to visit Body Positive in Greek Street. And yet he was here, checking out the new property as though it were a potentially fanciable man.

Obviously, it had to do with meeting Del McGowan this afternoon. Stephen's thoughts had become a bloody roll call of new impressions over the past couple of days. And Del had been one hell of a shock. For a second, it had been Angel walking into the hotel bar, younger, broader, more delicately featured than he'd ever been in life, yet somehow himself nonetheless. But every gesture was wrong, the accent far cruder, an alien nervous energy possessing him. Del wasn't Angel.

Been hoping he would be, Cinderella? Yes, of course. Oddly, as Del had grown less like Angel, Bathsheba had taken on the likeness. Now if *she* had been a man, Stephen might have been in trouble this afternoon. Harder to protect yourself when your old love comes back in a new guise.

He took a mouthful of his drink. One had to say, Bathsheba McGowan was ruthless. When he'd introduced her the other day to Geoff, she'd had no compunction about arranging the bomb at the Holly Blue. As long as she felt she controlled it, a warning shot in a McGowan business apparently seemed to her a good idea after all. Stephen had guessed that would be the case, but part of him found it appalling. The way she'd delivered her brother today, too, had been with the cool triumph of an evangelical hanging judge. At least Del finally was going to hand over his shares, that was something. But not enough. Though Angel's brother had been only the first shock of the day.

Jacob Fox. Bathsheba's partner's sister's boyfriend. Angel's legatee. Stephen had never once heard Angel mention that name, he'd have remembered. *Always on the look out for anyone who might be more important to me than you, weren't you, Steve?* When Stephen had first confirmed absolutely the will and its details, he'd shared the information with fucking Bathsheba within a reasonably short time. The facts of the will had hurt Stephen, really bloody hurt him, but still he'd given them over in a professional manner as soon as he'd dealt with them emotionally. They'd even shared a wry laugh about the solicitor being related to that twat Clifford Black, the chap who'd got himself shot. Yet she hadn't been *quite* so open with him. Slippery whore. Until today, Stephen had been unaware of any family link with Fox, that the man wasn't simply holding the money for Lulu Dawson but was sleeping with the tart. He finished his drink. Another one? Why the hell not. Raising his arm to Action Tears, he leaned back in his chair. Couldn't help imagining there was a sticky deposit on the seat, this suit better go to the dry cleaner in the morning. Stephen was close to finding out about Angel's murderer, he could sense it, as though he were a sniffer dog hunting for drugs. Del would have more information on that side of the McGowan business, Bathsheba was getting increasingly single-minded, and now there was this Jacob Fox. If Fox was the technical beneficiary *and* sexually involved with the real intended recipient, it wasn't impossible that he knew something concrete concerning Angel's death.

'Can I get you anything *else*, sir?' Insinuation sickly as the incense this place favoured. Stephen shook his head.

'No, thank you.' Short. Turning towards the stage, where a polished young man was supposedly being whipped by a slightly older one. If that so much as stung, Stephen would be extremely surprised. He didn't understand how people could get off on fake pain; the real thing was so much more powerful, full sex as opposed to a solitary wank.

Like the way Angel had tied Stephen's tongue. After November, he could tell whom he liked, but that approaching freedom was tinged with regret. He'd been living with the chains since Angel had decided to sell, long before the April dividends when the papers were actually transferred, and after 18th May it had been Stephen's one erotic compulsion. *Tell before November, and you'll have let me down. It'll be like you never existed for me.* Angel had wanted secrecy, Stephen was starting to realize, in order to ensure this fucking Fox got the money unimpeded. Bloody Angel knew he'd been given bad gear, was selfish enough to decide to take it, and made his lover ease the path for the person who benefited from that death. Pathetic, being shackled by a living threat from a dead man. Balls. There was no afterlife, he knew that, but he also knew that Angel would speak to him until Stephen's own death; if he'd broken his word, the voice would stop. *You mad fucker.* Possibly. Yet what else did he have? Except Bathsheba McGowan and now Jacob Fox. *Reckon you've got paraphilia, anyway. Know what that is, Rugby boy?* Beyond love to absolute desire; how could you think that would be a new word in this mind? Revenge is yours, Angel. Then maybe they'd both be free.

*   *   *

Maggie was starting to feel trapped in here, like the furniture was breeding, trying to overtake her. Biggest excitement of her week was another paranoid shuffle to the bins and back. Stupid, since that torn heart there hadn't been nothing to scare her, and even that, when you come to think, was more like a goodbye message than a threat. Though from who was another question. But she'd got in the habit of being fearful, hard to break as the cigs. Still couldn't bring herself to put that flipping gun right away. Her thoughts wasn't her own, these days. Like with that bleeding filthy film, she kept getting too close to imagining details, just managing to swerve off of it in time. Made her so flaming wild that Lu and Garry would of done this to her. Mind, was bound to of been that Angel's fault. It'd never washed with Maggie that he hadn't got Lulu into them films in the first place. Unless she was very much mistaken, he'd of got some hold on Garry and all. Just had to be thankful Garry and Lu wasn't really brother and sister – didn't bear thinking about as it was.

That'd be Jacob with her bit of shopping. Maybe he'd stop for a quick cuppa before he went on to Lulu's. Place was so quiet with Fred asleep in the spare room, his cold'd knocked him out, for a wonder, most likely sleep right through if she let him. Should probably get him up soon, else he wouldn't be able to get off tonight. If Jacob'd remembered that Black Forest, Fred should be out of bed fast enough.

'Meals on wheels,' Jacob said, as she opened the front door. 'I've managed to lose the receipt, but it came to about twelve quid.' Looking well put-upon. Bli, it was only a few odds and sods, not like she'd asked him to bake the flipping cake or grow the carrots.

She unpacked the bag, made a pot of tea, opened the custard creams. Jacob was getting nearly as grump-pig as the rest of the family round her. Must be feeling right at home. Lu'd mentioned recent that she'd not met *his* family yet – struck Maggie as a bit peculiar, seeing as how him and Lulu was getting so serious.

'You don't take sugar, do you, Jacob?' she said, coming back through. Knowing full well he never, wanting to put him back to visitor, see how he liked that.

'I don't, no. Thanks.' Lifting the cup off the tray. Getting out his cigs.

'Was just wondering – you and Lu had any thoughts about Christmas, yet?'

'That's weeks away, Maggie.' Laughing. 'Don't really . . . I'm Jewish.'

'Yeah, but you ain't religious, are you?' She took a sip of her tea, reached for her own cigs. 'You'd be welcome to come here, though maybe your mum'd mind?'

'No, that's great,' he said. Well polite now.

'Your mum bothered by Lu not being Jewish and all?'

'Uh . . . No.' Fiddling with his lighter.

'You *have* told her?' Fixing him still with her stare.

'To be honest, I haven't yet, no.' More fiddling. 'My dad won't care, though.'

'Don't you think you should bleeding tell both of them?' Right, so the mother was a bit prejudiced, unless Maggie was mistaken. That explained things. 'You ain't mentioned Lu at all, have you? If you're serious about her—'

'Course I am.' But his eyes'd gone shifty.

'Don't want her messed about, Jake.' Checking her wig. Staring at him again.

'We're okay, for the minute,' Jacob said.

'What d'you mean, *for the minute*?' Maggie drew hard on her cig. 'If you ain't just playing with me girl, then you should tell your mum and dad.'

'I will. But . . . Lu's had a lot to deal with lately.' Giving her a right accusing look. 'I don't want my dreadful family inflicted on her when she's just getting used to her own.'

'What's that meant to mean?'

'Come on, Maggie.' Contemptuous nearly. 'Think about it.' A bit more gentle. 'What would you have done if you'd found out who your father was?'

284

'You saying she's . . . No, she'd of told me if she'd met Mickey McGowan.' Please God, no. Jacob must mean Lu'd fronted the idea of McGowan, not him in the flesh.

'She didn't want to worry you, with you being in hospital.'

'So she has, then.' Maggie's heart went over. 'You and all?'

'Yeah, sure.' Scraping his cigarette on the side the ashtray, he shook his head. 'Shouldn't have said that, wasn't down to me.' Reaching out his hand, then dropping it back on his lap. 'God, I'm sorry. You had me on the defensive, but that's no excuse, I know.' Pompous. Though his face was all concerned. Hypocritical so-and-so.

'No, it flaming ain't.' Everything was slipping away from her – Garry, Lu, Fred, she didn't have no power any more. They all lived lives that had bugger all to do with her. 'They getting close, or what?' she forced herself to ask.

'No. But he wants to meet Fred. She's not sure about that.'

'Over my dead body.' Her voice none too steady.

'It isn't your decision, Maggie,' he pointed out. Soft. Ruffling his curls. With a nice patronizing smile. Think he could charm his way out of this one?

'Not being funny,' she said, 'but you don't know what's my decision in this family.' And the family was still hern, even if the people in it wasn't. 'Not going to let him meet McGowan, if I can be off of it. You don't know the wicked begger.'

'He's really cut up by Angel's death.' He sipped his tea. 'Half-mad with it.'

'Believe you me, he didn't need no death to be more'n half mad.' But for a sec, she did feel a pang for McGowan. Couldn't be easy, he'd worshipped that boy. More fool him.

'Grief might have softened him.' Jacob put out his cig. 'In my experience, it–'

'Leave off, Jake,' Maggie said. 'You know what? You're so far up your own bleeding backside, you think the world better be grateful for your shit.'

Jacob looked well shocked, face like a *smacked* bleeding backside. Then he grinned.

'That told me,' he said. 'I'm making a real mess of this, aren't I?'

'Make you right.' But she didn't feel so angry now. 'I'm going to leave Lu to come to me about McGowan,' she added. 'And she will eventually, promise you that much for nothing. But do me a favour, and I don't want any old fanny about it.' Using the strict voice she done sometimes on Fred. 'She starts on about Fred and him, you get straight here.'

'As it happens, I do think you're right about that.' Finishing his tea. 'Sure, course I will. And I'll tell my parents about me and Lu, you're right about that too.' Pulling his funny brief-case towards him. 'Mind if I get off now?'

'You'll have another cup of tea first,' she told him. 'And let me know all about McGowan.' To be fair, Jacob never hesitated, just nodded, got out his ciggies again.

'I knew Angel,' he said. 'That's why I understand what Mickey must be feeling. I feel a bit of it, too.'

Chapter Fourteen

Already it wasn't precisely autumn any more, it was practically winter. Wet and sludgy-grey. Like a kid's painting water. Fred bringing home germs from school, as if they were something he'd made for her in class. Customers in Heaven Scent squeezing themselves into PVC two sizes too small, *It'll fit by Christmas,* said with panic in their eyes. Jake in a right wintry mood and all, going on about bloody Angel, hardly ever mentioning her, or them. Jesus, sometimes she wished her and Jake had met in any other way, would almost of preferred it if he'd been a stalker. Lulu was bloody glad to of had this hour on her own for a change, bit of breathing space after work. Nice of Maggie to take Fred when he had a stinking cold, loads of nans would of said no. Least Maggie wasn't punishing Lulu for the film. Silence was golden in this bloody family.

Lulu checked her roots in the bathroom mirror. Just about acceptable, but she'd better pick up some Nice 'n' Easy next time she was passing Boots's. Well, that was her done, Jake'd be here soon. She added another quick coat of lippy for luck, and went back through to the living room where she'd left her glass of wine. Hoped he was going to be a bit more cheerful tonight. Maybe he was just nervous about that show tomorrow. Even she'd heard of Parchman Farm, and the Ocean in Hackney was meant to be a great venue. He hadn't done many big gigs since she'd known him, she was quite excited, but it'd explain why he was acting so tense. Didn't have to be her fault, though you couldn't help worrying.

She sat on the settee, looked across at the bare cabinet. That was a point, the picture from Angel was still in the bottom cupboard, maybe she should get it out, prop it up on the empty shelves for now. Or was it a bit strange to have a nude painting on display that reminded her of Maggie? Perhaps she'd imagined the similarity. Lulu went over, opened the door, pulled out the carrier. She unwrapped the picture, feeling as if she'd bought a girly mag. But it was so pretty, didn't think she'd realized that before. The colours were soft as faded curtains, and the woman . . . you presumed she had a life inside the painted skin. When Lulu thought of Mickey McGowan, of the way he was alive but somehow not, and then looked at this, the difference was almost spooky. No doubt about it though, that face was a young Maggie's. Careful as she could, Lulu got it standing on one of the shelves, leaning it against Fred's dictionary, sticking the crystal ashtray in front so the painting didn't fall. No way could she leave it there, not with Fred – that'd really do his head in – but it could stay till she'd showed Jacob. Fred was going to school from Maggie's in the morning if he was well enough; long as she had it put away by the time he got home, it'd be fine.

Jacob let himself in. He came up behind her, put his arms round her waist. Perhaps he was in a better mood tonight.

'What's that?' he said. Then, 'Bloody hell.'

'I know, looks a bit like Mags, doesn't it?'

'Isn't that, Lu. Just . . . I know that picture.'

'You do?' Lulu turned round to face him. 'How?'

'It was Angel's.' Jacob moved her aside, picked up the painting. 'Haven't seen this for nearly twenty years,' he said. 'But I'm not wrong.'

'Bathsheba gave it me a while back. Said Angel left it for me.'

'Yeah?' He looked down at it in his hands. 'Well, he must have cared about you, baby. This is worth a lot of dough.'

'How much is a lot?' Lulu grabbed his arm. Jesus, was this little thing going to make Christmas easier? Was it Angel's way of making up for ignoring Fred all them years?

'Don't know.' Jake laid the picture on the shelf. 'But it was about ten grand even back then. Should think there's a possibility it's gone up quite a bit.' He touched her shoulder. 'You're right, though,' he added. 'Does look like Maggie, doesn't it?'

'*Ten* grand?' Lulu felt sick. When he'd said *a lot*, she'd vaguely thought a couple or three thousand.

'It was his graduation present,' Jacob told her. 'An investment for him, apparently.' He laughed. 'I got a watch from my dad, and another one from my mother.'

'What am I meant to do with it? I mean, should I sell it?'

'We should get it valued, anyway.' Touching the frame. 'It's incredible, isn't it? Very erotic, don't you think?'

'Not when it looks like my auntie, no.' She smiled. Men were funny – no way in this world Jake fancied Maggie, and yet here he was, getting excited over the painting just because it was of a woman with no clothes on. You couldn't even get offended – was like a toddler holding out its hand every time you took it past a sweetie counter. Automatic. Remembered Garry saying once that give him some jiggling titties to look at, and a beer in his hand, and he was happy. Simple minded, really. 'How *was* Mags?'

'Fine. I've got a couple of things for you,' Jacob said. 'Comparative to this, they're not anything much, but . . . ' He went over to the living-room door, where he'd left his music case. Took out some videos and a small jeweller's box. 'Five Lucinda Luscious,' he said. Oh Christ, not more of her bloody past, thought they'd done with all that. She tried to look pleased. 'They don't make up for the one we lost, maybe we'll never be able to trace another copy, but I thought . . . ' Smiling, his eyes gone even darker. 'And this is just to say thank you for being the only woman who could make me reach my full potential.' Was clear he meant in the sack. He was holding out the box to her. She took it, her heart speeding up. Had to be a ring. *Had* to be. Was he going to ask her to marry him? If he did do, she'd perform every bloody trick from any of those films, a thousand times over. Everything had a price, even happiness, and that one didn't seem too high. Maybe they'd even have a baby of their own, she wasn't too old – Lulu had always fancied having a little girl. But where had he got the videos from? 'Go on, open it,' he said.

It *was* a ring. Not a diamond, a ruby. Shit, rubies were bad luck for engagements, Maggie reckoned they meant blood. Yet it was gorgeous – plain, deep, expensive.

'Bloody Christ, Jake, it's lovely,' she said. Choked.

'Not sure which finger it'll fit. Do you want to try it?' Taking the box from her, he prised the ring out. *Not sure which finger it'll fit.* Was he teasing her? Jacob got hold of her left hand. Her heart was in her throat now. She spread out her fingers. 'Most beautiful hands in the world,' he said. 'First thing I loved about you.' Kissing the knuckles, one by one. 'That's why it had to be a ring.' Oh shit, what did that mean? He put her middle finger to his mouth, gently sucked it. Then slid the ring on. Her *middle* finger. No proposal at all. Lulu closed her eyes. She bloody wasn't going to cry. Was still a lovely present, it still meant he thought a lot of her – wasn't like he earned all that much, he'd of had to make sacrifices to buy it. And it couldn't just be to soften her up about the videos, he wasn't like that. Not Jacob. She kept her eyes closed for *one elephant, two elephants, three elephants, four elephants* more, then opened them with a big smile.

'Thanks, Jake,' she said. Her voice happy. 'Really. I love it. Love you.'

'Looks great on. How good am I at picking, then?' Obviously delighted. 'That, I know how to do for a woman. I mean, for you.' He kissed her, hard. 'Pleased with me, are you?' he said. Kissing her again. 'Shall we have a drink and put a film on?'

'Funny to think,' she said. Going over to the table, pouring him a glass of the Merlot she'd bought specially. She preferred white. 'When we were first together, you said you didn't get porn. As in you didn't understand it.'

'Came out with a lot of bullshit when we were first together,' he replied. Lulu felt he was pinching her heart. She knew he didn't mean it nasty, but she kept having to tiptoe round his words so's not to get stabbed by them. 'Things change, baby,' he went on. 'All the time. I'm not the same person I was back in July, thank God.'

'No, suppose you're not.'

'Most of that's down to you.' He picked out one of the videos. 'This is a really early one,' he said. 'You look about sixteen in it. *Rami Tardar and the Temple of Dong.*' Laughing. 'Dreadful title, I know, but the film's really cute.'

'Do we have to watch it now?' she asked. Jacob's face changed, just a bit, but enough for her to see he was getting pissed off.

'You know I need to relax tonight,' he said. 'Bloody hell, Lu, tomorrow's going to be a stressful one for me. You *know* that.' Cold.

'Yeah, sorry. Course.' But what was she apologizing for? A quiet life, that's what. 'Fred's been going on again about that bloke he saw with Bathsheba,' she said. Plonking herself on the settee.

'So?' Putting the tape into the machine. 'Thought we decided he'd been playing too many blow-'em-up computer games?'

'Yeah.'

'Right, let's forget about Fred for now. Okay?'

'So your stress is more important than mine? Leave off.' That was mean, sniping at him after getting the nice present. 'Sorry, love. Suppose I'm a bit nervous about the vid. Was my first proper one.'

'Sure, I understand.' Coming across to the settee carrying the remote, sitting with his arm round her like they were about to watch *Coronation Street*. 'Well, I've turned into a *chosid*. That means a rabid fan,' he said. 'We ought to hunt down your other films, must be lots of them.'

'Yeah.' She stared down at her hand, at the red stone glinting in the light from the opening credits. Remembered the only song Jake had ever played just for her.

> *You've no one else lined up tonight,*
> *It's in your interests to be blind . . .*

She understood that, now. But she wasn't blind, she knew this was a compromise. Lulu loved Jacob, so she had to go back into porn, in a manner of speaking. Least it was private, for them two alone. And there was that picture, worth ten grand, more maybe. Money, a man, Fred speaking to her again, a ring. There were worse lives.

Got to get in there, got to talk to her. Fucking bastard cunt bastard. Couldn't go back to Bathsheba like this, someone'd sewn his bastard eyelids to his eyebrows. And if he done this first, his girl'd forgive a lot. *Wish I could tell her, sweetie, but she's not going to listen to me, is she? I'm hardly flavour of any of her months.* Shit, why was the door still shut on him? Got to tell Lu she was rich, couldn't have that Jacob getting a right touch, her and Fred having fuck all, is it? Clean start. He'd have the job with ISU soon, B'd have what she wanted, she still loved him, it'd be all gravy for everyone. Except for Jacob. Sweet. Yeah. Come on, open the bastard door. Felt like smashing it down, but held hisself in. This shit was murder, no fucking doubt. Opposite of happy pills, more like angry powder. Heart speeding, as if it was on something different to his head. Struth, why'd anyone take this for fun? Have more fun banging his nut against Lulu's door.

'What do you want?' Lu was in the doorway, but Garry hadn't see it open. One of them tricks, messing with your mind. She'd most likely learned it off Angel.

'Can I come in?' Words sounded like they was miles away, being spoke to him instead of coming out his own mouth.

'Not in that state, you can't.' Folding her arms. 'Jake's here.'

'Jake's here?' Tugging at her elbow, trying to get her not to be folded up. Stronger'n he'd thought, them arms. 'Good, right, cool. Only want a nag.'

'Come back tomorrow, mate.' Pushing her face close to his. 'Jesus, what you on?'

'Nothing.' Grabbing both her elbows, yanking them open at last.

'Shit, you *prat*. Yeah, right, sure you're on nothing. Go home, let B deal with you.'

'No way, no fucking way. No way.' Giving her a little shove. 'Got to come in.'

'Piss off.' Angry. Trying to close the door on him. He'd tumbled *that* trick. Got past her into the hall.

'Talk to me, Lu.' Stroking her hair.

'Jake!' she called. As if that cunt'd be able to stop him.

'Cup of tea,' Garry said. 'Please, go on, just one cup.'

'You're lucky Fred's not around. State of you. Jesus.'

'What's going on?' Jacob had come out the hall, they was squashed in like a rush-hour Tube. 'You okay, Lulu?'

'Yeah . . . *shit*. Leave off, Garry, you're pulling my hair.'

'Sorry, yeah, sorry. Can I come in?'

'Oh, for fuck's sake. Come on, then.'

'You sure about this?' Jacob asked. Worried, is it? Right to be, mate.

Then they was all in the living room. Garry'd have to keep an eye, they'd slipped that one by him. Fucking fuming for a second, but he had to get that under – didn't want his feelings controlling him. Telly was on, *Millionaire*. Jacob turned it off.

'Sit down, mate,' Lulu said, touching Garry's arm. 'Making me feel sick, all that roaming about.' Went off out the kitchen. Garry sat on the settee.

'How are you doing, Garry?' Jacob moved over to the seat opposite.

'Yeah, bang on the *money*.' Last time he'd go near Super-Crank, B wouldn't have to worry about that. But she mustn't see him like this, didn't trust hisself. Might end up treating her wrong, and he'd never drowned his goldfish yet. Why the fuck had he used it? Must be off his head. Could be anything in it, anything. 'Got a fag?'

'Sure.' Jacob chucked over the packet. Garry took out his lighter, sparked one. Hadn't smoked straights in three year, not since B. She'd go mental, she found out.

'Aw, *mate* – I is what I is,' Garry said. That was from before Bathsheba and all. Since her, he'd been more what she was, living up to her expectations best he could. Let her down tonight, let them both down. So sorry, darling, speaking true he was. Had just wanted . . . help with his head, after coping with that look in her eyes when she asked about the film. Thanks to fucking Jacob.

'Watch it, you nearly burned Lu's cushion then,' Jacob said.

'You can fuck off, and all.' Garry put on a woman's voice, 'Ooh, the cushion's burning, ooh, I'm such a decent bloke, ooh, I forgive you for them awfully tewwible films.'

'Give me my cigarettes, Garry, I want one.'

'And what Jacob wants, Jacob gets.' Garry slung him the packet back. 'Must be a right result, being you.'

Jacob lit a fag, reached over to pick up a glass from some-where, top of the telly maybe, finished off the drink in it. Lanky cunt. Reckoned hisself, is it? Like Angel. Had another think coming and all.

'There you go, mate.' Lulu was in front of him, must of appeared while he was looking at Jacob, she was holding a mug out. He took it, burned his fingers. 'Did one for you Jake, didn't know if you wanted it.'

'Sure, thanks. Do you want to sit here?'

'No, I'll be okay on the settee.'

'Don't fucking bite,' Garry said. Snapping his teeth together. Shit, that hurt. He put out the bonfire-tasting fag. Got some of the tea down his neck. Better. Nice and sugary. Next door had a new kitten, he'd see Bathsheba stroke it. But no way was he going to worry her with the shit that come in his head. Them boxes by the telly, they was Lu's films. Been watching them together, dirty fuckers? Bet Jacob made her. Sick. 'Good vids?' he said.

'We're pleased with them.' Jacob pulled on his fag.

'Not cheap.' Garry stared hard at Lu. No, she never knew, without a shadow of, look at her. No wonder she'd gone red, though – must feel well embarrassed. And Jacob's face and

294

all, right bottle job. Least Garry was working for their future. Lulu didn't even know she had a future someone *could* work for.

'There's something I need to discuss with Lu,' Jacob said. Way too late, pal. 'In private,' he added. Stubbing his fag in the ashtray.

'We can't turn him out now,' said Lulu. 'He's off his face, he can't handle drugs.'

'We have to, baby. This can't wait. Not a possibility.'

'Presume it could wait before, couldn't it?' she pointed out. Yeah, Garry made her right – bet it *could* wait while Jacob made her watch the films. Would of waited for ever if it weren't obvious the geezer'd been caught with his pants down.

'Look, he's been sampling the merchandise–'

'And you ain't?' Garry said. Fucker.

'Bet it's not the same stuff you gave Angel, though,' said Jacob, giving him the evils. Fuck, was the bloke some, some sort of voodoo merchant?

'I never killed Angel,' Garry said.

'Who's saying you did?' asked Lu.

'That cunt is.'

'Had to be you gave him the bad gear,' Jacob insisted. Like a bastard teacher. Be saying next no one was to leave the room till Garry owned up.

'Look, right.' Fucking too many lies, too many lies, nearly lost B over lies. 'Got him some gear off Stan and Del *one time*. One time, months before he snuffed it. One time, Lu. After I heard he laughed about you being related. Done me head in.'

'He laughed?'

'Yeah. The boys got him stuff occasional, could of easy been them give it him. Yeah, right, I knew it weren't clean, was cut with–'

'Crystal meth. Bad crystal meth,' said Jacob. Voodoo bastard.

'Yeah, this new sort of Nazi Crank. Super-Crank. Thought it'd be like that Russian Roulette. Might of hurt him, most probably not. Bit like what he give me that time.'

'What the bloody hell you on about?' Lulu's eyes sending out rays. That Jacob'd got her on the magic, and all.

'The dates are all wrong, mate. Stuff I give him was *months* before.'

'He could have saved it,' said Jacob.

'Angel save gear? Do me a favour.'

'What d'you mean, what he gave you that time?' Lulu asked. Pressing her hands together, knocking them on her knees.

'You know, that bastard film.' That nearly made B go all away. 'Was out me box on some shit Angel give me.'

'What sort of shit?' Jacob put in. Leaning forward.

'Don't know, angel dust I think, funny enough. And it weren't no good.' He laughed. 'Reckon I'd go with me own sister without something making me, is it?'

'Wish you'd told me,' she said. Pulling her thumb back like B done.

'You was in love with the bloke.' Garry shrugged. 'Then after he pissed off, seemed an horrible thing to say. You know, with you having a goldfish in your bowl.'

'That was good of you,' said Lulu. Soft. Like she meant it.

'Don't be an idiot, Lu.' Jacob picked up his mug, put it down again.

'And you don't come it with that whiter-than-white shit.' Garry's eyes was more open than ever, full of bastard ants. 'You want to tell her how much them vids cost?'

Jacob cleared his throat. Give a sort of laugh down his beak. Wrapped one leg round the other, as if they was made of spaghetti.

'A hundred and fifty thousand pounds,' Jacob said. Slow.

'*How* much?' Lulu jumped up off the settee, went over to Jacob's chair. 'Since when d'you have that kind of dosh?'

'He don't,' Garry said. 'You do.' Got up hisself, moved round the room. Feet was restless, that kicky feeling you got when you was over-tired.

'*I* do?' Spinning round to face Garry. 'What the fuck are you on about?'

'Lu . . .' Jacob'd untangled hisself from that twisted leg thing, was on his feet now and all. Like they was playing Simon Says. 'It's Angel's money.'

'Angel's . . . Someone want to tell me what's going on?' Lulu looked as if she was going to cry, poor cow. B reckoned Lu could turn on the waterworks just like that, but Garry still felt horrible. Had to remind hisself was for her own good. He picked something up off the side. Picture. Oh, fuck. They was *all* against him. Shouldn't of bothered trying to help.

'Clifford Black,' he heard hisself say. 'Clifford Black.'

'What?' Lulu turned back to him, sounding all irritable, like he was getting in the way of something more important.

'This is his,' Garry told her.

'No, it's Angel's. Remember? B gave it me. At Mum's, in a carrier, that time.'

'Fuck off.' Bathsheba'd give her a couple of books out of Angel's stuff, sure that's what she'd said. 'Telling you, it's his.'

'Clifford Black?' said Jacob. 'Isn't that Maggie's friend, the one who was shot?'

'*Friend*, is it?' Garry laughed. 'She don't have friends, mate.'

'Never mind that, for fuck's sake.' Lulu slapped Jacob on the arm. 'What's this about Angel's money?' She held out her hand, looked at it. 'Jake . . . my ring?'

'That was kind of a prelude to telling you,' he reckoned. 'A way in.'

'Telling me what, precisely?'

'Struth, girl.' Garry'd had enough of this. He banged Clifford Black's picture down on the cabinet.

'Careful, that's worth money.' Lulu come over, grabbed it up.

'Not one and half hundred thou it ain't, *I* bet.' Took the painting back off her. 'But that's what you're worth, if he ain't spent it all.' Looked down at the little naked Mum. Why'd Lu have this? How? Jacob must of nicked it from wherever B'd hid it in their flat. Like they was all trying to send him up St Clements.

'Angel left me some money, to invest for you and Fred.' Jacob moved across the room to them. 'Me, not you. Didn't know about it until well after we got together, baby. And now Bathsheba's taken half to stop Mickey McGowan finding out and getting it all.'

Lulu looked from one to the other. Her face'd gone even whiter'n normal. She run her hands through her hair, making it stick up round her face like a demon thing. As if flames was coming out her head. Brought her hand up to her mouth, started rubbing the lipstick off, leaving streaks on her fingers like blood.

'You weren't going to tell me, Jake,' she said. 'Were you?' Laughing, mad cow.

'Course I bloody was.'

'He was going have it away,' Garry put in.

'Doubt it, mate. Would you, love? No.' Lulu scratched at the lipstick marks on her hand. 'Bet your sweet life me and Fred would of got stuff. You'd of made sure of that, wouldn't you, Jacob?' So slow, you'd think she was half-asleep. 'But it would all of come from you, not him. Because he was the love of my life, and you couldn't handle that.'

'There's no such thing,' Jacob said. Right panic in his voice. 'Only to do with times in your life, not who the people were. If someone else impressive enough had come along when Angel did, they'd be the love of your life instead. It's the timing that matters.'

'Bollocks,' said Garry. 'Bathsheba's the only one could of been mine.'

'Very interesting, mate.' Lulu took a few steps nearer to Jacob. 'Now would you mind telling me where the rest of the fucking money is?'

'You reckon he never knew when he asked you out, is it?' Garry said. 'Dream on.'

'Did you?' To Jacob.

'No. That, I promise.' Reaching out to touch her shoulder. She eyed him. Nodded.

'Right, fine,' she said. 'It's *your* money, I suppose, if it was really left to you.'

'Thanks for this, Garry,' Jacob said. 'Thanks a lot.'

'Owed you one.' Shit, the anger was back, running through his body like a fresh hit. He held the picture close to his chest. 'I'll just take this then, shall I? Commission, like.'

'I don't think so.' Jacob moved Lu aside, come up to Garry. 'That's Lu's.'

Cheek of the fucker, after what he'd tried to nick off her. Garry see that chin above him, couldn't resist. Waiting for it, it was. And he decked the cunt.

Jacob asked the breasts for a brandy, settled back in his chair. This place was a cut-price Holly Blue, the girls comparatively older, more tired, the punters shinier with embarrassment and lack of personal hygiene. Or maybe the difference was to do with Jacob's mood; right now, he couldn't imagine seeing anything that would give him even the pleasure of novelty. He was pissed off, feeling as though he were a human Swan Vesta box and every bloody person around was a match that needed striking. The thought made him want a cigarette; he shook one from the packet, fished in his pocket for his lighter. Bollocks, must have left it at home. Luckily, there was a match-book in the ashtray, one of those soft promotional things. *The Pussy Parlour*. Why not go the whole way and call it *Cunt*? Jacob glanced round the room. Name would be appropriate for the clientele, too. God, if he'd been worried about being mistaken for a customer at the Holly Blue, how much worse was it to be seen straightforwardly as a punter here? Except . . . as it happened, actually he didn't give a toss what some aging stripper might think. Not any more.

His brandy arrived. Jacob swallowed it down, ordered another, lit his cigarette. The action made him wince. Bloody Garry Dawson. The bastard had been too out-of-it, too weak to do any real damage, but it hadn't been much fun playing the Ocean last night with a massive bruise on his face. Lead guitarist had taken the piss right through the set. And Lu had refused to come to the gig, despite claiming she more or less understood why he'd kept the money secret. Jacob had a nagging feeling she was biding her time. Then at the bookshop today, Michelle had looked at him with what he had to think was pity and contempt, as though the other bloke would never be worth seeing. Even not shaving hadn't helped much with how visible the thing was, and it was stiff now, sore. One of his back teeth felt loose; he couldn't *stand* the dentist. Jacob hadn't been hit since his late teens, when Angel had got them into that fight with those Townies; was ridiculous to have been punched now at nearly forty-two. Had almost hit Garry back, but he had to think of his hands. And anyway, the sympathy he'd got from Lu at that point would have evaporated pretty bloody quickly if he'd lashed out. Then there was the guilt, the oblique feeling he deserved what had happened. *Oh yeah, Mitzy. Otherwise you'd have steamed right in there.*

Jacob's face throbbed, everywhere he turned were tits he wasn't particularly interested in, even his cigarette tasted stale. And the truth was, he looked in on himself and didn't know who he saw, beyond a collection of impulses and their nerve endings. Lulu had got to the heart of it, of him, with a dreadful ease he'd had no access to: *it would all of come from you, not him.* There had been times when Jacob had really wondered if he'd intended to keep the money, but the only part he'd spent, apart from what he'd given to that bitch Bathsheba, had been the grand on Lu's ring. He'd wanted to be what Angel hadn't dared to be, had wanted to be braver, better than his friend, the love of all their lives, God help them. Lu was right, he'd probably have invested the money, sure, but offered the profits as though he'd earned them and the right to distribute them; Angel's death would have been just that, then: a death. *Never happen, mate. I'll be with you all for ever.* Oh screw this. If Jacob could get his hands on an exorcist, he bloody well would. Even if he had to convert for it.

Garry had humiliated him. Forced him to speak, and then hit him. That undernourished fucked-up toe-rag had made Lulu watch, as meantime Jacob was stripped of any dignity. Like being a non-consensual participant in some fetish movie. Even two days on, Jacob could feel his face burn when he thought about that. Wouldn't have been so bad if he could have believed Garry had been consumed by righteous indignation on Lu's behalf, that, Jacob could have taken, but being consumed by drugs and selfish rage wasn't the same deal. Jacob could have lost Lulu, nearly did, maybe had even, and Garry had capped that by chinning him. *When all you wanted was to play the big man with Lu and my money. Shame. Still want her, do you, then?* Course he did. At least, he thought so. Pretty much. If he wasn't totally sure, that was Garry's fault, nothing to do with Jacob losing the money.

Jacob put out his cigarette, drank his second brandy, signalled to the topless waitress. Shit, he was a crap revenger, just like he was a crap boyfriend. The sense of dislocation would always prevent him living fully in any world, even one as amoral as this. Somehow, he could never feel quite enough. He envied Lu's quick feelings, even Fred's – bloody hell, even Garry's sometimes – yet Jacob had more in common with Bathsheba. Depressing thought. But her blank look when he'd told her about Garry being in that film, it had been more than her straightforwardly keeping her reactions in; Jacob couldn't help thinking it had to do with her not knowing how to respond. Of not feeling very much, comparative to the buzz of winning the cheque. The third brandy arrived; Jacob took a sip, lit another cigarette with one of the bendy matches. Glanced at his watch. Stephen Hopkins was late.

Didn't even know who he was looking out for. No suggestion of them both carrying a copy of the *London Review of Books* or whatever. For all he knew, Stephen Hopkins was something to do with Mickey McGowan, intended to bully Jacob into giving up the rest of the money. Way he felt at the moment, the McGowans could have the bloody lot, if it wasn't for Lu. She was so furious with him, hurt, although mostly trying to hold it back. Whenever he'd got it wrong before, she'd been totally forgiving, blowing up quickly and just as fast calming down. But this time . . . Jacob wasn't sure whether the only reason she hadn't kicked him into touch yet was that the dough was in his bank account. She probably thought he'd betrayed her. He thought he probably had, too.

'Mr Fox?'

'What? Oh, right, yeah.' Had been a very long time since anyone other than his bank manager had called Jacob *Mr*. Stephen Hopkins was black; on the phone, that rich public school voice had made Jacob assume a white man. *That's the way, start with some liberal guilt.* Confidence oozed from the bloke as though he'd put it on with his aftershave, enough that others could smell it. Obviously not forty yet, good looking, smart enough to make Jacob feel shabby instead of the chilled-out muso he'd almost convinced himself he'd seen in the mirror at home. The bruise definitely looked sad apparently, rather than dangerous. What the bloody hell did Stephen want? No one he hadn't met had ever summoned Jacob to a meeting before, unless it was to sound him out about work. Somehow, he doubted this bloke had a depping job for him.

They settled down with drinks and *Did you have any trouble finding the place* and *Sorry to be late* and a fresh ashtray. Jacob felt wary, shifting about in his seat, telling himself to keep still. But after being punched, anything could happen, no question: someone was always out to shaft you. Had taken him nearly forty-two years to see that.

'Thank you for coming at such short notice,' said Stephen. Managing to sound disparaging, as if it wasn't a possibility that Jacob could have anything better to do.

'No problem.' The second Stephen had said, *In connection with Angel McGowan*, Jacob would have moved anything to be here. Even if Angel's father did turn out to be the reason. 'Did you know Angel? Personally?' Jacob asked.

'Oh yes. You?'

'For sure.' Jacob caught Stephen's gaze; pain reached between them. Bloody hell, had this bloke been . . . God, he was hardly one of the kids Angel had gone for in the last few years. Or

302

maybe they'd just been close friends. *Yeah, like us, Mitzvah.*

'I know about the terms of the will, Mr Fox.'

'Jacob.' He looked away towards the stage. Could see the cellulite on that girl from here, and her nose made Jacob's look small. Crap, Bathsheba had said only she, Jacob and one of her associates knew about the will; did that make Stephen Hopkins something to do with her? Jacob should have seen this coming. Fred had told Lu that one of the men Bathsheba had met the other week was *well smart* and black; could that be a coincidence? *Told you, they don't exist, mate.* Maybe Stephen was Bathsheba's own revenge for what Jacob had made her face. Perhaps she did care, after all. Her boyfriend certainly did.

'You were the only one with a direct vested interest, weren't you?' said Stephen. Taking a mouthful of his Peroni. 'That's going to be awkward when the family realizes. After all, the Register of Members has to be updated, and Angel's name won't be on it.'

'I know, yeah.' Thanks to Bathsheba he felt quite the expert.

'Technically, Ian Silverman's will be.' As if Jacob hadn't spoken. 'Of ISU.'

'That, I think's *my* problem, isn't it?' Ian Silverman . . . Of course. Jacob really was a congenital idiot: the cheque had been signed by the bloke who now owned the shares.

'How close were you and Angel, Jacob?' Was it Jacob's imagination, or did Stephen look slightly less cool, as though he hadn't wanted to ask that question. *I give a lot of people Tourette's, Foxy.*

'I loved him,' Jacob said. 'But not like that.'

'Like what?'

'We weren't lovers. We were friends.'

'Utter balls.' Stephen laughed. 'Angel didn't have friends.'

'Sure he did. Once. Me.' *Best mate. Best mate.* The thing Angel had given him was a sense of inclusion; the only time Jacob had been confident around women was in those years at Cambridge. Having a fairly *frum* grandmother and a bitterly celibate mother and a single sex school and a father capable of pinching your girlfriends hadn't given Jacob a proper idea of his sexual ranking; being Angel's chosen friend had. Though what Angel had got out of it, Jacob couldn't be sure. Someone who'd always love him best, maybe. Someone he could torment for all time. 'Sorry, I spaced out there.'

'I said if that's true, you were lucky.' Stephen reached for his beer.

'What about you?'

'He was my . . . We were together, on and off, for five years. Mostly off.' Shrugging. 'If you knew him that well, you know fidelity wasn't his strong suit.' Leaning across the table. 'To be honest, I wish *I* could have been his friend. Would have been hard, because I did find him so . . . well, attractive frankly. I was obsessed with him, and that's not easy to admit. But I think the singularity of being his friend would have been . . . flattering enough to make up for what I'd have lost.'

'Sure.' Freaked now. Didn't get the feeling this man was in the habit of confiding in strangers. Meantime, Jacob was still worried about the possible connection between Stephen and Bathsheba. God, nothing was worth this much hassle, not even Lulu.

'The point is, I cared enough that parts of my life have been ruined by his death.' Stephen smiled. 'That's rather less true of you, isn't it?'

'Not too sure about that.' He closed his eyes for a second, saw Lulu's smile, framed by the screen of his lids. If he left her, what would he have to go back to? A life of pretending he hadn't fucked up, a life of just getting by, emotionally, financially. Of work that wasn't good enough for him being the only focus in his life. Opening his eyes again, he looked at Stephen. 'What do you want?' he asked. A wearily familiar question lately.

'How much do you know about drugs?'

'Fuck all. I smoke the *very* occasional joint. Used to do a bit of speed at college.'

'That's a nasty bruise you've got there.'

'Reckon I got it in a drug deal, do you?' Jacob touched his face. He was beginning to see where this was going: Stephen Hopkins, maybe on behalf of Bathsheba, or even Mickey McGowan, was suggesting Jacob might have had something to do with Angel's death. It was almost funny.

'You're not at all what I expected,' Stephen said. Thoughtfully. 'Angel's *friend*.'

'The money's to look after Lulu and Fred. I was never interested in it for myself.'

'Fred? I've been wondering what the connection was with that name.'

'Angel's son.' Jacob watched Stephen register that: he hadn't known; this, you could see. 'He's Lulu's boy. Nice kid, thirteen.' Realizing as he spoke how fond he'd somehow become of Fred. That made him feel panicky. He'd never wanted children.

'Angel had a son.' With disbelief.

'Sure.' Jacob lit another cigarette. 'And kind of entrusted him to me. Kind of.'

'You're on Angel's side.' Linking his huge hands together.

'Always.' Finishing his brandy. 'That's why I was so pissed off that Bathsheba McGowan conned me out of half his money. It was meant for Fred, she knew that.'

'She did *what*?'

'Didn't you know?' So this guy did have something to do with Bathsheba.

'Technically, no. Though I should have realized . . . Not that I knew who Fred was.' Stephen leaned forward. 'Couldn't let me have a cigarette, could you?' he said. Jacob pushed the packet across the table. 'No, forget it. Look, I'll ask you this once.' His voice urgent. 'Do you really have a relationship with Angel's son?'

'I do, yeah.' Scraping his cigarette against the side of the ashtray. 'His mother's my girlfriend, and Fred's a big part of my life.' That was still true. For now.

'Did you know Angel's heart was enlarged?' Stephen laughed. 'Can't make my mind up whether that's appropriate or ironic.'

'I didn't, no.' Parodic, for sure. 'Thought he had AIDS.'

'He was HIV, but that was the least of his problems, frankly.' Putting his hand over his own heart. 'Do you think the McGowans gave Angel the stuff that killed him?'

'No.' Jacob's heart was pounding. He could do here what he'd always done, stay being an observer, threatening action in his head that never materialized. Or. Bollocks, if he spoke, that was Lulu's brother he'd be implicating. Jacob stroked his bruise. Well, tough shit, her other brother was dead. 'I think . . . ' Wished his glass wasn't empty. 'I think, no, I'm pretty sure it was Garry Dawson.' *Nice one, Jacob. I mean that, man.*

'Garry Dawson. Maybe you *would* say that.' Stephen sucked in breath, then his lips. And suddenly, Jacob became aware again of being in the club, the cricket beat of a backing track, the desperate gyrations of that poor woman on the tiny stage. Something wasn't right. If Stephen Hopkins knew Bathsheba, it probably meant he knew Garry.

'I've got a card I could show you,' Jacob said. 'Evidence, really.' Weirdly calm.

'Naturally, Angel died *after* Bathsheba countersigned the transfer of his shares to us,' Stephen said. As if he were thinking aloud. 'She told me only recently that she'd seen him for the first time in a very long time when he'd just decided to sell.' He rubbed his eyes. 'How sure are you?' he asked. 'About Garry Dawson?'

'Sure.' Okay, so he'd have to be sure now. Have to stay that way, too.

'My advice is, protect yourself.' Stephen reached across the table, patted Jacob's arm. 'Bathsheba McGowan's . . . Well, you probably know what she is. And I haven't discounted that you might be stringing me along.'

'I need another drink,' Jacob said.

'While you're having it, I need some facts.' Smiling, sadly. 'Then perhaps there's a few things I should tell you about business.'

Chapter Fifteen

Bathsheba felt she was going to be blown off this bridge. If she were even a tad lighter (let's face it, she could afford to lose a couple of pounds), she'd be swept into the Thames like that empty Coke can. There was something exciting about the way the wind pressed against your body, as if desperate to have you. She remembered when it had been like that with her and Garry. Hadn't made love for weeks now, not since the morning after Clifford Black – until then, there hadn't been too many days when they'd avoided each other in bed. Since Jacob had told her about the poxy film, she wasn't sure who was doing the most avoiding. She *knew*, of course she knew, that it was all long, long, long ago. And she knew as well what Angel could be like. *Let me feel how well the woman waxed you.* Hard to say no to him, snake, charmer. Anyway, Angel had got Garry on something, the poppet so never could do drugs. Though (sweet Jesus) she did wish she hadn't persuaded Garry to hold on to those other tapes (despite her foresight being proven in selling them back to Jacob). What if . . . She could kill Lulu. Trashy overweight tart, making Bathsheba imagine the unimaginable. And producing that nosy kid. Although she'd thought masses about it, she couldn't see how Fred had been able to give Jacob enough information to make that crack about *bomb disposal.* Child was turning into the devil himself, not to mention what he'd got from his bloody mother. Well, if Lulu and Jacob were going to win, then Bathsheba was Waterloo Bridge.

Garry and she just needed to get their relationship back on track, make it central to their lives again. Could do with a mini-breaklette (mm, somewhere warm) where he could forget London and all that had happened recently. Few days in the sun, that would get his appetites back. All of them. And where she could forget that bloody triumphant note in Jacob's voice. Maybe in a couple of weeks, when the dividends and the AGM were due – they'd have a quorum without her and it *so* wouldn't hurt to be away around then. She'd dig out the vaginal barbell. Didn't do to neglect any part of your toning, though when you weren't on display it was too easy to get scandalously flabby. The scales were nudging seven stone one lately, and (admit it) only God knew the state her pelvic muscles were in.

Those waves were bizarre, like something out of a film God was making for His own amusement. A little boat moored to the bank was being tossed about as if it weighed nothing. If she watched long enough, it would be smashed to pieces. The London Eye was still, frozen, staring unblinking over the city. Bet there were squillions of disappointed tourists today. Bathsheba turned her back on the scene, leaned against the bridge, anchoring herself with her hands. Fab day for Hopkins to suggest meeting outdoors. What that Geoff had said to Hopkins was still bothering her, *You're a mental bastard* – and that was coming from a man who made his living destroying things. Even she so wouldn't want to get on the wrong side of Geoff, yet she'd seen he hadn't just respected Hopkins, but feared him. Had been playing on her mind all week. Masses. *Got a mind now, have you?* Jesus, the closer she got to what she wanted, the more Angel tried to undermine her. Daddy's boy, all right.

She shook her head, to get her hair out of her face. There was Hopkins now, walking along Lancaster Place. Even he was windswept (thank God, not perfect after all), his overcoat billowing out around him, making him look fat. She fought the wind to put a smile on her face, waited for Hopkins to get within a couple of steps of her before moving.

'Lovely to see you, sweetie,' she said. 'But you so could have picked a better day.'

'Looks fine to me.' If that face was offering his version of fine, then she'd hate to see it when he was a weeny bit unfine. The darkest cloud up there wasn't as black as that expression, even his skin didn't have any other tones in it today. All she needed, poxy temperament from a civilian.

'Outdoorsy type, are you?' Bathsheba tried a giggle. Had bloody Del reneged? Maybe Hopkins was just stressy, he had a lot of deals going at any one time. Power meant responsibility, she'd have to get used to that herself. *Thought you hated fantasists, B?* Hopkins was staring down at her as though the weather was her fault. 'Never would have guessed you were hearty,' she added. 'Imagined you like your creature comforts too much.'

'Come on.' Grabbing her arm. 'We're going to take a little walk.'

'What?' That bloody well hurt, the sod. 'Something the matter? Is it Del?'

'Don't speak, Bathsheba. I *so* never liked your voice.' Pulling her along, over the bridge towards Waterloo.

'Charming.' *You're a mental bastard.* And suddenly, Bathsheba was scared. Something had gone wrong, that was clear, but what? She'd been as close as close – Daddy was practically a dribbling fool now, Del was transferring his shares, there was going to be that little nudgelette for Stan with the explosion at the Holly Blue (*and* there was her hundred and fifty in hand as a weeny extra). So close she could reach out and touch it. Bathsheba needed her Daddy's advice, but, of course, that was the one thing she'd never get, even if it had been worth taking these days. Her flesh went goosey, but this time it told her something bad was about to happen. 'Where are we going?' she chanced.

'You don't get to ask the questions any more.'

'But . . . ' This so couldn't be the end. She was the brightest McGowan, the only one in a functional relationship, the only one with a chance of survival. Her plans couldn't be ending like this, there was no reason for it. Everything she'd ever wanted was being squeezed away by that hard black hand dragging on her arm. 'You're hurting me.'

'Good.' Stephen Hopkins was walking so fast, she was having trouble staying on her feet. It had to be a misunderstanding, someone must have told Hopkins lies about her. But that grip felt personal, focused. Assured. As they reached the end of the bridge, she turned her head to look back at the river. There must be someone left she could sell.

'ISU Holdings? What's that?'

'More like what isn't it. They've got loads of businesses and stuff.'

'And you've bought shares in my name?'

'A guy called Stephen Hopkins is sorting it out for me. You won't straightforwardly be part of ISU, you'll be on . . . uh . . . the Register of Members for one or two smallish things.'

Lulu tried to take that in. Members of *what*? But as far as she could see, it would mean she'd be in charge of any money the shares brought in. She pushed herself back in her chair, looked round the club at the people laughing, enjoying themselves.

'Presume you've invested all of it?' she asked.

'Stephen advised a hundred and forty, so that gives us . . . you . . . something to play with meantime.'

'Right.' Lulu rubbed her ring on her skirt. If she stayed with Jacob, at least she'd be certain it'd be of her own free will now. That had to be good – didn't like thinking bad things about herself, even if she was fairly sure they weren't true.

'You won't make a fortune, but it'll help a lot on top of Heaven Scent.'

'Right.' Three hundred would of helped more, mate. Funny to think how excited she'd been when Jacob had first brought her here to watch him play. Seemed years ago, not four months. Couldn't imagine getting really excited about anything now, since the other night. She didn't believe Jacob had been going to keep the money, not precisely, but he'd wanted to control it. Her. Was as though Jake didn't see the difference between looking after her and looking after Fred. Bloody Christ, she'd just found one rubbish father, last thing she needed was two. Roles in this family were getting too sodding confusing. Lover-father was quite literally not sayable. Bet even Fred couldn't look up a word for that.

Lulu picked up her wine. Tasted a bit off, though it most probably wasn't. Had Garry really given Angel bad gear? But he'd said that was months before Angel died, though Jake didn't seem so sure. Could tell by the way he didn't want to talk about it, like he was protecting her from his thoughts. He was sparking a cigarette now, seemed he always had one on these days, the flame from his lighter showing up the bruise. Gone yellowish. Why the bloody hell had Garry smacked him one? Be truthful, she'd looked at it every which way, and knew her brother wasn't defending her honour, that was for certain sure. Them days were well over, if they'd ever existed, *and* he'd gone off with her picture. What if Jacob *had* meant to keep the money? No. If she kept thinking like that, might as well tell him to fuck off, and mean it. That wasn't an option. She loved him, loved the way he'd made her feel – mostly – in the time they'd been together. Even Fred had come round to him. She was too bloody old, too knackered, to start again looking for another new life.

'You okay, Lu? Miles away, there.'

'Fine. Ought to be celebrating.'

'We'll go out after my second set. Dinner, my treat.'

'Right.' Treating on whose money?

'We should go back to that Indian. Where we went the first proper time?'

'Yeah, that'd be nice.' The place where she'd waited and waited for him to kiss her, and he never had. Where she'd practically had to ask *him* out. Lulu felt in her bag for her mirror, touched up her lip-gloss. Come on, girl, try and put his mistakes behind you. Might as well go for it, if he *is* precisely what you want. *Love belongs to them, not to you.*

311

Did Jacob love her? *They're limited creatures, girl. Remember that.* He must do, else why stay with her? *A hundred and fifty reasons, Lu.* Great. Jacob had once told her Angel lived in his head, spoke to him – well, Maggie lived in Lulu's. Pity Angel and Mags never liked each other, they could of had a party.

'What's funny?' Jacob smiled at her, took her hand across the table. She loved them creases in his face.

'Nothing. Sorry I've been a moody cow.'

'Don't be daft, me should be sorry.' Squeezing her hand. 'You do like the ring?'

'Yeah, course I do.' Leaning forward in her chair, to stop the man behind her earwigging. Stank he did, and all. Didn't normally get dirty types in here.

'I've been meaning to say.' Taking a drag of his fag. 'Hope this doesn't sound dreadful, seeing as it was your money and I didn't have much choice anyway, but those films are worth every thousand we paid.'

'Jesus, Jake.' She had to laugh. 'What are you like?' Christ, he got it so wrong sometimes, it was – what's the word? – endearing. Nearly.

'Looks like you're having fun,' a woman commented as she passed their table. Lulu recognized her: she was the one who'd said in the loos once that a lot of them in here fancied Jacob Fox. Asked what Lulu was doing right.

'Tell you what, Lu,' Jake said. 'Listen out for "Shake Your Money Maker" tonight.' Grinning. 'I'll play it for you, especially. Told you I was a romantic.'

'Piss off.' But she was really laughing now. How could he be this sure of himself? This certain she'd forgive him about the money. Hard to think where that sort of confidence came from – she'd never had it. Nothing like. Wasn't just a male thing, look at Bathsheba. *She* walked through the world as if it'd been created to her exact . . . specifications. Even Garry wasn't as sure of his place in it. Though when Lulu had met Jake, she wouldn't of had him down as being sure, neither.

312

'I love that top,' Jacob told her. Running his fingers over the sleeve. 'Very sexy.'

'Yeah, well, it's meant to be.' Trying to fake that sort of knowing self-belief.

'You do make me happy.'

'Yeah?' she said.

'This is the first time ever I've worked with what's there, not made something up.'

'Good.' Though it didn't sound much of a compliment. Lulu took another mouthful of her wine. Getting used to the taste, now. Jake finished his pint, looked at his watch.

'I'm on in a minute,' he said. 'Can't help wishing we were at home, though. I can't stop thinking about those films. God, baby, why didn't I know you then?'

'Instead of now?' Sharp.

'That's bloody harsh. No, as well as now. Always.'

'You mean that?'

'I do, yeah. It's my number one fantasy, even though I know it's not a possibility.' Kissing her hand. 'The past isn't, anyway.'

'Sod the past.' Smiling. 'Got it in five boxes, if we want it.'

'For sure.' He stood up. 'See you in about an hour, then. I'll order you another drink on my way across.' Jacob began to move towards the piano, then stopped, turned back to her. 'Forgot to ask,' he said. 'How's Fred's cold doing?'

She didn't know yet how she precisely felt about the vids, but him saying that was worth a hundred and fifty grand of anyone's money. *You great soft baggage.* For once, Lulu almost felt she could tell her auntie to get lost.

Maggie weren't at all sure she could do this. Stood outside her front door, grabbing at the early morning air as if it was in the sales, her legs turned into something what felt like bowls of jellied eels. Was she having heart attack? No, don't be daft, it was one of them anxiety things, if she weren't very much mistaken. Let's be honest, she hadn't left the flat in going on two month, how could she expect to bleeding feel? That's it, nice and steady. Flipping hell, if someone *was* going to clonk her over the head again, couldn't be more worst than feeling like this. Not that she really thought it was a trap.

'You all right, Nan?'

'Anything's better'n being indoors listening to your radio.' Crikey, that music he'd had on – couldn't even make out the words and the ones she could make out she never liked.

'No, I mean you sure it's okay, taking me there? Can you handle going out?'

'It's important to you, love.' Bet your sweet life Lulu would of messed it up if *she'd* tried to take him there. Jacob reckoned Lu went all silly round the bleeder. 'And if I never, you'd go on your own, wouldn't you?' Wouldn't put it past Lu to of let him, neither. 'Sooner or later.'

'Probably,' he said. Could hear that cold of his was hanging around a bit.

'Just have to manage then, won't I? Was me what was invited, end of the day.' But was it too risky? When she thought about that kitten . . . Though Fred ought to get to know his family, only right, and least this way Maggie was back in charge. Might make all the difference, if Fred was more'n an idea. Any funny business, she had McGowan's gun safe in her bag. Just wished she could get her breath.

Get a grip, woman, at least. Most probably she should of been practising, making herself more used to being out, bit by bit. She was only going by what she see on that programme, but the doctor on there seemed sensible, for a wonder. Mind, too flaming late now. She had to get on with it, and that was that. Long old way to go, though. Right out of London. Thought made her come over all floaty, like she'd been cut off at the neck. Come on, you been through tougher stuff than this, Maggie girl.

Even with her arm tucked in Fred's, was a nightmare journey. Felt it was happening to someone else. Couldn't of took the District, that would of been *too* hard. Taxi over to the station hadn't been bad as the Tube would of, though right take-on, psychiatrist would of been cheaper. But Waterloo . . . Had London always been this noisy, this full? Everyone bigger'n her, even the kids, everyone with wickedness in their eyes. Blimey, her men seemed gentle as, well, kittens compared with the hardness out on the street. And it was so bright and all – near on the end of autumn, you'd of thought the world'd be less shiny, less shimmering, than this. Such a job, getting her breath, keeping it.

'You're meant to breathe into a paper bag, Nana?' Sniffing. 'Hyperventilating, you are. Looked that up once. Want me to get you one?' But even Fred weren't quite his normal thoughtful self. Had a touch of the umps, nerves if you asked her. He hadn't hardly said more'n one word about where they was going, after begging her for him to come with, but he might as well of had *Blow this for a game of soldiers* tattooed on his forehead. Might of changed his mind. She should never of told him who that phone call was from – part of her wondered now if she'd just been being selfish, wanting company for her first trip out. No, it was so's Lulu wouldn't get it sudden into her head to take a chance with their boy. But maybe Maggie should of said for him to come down Tescos with her instead.

Fred stared up at the man. Taller than Jake, and twice as ugly. *Grandad.* The word didn't sound right even in his head. Bloke crouched down a bit, put a finger out as if he was going to touch Fred's face, but then he didn't.

'Angel,' the bloke said.

'No, I'm Fred?'

'Angel.' Eyes full of tears. Fred felt well embarrassed. *He* was the one should be tearful, but he didn't feel anything, only sort of nervous. Nan had always hated Mickey McGowan – why'd he gone from bad news to good all of a sudden?

'Needn't think you can try nothing funny, Mickey.' Nan pushed in front of Fred. Mickey stood up. Eyed Nan.

'You look well, Maggie.'

'Yeah, you and all.' Then she laughed. 'Right pair of bleeding liars, ain't we?'

'You haven't changed.' He smiled. Wiped his eyes. 'Bit of a shock, the little one, do you know?'

'He wanted to come.'

'Well, I've wanted to meet him a while.' Did touch Fred then, on the head. 'Though children break your heart.'

'Make you right, there.'

House was way posh – Fred didn't know his grandad had money. Nearly as clean as Nan's, and all. Maybe he had servants, rang bells to tell them what to do. Wicked. Did his dad look like Mickey? Shit, might mean Fred would, when he was older. Though B was well buff, and course, Angel looked similar to Del, so perhaps Fred would be okay. God, kitchen was something out of Nan's magazines. But Mickey didn't sound snobbo.

'I've a pot of coffee on. You want an orange juice or something, Fred?'

'Yeah, please.'

'Sit down, both.' Mickey nodded to a big round, silver box on the table. Like one of the film reel cases you saw in . . . well, films. Ancient films. 'That's for you, Maggie. There's no copies, on me life,' he said.

'Meant to believe that, am I?' Nan asked. But she sat, and put the box down by her feet. 'Thanks,' she added. Bit of a mystery – was blatant they knew each other miles more than Fred had thought. Maybe they'd had a row once, that's why she slagged Mickey. Shit, what if that film was like Mum's . . . Don't be stupid, they probably didn't have that sort of thing back then. Jake was always telling him how different the world had got in a really short time, even since he was young, and Nan was loads older than Jacob. They'd had paintings though, in it.

Nan looked a bit better now. Had been well horrible, coming here with her hyperventilating and that scared thing in her eyes. Made him feel Mickey really was something to worry

316

about. A *murderer*, she'd said to Uncle Garry that time. But this was just some sad old bloke who missed his dead son. Anyone could tell that, looking at his eyes. Even Nan seemed to of gone all soft, as if she felt sorry for him. Weird to think they'd known each other years ago. Maybe when she'd looked like she did in that painting, only with her clothes on. Though knowing this family . . . But Fred didn't want to make this all crap, he wanted to like his grandad. Least not hate him.

'You're a fine-looking boy, so,' Mickey said. Putting the drinks on the table, sitting down to light his cigar.

'Um . . . cheers.'

'The very spit.'

'Only in looks, Mickey,' Nan said. Bit snide.

'Brains and all, I bet.'

'Yeah, he's clever.' She lit a fag.

'What should I call you?' Fred put in quick. Grown ups could get *way* sloppy. But it felt sort of nice, like some things you could count on, your nan boasting about you.

'Whatever you want, boy. Mickey or . . . Grandad.' Grabbing Fred's wrist. Fred's heart sped up. Didn't dare move. 'You don't have to decide now, mate.' Letting him go. Nothing to be scared about after all. Then, 'Thanks for this, Maggie. Believe you me, don't deserve it. But I appreciate . . . ' Tears coming down his cheeks, now. This was shitty, Fred didn't know where to look? Right, it was good that *Grandad* liked seeing him, but couldn't he of kept the waterworks for later, when they'd gone? Everyone had to spoil stuff. Only thing he'd wanted was to meet the bloke.

'We all got a lot of making up to do,' said Nan. Soft.

'More than you know, Maggie girl. Fuck me . . . Sorry, Fred.' Still crying, though he didn't sound as if he was. Like someone was behind his eyes, just pouring water out. 'We been betrayed, my Maggie. And I pulled some strokes, and all—'

'Betrayed?'

'God help us all, yeah. Mother of God, I don't know how to tell you.' Wiping his nose on the back of his hand, like a kid. 'But there's more I got to do.'

317

Nan put out her fag, pulled her massive bag across the table. Stuck it on her lap, put her hand in, but not like she was looking for something, more as if it was a giant glove.

'Fred shouldn't hear this, Mickey.'

'No. Course not.' He got out his wallet. 'Here's twenty quid. There's shops at the end of the road, son, go get some sweets.'

'Can I have a look round outside?' Buying sweets wouldn't take five minutes, even with a twenty. He'd had enough scenes to last him till he was as old as them two, wanted to leave them to it. Looked at his nan, his grandad. Family was getting bigger practically every day, but the new ones weren't babies, and that wasn't the way it was meant to be. Sometimes, Fred wished he could turn back to being twelve. 'Well, can I go, Nan?'

'Will he be safe?' Nan eyed Mickey.

'He's Angel's boy.' Like that was an answer. Maybe Angel had a massive rep round here, he might of been an hard man. Fred didn't mind that thought. But Richmond was a pants place from what he'd seen, nothing to get wound up about anyway.

'Fine. Be back here in half hour sharp, Fred,' said Nan. 'Here, take me mobile. Program your number in it for him, Mickey. Case he gets lost,' she added.

'I'm not Jake,' Fred told her. He finished off his juice. 'Everyone at school's got their own.'

'Half hour, Fred – I mean it. Don't take liberties. Don't answer the mobile if it rings. And wrap your scarf round that throat, else you'll be poorly again.'

As Fred was leaving the room, he heard Mickey tell Nan, *Sorry*, about ten squillion times. Seemed to him people were always sorry for stuff they could easy not of done in the first place.

'Sorry, no. That's gonzo porn, Jake.'

Jacob picked up one of her overstuffed cushions, put it behind his back. Lu's settee was even more uncomfortable than his. He looked up at her.

'What's gonzo porn?' he asked.

'When a bloke holds the camera and he's in the film and

all.' Sneering. 'One step up from home movies. Leave off, you haven't even *got* a camera.'

'I have now, back at my place. And lights. Second-hand, but you know . . . '

'Did *I* pay for that?' Running her fingers through her hair.

'Course not. Shit.' Felt himself flush. 'Parchman Farm did.'

'Bet it's a crappy one, then.' Fiddling with her skirt. God, why didn't the woman just sit down? 'Jumping the gun, weren't you?' she added, under her breath.

'So are you saying if I got a proper studio and a crew—'

'No I'm bloody not.'

'Be a way of you giving me all of you, baby.' Jacob couldn't stand this; he was so close to everything he wanted now: retribution, plus the whole of Lulu, every part she'd offered to other people, all he hadn't had access to. And she was telling him no. Who the bloody hell did she think she was? If it wasn't for Jacob, she'd still be struggling with Fred on her own. Or maybe worse, stuck with some dickhead who'd abuse her. He'd invested time, care, gone wholly into her world meantime; if that wasn't love, what was? And now he'd met Stephen Hopkins, Angel's money would be safe for her, too. There was even a chance they'd get back what Bathsheba had stolen. *What you gave her. I'd say Lu was already stuck with a dickhead, wouldn't you?* Jacob moved the cushion, fished for his cigarettes. 'Why are you being like this?' he said.

'Like what? Don't be a prat, all I said was I don't fancy it.' Sitting next to him, pushing her fingers through her hair again. He could see the roots coming through, dark with threads of silver. Saw the flesh wobble through her shirt with the movement of her arm. If they didn't make a film soon, she'd be too old. Wasn't as though he was asking her to go back into it for anyone else, just for them. Then they could look behind them and remember before sleep became the only thing they cared about. His grandmother would have been shocked beyond reason, would have thought Lulu a *nafkeh*, himself close to a pimp, but sex had always been a weird one in their family.

Other than him, only Dad had gone for it in a big way, as far as Jacob was aware. That, for sure, was one person who'd understand. It was the bloody digital age; if you couldn't manipulate your own narrative now, then there was no point living in the twenty-first century.

'Would only be the once, Lu.'

'Heard that before. Didn't hire the camera, did you? You *bought* it.'

'Isn't there anything I can say?' Putting his unlit cigarette on the floor, taking her hand. 'If you do this, I won't have any reason to be jealous of your past. Even of Angel.'

'Don't give me that emotional blackmail, mate.' But then she turned to him, her smile taking all the crossness from her face. Shit, was she going to agree after all? 'You reckon you love me, yeah?' she said. He nodded, not trusting himself to speak in case he fucked up. 'Look, Jake, I'm nearly thirty-seven years old. You're nearly forty-two—'

'We still look good,' he said. Almost whispering in his anxiety.

'Not what I meant. I . . . How serious are you about me?'

'What kind of question's that?'

'You came to me because of Angel.' Kissing his cheek. 'I'm okay with that. You had a thing about his and my film. Fair enough.' Another kiss, on the edge of his mouth. Jacob was getting a hard-on; if she were still going to refuse, he'd fucking implode. 'You've bent over backwards to look out for Fred for him.' Running her tongue over his top lip. 'You even wanted to pretend in your head his money was yours, so we'd love you instead of him.' Flicking her tongue into his mouth. 'Seems to me you . . . not that you want to be him, precisely, but you want what he had.'

'I do, yeah.' *Now the boy admits it. Be getting your foreskin sewn back on next.*

'I'll do your film, love.' Oh God. 'If you got the bottle to go all the way.'

'What do you mean?' Please, don't let her say she wanted Garry in the video.

'I get my coil taken out, you don't use a condom. We take a chance. Most probably won't work, but it did for me and Angel.'

'A *baby*? You never said you wanted more kids.'

'Well, precisely. That's because I didn't, not really. Most likely won't happen, anyway.' Pressing her body into his, her mouth on his neck. 'But if you want this as much as you say you do, you'll go for it.'

'What if I left you holding the baby?'

'Presuming you wouldn't.' Nipping his flesh. 'You might say no to doing it, but if you did it and it happened, you'd stick around. You can't help being a decent bloke.'

'You trying to put me off the idea?'

'Just suddenly seemed the logical thing, d'you get me?'

'No.' *You fucking deaf, Foxy? She's saying you'd be taking my place. For good.* 'You've not thought this one through,' Jacob tried.

'I know. Not had a chance to, have I?' Running her hand along his thigh to the crotch of his jeans. 'But I've had fantasies about us having a baby before.'

'Sure, that's totally understandable, but babies are bloody real, Lu.'

'Think I know that better than you, love.'

'I've never wanted kids. Never, not with anyone.' But the old panic was mixed up with wanting what only she could give him. Oh God, don't let him say yes. No Fox should be allowed to reproduce; each of them walked uncomprehending through the world, so none could make it explicable for the ones who came after. That, he was sure of. Jacob didn't hate his life, but it had never had enough point to want to pass it on. 'Fred's a bonus for me,' he said. 'Don't want one of my own. I'm just about getting used to being around a kid at all.' Trying not to feel her hand pressing down on his cock.

'Fair enough,' Lulu said. 'Want to make love? Sorry there's no films here, but–'

'See? You can't even have your own films around because of Fred.'

'Yeah, I know that. I said, fair enough.' Pulling up her skirt for him; he could see the tops of her stockings, the soft flesh above, thought he could even smell her cunt. 'Come on, he'll be with Maggie for ages yet,' she said.

God, the idea of fucking her while having control over the camera . . . Angel hadn't directed his own film. But it would be a bloody stupid thing to do. Irresponsible. Not to mention the fact that he'd never have choices again, would be stuck with the one life for ever. Angel's life. Even Jacob's revenge for Angel was going to be by proxy, exactly the way it was for Angel himself. Would *Jacob Fox* be meaningful, if he went further? Pretty much a dreadful thought, either way. *Semantics again, Jakey boy. You want my life or you don't.* No. If Jacob was even going to consider this, it had to be as himself. Straightforwardly. Screw Angel. The baby, if there ever was a baby, would have nothing to do with Angel McGowan. *Be my money financing the little bastard, though, won't it?* Hundred and fifty grand didn't go as far as all that, mate.

'Show me yourself,' he said to Lulu. 'Come on, baby, act for me.'

Weren't till she heard the door properly close that Maggie turned back to McGowan. She kept her hand in her bag, round the handle of the gun, the metal warm now where she'd been gripping it so long. Dying for a ciggie, but no way was she going to let her guard down. If she was ever going to give this shooter back to him, wouldn't be by handing it over. Mind, he looked about as dangerous as a jelly at the minute, pain leaking out his eyes like the mould'd overrun.

'What d'you mean, *betrayed*?' she said.

'It's all about betrayal, ain't it?' Fumbling for his hanky, blowing his nose. 'Life. Jesus, Maggie, you of all people should know that.'

'You mean what I did to you?' Maybe a grudge could last near on half a lifetime.

322

'No, not me.' He laughed. 'Should of made a go of it with you. Two of a kind.'

'We was never together, Mick.' Blokes just had to make up a different version of the past, as if it was something you could invent. All of a sudden, come into her head that McGowan was the last man to kiss her, till Clifford.

'Don't be too sure about that.' Re-lighting his cigar. 'I give me Angel a picture for his graduation present, old picture, worth a few bob. It looked like you, that's what made me buy it. Call it me fancy.' A half smile. 'Bet the bugger flogged it.'

'Oh, do me a favour.' Had he been that sentimental over the film of her and that *special* bloke? Over his wickedness. Lovely picture, that. Was he really going to let her walk out of here with it? 'Be telling me next you wanted to marry me,' she said.

'You was the only woman strong enough to take me on.' Staring at her. 'The only one hard enough. But you was a brass.'

'That's what made me strong, you stupid beggar.' Bleeding typical – she'd of been loveable if she hadn't been the thing what made her who they wanted to love. Might as well of been Clifford hisself sitting there. Hard, though? She weren't hard. 'You was bleeding married, don't forget that.' Bet he never carried on when his wife died like he was over his son. 'Sorry to disappoint you, but I was never interested in you, dear.'

'Wear your mark on me fucking arse, lady.' Slapping the table with his great meat-hook. 'I limp because of you. We've always been the same, me and you.'

'Just tell me why you invited me here,' she said. Maybe handing over that film was meant to be a reminder of his power.

'Right good of you to bring Fred.' McGowan smiled. 'He's Angel all over again.'

'He's flaming not.' Shouldn't of brung him. Soup for brains.

'Don't come over all superior, Maggie love.' His baggy face losing any tightness it had left. Cleared his throat. Twice. 'You ain't got a leg to stand on, warning you.'

'Don't *take* your warnings, remember?' Putting her finger in the trigger. She'd pull it before she let him touch her, swear to God.

'Jesus, you're a fool.' Said bitter. 'Maggie, *I* arranged to have you attacked.'

'What?' Insides turned liquid. Tightening her hand more round the gun. Should of known. Hadn't bleeding occurred to her. But who else'd get a kick trapping her in her flat, making her scared of living case she died. Her pussycat. What'd she flaming walked into?

'Yeah,' he said. 'Your woman Lulu was me alibi, though course she don't know that. Even used someone you know to do it, cunt that I am. Excuse me language.'

'Who?' Swallowing bile.

'Don't matter. Just wanted to make it as personal as I could.'

'Why?' And why tell her now, less he was going to have another go? 'After all them years—'

'Was told you was responsible for me boy. For Angel.' Tears coming again. 'God forgive me, was looking for someone to blame, and I was offered you on a plate.'

'How could I of had anything to do with Angel?' Voice shaking. Don't let him see your fear, girl.

'Realize that now.'

'That why you sent me the messages? To warn me?'

'What messages?' Looking baffled. Suppose he had no more reason to lie. But why'd Bathsheba give Maggie to understand he'd sent them, then?

'I hadn't see Angel in more'n twelve year,' Maggie told him.

'That right?' Mickey pushed his finger into the pouch under his left eye. 'Should of asked you, shouldn't I? Fair play. But way I heard it, you told Angel who Lulu's dad was, and you done it not long before we lost him.'

'What, and it drove him to off hisself?' Watching his ugly mug flinch. 'Do me a favour,' she added. Sounding more normal now. Though she *had* told Angel – not when McGowan thought, she'd nothing to do with the death, yet she could hardly give it the innocent. 'Must be a terrible thing to lose a child. I'm sorry, Mickey.'

'So . . . Well, weren't so much I heard it like that, though enough big hints and bollocks come up, seemed . . . I'm not a well man, Maggie.'

'No, you're bleeding not.' *I'm not a well man* – yet another Clifford thing. But . . . if McGowan hadn't had her beaten up, Clifford would still be alive. And Garry would be normal. Careful to keep her bag balanced on her lap, Maggie let go of the gun, took her hand out to light a cig. 'That what you meant by betrayed?'

'Was me little girl, love. She's been schmoozing with a geezer called Stephen Hopkins, trying to make me business collapse so the legit boys can move in, do you know?'

'Bathsheba? You mean that madam's been working for the takeover thingy?'

'Fraid so. And . . . Well, Hopkins brung her here, yesterday. She held her hands up, and not just hern. Fred got sent a dead kitten, didn't he?'

'That weren't you?'

'What d'you take me for?' Outraged. 'Wouldn't harm one fingernail of Angel's boy, so I wouldn't. No . . . Love, it was your Garry.'

'Don't be stupid.' Almost enough to make you laugh.

'It was.' Reaching across the table to her. She ignored that. 'I'm so sorry, lady, but . . . he give Angel the stuff what killed him. Your son killed my son, Maggie.'

'Killed . . . He couldn't of done.'

'For Bathsheba he could.'

'No.' This couldn't be happening. *Garry* killing Angel? But . . . he'd shot Clifford, even though that *was* bleeding McGowan's fault. And done for the kitten and all, looked like, what wasn't. Maggie put out her cig, stuck her hand back in her bag.

'You know I can't let this go,' McGowan said. 'You know that. I'm giving you fair warning cos of Angel's boy. Didn't

325

want it coming out the blue, you had to know why, make sense of it for Fred best you can.' He coughed. 'And, love, Stephen Hopkins was a big mate of Angel's – if I don't sort it, he will. Could be out me hands.'

'I'll go to the Old Bill.' Torture. That was McGowan's thing. Dear God.

'You reckon I give a shit? Me life's over, Maggie.'

'There's Fred. You just said so.'

'He'll be okay. Turns out Angel sold his shares . . . ' Fresh wash of grief in his eyes. 'Anyway, him and Lu of got the money. God willing, I'll live long enough to leave me own money to the boy. If not, three hundred grand'll have to do him.'

'Can't let you do it, Mickey.' *Pulling out the shooter. Recognize this?* But she could do that only in her head. More likely to hit him round the bonce with the flaming handbag. Any real pain today would be hern. Torn heart was right – whoever'd sent it her had been a bit previous, that's all – and it weren't McGowan, she was sure of that now. Too fancy for Garry to of done it, would say it had a woman's touch. Should of seen that. Garry. He was just a baby. Mickey smiled.

'What you got in there, Mags?'

'Nothing.' Though she could see he knew. Most probably from the first.

'You want Fred's nan inside?' he said. 'Go ahead. Told you, I'm finished. But it won't help Garry, love. Like I said, Hopkins'll see to it.'

'What if you're wrong? Maybe Bathsheba give Angel the stuff.'

'Bitch had an hand in it, I'm sure.' Big sigh. 'She helped Angel transfer his shares, and that's . . . Hopkins found out from somewhere else about your Garry. There's proof.'

'You was wrong about me.'

'Yeah, and I'll probably burn in hell for that. But Hopkins plays the white man.' Giving a laugh. 'Life's not worth having, do you know?' Pushing aside an envelope that was lying by his elbow. 'Not worth the paper it's printed on. God's one sick bastard.'

'You believe in God?' *She* believed in the Devil, knew that much.

'He's a malicious bugger, putting the idea of heaven in us just so's the shock of it not being there'll kill us.'

'What you going to do?'

'What I have to.' He laughed again.

'No, wait.' The gun shaking against her keys, her purse, her make-up. 'There's another way, promise you on me life. On Fred's life.'

'I pray to God He lets that boy off light.' The doorbell went. 'Talk of the devil,' McGowan said. 'No, that sweet boy's no devil. Send him home, so. He's old enough to get the train by hisself. I'm listening.'

'Be warned, Mickey. I don't mind crying, as long as you don't laugh.'

Jacob could hardly see through the viewfinder, his eyes were so full of tears. He offered up a silent prayer to the God he didn't know, for giving him this gift. *Should be me you're thanking, mate.* Fair point. The journey had led him from Angel's first letter to here; a tyrannical and amoral psychology had been, meantime, the most generous. Over the past couple of days, giving Lu permission to have her coil removed, dealing with Fred's suddenly developed teenage moods, Maggie disappearing to stay with a mysterious friend and ringing Jacob asking him to tell the others, he'd felt *he* was the linchpin of the family. Perhaps this was the legacy: all the moral and emotional tests had led, inevitably, to this moment.

'And . . . Action!'

'Bloody Christ, Jake.' Lulu giggled. 'Who d'you think you are, Tarantino? Your flat's not precisely Hollywood.'

'No, but I've always fancied saying that.' He took the video camera away from his face, smiled at her. She looked great, so happy. Glowing. Even without the Vaseline she'd insisted he rub on the lens, her skin was white and plumped out, her big blue eyes shining, her hair, that she'd dyed a darker shade of red than usual, glossy as an actress's. Thank God for Heaven Scent: that costume was perfect, the cream lace soft against the dark brown leather, a mixture of innocence and wicked sensuality. He could never understand why people likened breasts to anything else; when they were that amazing, the highest compliment was to say they were breasts. The ideal form. She *was* sex: Lucinda Luscious from her nail extensions to her pedicure. A star. 'You ready?' he asked.

'Presume so.' She came over to him, put her arm round his neck. 'Give us a kiss for luck, love.'

'Sure. Then I'll stop calling you Lu, okay? And you call me . . . ' *Angel.* He kissed her, hard. 'Anything except Jacob. I know, call me Mitzvah.'

'Mitzvah? If you like. Funny name, though.' Moving away a little. 'Suppose you want me to be Luscious.'

'You're already that, baby.'

'Baby.' Stroking her stomach. 'Well, you never know.'

She could see that her stroking her tummy made her back into Lulu for him, so she adjusted one of the lights he'd bought, went over to the bed, sat on the edge of it. Wonder if they'd live here or at her place? No, his flat was too small with only this one bedroom; they had to have a room for Fred. Maybe they'd move somewhere else altogether, somewhere light and airy, that they could paint lovely bright colours. Jake was too addicted to browns and beiges. And a new bed had to be first on the list, for definite. This one was a good size, but lumpy, shaped by other women's bodies. Not having that.

Jacob put the video camera up to his face. All of a sudden, he could be anyone, any of them nameless crews who worked in Soho or Essex or North London. The light on the camera went green. Mitzvah it was, then. She shook her hair back, smiled into the lens, ran her hand up her leg.

'You really know the big film people, Mitzvah?' she said.

'Lies, I wouldn't tell you.' With a funny lilt he didn't have as a rule.

'You think they'd like me?' Putting her finger in her mouth.

'The camera loves you,' he said.

And the camera *never* lies. She feels the years rub away from her like dry skin, all the suppleness comes back into her body, stretching and pulling her muscles back into shape. Smiling, always smiling, into that single eye. Focused on her, on the one thing she still knows how to do. Her own hands and tongue belong to him as she grabs roughly at her tits, teases the straps of her costume from her shoulders, pushes her boobs up to lick her nipples, forces her fingers deep inside herself.

And he's directing her, not with his voice, but with what she knows he wants to see through the lens. Reward for his commitment. She turns her back to the camera, slips her finger into her bum, feels his direction bore into her. Easy. Presume the body never forgets.

And when he puts the camera on its stand, joins her on the bed, still the eye watches them. Never satisfied, nothing's enough, yet the gaze remains steady, waiting for him to call the pace. She's excited now, not precisely for herself but for the camera, because it knows how to love her, wants her and no one else. Then he's fucking her, her ankles round his neck, his hands under her bum, the nails tearing at her flesh. She starts counting elephants, but realizes she doesn't need to. Jesus bloody Christ, she's going to come for the camera.

She didn't. But it had been so close, almost felt she had. Lulu was giving something to Jake that he wanted more than anything in this world or the next, and she was bloody determined she was going to feel good about that. And that after this film was finished, she'd never do it again.

He was grateful she'd had to get back for Fred. Probably they should have watched the film together first, but he wanted it for himself. Didn't seem to have to do with her just at this moment, nor with him either: the video was for him but not of him, as if he was the creator of a separate world. When she'd left, he'd kissed her goodbye, tasting them both on his tongue. But now, with a lighted cigarette, a glass of brandy, his mouth was straightforwardly his own again. Jacob pressed the remote; he'd get round to editing it soon, but meantime he just wanted to see what he'd shot. *Her down in flames is my guess, Mitzvah.*

Even though he'd had those couple of professional lights, the screen was too dark, amateur looking. *Like the woman said, you're no Tarantino, mate.* It was Lulu touching herself on the bed, not Lucinda Luscious; this, he couldn't get hold of, nothing in the viewfinder had prepared him for that. Was as though he'd made this to send to that programme they raved about down the club, some digital show where ordinary women took their clothes off in the misguided hope of becoming famous. No, that was harsh: Lu knew exactly how to move, what to make a camera see. Was hardly her fault he was bollocks with a video. Why hadn't he practised with it? *What, tape yourself tossing off, would you?* Or maybe, given he'd made this happen, that was something to be proud of in itself. He watched as the scene jumped, and he was on the bed with her. Jacob started to get turned on, his hand automatically going to his cock. A three-wank film, Lu reckoned, though that wasn't a possibility tonight.

As it turned out, even the one wank was a pitiful thing, risible, a middle-aged man getting mildly excited by images where the real power had been in the making of them. Thin trickle of spunk, barely an impression of what had gone before.

He'd never felt so disappointed in his life. Furious. The thing he'd wanted so badly had turned into this, a pathetic attempt to recreate the moment. But that was gone.

Trouble was, porn in a sense limited sexuality; it was all . . . yeah, linear, plod, plod, plod to an inevitable conclusion, single-focused by the lens, not wild and unpredictable and dangerous comparative to real sex. Not messy. Too . . . sanitized. Finite. The people in it, even Lu, even him, were disposable. God, look what happened to Angel's film, history ripped and thrown away as if it were a fucking pizza box. Now Jacob had made his own narrative, there didn't seem to be anywhere else to go; if he made more, there wouldn't be any significant variation on a theme. Like playing twelve-bar for the rest of his life, only the key changing. Dreadful thought.

So where *did* he go from here? Jacob got up to pour himself another brandy, find another cigarette. A baby? Had he written that in, too? His stomach turned over; he'd bloody told Lulu he'd never wanted a child. Even Fred, when it came down to it, all Jacob was good for there was warding off sulks. Well, tough shit, Angel had landed Fred on him and that was the best Jacob could do. He'd avenged his friend, or nearly, he'd met Lulu and kind of loved her, he'd got Maggie to trust him – *Yeah, then dropped her son in it* – invested the money, taught Fred guitar. For sure, he deserved to keep some of his life to himself. Garry wasn't his bloody responsibility. Angel couldn't have it both ways.

Jacob wandered over to the window, pulled open the curtains. Shit, his back ached; Lu had been in premier hypermobility mode today, Garry must feel like hell after a night with Bathsheba. *Not for much longer, Foxy.* Someone was letting off a few fireworks, greens and pinks squibbing across the sky, the bloody definition of disappointment. What if he could make the past few months disappear like that? Sure, his old life couldn't accommodate a lot of what he'd learned, even about himself, but would that be so dreadful? He took a deep drag on his cigarette, bent to put it out. Swilled his brandy round his mouth. Jacob had always made women up, maybe that included Lu after all. She was sweet and generous and loving, but . . . Every time he'd made her furious, where had the anger gone? Dissolved too easily, Alka-Seltzer emotions. The fucking woman was so terrified of losing him, she wouldn't let anything come between them, not even a film she probably didn't want to make. Bargaining for a baby . . . well, screw that. And yet, that smile, that infinite hospitality she offered with her body, those, he hadn't invented. Those, he loved.

Perhaps he should take another look at the film, see how he could improve it somehow with cutting. Closing the curtains again, Jacob finished his drink, went back to the settee. He rewound the video. God, wouldn't it be great if you could rewind life like that, go back to the point where he'd been shooting the thing? For that couple of hours, he'd been more sure than of anything before. Cambridge, he'd drifted into; playing the piano for money, he'd taken up just while he thought what else he could do; Becca, Maria, Susie, they'd all found him. *And I took you to Luscious.* But behind that camera, Jacob had been in control. Yawning, he pressed the play button. One quick flick through, then he'd go to bed.

Realization hit him as though he'd suddenly seen Jesus Christ. Treacherous, hideous vision. Defiled revelation. Oh, Lulu. *Fuck me. Better grow a moustache so you can twirl it.* Of course she'd been yet another fantasy, the latest in a very long line; he could see that now, see her now. This was the close of Angel's planned journey for him, taking him through from the beginning of the dream to the end, maybe the very road Angel had gone on himself. *No moves left from here, mate.* What the hell was Jacob going to do? There was still Fred, this new life, this travesty of a family. Was still his self-reputation to consider. Inflating then reducing Lulu like that, might as well have nailed her to a cross. *Tasteful analogy, Jewboy. Inflating who, was that?* Though he couldn't stop looking into his open heart: just couldn't see there what was left, how to need her any more.

But it had been a long day.

Chapter Sixteen

'What do you mean, over?' Screwing up her eyes against the unforgiving strip lighting. Seen like that, the bars looked like their kitchen wallpaper. Only not. 'Because of this?' She gestured round the vast, vile room. Hot drinks, table between them as if they really were in their kitchen. But theirs didn't have forty other kitchens openly planned next to it. 'On remand doesn't mean convicted, sweetie.'

'Fucking well will do, we both know that, girl.' He touched his cold sore. Bathsheba had to fight the urge to slap his fingers away. Mother of God, it was hellish in here. Their conversation simply didn't smell right, no paco rabanne, no Cif, no wonder he hadn't wanted her to visit sooner. Why were the people who got caught all ugly, brutal? And the women visiting them were either serious tarts or overweight muttons dressed as lambs. One lardy woman's great arse was totally in Bathsheba's eyeline if she moved her head even a wee bit. After only ten days, Garry's skin was sickly grey. He had a beautiful skull though, she could see just how perfect it was now it had only that skin covering it. Garry so didn't belong in here, he needed Bathsheba to interpret the world for him. Should be able to run him a bath, but those bars *weren't* their wallpaper, this might be his home for the moment but it wasn't hers, she had to keep that straight. Keep strong.

'Do you think I won't wait for you?' she asked.

'On what, fresh air?' Picking up his plastic mug with both hands. That vest they had him wearing over his clothes made him look as though he was about to take part in a five-a-side match. She'd never known him so much as jog. Her own soft sweater and cords, chosen because they were the most casual things in her wardrobe, presented in here like she was trying to be flash. He must feel terrible, bless him, knowing how much they cost.

'I could pick up more work,' she said at last. But the thought of being thirty years old and back on the circuit made her muscles cringe. Fab, she'd end up one of those novelty acts, a wrinkly in a lumpy leotard balancing a candelabra on the soles of her shrivelled feet. Hardly the Chinese State Circus, more like one of Billy Smart's chimps. Garry eyed her.

'Your old man's going to let that happen, is it?' he said. 'You reckon he'll let you just carry on? Turn it in.' Taking a sip of his tea. 'You'll have to get away from the agg, B. Ain't going to die down, promise you that much for nothing.'

'I'm so not running.' Laying her hand on his arm. The wrong smell, like a hospital crossed with a school gym, was making her feel a teeny bit sick. 'I'd rather have a short life with you in it than a long one without, my love,' she added.

'I'll *get* fucking life. Struth.' Shaking his head. 'They got the painting.'

'I know that.' Trying not to be distracted by the conversation at the next table, about how bloody *little Kylie* was doing. Tragic. Even if they thought Garry didn't have the right to privacy, surely she still did. The noise levels were excruciating, Bathsheba wanted to tell Garry to turn them down, hard to believe neither of them had any control over the volume. How did anyone stay sane in here? 'Why did you have to take the poxy thing off Lulu?' she said. Had really thought Lulu owning it might stitch the slapper up, if that became necessary. No one had such bad luck as Bathsheba and Garry.

'Fuck knows,' he said. 'Clifford Black had it away from Angel's brief's office. They was cousins.' He laughed. 'Geezer's going to testify Black had it, bent cunt.'

'Circumstantial, darling. Even if the DNA—'

'Not when I plead Guilty.'

'*What?*' But she'd known this was coming when Daddy hadn't done anything worse to Garry, when the family solicitor was retained, when the Magistrates hadn't granted bail, when police bail hadn't even been attempted (ISU so *was* involved with the Freemasons or similar). Daddy must intend to prolong the punishment. Always was his style.

'When me case comes up, I'll change me plea. That's the score.' He looked straight at her, his eyes blank. 'Picture's only their icing, anyway. Deal's I hold me hands up to Black's murder. Me mum bought me life. Remind me to send her a thank you.'

'Maggie did?' More and more bizarre, Maggie in here with them, as though this was their flat after all. 'How?'

'Fuck knows. Anyway, it gives you time to get away.'

'*I'm* part of the deal? That's scandalous.'

'Was the only thing I had on offer, speaking true.' He shrugged. 'But I don't trust it, you know? Trust me mum to a point, even though she done me up like a kipper, but your old man's bastard mental. And your mate Hopkins, and all.'

'He's no friend of mine.'

'No?'

'I told you what happened, sweetie-pie.' Jesus, he wasn't starting to believe that she'd stitched him up? She adored him, but even the Bible said you'd to put your own salvation before relationships. Bathsheba watched Garry stick a roll-up together (so wasn't the time to get even a tad shirty over him smoking cigarettes). Only a couple of weeks ago, she'd had her world at her feet, and now . . . It was finished. Lulu had everything, Bathsheba nothing. Not the hundred and fifty, nothing. Even her shares; Daddy had forced her to transfer them. Let's face it, she'd be lucky to stay breathing – Daddy's idea of family loyalty was to build Angel's incestuous bastard into the equation, and out everyone else (except maybe Stan). Wouldn't astonish Bathsheba if that grassing little kid had something to do with Daddy's OTT reaction. *Bomb disposal.* Him and Jacob had probably got to Daddy, before bloody Hopkins had. You

335

could work your butt off, and end up without your man, your money, your future, while other people could sit on their own (fat) bums and have masses of everything given to them. Her one serious mistake had been not to foresee sooner that Daddy would want Fred as a replacement Angel. *Always said you were a loser, B.* And everything she'd done for Hopkins, this was how he repaid her. Betrayal. No other word for it. Oh Jesus, what was she going to do without Garry? Break in another man? The sweetheart must be trying to finish with her to give her a life. But (admit it) he so didn't have a life to offer, only the illusion of one. She'd prepared emotionally for his death, not for this. Mourning had a purpose, you could still love and be loved by your dead.

'You might as well go,' Garry said. 'We ain't doing each other no good.'

'Don't say that, darling. We've got a lot of things to think about.'

'Do too much fucking thinking.' Laying his roll-up in the foil ashtray. Suppose you couldn't do anyone damage with tinfoil. 'Had a dream last night, mate. About that kitten.'

'We've so got bigger things to worry about than that,' she said. A bit sharp, though her tone was immediately gobbled by the cacophony in here. She smiled. 'Come on, poppet, don't collapse on me.'

'Just a little thing, is it?' Picking at his scab. 'Tried to think that for months, B. Ain't, though. You was me goldfish and you—'

'Was?' Catching sight of the lardy woman's thong as the slobby cow leaned forward to whisper to the orangutan opposite. Might as well have gone to the zoo.

'Aw *ma*te, whatever way you look at it, we can't be together no more.' Garry rubbed his eyes. 'Breaks me fucking heart, what's left to break. But we done something to us then, darling. You killed the kitten, I killed a bloke.'

'Thank you, Dr Freud. Christ.' If that was profound, then Bathsheba was illiterate. 'Hopkins did for us, sweetie. And your sister's getting all the profit.' *Don't forget me, darling. Hopkins did what he did because I'm so fucking loveable.*

'Not going to send you no VOs, B. Don't want you visiting me, writing to me, just . . . Shit.' Playing with his uneaten Mars bar. 'Need to forget each other, without a shadow.' Flat. As though he'd never begged her to marry him, said he couldn't live without her. As though he hadn't screamed out her name when the police had come to arrest him. As though he'd never been the person whose devotion was so great he'd kill for her. Suddenly, Bathsheba was terrified – she was alone. Well, it wasn't going to end here, it so wasn't. She stood up, leaned across the table to kiss Garry's cheek.

'I love you, sweetie,' she said. 'Ring me, please.'

'No.' He looked up at her, the veins stringing his head like blue pearls. 'Love you too, B. Make no fucking mistake about that.' Still his voice was flat.

The longing had gone from shattering to shattered. Jacob could hardly bear to look at himself, at the inside of his head; there were no excuses, not a possibility of any, he was a bastard. Or maybe violence had killed passion. Garry would go down for murder, though not for the right one. For bloody Clifford Black, someone nobody gave a toss about. *Come on, you're disappointed. You thought my old man would make you an accessory to murder. Proud of you, boy.* God no, that's not what Jacob had wanted, at all. At least this way, he could live with himself. Had got a kind of watery revenge for Angel, but even that had left him feeling death was everywhere, bigger and stronger than life. No wonder love was impossible to sustain. *Love? You reckon that's what it was?* Hard to be sure. Whatever, passion always fades, he'd just not thought it would be that . . . sudden. This brutal. For the past two weeks, he knew he'd been faking it; might have admitted it fully to himself sooner if it hadn't been for the furore round Garry, taking up the space in all their heads, leaving no room for any kind of doubts. But today, Jacob was sure. He didn't want her any more. Didn't even want the film they'd made together; he'd wrapped it in blue shiny paper, intending to give it to her, but sense had hit him before she arrived and he thought he'd better keep it in his music case.

Disgraceful pub, this: even the barmaid looked worn, sticky. Given him the wrong change, too, though he hadn't said anything about it. But it was close to Heaven Scent, and he hadn't wanted to let Lulu get all the way home in the bitter cold anticipating one set of things, only to get another mean-time. He glanced at his watch. Quarter to seven. She finished at half past six today, should be here by now. At least it wasn't crowded yet. He swallowed the rest of his brandy, pulled his pint towards him.

'Hi, love. Sorry, Mags rang my mobile just as I was coming out. Been sitting here long?' Lulu bent over him for a kiss. His lips brushed her cheek, but even that felt too much. 'Great, you got them in. Cheers.' Sitting opposite, picking up her wine. There were dark bags under her eyes; crap, how could he do this, when she needed support? Bastard. *Knew you had it in you, man.* Jacob lit a cigarette.

'What did Maggie have to say?' he asked.

'Nothing much.' Taking a huge gulp of her drink. 'Just that Garry's solicitor's still the McGowan one, for some strange reason. Thought Garry reckoned it was better to change. Keep wondering if I should have a word with Mickey, but Mags says no.'

'She probably knows best. How is she?' Surprised to find that he still cared.

'Same. Too calm.' A tiny smile. 'She said for you to go round tomorrow, though nothing to do with her birthday. Think she thinks you're clever, you must know what to do.'

'Sure.' He shrugged, pulled on his cigarette. 'But what I know about murder could be written on this Gitanes packet.' Yet five months ago, it wouldn't have filled a matchbox. He took a mouthful of his pint. The London Pride was greasy or the glass was; either way, it left his mouth feeling slimy.

'D'you reckon he did it, really?' For the hundredth time. 'Still can't believe it.' Sticking her finger into her wine. 'Well, no, I can, but . . . wish I couldn't, d'you get me?'

'I do, yeah.' Rubbing his eyes. 'Seems like nothing's straightforward any more. I can't even deal with myself, Lu. Manager at Padley's said if I don't get my act together, they'd have to think again.' For one bad night, that was totally harsh. But he'd played crap, no question, coming over like a rank amateur.

'Jesus, Jake – what you going to do?' Concern for him written over whatever she was feeling about her brother.

'I need to concentrate on me for a bit, sweetheart,' he said. 'Since Angel died, I've not exactly been giving it a hundred per cent. Anywhere. Can't afford for everything to fall in on me.'

'Yeah, presume you've not had much time to practise. Once Garry's sorted–'

'It's not just about practice, it's about time for me.' God, wasn't as if he'd even chosen Lulu, she'd been forced on him. 'I didn't ask for this.'

'You reckon I did?' Scratching her head, so hard he could hear it.

'No, course not,' he said. Though she'd been bloody quick enough to grab at the security. Maybe she'd made him up, as much as the other way around. Bloody hell, everything they'd ever had in common was in Angel. 'But this is your world, not mine.'

'What you saying?' Pressing her palm flat on the table.

'Just . . . ' This was the hardest thing he'd ever had to do; understood now why Susie had cried when she'd moved out, even though clearly by that time she'd despised him. 'I'm knackered all the time. There's Fred to think about . . . ' Yet he was desperately trying not to. 'And Maggie, now all this shit with Garry. Plus your investments . . . It's a lot, baby.'

'It's a lot for all of us,' she said. Snapped.

'Sure, yeah, I know that. But . . . I can't do anything about what it's like for other people. No good to anyone if I can't hold it together.'

'You seem okay to me.' Bitter.

'Believe me, I'm not.' Lighting another cigarette from the stub of the one he had on. 'Don't think I've been right since he died. This isn't who I want to be, Lu.'

'But . . . Is this because of the other week?' Leaning forward. 'The film?'

'No, course not.'

'Because *you* wanted that, Jake.' Lulu pulled the ribbon from her ponytail, shook her hair. Just one of a million sexy women in London now, nothing about her disturbed him.

'I know I wanted it,' he admitted. Pushing his chair back from the table.

'Look, I'm not pregnant.' Hint of desperation.

'Just as well.' Thank you, God. Thank you. Was almost enough to make Jacob think about making next Yom Kippur. As it was, what he was doing amounted to a protracted fast: he couldn't imagine going through all that shit with someone else to get a sexual relationship. Never had the courage really to go with it full on, either with women or in his so-called career, and maybe there was a good reason for that. Maybe he wasn't built to take on all the bollocks of another person; perhaps without that, he'd be able to put his energies into finding better gigs. *Yeah, or maybe Lulu was your walk just inside the wild side, boy. Time for a long run with that nice Yiddisher girl, now.* No, Angel was wrong: if Jacob couldn't make it with Lulu, when they'd come so close, doubted he could be bothered to try again with anyone else. Disappointment was built in, for him at least. He wasn't planning a lifetime's celibacy, necessarily, but he pretty much knew he couldn't handle another permanent girlfriend. Or maybe he *would* meet someone he couldn't resist trying with, even knowing what he did about himself, but either way that had nothing to do with how he felt right now. 'Sorry,' he said, as someone banged into the back of his chair. Lulu was staring at Jacob, just bloody staring, her eyes peering weirdly above the bags. 'What?'

'You have to do this in public?' she said.

'Do what?' For God's sake, he'd saved her the humiliation of travelling hopefully.

'You're leaving me.'

'That's not quite true.' You couldn't leave what you'd only borrowed.

'Isn't it?' Finishing her wine. 'Well, what is it then, mate?'

'I do love you.' Knowing that this time, it was for sure not totally right. Wasn't that he'd stopped caring, not straightforwardly, but he couldn't stop the not wanting. 'We still could be good friends,' he added. *That's original. Want that really, do you?*

'Friends?' She laughed. 'Jesus, mate, what we going to do? Hang out and talk about music? Get some porn and Pringles in, have a boys' night? Few lagers, eyeing up the birds in the Holly Blue? My brother's most likely going down, you know that. Did you have to do this yet awhile? Couldn't you of waited a bit?'

'No. That wasn't—'

'A possibility, don't tell me.' Tapping her fingers against her empty glass, her eyes teary, pleading, lurking, bloody furtive, behind the anger. 'You didn't even have the bottle to tell me properly, did you?' She said. 'I had to pick it out from all the crap you were waffling about.'

'Was trying to explain—'

'Well, precisely. Trying. Not bloody doing it.' Reaching across the table, she grabbed his pint, swallowed a mouthful. 'This got to do with me getting the money?'

'God, no.'

'What if I *had* been pregnant?'

'We'd have dealt with that. Wouldn't just have left you to it.' Hoping that was true. Shit, he'd barely given it a thought. 'Another drink?' he asked. Putting out his cigarette, pushing the ashtray to one side.

'Yeah. Not wine, gin. A large one.' Picking at her nails. 'You always reckon you know what people want, Jacob. But you

341

don't.' Rummaging in her bag, getting out a tissue. 'Just tell me one thing, though. Why don't you want me?'

'I don't know.' He leaned across the table to touch her face; she jerked her head away. 'You were everything,' he said. 'You were stuff I didn't even know I wanted till I met you. But it's too complicated, baby. You're right, I've got no bottle.'

'Yeah, I know, it's not me, it's you. Leave off. Heard that one before.'

'Not from me, you haven't. Shit, Luniu—'

'Don't. Just bloody don't start with that, all right?' She scraped her chair back, crossed her legs, her arms. 'Don't tell me you love me, Jake. Don't come it with the pet names. Don't tell me it's not personal. Course it bloody is – how could it not be, you prat?'

'It's not.' But he had desired her, now he didn't; she was right, it wasn't some abstract thing, it was to do with her. And him. *And me, Jakey. Don't forget that.*

'Whatever you make out, it's my fault,' she said. As though she had a coin in her mouth. 'Hardly anyone's dream woman, am I?'

'But you *were*. That's the—'

'I'm not stupid, mate.' With a half smile. 'No, most probably am. Did what you wanted, and then you realized that was precisely what you didn't want.'

'That's not it.' He stood up. She always had to bloody simplify, as though people could be reduced to pop-psychology sound-bites. *And you're such an intellectual.* Maybe not, but his thoughts weren't formed entirely from cutting out the words in magazines. 'I'll get those drinks, yeah?'

The place was getting packed now. When the barmaid finally came over to serve Jacob, he indicated that the under-dressed woman next to him should be first. Stupid bint ordered without even thanking him; screw that, wished he'd taken her turn after all, instead he was having to listen to her shit-thick partner sounding off about bombing the Arabs. He'd miss Lu for sure, the way she'd opened up his closed mind, body; her

342

generous smile; her hands; the way when she was on form she made Fred laugh. That especially. Was he doing the right thing? *Taxonomy's a pretty twisted kind of love, Mitz.* It was, yeah, and he only felt like this because she wasn't in front of him now; when he'd been served, she'd turn back into someone who wasn't the sum of her parts. Who wasn't enough.

Almost spilt Lu's gin and tonic on the way over to the table, trying to avoid being crashed into by idiots. One of the few times he was quite glad he was so tall: he could hold the drinks above most people's heads. But it was a waste of time. Before he reached their table, he realized she was gone.

Maggie put her own sheets in the washing basket, spread the bottom work one on the mattress. Could do with a bit of a press, but she was shattered. Just pull it flat – there, that was better. Suddenly popped in her head the picture of that one orgy Welsh Adrian'd paid her to go to. Brown brushed-nylon sheets covering the hostess's three-piece suite, a cardboard sign in the bedroom stuck to the headboard, No High Heels On The Bed. How she'd kept a straight face . . . But it never seemed so funny now. Quick as she could, Maggie finished her job and went back through to the living room for a ciggie. Outside, could hear youngsters larking about, boys' voices, that bit older'n Fred, making their presence felt in a world they'd had nothing to do with messing up. Just like Garry and his mates, years ago – no real harm in them, but they loved giving it the bigun, testing out being little blokes. Mind, little blokes grew, took over the control, and there was plenty of harm in them then.

She drew hard on her cig, went across to the sideboard, picked up the china bear with the heart in its paws. Bleeding saucebox'd brought her that after the first time he'd come home drunk, as if she'd get all sentimental and forget what he done. She'd took the bear and give Garry the backhander she should of give him the night before. Always kept the flipping thing, though, despite it only had one ear left where Fred used t play with it when he was tiny. Stupid cow. Wished she had time for a nice cup of tea.

Sitting on the settee, Maggie finished her cig, put it out. Rubbed her knee. That was getting worse with the winter damp. Her eyes filled, but she blinked, hard. Didn't want to re-do her make-up, thank you very much. *You always look lovely, Maggie. Pristine.* No one'd ever say that to her, now Clifford was dead. She'd be sixty years old tomorrow. Useless feeling sorry for herself, too late for that. Better to keep busy, leave the thinking and the grieving till she weren't capable of doing nothing else. Come on, that's your lot, one more ciggie then Jack should be here. Funny, the difference a letter could make. Jack. Jake. Lulu had the better deal, if Maggie weren't very much mistaken. If a bloke like that was keen, Lu must have something about her. Maggie must of done that something right.

Only last Christmas, Maggie'd slapped Garry's legs for him for showing off. Heart had sharp, heavy stones in it, as if something in there was walling up the middle – most probably just as well. Good job Jack weren't as enthusiastic these days, she couldn't of played ride-a-cock-horse tonight. Even the picture of it in her head made her go squirmy – right lovely that'd be, couple of pensioners . . . Enough to turn your bleeding stomach. She glanced over to the mantelpiece at the clock. Any minute, he'd be here. Maggie touched her wig, check it was on straight. It was. Course it was. Like always.

She'd never been able to get rid of the thought that one day she'd wake up beautiful. When she was a little girl, she'd really presumed she would. And even after she was grown up, there'd been a part of her that somehow refused to give away hope. She'd never forgot the certainty, although it had faded into a vague dream. But now, she realized it wasn't ever going to happen. Oh, yeah, she knew she wasn't too bad for going on thirty-seven, even with being a bit podgy. But not close to beautiful. And she'd get further and further away from it, no escaping that. Wouldn't surprise her if that's what Jacob had seen, watching their video back, mentally comparing it with her earlier films. About the only thing that made sense to her, in getting chucked.

Had really started to believe it might not end this time. Lulu lay back on the settee, closed her eyes. She felt so sad. Not in Fred's sense of the word, but properly sad. Was a different feeling to, like, unhappy or miserable, it was heavier, softer, had less edges. Though it didn't stop her feeling bloody fucked around, and all. End of the day, she was more of a catch than she'd ever been, if this investment stuff came off. And there was Mickey McGowan saying he wanted to do this, that and the other for Fred. Be wanting to meet him, next – well, she couldn't put that off much longer. Another little treat Jake'd miss. But money obviously wasn't enough for Jacob, not when she was in charge of it. Though it couldn't be that putting him off, not precisely – he must know she'd of given him anything he asked for. Oh shit, felt like someone had drained off her blood and filled her veins up with . . . What was heavy and liquid? Something else, anyway, that made her sink into the cushions. She wasn't good enough, that was the fact of the matter. Jacob was gone, and it was really and truly her own fault. She should of read proper books, had professional waxes, gone on a strict diet, not been so snappy. Should of been . . . different.

Forcing herself to sit up, Lulu reached for her gin. Mother's ruin. Bloody Christ, what if she really had gone and got her coil taken out? That fucking bastard wouldn't give a shit if she was pregnant. Yeah, he'd of given it all the lip about looking after her, but he'd still of left. Thank God she'd had the sense not to take him serious when he'd said she could try for a baby – he'd soon got fed up of Fred, hadn't he? Couldn't of told you why she hadn't done it, except she didn't want another kid much as all that. Not enough to risk their relationship over, anyway. That was a bloody joke, now. Bastard wasn't just leaving her, he was leaving her boy and all. Right when all this Garry business . . . Suppose he thought the hassle wasn't worth sticking around for. Her brother might be a murderer, no way could you get your head round that, and Jacob . . . Even Angel couldn't of got out more sudden than Jake had. Lulu had always thought there was something funny about them being mates, but now it was obvious. They were both blokes, that was for certain sure.

Her throat ached with trying not to keep crying. She gulped her drink, pulled herself off the settee to go pour another. Stomach was all fluttery, panicky, as if there was something to be scared of with Jake gone. Like she'd just started to get a sense of who she was, and all of a sudden she wasn't that person any more. Lost inside her own head. Even the things she'd normally done when she'd split up with someone weren't suitable to this feeling. She couldn't put on sad records and bawl her eyes out, because Jacob was a musician. Music belonged to him, she couldn't use it for her own emotions. She couldn't go out and pick up a bloke for the night, because that wouldn't give her back any confidence. Sex belonged to him and all, fixed in that bloody film. And she couldn't stuff her face with biscuits and ice cream, because she'd never been chucked at nearly thirty-seven before. Weight didn't come off so easy, now. Felt as though Jacob had taken away with him the very last of her being young, and she didn't know how to be middle-aged, wasn't at all sure she wanted to find out.

Always thought money should make a massive difference. Well, it did. But not to everything. Couldn't change that Jacob had gone from watching porn to doing it, that something in her had made that happen. And that when it had, she'd lost him. Mrs Thingummyjig, who'd had Fred in Primary, had told her a teacher would always lose her best pupils to the outside world, and it had sounded like poncy gobbledygook to Lulu then. But now it seemed a dark thing to say, morbid and true. Lulu had never wanted to teach anyone anything. *I'll be devoted to you for ever.* Yeah, but for ever was shorter than it used to be. Porn always did date quick. Wasn't bloody *fair.*

Her life wasn't over. It never was, no matter how bad it felt.

And this, this was the worst she'd felt since Angel went. As if she'd been left with them blistering burns all over her skin that everyone could see, and ones inside her that might well leak through, yellow and poisonous with sad. Jake was the only person who wouldn't think she'd gone mental if she said that out loud. But. Lulu finished her drink, realized she was still standing by the bottle, poured out more. Fuck it. That was one traditional thing when a bloke left you that she wasn't going to let Jacob take off her.

Bloody Christ, the things she'd put up with from him. All the lies, the porn, the sulks, the lectures. Every time, she'd forgive him, quick as that. Must of seemed right desperate. Like Maggie always said, *You want dog dirt from their shoes on you, girl?* Even the legacy, Lulu had come up with excuses for him before *he'd* thought of any. She must look a total prat. Most probably had to do with why he'd fucked off – likely thinking he should of skagged the money anyway, she'd of just found reasons why, offered him them with chips. Well, if that's what he thought, she was bloody well better off without him.

Maybe that was him at the door, coming to say he'd changed his mind. Perhaps he'd only had a sudden panic about getting serious – seen that in blokes before. He *had* said he still loved her. But he hadn't given her back his key, he could of walked straight in. Then, maybe he didn't think she'd appreciate that. He was right, she wouldn't. Lulu went out the hall, looked through the spyhole. Disappointment punched her in the tummy. What the bloody hell was Bathsheba doing here? Christ, had something else happened to Garry?

'What's the matter?' Lulu said, almost before she'd got the door properly open.

'I need to talk to you. Can I come in?'

'Yeah, course. Want a drink? I'm on the gin.'

'No, thanks.' Bathsheba followed Lulu back through to the living room. Too close behind. Felt like her shadow had stood up.

'Where's Jacob? Working?'

'Yeah.' She wasn't about to swap lonely hearts stories with Bathsheba. 'What's wrong, B?' Lulu edged away to the cabinet, sloshed some more gin into her glass, turned so she was facing the other woman. 'Shit, you don't look right.' Hadn't seen her since the Magistrates' Court ten days ago, and they hadn't spoken then because Lu had felt awkward about the money. Course, Bathsheba was as immaculate as ever tonight, but was obvious she'd been crying, even though her make-up was perfect again.

'You really can't guess?' B took the new school photo of Fred off the wall, stood looking at it in her hands. 'Always wondered if you were a teeny bit stupid.'

'Frigging *cheek*.' Chin the bloody midget, she wasn't careful. 'Look, I don't need this tonight, mate. You better go. And give that picture here.'

'Pity you didn't say that to my Garry.' Bathsheba slung the photo on to the cabinet. 'You do know your painting's being used in evidence?'

'Tell the Old Bill you gave it me, shall I?' Wouldn't surprise Lulu if Bathsheba had shot the bloke herself.

'Your word against mine.' Raising her voice. 'Though seeing as you're *so* everyone's pet at the moment, they might bloody believe you.'

'Keep it down, Fred's asleep.'

'Oh, right, I really give a fuck.' Laughing. 'That bloody kid's taken my life. You think I care even a tad about his beauty sleep? You should have warned him never to grass, Lu. Boys without dads need more strict lessons in life.'

'What you on about?' Lulu sipped her drink. She didn't like the look of this. Bathsheba was acting as if one of them was round the twist. You could make excuses up to a point, with Garry being inside, but there had to be limits and Fred was one of them. Christ, why did Jacob have to of left her today? Thought musicians were meant to have timing.

'Everything comes back to you and Angel,' Bathsheba said.

Unbuttoning her coat, her leather gloves evidently making it tricky. It was beautiful, that Afghan – Lulu could afford the odd thing like that soon.

'What's that to you?' Lulu said.

'Nothing, *sister*.' Curling her lip, like a miniature Elvis. 'Only everything I worked for ends up in your pocket because of it. That's all. Or in Fred's.'

'This about the dosh you tried to nick off me?'

'It was a transaction, sweetie.' Opening her bag. 'Five grubby videos it cost us, for our part of the equation.'

'Leave off, B. That money was mine, and you know it.'

'You had no right to it. You're a poxy *freak*.' Practically screeching.

'Told you, keep your bloody voice down.' Hissing.

'Freds!' Bathsheba called. 'It's me, sweetie-pie.'

'Shut the fuck up. *Now*.' Lulu moved quick, grabbed B's arm, shook her, let go.

'What makes you think you've got any power?' Bathsheba stepped further away.

Lulu almost laughed. Was just like Fred giving it, *You're not the boss of me*.

'Go away, Bathsheba,' she said. Was beginning to look as though Lulu would have to throw the woman out physically – good job B was so tiny. Lulu finished her drink, listened out for Fred. Seemed he hadn't stirred, that boy could sleep through an explosion. Better not have any more gin till she'd got rid of the witch. This was all she needed, when she only wanted to be alone with her sad.

'I'm so not going anywhere,' said Bathsheba. 'Not until I've done what I came to do.' She took a little gun out her bag.

The Holly Blue was empty at last. Stan actually nodded to him in passing. Five a.m. Stephen stood in the freezing street, looking at the club's neon sign; he certainly shouldn't be here, his presence technically negated the point of hiring Geoff. But he felt this one was both for Angel and in spite of him. It had already been put on hold for a week, Stephen wanted to see it done. *How's having a pop at my family's business going to help me now, Stevie baby?* Stephen had been delusional if he'd thought avenging Angel's death would make that voice any kinder. All right, Bathsheba's grand plan was dead in the water, she'd served her purpose, but business was business: ISU still wanted the Holly Blue, the McGowan shops, the distribution, desk-top, and with Del McGowan sold up and disappeared, the bomb would make Stan think twice about wanting to hang on to the props. A quarter of Soho in four years. Perhaps it was possible, especially given that they had the Wilson properties as of Friday. In time, Stephen might even care about that again. It was the kind of thing one lied about to oneself, anyway, and maybe if you did so enough, it became true. *Never heard that one before, boy.*

A man was moving towards him. Geoff, jangling what was probably the 'borrowed' keys to the club. That man must spend a fortune on briefcases, not as if he'd *consider* anything less than Gucci, even though none of them lasted him longer than twenty-four hours. Stephen ducked into the side street, went down it as far as he could while still being able to see. He'd easily be safe here, and even if he wasn't, he didn't really give much of a damn. Stephen could understand now what had made Mickey McGowan leave to his remaining sons decisions he'd once scrupulously have overseen. It would be almost too easy to feel sorry for the man; after all, they'd both lost Angel. And Mickey was arranging for Garry Dawson to have a less than pleasant time inside, which was more than Stephen would have been able to do. But the bloody father could have done so much more still: one of them should have taken Garry out of this life, the way Garry had taken Angel. It felt like failure. *That's because it is, you dickhead.* Well, at least Angel's son would be cared for; Stephen didn't want ever to see the boy, but it was good to know Angel had left something warm and human behind. Something uncorrupted. *Yeah, and you don't want to meet him in case you want to fuck him. Nice little Hobby.* That was sick, Angel. Even for you.

Geoff walked empty-handed back across the end of the street, heading off for home no doubt. He had a rather attractive wife; must be nice to have someone to go back to. That youngish white man this evening, he'd been seriously interested, and head-to-toe Paul Smith certainly didn't signal gold-digger. Stephen fingered the card in his pocket. Maybe he'd give the chap a call tomorrow, although the HIV conversation would be a bore, embarrassing, as though Stephen were one of those careless macho types. Yet, a drink didn't commit one to anything. *Life must gone on, what? Do me a favour.* Life does go on, Angel; no point in dying before you're dead. Maybe Stephen would never get it up for a live body again, though how did he know unless he tried? Five years of torment might have been delicious in some ways, but perhaps it didn't mean normality was out of his grasp for ever.

The world shook, dark with brickish cloud.

He was on his knees.

Better to die on your feet, mate.

Stephen coughed, struggled to stand, to see through to the building. Oh balls, Christ, looked like that might be a bigger bomb than he'd requested. Damn Geoff. Bloody trigger-happy twat, Stephen would have to have a word with him. ISU wouldn't be impressed if the damage was too great.

But who was to say what damage was too great.

Epilogue

Lulu added another coat of lippy. Lovely evening, would only need to take her thin jacket. Spring had always been her best season – you didn't have to go out all bulky, the way you did most of the year, yet you weren't right exposed like you briefly were in summer. She was still self-conscious about her arm anyway, was dreading the strappy dresses she'd have to dig out in a couple of months. But maybe it wouldn't be as bad as she was making out – least the scar did remind her how lucky she'd been. Even losing Jake hadn't been important compared with that. Not when she properly thought about it. That's you done, girl. Christ, this jacket was gorgeous, made her seem almost slim. Just showed you, labels did make all the difference, didn't care what Maggie said.

'How do I look, Freddie?'

'Scutters.' He grinned. 'No, you look all right? Nice, you look nice.'

'Don't knock yourself out, kid.' Ruffling his hair. 'You be okay on your own?' Stupid, been months now, and besides, you had to presume Bathsheba could come back any old time, not just at night, but Lulu's heart went too fast as she asked Fred the question. *Always told you, no point to life if you live it in fear.* 'If you do go out, with your mobile with.'

'Course,' he said. 'And . . . Jenny said she might knock for me, yeah?' Obvious he was trying to sound casual. 'Can I ask her in, if she does?'

'Yeah, you know you can.' Lulu couldn't resist. '*Fred and Jenny, sitting in a tree. K-i-s-s-i-n-g.*'

'God, Mum. You need to grow up, in it.'

'Might have to make you right there, boy.' Grabbing him, she kissed his cheek. 'Love you.' Ought to have Angel's advice tattooed under the puckered skin of her scar. Though, of course, Fred had already proved how brave he was – she could well be dead, weren't for him. And if they were lucky, maybe B was dead herself. Garry seemed to think that was possible. Lulu kissed Fred again.

'Get off, you minger.'

'Mr Sweet Talk, you.' Did she really look all right? Bloody Christ, she was nervous. Paul seemed a nice enough bloke, but she'd been wrong a hell of a lot. Get a grip, Lu – you're bound to feel a bit funny, first date in a long time. Well, suppose it wasn't *that* long, but she felt new, as if her arm branded her as someone different, someone who'd never had a bloke at all. Maggie said she'd to get back on the horse, and that was true, though . . . made her wonder what Jake was doing, who he was doing it with. And she hadn't thought about him in weeks, not precisely. A backwards step, even though there was nothing to go back to, not even the old Lulu. Made her think about the shooting more and all, for some strange reason. Had a nightmare last night, first one in ages, where Bathsheba and Jacob had both been waving guns at her, and Fred was trying to save her but was tied to the door-knob. Though nightmares couldn't kill you, that's what she'd always said to Fred when he was little. 'Won't be back late,' she told Fred now. Glancing over to where the blood had been. Good move, to of got a new carpet.

'Heard that before.' He tapped her on the arm. 'Be careful, right.'

'Definitely.' But it hurt, to hear him sound so old.

'Don't mean . . . You know, we're okay like we are.'

'Know what you're getting at, love.' Lulu ran her tongue over her teeth, in case any lippy had strayed there. 'It's just dinner, promise you. Presuming he's a decent fella, but if not I'll cut my losses and come home early. Fair enough?'

'Yeah, suppose.' Pulling on his baseball cap. 'This look right?'

'Beats me why you need that on indoors,' she said. 'You're a stunner, boy, getting just like your dad.' Nodding to the photo Mickey had given them. Lulu hadn't wanted it kept out, but Fred did, so that was that. 'Don't know why you want to hide yourself.'

'You miss him?'

'Angel?'

'No. Jake.'

'Sometimes, yeah.' Though that was mental, you couldn't love someone who was only a memory. Specially when the thing you remembered most was that he believed you weren't good enough for him. Not much to miss in losing that. 'Why, do you?' she asked.

'No, he was way flicky, did your head in with not being able to find stuff and that.' Sticking a chewing gum in his gob. 'Least he left his guitar, that was the best thing about him.' But his laugh sounded forced. Lulu was buggered if she was going to feel guilty, though – nor stay indoors for the rest of her life.

'It's okay to miss Jacob,' she said. 'Sure he does you, and all.'

'That's up to him. Can I open my Easter Egg?'

'Bit previous.' But what did it bloody matter? You might as well grab what you could while you could. 'Go on, then. Only if I can have a bit.' Wouldn't sleep with Paul tonight though, even if he was as nice looking and funny as she remembered, not on the first date. Most probably. After B had disappeared off the face of the planet, Garry had asked Lulu why any of them bothered to carry on, and she hadn't had an answer for him then, not with her being free. Not with her feeling she'd be looking over her shoulder the rest of her life, neither. But she had one for him now – why the hell not? She picked Fred's Coke can off the cabinet, took a swig.

'Here's to life, mate,' she said.

'That's *mine*.'

* * *

They were a family. It was the first thing he'd learned about them, and almost the last thing he could be sure of about them. Even now, as he stared at the decapitated bodies, a muddled excess of limbs on the silent screen, he thought mean-time more of what the Dawsons had come to mean for him, of how they had come to mean for him, than he did about any sexual response he might be having. The shot panned to a female head, a rictus of dead pleasure. He knew too much to get anything but the comfort of the familiar from the view, a safe place from which to think about them. Seemed as though he'd always privilege that family, never be able to wrench himself away; eating, drinking, sex, almost nothing would hold his attention except what he'd found in them. Screw this, he was a castrato. The dead had taken his will and the living his desire; he had no autonomy left, replaced by this relentless, unwanted attachment to something he was bloody sure he'd never understand. That he'd rejected, for God's sake. Even his dreadful resentment couldn't possess him. There was nothing could give him any purchase on what remained of his exis-tence. He was finished, and it didn't look like there'd be a miraculous resurrection any time soon. Always did think the Christians were a gullible lot.

Why don't Jews drink?

It dulls the pain.

Without taking his gaze from the screen, he poured himself some more brandy, dropped the burned-down butt of his ciga-rette into the saucer, lit a fresh one. *You minger.* Fred would find it hard to keep hold of any moral advantage, growing up in that family. But maybe Maggie was right: Jacob was just some ponce who'd spent his life assuming he was cleverer, more talented than most, without have the bollocks to prove it; not that she'd put it quite like that, but it's what she'd meant. *You're so far up your own bleeding backside, you think the world better be grateful for your shit.* Took a lot for Maggie Dawson to say shit. Despite everything, he laughed as he thought of that. Remembered her telling him about when she was young, how her sister would twist Maggie's arm up her back, hissing, *Say it. Go on, say fuck.* According to Maggie, she'd never given in; he could totally believe it. Was difficult, dreadful, to think about Fred's world now being exclusively female. There was no doubt that Garry was in the right place, but the fact remained that Jacob had taken both Garry and himself out of Fred's life; that wasn't a remotely comfortable truth. Even though Fred was probably better off without either of them. Perhaps it was Jacob's loss.

Warm evening. Jacob tugged off his fleece, pulled his tee-shirt down over his stomach. His heart fluttered; he put a hand on his chest to soothe it. Angel's heart had been enlarged, maybe that was a necessary and sufficient condition for anyone who got involved with him; Angel himself probably needed more space for his self-love. God, the journey's answers had been implied all the time, rhetorical questions, about how much Jacob loved him, how far he'd go. Yet if he could go as far as back to last year, knowing the consequences, he'd still do everything more or less the same, except for the last part. Leaving Fred, even leaving Lulu, hadn't proved to be that simple, comparatively. Or maybe that was guilt talking. After all, they could have been killed, and he hadn't ever gone to pick up the stuff he'd left at her place, which would have been the perfect excuse to ask how they were doing. He'd thought about them all the time, of course, listened to newspaper gossip down the club, taken the sympathetic looks that quickly turned scathing when people realized he wasn't with Lu any more, but the sort of care he'd felt hadn't been motivating. Still wasn't. They could be in any kind of state now, and probably they were, especially as the papers had obviously given up the search for Bathsheba, although the police might not have done, officially. Suppose if Lu had died, the story would have run for longer: the family angle could only sell so many copies without a body. Fred had been fearless, the way he'd apparently rushed in and tackled Bathsheba, even the *Guardian* admitted that, succumbed to tabloid approval; Jacob had felt proud, until he realized he didn't have the right. But Lulu didn't strike him as a survivor, even with a bit of money behind her: she'd been too soft for the world she found herself in. *Why don't you want me?* He still couldn't answer her, wasn't even sure if it was still true. Didn't seem to matter much now. Was irrelevant.

Outside the window, the world had moved on from the late afternoon pseudo-night he hated to the real thing. Forced himself to get up, close the curtains. Legs and back felt stiff from sitting too long in one position; almost certainly more than halfway to his bloody grave, even supposing he outlasted his allotted span. I die, you die, he/she/it dies, we die, they die. That, he knew would drive him mad if he didn't stop thinking, would go round and round, he would put a beat to it, even a tune, until it seemed any other words weren't a possibility. Enough was enough. He pulled open the drawer under the coffee table, took out his works. From the corner of his eye, he caught a glimpse of white, dimpled flesh, garishly lit; abruptly, he turned his back on it.

Mix the smack with juice from the squeezy lemon, using the matchstick. Cook up the gear on one of Babu's best spoons, over the candle; *crap*, burned his finger. Nothing comparative to the state of the blackened silver, though. Place the butt of a clean cigarette in the spoon, draw up the brackish solution into the syringe through the filter. Using his teeth to tighten the leather strap about his bare arm, he listened to the sounds he couldn't hear to the images going on behind him, making a tape in his head from too much experience. He worked his hand several times to raise a vein, dug around to get show of blood. As the needle went in, apparently of its own volition, he moved so he could see the screen while the rush filled him. Better than sex, some users said. Better than death, so far as he knew. And for sure, it had to be better than obsession, for anyone.

L'chei-im.